EyeCue Productions
Presents

I0678812

TRAPPED WITHIN

- A HORROR ANTHOLOGY -

Trapped Within First Published in 2017

Published by EyeCue Productions

Trapped Within Copyright © 2017 Duncan P. Bradshaw

The EyeCue Logo Copyright © 2016 Duncan P. Bradshaw

Copyright of each story belongs to its listed author.

All rights reserved. No part of this publication may be reproduced, stored in a retrieval system, or transmitted, in any form or by any means without the prior written permission of the author, nor be otherwise circulated in any form of binding or cover other than that in which it is published and without a similar condition being imposed on the subsequent purchaser.

All characters in this publication are fictitious and any resemblance to real persons, living or dead is purely coincidental.

Cover and Internal Design by EyeCue Productions

ISBN 978-1-9997512-0-3

CONTENTS

DEDICATION

For Mike.

INTRODUCTION

DEBBIE BRADSHAW

The choice of the Stroke Association as the charity to benefit from the proceeds of this anthology has huge significance to me. My dad suffered a severe stroke over ten years ago and I've witnessed first-hand the devastating effects it can have on someone. He was only 63 at the time, young enough that he would still have been working on the farm he had run for most his life if he hadn't been fortunate enough to take early retirement a few years beforehand.

I will never forget the day it happened. I was at work when I got the call from my brother to say that my dad had suffered a severe stroke and had been taken to hospital. A colleague took me home as I was in a state of shock, before I then drove to the hospital; the two and a half hour journey a blur, fear took over, as I didn't know what to expect or what state he would be in.

Seeing him, I was at a loss as to how to react, what to say or do. He was pale, drawn, vacant and whether he even recognised us, his family, was anyone's guess. The stroke had caused part-paralysis of his right-hand side and impeded all ability to communicate. As upsetting as it was, I can't begin to imagine what my mum was going through, let alone my dad.

Following months in hospital, it was a relief when my dad was finally able to go home to familiar, albeit adapted, surroundings. My mum helped my dad to get into a new routine, as they continued his rehabilitation with exercises each morning, followed by the daily ritual of laps around the garden with his little tripod walking stick. For a while my mum was able to take my dad out for occasional trips, but the after-effects of the stroke meant they couldn't go far or stay out too long.

In the years following the stroke, glimpses of his personality, old habits, likes and dislikes would come through, along with the occasional, bizarre change.

You would often find him on the way back from the downstairs bathroom, stopping to raid the fridge and kitchen cupboards (something he would do before the stroke), sneakily filling his jumper pockets with ham, biscuits or jam tarts. By the time he got back to his chair, he'd often forgot about his stash, leaving the collection of goodies to amalgamate in his pocket, only to be found when the incriminating jumper was put in the wash. If you managed to catch him in the act, he'd give you his 'I'm not guilty' smile, his old personality making a fleeting appearance.

With football, interest in his boyhood club Blackpool and subsequently Arsenal waned with Man Utd disappointingly becoming his team of choice. Similarly with TV, Only Fools and Horses and Bond movies would be on constant loop, while the westerns and quiz shows he used to enjoy were no longer of any interest.

As a result of the stroke my dad became a shell of his former self and as Duncan and I didn't get together until a year after it happened, it meant he never got to meet the down to earth, confident, talkative and funny man my dad once was. The man who, rightly or wrongly, would stubbornly stand his ground on the things he had an opinion on. He also didn't experience the constant worrying my dad, and consequently my mum, suffered, often due to the stresses of the farm. Sharing this trait with him, it became a common bond that allowed us to relate to each other in the years running up to the stroke.

When growing up, we weren't especially close and

certainly didn't have the stereotypical close father-daughter relationship you see on TV or movies. But along with my two brothers, we were always made to feel safe, cared for and loved in our own, perhaps less emotional, way. A man of his era, it was also left to my mum to run the household and look after the children, in addition to pitching in with the day to day running of the farm. I deeply regret that it wasn't until my twenties, after my parents had retired, that we were able to grow closer. Then the stroke happened and stole that away.

In recent years, my dad's health has deteriorated even further. A few years ago he had another spell in hospital, following a suspected, but never confirmed, further stroke or set of mini-strokes. At one point we feared he may never come home, which made me worry about my mum and how she would cope without having my dad to focus on.

Luckily, he was able to recover enough to come home, though since that point he has been bed ridden, no longer able to get from the bed to his chair or to walk from room to room. He suffers even more from tiredness; just watching a sports match or having the family round to visit takes it out of him. Coupled with an array of other symptoms, it all takes its toll on my dad and consequently, my mum.

When visiting my parents, it makes me smile to see how pleased my dad is to see us, even if I'm not 100% certain he recognises us. On the flipside, it's heart breaking not to be able to talk with him, even over something as simple as the football or what's on TV. It's impossible to know how much he understands of what you are saying and seeing him struggle to get a sentence out is incredibly upsetting. He will often get part way through, before getting completely stuck, his mind getting confused or going blank. You can visibly see the frustration and upset it causes.

Ultimately, I resent the way the stroke took away my

dad and the essence of who he was. The way it stripped him of the ability to do things so many of us take for granted, whether it be to go places, join in a conversation or see his grandchildren grow up. The way it stole from my mum and dad the time they had earned to spend together, having worked so hard to enjoy their retirement. The way it meant my dad couldn't be at mine and Duncan's wedding, leaving a gaping hole in what was otherwise an amazing day.

From my experience a stroke is cruel. It leads to a complete loss of independence, as it cuts off control of your own body. It stops you being able to do what you want, speak to those you love, and spend time with those closest to you. It strips a person of their humanity, as they are left to just sit there, unable to join in conversations, or to share a joke.

It does all of this, and so much more. Slowly stealing everything that someone once was, and replacing it with a void. I cannot imagine looking out at a world that must have a semblance of familiarity, but feels so utterly alien. Struggling to do the most basic of tasks, with a body that is no longer your own. This is the cruellest thing that a stroke inflicts upon a person. You are a captive, forever looking out, forever trapped within.

THAT DAMN SLIT

JAMES NEWMAN

I was twelve years old when I first seen it, in the summer of '67.

That was the day Granpappy went missin' for the last time… the day the thing in the woods took him, and left nothin' behind but his shoe.

He did that a lot, wandered off when we wasn't watchin' him close enough. One minute he'd be sittin' in the livin' room, mumblin' to himself while he watched *The Andy Griffith Show* on our battered old Zenith. The next minute, you turned your back and he was gone. Like he just vanished into thin air.

Granpappy had come to live with us the previous winter. He used to have his own place across town, but he'd slipped on some ice, hit his head, and he hadn't been the same since. At least once a week he forgot where he was, or who we were. He was nothin' but a nuisance to Daddy. I heard my folks arguing about that a lot, especially when Daddy got to drinkin'. Mama said the old man probably didn't have too many years left, so it'd be wrong to throw him in some rest home and just pretend he never existed. That was the only thing Mama never would budge on. Usually, Daddy got his way about everything, 'cause it never took too long for him to use his fists to settle whatever they were fightin' about.

On the day in question, Daddy had just come home from work to find the front door wide open. No sign of Granpappy. Me and my sister Shelly was playin' outside in the backyard, and we heard Daddy yellin' at Mama all the way out there. That's the way most of our evenin's started when we was kids. With a whole lot of yellin'.

As always, it was me and Shelly who were given the task of findin' Granpappy. I guess it never occurred to our parents that we was just a couple of kids, and if we did find Granpappy and he didn't wanna come it wasn't like we could *force* him to follow us back to the house. There wasn't any guarantee that he'd even know who the hell he was talking to. But he came. He always did. Like a scolded puppy, he'd follow us back home, and he'd sit on his bed with tears in his eyes while Daddy hollered at him, "For Chrissake, Pop, what if we never found you? You'd be dead, and since I'm supposed to be the one takin' care of you I'd probably go to jail. You think I wanna go to jail 'cause of you?"

Granpappy's lip would quiver, and judgin' by the look on his face he woulda liked that just fine. He didn't know much, but he had to sense that nobody really wanted him around. I guess that's what made him walk off in the first place. Not his feeble old brain. But a brain that knew he'd be better off someplace else, where he wasn't a nuisance to anyone.

"These damn skeeters are eatin' me alive, Jesse," Shelly said as we made our way through the woods in search of our grandfather. My sister was twelve years old, same as me, but when we was alone she cussed worse than most grown-ups I knew.

"Why don't they suck on you for a while?" she said.

"For some reason they never bother you. Your blood must taste like shit."

"We're twins," I reminded her. "We've got the same blood runnin' through our veins."

"I don't think it works that way. Why do you reckon God invented skeeters? The sons-a-bitches don't serve no useful purpose."

"Shelly, I wish you wouldn't cuss all the time," I said. "It makes you sound like poor white trash."

"We *are* poor white trash, little brother."

Despite the fact that we was twins, she always got a kick out of remindin' me that she was born a few seconds before me.

She slapped at another skeeter, leaving a chunky red smear on her arm that looked like a half-chewed cherry. "Oh, well... guess I learned from the best, didn't I?"

"He ain't much of a role model, you ask me."

She laughed, but there was no humor in it. "You got that right. He ain't much of anything."

I watched my sister walk on ahead of me, her pretty brown hair swishin' back and forth, and I tried my best not to hate our father. His drinkin' wasn't the worst of it, nor the way he hit Mama when she did something he didn't like. There was things about Shelly's relationship with Daddy that bothered me somethin' awful, things I couldn't explain at that age. I just knew they didn't feel right. Daddy seemed to love Shelly a little too much. One time, a few months before all of this happened, I seen him sneakin' out of her room one night. He didn't know I seen him, but I did. He was adjustin' his pajama bottoms, and when a snatch of moonlight struck his face I could tell he was all sweaty.

I never asked Shelly about it.

We trudged on through the woods. Twigs and dead leaves crunched beneath our feet. Overhead, through the canopy of trees, we could see that the sky was the color of ripe peaches. Soon it would be dark.

We wasn't far from home. A quarter of a mile at the most. But the woods around our house were thick. It was like we was walkin' through another world, one covered with nothing but thick forest. This had always been our favorite place to play, as far back as I could remember, but at times like these, when it was gettin' dark and it had been left up to us to find our lost grandfather, the woods could be more than a little scary.

Shelly said, "One of these days I'm afraid to death he's gonna wander off, fall and break his neck or bust his head open on a rock. Maybe a mountain lion will get him, eat him up before anybody has a chance to save him. I think about that every time we have to come find him, Jesse. Like this time's gonna be it."

"Maybe Daddy's right," I said. "Maybe we should put him in a home somewhere. For his own good. Where people could look after him, make sure he don't hurt himself."

"Don't talk like that, little brother! Don't you dare talk like that. He needs us."

"I don't mean nothin' by it. I'm just sayin'… "

"Who's soundin' like Daddy now?"

I didn't get a chance to retort. 'Cause that's when we found it, in a small clearing smack-dab in the middle of the woods.

I was lookin' down at my feet, makin' sure I didn't trip over a root as we hurried along, so Shelly saw it first.

"What the hell… is *that*?"

The first thing we'd noticed was one of Granpappy's shoes, lyin' there on the forest floor. We knew it was his 'cause we had bought those shoes for him last Christmas. I had used my own money, money I earned for helpin' Mr. Henderson down the road split firewood.

But it wasn't Granpappy's shoe that made me and Shelly stand there with our mouths hangin' open like a couple of starvin' catfish.

It was the thing a few feet away from that single brown

loafer.

The thing in the rock.

Instantly we both knew—without a doubt—that it had gobbled up Granpappy.

It was a thin, vertical slit, about six feet tall, on the underside of a rocky hillock. It looked like a tumor on the back of Mother Nature, I remember thinkin'. There was some moss growin' on either side of it. It looked wet. At first, I thought it was the muddy openin' to a cave, but the longer I looked at it I knew that wasn't quite right.

I was pretty sure I felt a strange warmth radiatin' from it as me and Shelly stood there starin' at it.

I stepped toward it.

"Jesse, don't—"

"It's okay," I said. "It's… not hungry anymore."

I don't know how I knew that. But I did.

Just like I knew that it had eaten Granpappy.

His shoe lay on the forest floor just a few feet away from the slit.

I picked it up, threw it.

The slit sucked it up with a sound like somebody steppin' into a fresh pile of dog crap.

And that was the last of Granpappy.

They never found any trace of him. Not that they tried too hard.

Even at the age of twelve, I knew somethin' wasn't right about the whole thing. I didn't know about stuff like waitin' periods and bodies bein' pronounced dead when there wasn't a body to pronounce, but I was smart enough to know there was somethin' suspicious about the way it all went down.

And I knew it was 'cause of the sheriff.

Daddy had been friends with him since they was little

boys. I might've even heard Daddy say at some point that they was distantly related. In any event, I knew he didn't help Daddy out of the goodness of his heart. The kind of men Daddy hung out with didn't have no goodness, you could tell just by lookin' at 'em.

Any fool could see why the sheriff had Granpappy pronounced dead within a matter of just three or four weeks after he went missing.

Our parents were cleanin' up Granpappy's house, preparin' to put it on the market, when Daddy found an old lockbox under Granpappy's bed. It had some money in it. A lot of money. More money than anybody in my family had ever seen before. I guess Granpappy had been hoardin' it away for years, and when his mind started goin' feeble he forgot all about it.

It was like we had won the lottery. For the first time in years I saw Daddy smile. Mama too.

Once he found the money, Daddy didn't push for a big investigation into Granpappy's disappearance. The sheriff put together a search party for Granpappy, but that lasted all of about four hours before they called it quits.

Daddy used his newfound wealth to do a bunch of renovations to our home (by that I mean he paid some guys; he didn't lift a finger, of course). The place actually started lookin' pretty decent after a month or two. For the first time, we had a roof that didn't look like it might blow off the house in a heavy downpour. The holes Daddy had punched in the walls through the years were patched up and painted over. We had air-conditioning that kept us cool in the summer like it was supposed to and a furnace that kept us from shiverin' in the winter.

I figured the sheriff got some of that money too, when all was said and done.

I saw him drivin' a fancy new Cadillac around town. One that looked just like Daddy's.

Shelly and me, we never told anybody what we saw out there in the woods. We didn't speak a word about it to anybody except each other.

We spent many a night lyin' awake, theorizin' about its origins. We had devised a way of communicatin' that Mama and Daddy didn't know about; at some point we had discovered that we could sit there in our own rooms, on opposite sides of the house, and talk through the furnace vents. Somehow our voices didn't reach our parents' room. It was somethin' special, and a whole lot better than two Dixie cups on an old piece of string.

What *was* the slit, we wondered? Where did it come from?

Was it from another galaxy? Somethin' supernatural? Maybe it was some kinda new species of plant or animal, or a combination of the two?

What did it eat, before Granpappy came along? Did small forest animals keep it from starvin'? How often did it need to eat?

We eventually learned the answers to some of our questions. Not all of 'em. But some.

Two years to the day we found it out there in the woods, tragedy hit our family again.

We shoulda known Daddy would go too far, sooner or later. We had seen him hurt Mama one too many times.

We shouldn't have been surprised when he killed her.

Once again, Daddy's old pal the sheriff was kind enough to help him out.

The case was closed after only a week or so. The official word was that Mama was bringin' Daddy a cup of coffee while he was working in the yard, she spilled some of it, and then she slipped in the puddle and fell, hittin' her head on the corner of the porch.

I guess nobody cared to look any deeper into the whole thing. Nobody bothered to ask why there wasn't a cup of coffee anywhere to be found, or why the porch didn't have any of Mama's blood on it but that old broken axe-handle Daddy kept by the door sure did. Times was different back then. In those days, a woman was expected to obey her husband, and if he slapped her around a little she must have had it comin'. We was poor, Daddy was good buddies with the only lawman in town, and Mama didn't have any family to make sure her killer was held accountable for what he'd done.

Once the sheriff said the case was closed, the case was closed.

One night, not long after they buried her, me and Shelly was layin' in our beds, talkin' through the vents.

"Jesse," Shelly's voice came to me. "You reckon I'm gonna grow up to be just like her one day? Married to a man who hits me every chance he gets, always dreamin' about somethin' better for me and my kids… "

"No," I said. "You ain't gonna be like that."

She didn't say anything for several minutes. I wasn't sure she believed me. *I* wasn't sure I believed me.

"It ain't right, is it? He's gonna get away with it."

"No, sis, it ain't right."

"It's hungry," Shelly said. "And it's up to us to feed it."

We was lyin' outside in the yard on an old blanket, starin' up at the stars and listenin' to the crickets. Fireflies blinked all around us like the eyes of the night itself eavesdroppin' on our conversation. Behind us, through the house's front windows, we could see the flickerin' blue glow of the television—Daddy passed out in front of *The Twilight Zone*.

"What in the world are you talkin' about?" I asked her.

She chewed at her bottom lip, tryin' to find the right words. The look on her face suggested that she had been givin' this a lot of thought lately.

"It gives you things, when you feed it. When you don't, it takes things away. Like... once it gets your attention you'd better not forget. If you do, it... punishes you."

"It was survivin' just fine out there before Granpappy came along," I said.

"All I know is, once you give it something it becomes a part of you. It took Granpappy from us, and now we've got more money than we've ever seen before. But we've forgotten about it over the last couple years. We've left it out there to fend for itself. So it took Mama away from us."

"You're talkin' crazy," I said.

"Maybe," she said.

"Daddy's the one who took Mama away from us," I reminded her. "He hit her in the head with his axe handle."

She shot a nervous glance toward the house.

I had to admit—there was a strange sorta logic to her words. I didn't know why. But it all made sense. Goosebumps crawled up my skinny forearms.

She said, "I dream about it, you know."

"You dream about it?"

"All the time. That's how I know it's pissed off."

I was silent.

"You don't?" she asked me. "You've never dreamed about it?"

"No."

"Weird. I figured you did too."

A chill ran down my spine. I wasn't sure why, but it bothered me to think that the thing in the woods had been visitin' Shelly in her dreams.

Something else disturbed me more, though.

For those first few seconds after she told me she'd been dreamin' about it… I was so jealous I wanted to hit her.

Mama had been in the ground a little over a month when Shelly's voice came to me through the vent one night.

"Jesse," she said. "You awake?"

"Yeah."

"You still talk to that Mayhew boy?"

"Sometimes," I said. "Why?"

"I know what we've gotta do… "

There was a kid who lived down the road, went to the same school as us till he was finally kicked out for good. His name was Ellis Mayhew.

Ellis had brought a gun to school earlier that year. He'd pulled it out durin' recess, started flashin' it around, showin' off. To all the other boys in my class, includin' me, Ellis was a legend for a while. Didn't matter that it wasn't even a real gun. Ellis's dad was into breeding European deer or something like that; Ellis had stolen one of his tranquilizer guns.

The day after me and Shelly decided on our course of action, I paid Ellis Mayhew a visit.

I told him I'd give him three hundred bucks for that

gun.

He told me he'd take six. Said he already got his ass beat one time already; if he was gonna risk that by stealin' the gun again then it better be worth his trouble.

I took the money from Daddy's wallet while he slept, and the next morning the deal was sealed.

The day was slowly dyin'. It would be dark soon. I was startin' to worry that Shelly had lost her nerve. It was so quiet I could hear my own heartbeat in my ears.

I hid behind a giant oak tree on the edge of the clearing, about twenty feet from the slit. I held the tranquilizer gun tightly, with both hands... Its presence made me feel a little better, but not much.

Finally I heard them approachin'. Dead leaves and twigs crunched beneath their shoes. I could already tell by the slur in Daddy's voice that he had been drinkin'. It was all he ever did in those days, especially since he didn't have to worry about money anymore.

"This better be worth it, girl, whatever you wanna show me," I heard him say. "It's been a long damn day, and I ain't got time for games."

"Oh, it'll be worth it, Daddy," Shelly replied. "I promise."

I waited, listened as they drew closer. I didn't move, tried to breathe as quietly as possible.

Meanwhile, I was pretty sure I saw the slit pulse gently, as if it knew what was about to happen. I saw this out of the corner of my eye. I didn't look directly at it. I wasn't too fond of bein' alone with it.

When they stepped into the clearing, I felt sick. Shelly's shirt was torn, and I could see a hint of her bra underneath. I hadn't even known before that moment that my sister wore a bra. She had a touch of make-up on. She looked a lot like Mama.

She had lured Daddy out here with promises of something more.

"Well, girl, what is it?" he said when they stood in the middle of the clearing, about ten feet from the slit.

"It's time for you to go, Daddy," Shelly said.

"What?"

"Do it, Jesse! Do it now!"

I stepped out from behind the tree.

"What the hell is this?" said Daddy.

I pointed the gun at him, squeezed the trigger.

The gun bucked in my hands.

At first I thought I had missed. But then I saw the dart sticking out of Daddy's thigh.

He reached down, pulled it out. Stared at it.

He took several steps toward me, but then listed from side to side like a man on a ship caught in a violent storm.

"You kids... you're gonna get it... "

He blinked at us. Dropped the dart.

And then he toppled forward, face-first, into a pile of leaves.

We didn't say anything for several seconds. I don't think either one of us expected it to be so easy.

"Holy shit, Jesse," Shelly said. "We did it."

"It ain't done yet," I said.

I rushed across the clearing to stand beside her, over Daddy.

She said, "How long do you think—"

"Not long. We gotta hurry."

I took one of Daddy's arms then. She took the other.

We grunted as we dragged him across the forest floor, toward the slit. He was heavy, and it took all of our strength to get him over there.

"Shelly," I said, "Are we sure about this?"

"Damn right we are."

We propped him up against the slit. He let out a little moan. For the next minute or so, he just looked like a drunk passed out on somebody's front porch.

"Nothing's happenin'," I said.

"Just... wait."

We didn't have to wait long.

The slit parted slowly, like two thick brown curtains slowly drawin' back from one another, and it began to suck Daddy inside. It took his head first. Watchin' it made me think of something bein' gradually consumed by quicksand. Daddy's head tilted back, almost like he was raisin' his face toward the heavens to say a silent prayer, but he didn't wake up as he was sucked inside.

He looked peaceful.

Thirty or forty seconds passed, and then we could no longer see the top half of body.

About the time it got to his knees, I guess he woke up. He started kickin'. His workboots thumped against the forest floor. But it didn't do any good.

A minute later he was gone. Every bit of Daddy had been sucked inside of the slit. As if he had never been there at all.

The woods were silent.

"Good riddance, you son-of-a-bitch," said Shelly.

Her expression gave me chills. She didn't look angry. She didn't look glad to see him go. She just looked numb. As if her mind was somewhere else, far away.

I stared at the slit.

It didn't move.

But a couple seconds later I was pretty sure I heard it burp.

We was adopted by a local couple who lived a mile or so from the house where me and Shelly grew up. They owned a chain of furniture stores in the area, and they was the sweetest people you could ever meet. Before long we was livin' in a three-story house with fancy knickknacks in every room, a carpet that felt like cat's fur when you walked across it barefooted, and a fancy blacktopped driveway. I remember Shelly sayin' one time how she felt kinda like the main character from *Annie*, that lucky orphan girl from the funny pages that used to make our real Mama laugh.

Life was good, for now. Really good.

It was like we had been blessed by some higher power.

It was a Christmas night a few months later, I remember, when me and Shelly found ourselves discussin' everything that had happened. I don't know what brought it on, or who even raised the subject. The house was warm, our bellies were full. Both of our bedrooms were nearly overflowing with new toys and clothes. We had never felt so loved. So blessed.

"Everything that's happened, it's 'cause of the thing in the woods," Shelly said. "That damn slit."

"What are you talkin' about?" I asked her.

We sat on her bed this time, talkin' by the dim glow of the lamp on her bedside table. The days of havin' to conspire through the vents like convicts, the way we used to do when we lived with Mama and Daddy, were long gone.

"She takes a sacrifice. And then she gives you things in return. That's what I think."

"There you go again," I said. "Who says that's so bad? And what's this *she* business?"

Shelly shrugged. "I don't know. I just started thinkin' of it like that. And I decided it's a female."

I frowned, shook my head. I hadn't thought about the thing's gender at all. I'm not even sure I ever considered it a livin', breathin' thing. It just *was*.

"She gives you things. Makes you rich. But I'm not sure I want 'em, Jesse. I don't want 'em, if this is what it takes to get 'em."

"Don't tell me you're feelin' guilty," I said. "He got what he deserv—"

"No," she said. "I don't feel guilty about him. I'd never feel guilty about what we did to him."

"We've got it good now, Shelly. We've got two foster parents who care about us. The kids at school don't point and laugh 'cause we're always wearin' hand-me-down clothes with holes in 'em. And... *he's* gone. You've gotta be happier about that than anybody."

It was the closest I ever came to lettin' on that I knew about what Daddy used to do to her.

"Mama's still gone," she said. "There ain't no bringin' her back."

I couldn't argue with that.

"I'm just afraid, Jesse," she said. "I feel like something's comin'. Something bad. I don't know how to explain it. She makes things worse than they were before, I think, if you go too long without feedin' her. Don't you feel it too, little brother?"

I swallowed loudly, looked out her bedroom window at the thick, black night. I imagined it—*her?*—out there in the woods.

I saw tears in my sister's eyes.

Was she aware, even then, of what lay ahead for her? Did she know?

Two months after our sixteenth birthday, my sister was diagnosed with leukemia.

One minute, Shelly and I was walkin' into the school together, laughin' about some dirty joke a kid on the bus had told us.

The next thing I know, I'm gettin' pulled out of fifth-period Social Studies and called into the Guidance Counselor's office. I was informed that my sister had collapsed during P.E., and our foster parents had come to pick her up.

Three days later, the doctors told our new Mom and Dad that Shelly had a year or two to live, at best.

But Shelly didn't even want that.

She had other plans.

A few months after she was diagnosed, I heard her callin' me into her room. She'd had a few treatments by this time, but she hadn't started to waste away yet, so at that point her voice was still loud and strong.

I ran into her room, thinkin' something was wrong. I always thought something was wrong, ever since I got the news of her sickness. Like we had always been so close that she might know the exact moment she was about to die, and she would make sure she called me in to say goodbye before it happened.

She sat up in her bed, smiled sadly at me when I stepped into her room. "Close the door."

I did as she asked. "What is it, Shelly? What's goin' on?"

"Come here." She patted the bed. "Come sit beside me, little brother."

"Okay."

"Can you hand me my glass of water?"

"Sure." I got it for her, from her bedside table.

She sipped at it. I got a chill, watchin' her cheeks sink

in as she sucked at the straw. For a second I thought I could clearly see the outline of my sister's skull, and I wondered how long it would be before she looked like that all the time.

She handed the cup back to me.

"Jesse," she said, "do you love me?"

"What kinda question is that?" I said. "I love you more than anything else in the world. You know that."

"Then you'd do anything for me, right? Even if it sounded crazy as hell. You'd do anything to make me happy?"

"Yeah," I said. "Within reason. I mean, I doubt I'd set myself on fire for you. But I would hope you wouldn't ask me too."

She laughed weakly. "Silly. More water."

This time I held the cup for her as she drank.

"What's goin' on, Shelly? What are you gettin' at?"

"I need you to do somethin' for me, Jesse. It would mean a lot to me. And it's what I want. So even if it sounds crazy, I want you to do it. I *need* you to do it."

"What is it?" I asked her.

"I want you to take me out into the woods."

I waited for it. Somehow I knew exactly what she was gonna say before the words fell from her tiny mouth.

"I want you to feed me to her."

"What?"

"You heard me. I want you to feed me to the slit."

I told her I couldn't do it. I lost count of how many times we argued about it over the next year or so. I think she hated me because I wouldn't do what she asked me to do.

"I want it," she said. "Don't you understand, Jesse? It's okay, because it's what I *want* you to do!"

"You're obsessed with it," I said.

21

"Her."

I ignored that. "It *eats* you, Shelly! You don't come back. It ain't like you step into it, and a few minutes later it shits you out on the other side. Is that what you think is gonna happen? Maybe you think you step out of it and all of a sudden you're in a better place?"

She looked at me like I'd just insulted her. "I'm tellin' you... this is what I want. I want to know what happens. Whatever she does to me, wherever she takes me, it's got to be better than *this!*"

I looked at her, lyin' there all frail and sick, attached to needles and tubes like somethin' out of a bad science-fiction movie. She was gettin' worse every day. She barely even looked like herself.

It broke my heart.

"You go somewhere else," she said. "But when she takes you, I don't think you suffer. I think you're just... gone. You cease to exist." Again, she said, "Whatever happens, it's gotta be better than this, Jesse. This way, I know I'm gonna suffer. The whole family's gonna suffer. I don't want that."

My eyes grew wet with tears. I swallowed back a sob.

"You *have* to do this for me," she said.

"I'm sorry," I told her for what must have been the millionth time. It seemed that was all I said to her these days.

"Dammit, Jesse, you told me you'd do anything—"

"Not that," I said. "I can't."

I couldn't murder my sister.

So I let the leukemia kill her slowly.

I know she never forgave me.

And neither did the slit.

Here I sit, decades later.

My trailer smells like stale beer, mildew, and cigarettes. It's about to be repo'd soon, but I don't give a shit.

I finish off the can of Natty Light in my work-calloused hand. Some of the beer trickles down my chin, into my beard. I don't bother to wipe it away.

I think about what I have become...

I swore I would never be like him. But look at me.

I'm a loser. A drunk. I have no job. I've been married four times—five? Hell, at this point I've nearly lost count. All of them ended badly. I've been in and out of prison for beatin' on my exes 'cause I couldn't control my temper. My kids don't even speak to me anymore. One of them, a three-year-old named Shelly, I've never even met in person.

I have become what I despised.

I am my father's son.

Every day I ask myself: was this my destiny all along? Would I have been unable to escape it even if I tried?

Or did my life turn out like this 'cause I didn't give my sister what she wanted? Was she right about the thing in the woods? Has it waited out there all this time, hungry and neglected?

The slit giveth, but she also taketh away.

That's what Shelly said, so many years ago. Maybe those weren't her exact words, but the message was the same.

And more and more these days, I believe she was right.

I have nothing. I am nothing.

I'm sorry, big sister. I'm sorry I let you suffer.

I know it's still out there. I can feel it, calling to me.

Her.

It's been too long. The slit is hungry.

So I'm going back. I'll give the bitch what she wants, by God...

I will step inside.

I hope Shelly was right, all those years ago, on that night when the skeeters wouldn't leave her alone but for some reason they kept avoidin' me.

I hope I taste like shit.
And I hope the thing friggin' *chokes* on me.

JAMES NEWMAN

James Newman lives in North Carolina with his wife and their two sons. His published work includes the novels MIDNIGHT RAIN, ANIMOSITY, THE WICKED, and UGLY AS SIN, and the collection PEOPLE ARE STRANGE. Next up are two new novels, DOG DAYS O' SUMMER and SCAPEGOAT (co-written with Mark Allan Gunnells and Adam Howe, respectively). When he isn't writing, James loves listening to loud rock n' roll and watching University of North Carolina basketball.

WITH BLACKEST MOSS

CHRISTINE MORGAN

Maude promised herself that if it turned out to be wall-to-wall spiders in her mother's old gardening shed, she'd take up some different hobby.

Scrapbooking, maybe. Crocheting. Something, anything, some way to fill the waiting hours.

Let go. Downsized. Fired. Taking involuntary advantage of the early retirement program. No matter what you called it, out of work was out of work.

She wasn't sure when anybody had last been inside the shed, but she ought to at least see what there was before she went spending a bunch of money on tools.

The door stuck. Maude pulled. She heard and felt a soft ripping giving-way, like muffled Velcro, as it opened. She backed up in case those anticipated, wall-to-wall spiders came out in a swarming flood.

Nothing came out, no spiders, swarming or otherwise. Only a draft of air, cool, heavy, and musty-smelling. Not stuffy and sweltering like she would have expected, but a basementy smell, a subterranean cellar-like smell.

The doorway showed only a rectangle of shadow in the hazy, sepia-toned smoglight of yet another southern California summer. Maude squinted through her sunglasses, waiting for her vision to adjust.

This wasn't the way things were supposed to be. This wasn't how her life should have turned out.

All those things she'd wanted to do, meant to do... but kept putting off... until the time was right, until the money was better, until the divorce was final, until the kids were out of the house…

Maude sighed.

Too late now.

At her age? In this economy? What, go back to college, get her degree? Start her own business? Begin a new career? Travel? Date? Remarry?

Have a life?

Yeah. Yeah, that'd happen.

"Oh but Maude," everyone told her, "you're always *so* good about putting your family first."

Married right out of high school, divorced fifteen years and three kids later. Custody battles and child-support hassles. Working full-time to keep their heads above water and stay a step ahead of the expenses both expected and unexpected.

Putting your family first.

Telling yourself that, once they were grown, once they were settled and on their own… once the nest was empty… there'd be the chance for something else.

Maude sighed again.

Instead, here she was. Back home right where she'd started. Pushing fifty and already washed up. A dead end with nothing to look forward to but getting older, maybe with the hereditary dementia into the bargain, like a bad bonus prize.

She noticed a black, fuzzy smudge along the shed door's edge. Thready in fine straggling wisps, like a torn piece of linen, or a skein of brushed wool, it ran all the way down, as well as along the top and bottom… in fact, the entire inside of the door was covered.

Maude touched the stuff. It felt fibrous, a little crumbly, a little springy, a little furry and a little… moist? No, not moist, not quite, but not dry.

She thought of dust, the greasy but fluffy dust that accumulated in range hood fans and under stoves. Or soot, ash, the waxy char-black residue that came off a burnt candle wick. Those were close, but not quite right.

Weird, not unpleasant, but odd and foreign and... strange.

She poked a fingertip into it, made a divot, pulled her finger back, and watched as the whatever-it-was filled the depression slowly back out. Like one of those fancy foam mattresses, the kind that, on the commercials, suggested you could jump on the bed without spilling your wineglass.

Spongy, sort of. And thick. An inch-thick layer, coating the inside of the door. Top to bottom and side to side. With a rounded hump where the inner half of the doorknob mechanism was, and longer narrower humps over the hinges.

When she looked at the jamb and saw it there, too, all the way around, the Velcro sensation made sense. She'd pulled until the stuff had... had just torn along the seam, like an old pair of pants.

She scraped at it with her nail, scratched at it. She pinched a tuft, plucked it off the way she'd pluck a lint puff off a sweater, and rolled it between her forefinger and thumb. The texture made her think of oily strands of hair wadding into a ball... or the clumps of fur that used to be left in the comb after she groomed the dog.

Rubbing her palm back and forth over the strange black layer was almost like petting Woozles again... the woolly feel of his coat... smoothish one way, nappier the other.

A tickle on her cheek startled her, and only when she wiped away a tear did Maude realize she was crying. Standing here in the hot, midday smoglight, crying over a dumb, sweet goof of a dog who'd gotten out one day and run off when the gate had been left unlatched. Hadn't she been wondering just a few minutes ago when that hereditary dementia would catch up with her?

Maude snapped herself out of it and took a closer look, as well as an experimental sniff. The scent of the stuff was the same as she'd smelled on that cool draft... musty, heavy... an earthy plant smell...

It was some kind of moss, or mildew, or mold.

Her nose wrinkled. She thought of the nasty brownish slimy spots that appeared in the bathroom corners, no matter how often she sprayed and scrubbed.

Only this stuff wasn't nasty, wasn't slimy.

It reminded her of the ground-covers people might choose for their gardens, something that would spread in a nice low pad. Hardy, durable, not needing a lot of fuss and maintenance.

The moss, or whatever it was, had overtaken the whole interior—door, walls, floor, ceiling—in carpets and cascades. Here and there, it bunched up in hummocks, dotted with little shiny-black domes like mushroom caps. It was so thick over the windows that not a single pencil-thin ray made it through the shutter-slats. Long feathery-fine tendrils dangled from the ceiling, stirring in the desultory breeze.

The shed was much cooler than the yard outside... cooler than it'd be in the house, for that matter. The old house had no air conditioning, just fans that made a constant stuffy whirr all summer.

Out here it was cool, and quiet. Muffled-quiet, padded-quiet. No whirring fans. No unsynchronized ticking of clocks. No yellowish-miasma nicotine buildup on the wallpaper. The musty, earthy smell was... pleasant. Comforting.

If she closed the door behind her, she'd be isolated in this cool, quiet, comforting, fragrant darkness. The way the moss sank under her feet told her that it really would be as soft as one of those foam mattresses.

What a wonderful thing it would be to sleep, to sink into a full, real, restful sleep for a change. For the first time in a long time. For the first time since she'd come home again. Sleep without the subliminal anxiety of listening for her brother... without being on alert for the next outburst or disturbance... how nice that would be!

"Oh but Maude, you were always *so* good about putting your family first."

Yes, it would be nice, but she couldn't. Sleep? Out here? That was crazy.

She pushed the door closed.

Besides, it was Friday. Friday was grocery day. She went into the house for her purse, list, and keys.

"I'm going shopping now," she called.

No answer from the den down the hall.

Two hours later, Maude pulled into the driveway, turned off the ignition, and listened to the engine clunk-chug-wheeze its way to silence. She got out, popped the trunk, and hauled in the groceries in one trip by laddering the plastic bag handles up her arms. They dug into the flesh and left sweaty red marks.

"I'm home!"

"Did you bring chicken?"

"Chicken's for Monday!"

"It isn't Monday?"

"No."

"Didn't you go to work?"

"I don't go to work anymore, remember?"

Fred's reply was a disinterested snort, signaling the end of the conversation.

The groceries got put where they belonged, a place for everything and everything in its place, where they'd gone for as long as Maude could remember.

Clocks ticked. Fans whirred. Pipes gurgled. The house was as stuffy and sweltering as ever. Furniture sat and pictures hung where furniture had sat and pictures had hung for over half a century. The same knickknacks gathered the same dust. Each year, the rug got a little more worn, the wallpaper a little more yellowed.

She set frozen fish fillets onto a baking sheet because it was Friday; chicken was for Monday, take-out rotisserie chicken; frozen fish fillets were for Friday. Saturday, their big day, they'd go out to the smoke shop and beer barn to stock up, then have an early dinner at the Heartland Buffet.

As the oven pre-heated, she poured herself a soda and went to check messages.

Nothing from any of the kids. She wasn't surprised, had no reason to be—they never called; they'd write sometimes but they *never* called because Fred might answer.

"He's dead to us," they'd told her. "As far as we're concerned, he's your brother, not our uncle. He's no relation of ours. He's not welcome in our homes, and we don't want him anywhere near *our* children."

Maude thought they were being a little extreme. Okay, they didn't like him, he gave them the creeps, but he'd never *done* anything to them.

"He beat up Grandma," they'd said.

"He didn't beat her up," Maude tried to explain. "He slapped her once, and you know how she was toward the end, she was out of control."

"She was eighty years old and about eighty pounds total, and he *hit* her and now you're defending him just like *she* always used to do! Like you *promised* you wouldn't!"

Maude's hand had been on the telephone, ready to pick up and dial—elder abuse, domestic violence, assault!—when her mother, already bruising, said "Maudie-don't-you-*dare*!"

Couldn't anybody understand she didn't have any choice? What else was she supposed to do? Later, her mother had begged, from her very deathbed, that Maude "look after my Freddie." How could she refuse?

"He can't live by himself," she'd said, trying to reason with her kids. "Without me, he'd end up—"

"In prison? Dead? Rehab? In a loony bin? On the streets?"

"That, or some kind of adult care home—"

"So what? Let him!"

"He's your uncle—"

"He's a shitbag alcoholic racist sexist homophobic asshole parasite waste of space!"

They insisted duty and obligation only went so far. They said they wished Fred would need a transplant and one of them the only donor match, so they could refuse and watch him die.

"What about you, Mom?" they'd asked. "What if something happens to you? He's in for one hell of a rude awakening if he thinks any of *us* are going to take care of him!"

Furthermore, if it fell to any of them to make Fred's final arrangements? They'd donate him to one of those cadaver farms like you saw on *CSI* or *Dirty Jobs*, and the only pity was, a place like that would expect him to be dead first.

"He knew Grandma was getting worse," they'd said. "He didn't do a goddamn thing."

"He didn't want to worry me," replied Maude.

"He didn't give a shit."

Her mother had eventually been pulled over by the Highway Patrol for erratic driving, halfway to San Diego when she'd only been going to the beauty parlor. When she'd been too confused to answer their questions, they called the house and got Fred, whose main concern had been that "the dumb old biddy" was supposed to bring rotisserie chicken, and asked if the cops would stop and pick some up when they brought her back.

Hiring someone, that was out of the question. So were nursing homes, retirement facilities, assisted living, anything of the sort was met with mulish stubbornness.

So, Maude, always *so* good about putting her family first, went to stay with them for a while to help out.

For a while. That had been the plan. Her mother deteriorated rapidly after the highway incident, and Maude told herself it'd be a matter of months, maybe a year at the most.

On that count, she'd been right.

Those final words, though, that deathbed plea …

"Maudie, you have to take care of him, you have to look after my Freddie."

"He cost us our grandmother," her children said. "Now he's costing *our* kids *theirs*!"

They wouldn't visit her, and she couldn't visit them. They kept inviting her for Thanksgivings and Christmases, but was she going to leave him alone on the *holidays*? What would her mother have thought of *that*?

She was stuck, and why was that so hard for her kids to understand? Why did they think she could throw Fred to the wolves, let him sink or swim, fend for himself? Sure, he largely ignored her when she was around, but he didn't like it when she was gone. He'd accepted her going to work out of necessity. Anything else was abandonment.

Why should she put her selfish wishes against his legitimate needs?

"Why not?" they'd say.

So, she needed something to keep her busy, a hobby, but one that would also be homebound, keep her near at hand. Something like gardening.

Their mother had gardened. The roses, the geraniums, the flower beds and rows of terra-cotta flower pots she'd set along the porch rail... Maude didn't know if she had inherited the green thumb, but she didn't think Fred would object the way he objected to other proposed changes.

The way he'd object to another pet, for instance. Neither he or their mother had warmed to Woozles— "that damn dog," was how they'd peevishly referred to him.

And, of course, any suggestion of selling, moving, remodeling, even clearing out the garage or attic of a half century's worth of clutter was out of the question.

The smell of baking fish fillets and boxed Parmesan noodles drew him from his lair in the den. He shuffled into the kitchen, filled his plate without a word, grabbed the hot sauce from the cupboard—he doused everything in hot sauce, pepper or both—and went to the fridge.

"Where's the beer?"

"Right where it belongs?"

"I finished the last one earlier."

"Then we're out."

"We can't be out!"

"If you finished the last one, then we're out."

"Why didn't you get more?"

"We'll go to the smoke shop and beer barn tomorrow."

"But we're out!"

"Can't you drink something else?"

"I don't want something else!"

"It's only until tomorrow—"

He flung his plate against the wall. It smashed beside one of the cuckoo clocks and fell in pieces to the brick-tiled floor. Fish fillets and noodles went everywhere. The clock let out a surprised chirp.

"*There*, look! Are you happy *now*?"

"Fred—"

"What good are you, can't even keep enough beer in the house?" He stormed out, stomping down the hall hard enough to make the floor shake.

Maude looked at the mess. Her appetite was gone. She just felt so damn tired, so damn used up. All she wanted to do was crawl into some cool, dark, quiet place and let the world go away.

She knew just where.

Okay, maybe it *was* crazy, but so what? She didn't care anymore.

The sky had the color of an old penny beginning to corrode and go green. The air hung flat, limp and humid. Planes droned overhead. Traffic made its steady snarl.

The shed door peeled open not with a Velcro sound but a barely-sticky-tape sound, from where the tattered mossy threads had already started knitting back together. The cool, musty draft washed over Maude.

She stepped inside, feet sinking into that spongy

cushion. She closed the door. Blackness enveloped her. Soft, silent blackness. Wispy tendrils whispered against her face as she moved. The layer of moss at the shed's center was deep, thick, a plush upholstery.

The tiny mushroom-cap things pop-pop-pippety-popped with a delightful bubble-wrap sensation when touched, and gave off whiffs of that mild, earthy fragrance.

Maude sat down, then reclined and stretched out. The moss supported and conformed, it molded itself around her in marvelous comfort. It was goosedown and fleece, clouds and cashmere.

Eventually, she noticed that the darkness wasn't as total as she'd thought. No light seeped in from outside, but, faint speckles of some sort seemed to float, to drift, to waft effortlessly above her. Faint, pale speckles... like dust motes... spores that eddied on the currents of her breath, swept toward her in whorls when she inhaled, billowed spiraling upward when she exhaled.

She was breathing the stuff, and that might not be so good, but this was too peaceful, too restful, too relaxing for her to worry about possible adverse effects.

Her fingers sank into the moss, combing through it, the substance parting and closing back in to fill the channels. Soothing... it was so soothing... it would make everything all right again. Shouldn't she be the one taken care of for a change?

This sweet, simple, undemanding, unconditional welcome... affection, almost... no judging, no anger...

Then her slowly dredging fingers snagged on something not-moss, and Maude brought it up with a vague dreamlike sense that she should have known, or that, deep down, she'd known all along. The collar's imitation leather was moss-caked now, the encrusted tag dangling.

More tears slipped from the corners of her eyes. Gotten out, they'd told her. Must have gotten out and run off. The gate left unlatched, an accident, such a shame.

That damn dog. Her Woozles.

Not even when she felt the moss creeping over her could she dredge up the energy to be concerned. It not-quite-tickled on her skin, a gentle spreading embrace as it enfolded her limbs. It wove through her hair like a million filament fingers massaging her scalp, and made fluffy earplugs. It blanketed her body.

So quiet. So private. So cool and dark and comfortable.

The moss crept to her cheeks, her forehead, her chin. Tendrils followed the tracks of her tears. Maude closed her eyes to what felt like the delicate brushing of an eyeshadow applicator. She suppressed a slight urge to sneeze as the moss tickled into her nose.

It reached her lips. Her mouth. It cocooned her completely.

The silence held.

The cool air in the shed grew cooler still as the sun finally descended and the sky turned the murky purple-orange of a Los Angeles dusk, heading for the muddy denim that was the closest it ever got to full dark. In the bushes, crickets commenced their chorus.

Later still, as a famous nearby theme park set off its nightly fireworks extravaganza, the vibrations of their thum-*thud* echoing explosive concussion blasts penetrated into the shed, causing the mossy mass at the center to quiver, and rustle, and stir, and rise.

Maude crossed the backyard and patio. The crickets hushed as she passed. The bugs flitting and flicking against the porch light dispersed in a panicky scatter.

She went into the stuffy house. Fans whirred, clocks ticked. Fish fillets sat room temperature on the baking sheet; the pot of noodles had congealed into a Parmesan clump. Pieces of plate and spilled food still littered the floor.

Her footsteps were as muffled and silent as if she wore thick wool slippers, but that didn't stop the old floorboards from creaking as she went down the hall. The den's door stood ajar, the television tuned to a right-wing rant-a-thon about gay marriage and immigration.

The smoke-filled room smelled of alcohol... not beer, but the harder stuff he swore he'd given up on and she thought she'd gotten out of the house. Fred, slumped in his recliner with the remote in one hand and bottle in the other, didn't turn as she came in. A full ashtray rested on the arm of the chair, a butt smoldering in the ashy heap.

"*There* you are, about damn time," he said. "Did you want me to sit here and starve all night while you sulked?"

When he didn't get the expected contrite reply he turned, but by then Maude was to the recliner. He saw her and gaped.

She grasped him by the head.

Moss rippled along her arms and hands... moldy, fuzzy, living black gloves. It rushed over his face with surging, rapid, hideous eagerness. It seethed up his nose and into his mouth, choking off his scream. Fibrous, expanding like a dark fungal form of spray insulation, it clogged his throat and filled his lungs.

Fred thrashed in the chair. Always florid, he went maroon. His bloodshot eyes bulged. His body heaved and lurched. His chest swelled up like that of an enraged bull. One flailing arm hit the recliner's lever, pitching him backwards, kicking his feet up on the footrest. With the other hand, he clutched at Maude and only came away with an oily, fetid fistful.

His spine stiffened, arching him up from the seat. His heels drummed. Then he collapsed, loose and slack, limp deadweight. He shuddered. His fingers twitched.

Then... nothing.

Maude waited.

The moss plugging his nostrils and windpipe dissolved, with a foamy hissing bubbling sizzle like hydrogen peroxide. The wad clenched in his fist withered, going brittle and white, disintegrating into powder. Fred's swollen chest deflated, expelling a sickly gas of alcohol fumes, cigarette smoke and decay.

Soon, no traces remained, no residue.

Heart failure, they'd decide. Stroke, or embolism. Unsurprising in a man of his habits, who hadn't been to the doctor in years because he knew what they'd tell him to do and had no intention of doing it. A pity poor Maude had to find her brother this way, but, at least it had been quick.

She'd taken care of Freddie right up until the very end, and isn't that what their mother would have wanted?

The moss prickled and tickled as it crept down her body, the hairlike little rootlets withdrawing from her skin. It flowed onto the den rug, forming a fuzzy lump that grew and coalesced into the semblance of a little black dog. Maude picked it up, stroking the woolly coat. It wiggled with happiness, wagging its stub of a tail.

There'd be so much to do… selling the house, starting over… but before beginning any of that, she'd call the kids to chat and catch up and apologize.

After all, as people liked to tell her, she'd always been *so* good about putting her family first…

CHRISTINE MORGAN

Christine Morgan recently relocated from the Seattle area to the Portland area, beginning a new, more-social phase of her life among the local horror/bizarro weirdo creative community. They like how she brings goodies to readings and events. In addition to her several books and dozens of short stories in print, she's a regular contributor to The Horror Fiction Review, the editor and publisher of the Fossil Lake Anthologies, and dabbles in many various other writing-related projects. Her other interests include history, mythology, cooking shows, crafts, superheroes, gaming, and spoiling her four cats as she trains toward eventual crazy-cat-lady status. She can be found online at https://www.facebook.com/christinemorganauthor and https://christinemariemorgan.wordpress.com/

CHAGRIN

JONATHAN BUTCHER

Chagrin (noun) – frustration or distress at having been humiliated or failed

"Quit scratching your fucking shoulders," Nigel said from the armchair. "It's like you've got fleas or something."

James, still a little stoned from the joint he'd smoked earlier, rubbed the skin beneath the sleeves of his black "Scum" t-shirt, with one hand on either shoulder. He tried not to scowl as he looked at his stepdad.

Step*twat*, more like.

"They're itchy," James said, fighting the urge to get up from the couch and hurl Nigel's open super-strength beer at him. James was only sharing the same breathing space as this douchebag because he liked his mum believing that they got along.

Nigel settled back into the armchair that James's late dad had paid for. Its plush brown leather had once seemed like luxury compared to the lounge's stained carpet and nicotine-yellowed walls. After Nigel had moved in a couple of years back the seat had lost its sheen, and the armrests were now peppered with coarse, plasticky fag burns.

Slouching, Nigel bent one knee and tugged off a sports sock. A rank odour wafted over James, smothering the baking smells drifting from the kitchen. Nigel's foot was grey, bristly, its nails so jagged that they would have shamed a hobbit. Keeping his eyes on the TV, Nigel said, "You're putting me off the snooker."

Trying not to heave, James said, "It's a crap game anyway. Just two blokes playing with their balls."

Nigel narrowed his eyes. "Don't start that queer talk today, Shitpool."

"Shitpool" was Nigel's attempt at a twist on James's favourite superhero, Deadpool. It referred to James's birthmark: a wide patch of dark-brown skin covering the lower half of one cheek. James had always suffered playground insults and laughter, but never so badly as after the day that Nigel had picked him up from school and called him 'Shitpool' in front of the other students. Even now, just a few months from his final exams and his 18th birthday, the name still stuck.

"Snooker is a game," James said, improvising, "where two guys grasp their long poles and push balls into someone else's holes."

"Something wrong with you, boy," Nigel said, his face darkening. "Why don't you go play with your imaginary computer friends?"

"The best part is when someone wins the championship," James went on. He had nothing against gays himself, but he knew just how to piss off his stepdad. "That's when they pop their champagne corks and squirt white foam all over their mates. Sounds a bit like an outlet for closet-cases, doesn't it?"

Nigel's breath whistled in his nose. When he stared back at James he wore a hateful, boozy leer. "Keep talking, Shitpool. See where it gets you. All I've gotta do is wait a couple more months, and then you'll be gone."

"Ha! Dream the fuck *on*."

"Don't matter what you think, boy," Nigel said. "Coz I've convinced your ma what's *best* for you. And, you know what? We both think that you need to stand on your own two feet. Become independent."

James's chest went cold. "What are you on about?"

Nigel lowered his voice. "You're outta here, boy. And while mummy thinks that you'll be prepped an' ready to take care o' yourself, I'm willing to bet that in two shakes of a lamb's bollock, you'll be out on the streets, fiendin' for brown, an' suckin' off old men for change. Probably be dead in a year or so, just like *daddy*. Now there's a nice thought."

James stood up, ready to launch himself at the alcoholic bastard, but then his mum bustled into the lounge, followed by the smell of charred sugar. Her hair was a bushy mess at the best of times, but today it was even wilder than usual.

"Enjoying the match?" she asked. Her eyes didn't quite focus on James. Onto the coffee table she placed a tray bearing two rows of black lumps that might once have been biscuits. "Here, I've baked some cookies." She smiled blearily and took a sip of Nigel's beer. "May have left them in a little long, but that'll just add to the flavour."

When James had been young, his mum had baked brownies and crumbles, muffins and shortcake. She'd been much better at it back when James's dad had still been around.

"They look wonderful, Susie, love," Nigel said. He stood up, threw his arms around her and leaned in close. She pecked his lips but Nigel made a pantomime of slipping his tongue into her mouth.

James's mum's cheeks became even rosier. "Nigel!"

James felt sick.

"Sorry, Susie, love," Nigel said. "Jus' can't keep my hands off you."

"Well, you just enjoy the snooker, and save anything else for later!"

As she turned to leave again, Nigel hit her backside with a *whap*. When she was out of earshot, he said to James, "She's no cook, but trust me: your mummy fucks like a demon."

James kept his gaze level, imagining Nigel's head bursting into flames.

And his shoulders continued to itch.

As James settled into his bed in the darkness of his little room, he heard a knock. His stomach clenched as he imagined his steptwat popping his head in for one last insult, inspired by the end-of-session rum that he guzzled before bed every night.

When the door opened, James saw the silhouette of his mum's tangled hair.

"Jusssst thought I'd say nuh-night," she said, her voice slippery with wine.

"Um. Okay."

The door closed. She didn't turn on the light, and when the room was just greys and blacks again James heard three steps before her weight flopped onto the bed beside him. After a brief silence, James's mum said, "I know that you two don't always get along."

James smelled the brewery waft of her breath, felt the weeble-wobble of her weight.

"But Nigel makessss me better. He makes me alright."

James couldn't remember the last time he'd felt so awkward. It was like being a kid again.

"He'ssss not... not like your dad, I know." James felt a movement that was probably his mum shrugging. "But he's better than nothing."

James wanted her to know how much of an arse Nigel was, but he was no good at arguing. It wasn't as if his dad had been much of a role model, either—he'd just been... nice. It was that simple. He'd been a smackhead towards the end, yes, but James felt that his dad had always tried. Before everything had gone downhill, James remembered his dad making his mum smile, with no need to load her with wine or super-strength beer.

"I know you'll be allllright when you go," she added. Her shadow loomed over James and he felt her squeeze his wrist. "When you get your own place, you'll be a man, won't you? A big man."

James wanted to yell that he already *was* a man. He wanted to punch the walls. But he just lay there stiff and tense and bitter as his mum pressed her lips to his cheek.

She rose, fell back, and then rose again, and he heard her totter through the dark to the door. The yellow crack of light reappeared and vanished again as she left.

James swallowed hard.

"Don't do it, don't do it... " he told himself.

But then, for the first time since his dad's funeral four years ago, James began to cry. He never let Nigel, or the assholes at school, or even his mum see that he was hurting. He turned over and muffled his sobs with the pillow.

"Grow up, you prick," he growled through the tears.

He thought back to everything his steptwat had said. His dad had been an addict, so what was to stop James from becoming the same, without a roof over his head? He'd never had a job. He wasn't a great student at school. All he really knew was playing massive online multiplayers and smoking weed.

He imagined trying to convince his mum that Nigel was playing her like an idiot, but he'd heard what she'd said. She hardly believed that the sun shone out of Nigel's beer-farty arse, but she didn't seem to think that she could do any better, now that dad was gone.

James's mum deserved a man to *support* her, though, not to drown her in booze.

"I'm more of a man than him," James muttered, wiping his eyes and shifting onto his side.

He jumped when his shoulder touched the mattress.

Both his shoulders had become tender, red and blotchy as the day had gone by, so he had used two dollops of his mum's face cream on them before getting into bed. It had done nothing to soothe him.

James's mum's headboard began to thud against the

wall. Her mewling came between the sounds of what James assumed were spanks, like the ones he'd seen people doing on the internet. His stomach turned at the familiar noises.

James remembered his dad nodding off in the armchair, not even bothering to hide the greasy track-marks that dotted his arm. Then he pictured Nigel in the same chair, supping his beer and leering at James's mum.

Did James want to follow either of their footsteps—or was there a better way?

He sat up panting, brow damp and shoulders prickling like nettle stings. He ripped at the itchy spots with his nails while his mother and steptwat humped and bumped in the next room. As he scratched he stared up through the darkness, wishing that he believed in God or that he had someone else to reach out to. There was no one, though. James needed to take things into his own hands—he had to become the *real* man of the house.

It would be Saturday tomorrow. Nigel would head out early for a day at the bookies, followed by a heavy night at the pub.

He'd come home wasted.

He'd be slow, weak, and even dumber than usual.

James decided that if nothing convinced him differently, he would take this as an opportunity to deal with his awful steptwat.

James awoke to the hiss of a woman's voice: "*You shouldn't.*"

He sat up, twisting his head to the right so fast that the joints clicked.

No one.

He peered over the edge of the bed. Still nothing; just his glass of Pepsi on the carpet—never booze—and a bed so close to the floor that not even a kitten could squeeze beneath it.

The clipped, female voice came again, inches from his ear: "Apologies for waking you like that, but I couldn't hold it in any longer."

James lowered his eyes to his right shoulder and the short, loose sleeve of his "Scum" t-shirt.

"Yes, that's right," the voice said.

Frowning, still half-asleep, James lifted the black material.

His shoulder grinned.

James stared, struggling to process the sight.

Overnight, a pair of plump, pink lips had risen from the ridge of his collarbone, breaking through the skin between his neck and the curve of his hairy shoulder.

The mouth beamed, its teeth immaculate.

"Hello," it said, primly. The voice almost reminded him of his mother.

James squawked. He leapt out of bed, despite the fact that the thing he wanted to escape was attached to him.

"What the hell?" he demanded, standing in his pants and t-shirt.

"Come on now, James," the mouth told him. "Calm down."

"You aren't real. You can't be."

"Stop talking then," the mouth replied. "You *do* look rather silly, arguing with your own shoulder."

"Shut up, shut up, shut up!"

"I'm not talking though, am I, James? As you said, I'm not real. I... "

"*I said shut up!*"

James slammed a hand over his shoulder. The mouth nipped him, and he yelped.

"Don't do that," the mouth snapped, no longer playful.

James sat down on his bed and stared at the wall, counting to 10. If he reached 10 and the mouth had vanished, he would put the sight down to tiredness, or a dream. But if it was still there when he reached 10...

He reached 10.

When he looked down, the lips were pursed cockily.

"Well?" the mouth asked. "Real enough?"

James looked at the palm of his left hand. There were two rows of angry teeth marks. He felt like running from the room to either dial 999 or tell his mum, but something stopped him. His legs and arms felt unsteady.

If Nigel had spiked last night's omelette, James would *murder him*.

"You won't be *murdering* anyone," the mouth said, as if in reply. "And this, young man, is exactly why I'm here."

James focused on his drawn curtains. "What are you talking about?"

"Oh, I have permission to speak now, do I?"

James neither replied nor argued.

"Well then. Lately, James, you've been having some rather dark thoughts, haven't you? 'Shoot this bastard'. 'Hang that bitch'. And, more significantly, 'Let's *deal with* my step-daddy'."

"How do you... "

"Because I'm part of you, silly." The mouth clacked its teeth. "I know it all. I... " The voice became muffled: his sleeve had dropped down again. "Do you mind?"

James lifted the fabric.

"Thank you. As I was saying, I know everything about you. I know about the time that you pushed little Kenny Thistlethwaite out of his wheelchair, and said that if he told anyone, you would get your dad to beat him up."

"I was nine!" James said.

The lips smiled again. "I know about that time when you were left alone in class, and decided to sniff your French teacher Mrs Clacton's seat."

Ashamed, James had no response. The morning felt dreamlike but the pain in his hand told him that he was awake, and he *still* could not bring himself to leave the room.

The steptwat had probably left the house by now, but James's mum would be downstairs, probably watching Jeremy Kyle on catch-up. James had planned to make the most of his Saturday morning, either by working out what to do about the steptwat, or sending pictures of his knob to girls online. But now he found himself locked in debate with…

With?

"You've been a naughty boy," the mouth continued. "Shoplifting to impress the other students. MDMA and amphetamines. Fighting the other lads. But so far you've done nothing compared to what you're considering now."

"Nigel's a prick, though."

"Stepfathers are always… difficult."

"Oh, so it's okay to threaten me, like last night?" James said, antagonised. "You heard what he said? About kicking me out?"

"I did," the mouth said. "But do you really want to sink to his level—*or lower?*"

James didn't generally think in 'levels'. In Social Health at school, Mr Hopkins often talked about morals and stuff. While James understood that most people believed in 'right' and 'wrong', he struggled with the finer details. 'When is abortion acceptable?' Mr Hopkins had once asked. 'Is it right to murder one human in order to save a hundred?'

And James had thought, 'Depends if you get away with it.'

"But there is more to life than 'getting away with it', young man," the mouth told him.

"Will you *please* get the hell out of my head?"

The mouth ignored him. "There are certain things that you simply shouldn't do. Rape, for example. Torture. And, in your case, cold-blooded murder."

"But he's a prick!" James repeated. "He deserves whatever he gets! He comes into my house, sits in my dad's chair, keeps me awake at night when he and mum are... eurgh... and he's gonna chuck me out! So don't you think that—?"

The mouth yawned loudly. James closed his left eye and used his right eye to look down between the mouth's dazzling white teeth. Inside, he couldn't see any of the muscles or bones that helped him move his arm. But there also seemed to be no tongue, or gullet, or any of the pink that you would expect to see inside a mouth. Between those perfect white teeth James saw nothing but black. It was like looking into a deep well, and it made him dizzy.

Everything felt so wrong.

"*This* isn't wrong," the mouth countered. "*Killing someone* is wrong. And, more simply, you'll get caught."

A harsh male voice said: "Oh, blah, blah, fuckin' blah."

James jumped, but in a weird way wasn't even surprised. As he reached up to his left shoulder, he braced himself. He lifted the t-shirt's other sleeve and before he even saw what was underneath he was hit by a waft of gingivitis.

A second mouth had appeared overnight. This one was cracked and split, the lower lip coated with froth. Its teeth were a brown junkyard, and something grey oozed from the sides of its lips.

How had he not noticed *that* sooner?

"I might not be pretty," it told him, "but at least I'm honest."

"Don't listen to that troublemaker, James," said the right-hand mouth. "He'll just confuse you."

"How can I confuse him any more than you already have?" the left-hand mouth—Lefty?—demanded. "This poor bastard is being threatened with death, and you're telling him to hold back? If anything, he'd be showing restraint by killing his steptwat. That arsehole needs torturing!"

James's head swam. "I... I never said... "

"Oh come off it, Shitpool," Lefty said. "We all know what you was thinking."

James almost punched the rotten mouth at the sound of his nickname, but somehow he knew that he'd only bring himself pain. Again he wanted to jump from the bed and hurry downstairs to his mother, but when he tried his limbs disagreed. He was trapped by his own body.

Lefty said, "If you ask me, the question isn't *whether* you should do it—it's just *how*."

"Well... well no one's asking *you*," the right-hand mouth, or Righty, said. She sounded flustered. "James— you love your mother, yes? Then just think how she would feel, if—"

"Ah, quit your preachin'," Lefty said. "The longer you leave it, James, the more likely it is you'll just stand there and let that bastard chuck you onto the streets."

"James," Righty said. "Take a moment, and just *think-*"

"If you don't stop your yammering," Lefty warned, "I'll come over there, and—"

"Stop," James said.

Both Lefty and Righty clamped shut. James glanced at each in turn, waiting to see if they were going to start again.

As bizarre as his morning had become, James knew that the mouths were right about one thing: he had a decision to make. Everything had come to a head in a short time, and although he wasn't sure if he was going mad, hallucinating, or still dreaming, he planned to face things head-on. That's what the man of the house would do.

"Okay. This is what's going to happen," James said. "Both of you can tell me what I should do. State your case, like. You can each have a couple of minutes to speak, and then I'll weigh everything up and decide."

The mouths puffed irritably. "Fine," they said, almost together. Minty breath rose from James's right and a cloud of rotten gas filled the space to his left.

James stood up and went to the crack between his wardrobe and the corner of his room. The mirror, which he rarely used, was about half his height. He dragged it out, propped it onto the bed and leaned it against the wall. Then he tugged off his t-shirt and sat cross-legged before the glass on his mattress. He stared at his sleepy self: the birthmark on the side of his face, his pot-belly, his yellow boxers, and the new mouths that had grown from the skin of his shoulders.

"I'll go first," said Righty.

Lefty didn't object.

"You've had it tough, James," Righty began. "When your dad lost his job, he picked up an old bad habit again, and after a while, that brown filth took him away from you. Afterwards, your mother seemed to give up, didn't she? She sank down into herself and then fell into Nigel's arms—conniving, controlling, boozing, bullying Nigel. It's no surprise that you're angry."

James was. He felt madder than he could ever remember being before.

"But," Righty went on. "You've survived this long without doing anything dreadful, so why put your future at risk? If you do something silly, you'll let that monster win, and what would your father think of that? You can become a better man than the both of them—a *real* man, who takes responsibility and learns from his hardships, rather than letting them consume him. Take up a job now, while you still have time to save, and then rent your own place. Grow. Face the challenge. Become responsible, take ownership of what's happened to you, and break the cycle." Righty bit her lower lip. "I, um, rest my case."

James was silent for several moments. Then he said to Lefty, "Okay. Your turn."

He watched the other mouth in the mirror. Its discoloured teeth were clenched. "Alright then," Lefty said at last. "Here's my argument."

James felt his left shoulder joints shudder.

"James… " Righty said.

In the mirror, Lefty drew its lower lip up and over its

horrid dentures, opened wide, and *gnashed*. Pain erupted in James's shoulder, but somehow he managed to avoid crying out.

"*Get off,*" he gasped, instinctively snatching at the furled strip of muscle which Lefty had clamped between its teeth. Instead of simply releasing its lip, Lefty opened and chomped down again—this time into the palm of James's hand. The pain sharpened to a point. James breathed in with a whistle. Lefty bit down for several more seconds and then released him, hissing. The foul teeth, now tipped red, had left blood-welled ditches in James's hand, deeper and more painful than Righty's warning nip earlier.

James cringed when the mouth expelled a sticky, hateful snarl, exposing the hollow blackness inside.

"Stop," James pleaded, panicking. "This isn't an argument!"

Lefty, foamy with blood, clamped its jaws down over its own lip once again, apparently impervious to the pain it was causing, and then roared, "*Of course it's an argument, Shitpool! So argue back!*"

James shrank from the stench of its breath, wishing he could tear his eyes away from the mirror.

"Fight me, you fucking coward!" Lefty demanded, biting the sore skin once again. "Or aren't you *man enough?!*"

Rage bubbled up inside James and he finally retaliated: he ploughed his right fist into Lefty's teeth. There was an explosion of pain and the blow sheared skin from his knuckles. One of the mouth's filthy incisors broke and became a jagged fang. Blood rose from the back of James's hand, but even more rushed from Lefty's burst lip, down over James's collarbone.

Lefty spat. "That's what you have to do," it said. "When something threatens you, you don't just take it, and you don't just turn the fucking cheek. You *fight*."

Catching his breath, James watched Righty's reflection. The neater mouth was silent.

Lefty breathed a disgusting, satisfied breath. In the mirror, James saw another rivulet of blood emerge from its maw, catching speed as it joined the rest and ran down into his armpit hairs.

He knew what had to be done.

While James believed that his plan would benefit his mum in the long term, he felt as if something cruel and cancerous was squirming in his belly whenever he imagined how she would first react. Instead of eating lunch with her as he usually did, he munched a sandwich in town before visiting the hardware store. He needed to buy one item for his main plan, and another for his backup plan.

Although James could tell that Righty was irritated by his decision, at least it had stopped protesting. The pair of mouths could still not agree, but James was thankful when they hushed their bickering whenever they were near other customers.

After hiding a bottle in his pocket, James stood before a display of DIY tools.

"If you *have* to go through with this ghastliness," Righty said from beneath James's sweater, "then it is better to be quiet and underhanded than vicious and blatant."

"Such a coward," Lefty muttered. "If you're gonna do something, do it right. Imagine the satisfaction of smashing that fucker to pieces!"

"You said that this was about fighting back, not about sadism," Righty said. "James, think of your mother, please."

James thought of his mother. Then he thought about Nigel calling him Shitpool, and the sounds of the pair of them fucking in the next room.

So James slipped a second item under his top and hurried from the store.

When James returned home to prepare his backup plan, his mum was slouched asleep in his dad's armchair, the shrubbery of her hair hiding her eyes. He leaned over and kissed her cheek. She snuffled when his lips brushed her skin and he froze, hit by a gust of her alcoholic breath.

Relieved that she hadn't woken up, James surveyed the room. The TV blathered in the corner. James could smell the remnants of another morning's baking, perhaps to make up for yesterday's singed biscuits. He tidied up a couple of plates and a few empty cans and left his mum snoozing in his father's once-smart leather chair.

I could get used to this, he thought, smiling at his steptwat's absence. *First things first, though.*

Sometimes, James felt nervous passing beneath the underpass alone. It was only a short walk from his home, and while overhead lights coloured the tunnel interior a bright yellow, both entrances led onto sections of road unlit by streetlamps. One dark verge led down towards another road, while the other side sloped towards a section of river.

On the river side, at the entrance to the underpass, James waited in the darkness. He crouched and pressed himself against the wall, knowing that his steptwat was more likely to spend his last scraps of change on another drink than on a taxi ride home. Cars purred and belched by, headlights sweeping the shadows but never quite revealing James.

He itched all over but resisted raking the skin. Instead, he fingered the stolen claw hammer through one of his puffer jacket pockets. It had a satisfying weight and a sharp, curved hook made for prying nails. Back home he had made his backup preparations, just in case Nigel passed by with someone else in tow, or didn't show up, or, worse, James was too squeamish to go through with it.

"You can still change your mind," Righty said, muffled beneath the layers of his jumper and coat. "Just throw the hammer away, go home, and… "

"Oh shut your fucking hole," Lefty replied. "Stop sulking, just because you lost."

"I'm not sulking at all," Righty said.

"You're always sulking."

"Oh, for goodness'—"

"Hush, you two," James said.

A figure had entered the opposite end of the tunnel. James felt ill, but reminded himself that this was all for the best, and that it was for his mum as much as for him. Two wrongs probably made a right, and all that mattered was that he got away with his crime.

His steptwat Nigel was not quite staggering, but his feet threatened to tangle over every second step. His upper half leaned towards the road, as if magnetised by the tarmac. A lorry blustered by. James considered pushing Nigel beneath a vehicle instead.

"Fuck that," Lefty sneered. "Witnesses mean either getting caught or having to shut more people up."

"I hate to say it, but he's not wrong," Righty said.

James didn't want to kill anyone else, and he definitely didn't want to be caught. He peered around the corner again.

Nigel wore the thin brown trench-coat that James always thought made him look homeless. It was unbuttoned and James could see a pale football shirt half-shimmering in the rancid light of the underpass. Nigel's eyes were half-closed, like he was sleepwalking, and he carried a near-empty glass of what James assumed had once been a full pint of beer.

James heard his two extra mouths whispering, one in each ear, but he was done with debating. He drew the hammer from his pocket and glanced up at the stars. Nothing dissuaded him. He was overcome by a fierce certainty.

Nigel murmured as he neared; he sounded irritable. James kept hiding, counting his steptwat's steps, telling himself that on 13 he would pounce.

When James rounded the corner, Nigel jumped.

The pint glass shattered at their feet and his steptwat's lidded eyes sprang open. "*Shitpool?*"

James swung the hammer into Nigel's ribs. There was a crunch and a throaty gasp. James grabbed his steptwat by one shoulder and yanked him away from the road, onto the shadowed grass of the roadside verge.

Despite all the beer he must have drunk, Nigel was quick. James lashed out with the hammer again, aiming for the moonlit plate of Nigel's forehead, but Nigel batted his arm away.

"*What the FFFFFFFUCK do you think you're doing?*" Nigel yelled.

"Get him, James!" said Lefty.

Nigel stepped forwards but slipped on the grass, grabbing James's puffer jacket sleeve as he fell. They tumbled towards the moon-dappled river, a shadowy laundrette-spin. James's weapon-arm bounced against the ground. There was an impact and James lost his grip on the hammer.

Nigel, who had landed on top of James, howled into the night. He reared back onto his knees and the moonlight revealed his face. The hammer's claw had lodged above one of his steptwat's eyebrows and now dangled from his face like a wall hanging.

Above them on the road, a motorcycle buzzed by.

James's steptwat's forehead streamed black blood, and the eye not hidden by the protruding hammer kept batting in confusion.

"Don't just lie there—kill the prick!" Lefty shouted.

"No James—run!" Righty said.

James shoved Nigel but his steptwat was sturdier than he looked. Nigel raised a hand towards the hammer, wincing with his one visible eye as he wrenched it from his skull. There was a gritty squelch and blood waterfalled from the wound, coating half his face. "You... " he mumbled. "Youuuuuu... "

James was paralysed.

Nigel appeared dazed as he raised the hammer and, one-handed, swung the claw-end downwards. James tried to roll sideways but his legs were pinned under Nigel's knees. The hammer arced into the rear of James's hand. Knuckles shattered. Skin split wide.

And James's hand *screamed.*

James screamed too, as did both Lefty and Righty beneath his clothes.

Nigel seemed to regain his senses, frowning at the chorus coming from James's body. Ignoring the pain, James rammed the back of his injured hand into Nigel's face, pimp-smack-style. James felt a twinge of unfamiliar muscles as his hand clamped onto Nigel's cheek. Nigel shrieked and wrenched his head backwards, yanking James's arm as he went. The new mouth stayed attached to Nigel's scrawny jowl.

Nigel grunted, raised the weapon, and hailed hammer blows into James's chest, arms and sides. Wherever its claw broke through his jacket and skin, James saw the glitter of new teeth—some sharp, some jagged, some neat, some misshapen—and another voice joined the demented choir. Desperate to avoid further wounds, James did something he had never done before: he hugged his steptwat.

As they embraced, each mouth that had emerged across James's body gnashed through Nigel's clothes. All shouts—aside from Nigel's—made way for the clacking of molars, the ripping and spitting of fabric and the wet tearing of flesh. Lefty chomped into Nigel's still-swinging arm, holding it in place between its vile brown teeth. The hammer dropped to the grass and Nigel used his one free arm to punch and chop at James's back.

Wracked with agony, James used his one unoccupied mouth—the one he had always owned—to bite Nigel's throat. His steptwat tasted like bad aftershave and blood.

Even when Nigel had stopped fighting, James's many mouths continued to chew and swallow. Between mouthfuls, they commented on a job well done, and debated the taste of the sinewy snack that James's steptwat had become.

James walked home, a bleeding, gibbering wreck. The mouth in his head remained silent but the horde of fanged holes patchworking his torso argued and debated, discussed and bemoaned. He could barely follow his own feet, let alone discern which of the parroting lips made the strongest points. Now and again he heard a voice that reminded him of his father, or of teachers at school, or of the bullies that had plagued his lessons and lunchtimes.

He did not pass a soul, but when he arrived outside his home he saw that the curtains of his lounge were painted a faint green. His mother must have still been awake, perhaps worrying why Nigel hadn't returned. James had hoped to just go to bed, either to peacefully bleed to death or to sleep until morning, when maybe the mouths would have closed, sealing the wounds they'd sprung from for good.

"Be quiet, now," James said as he stepped through the door.

The mouths continued regardless.

James found his mother face down on the lounge floor, her face hidden by the fallen veil of her ridiculous hair. An orange halo of vomit circled her skull. His steptwat's cheap white rum stood open on the table, empty.

The backup plan had been to spike his steptwat's "night cap" rum with the paint thinner he had stolen. His mum must have finished her wine and taken some of Nigel's rip-off Bacardi, maybe to calm her nerves as she awaited his late return.

"Oh, James," Righty said. "If you need to cry... "

"Shut the fuck up, you," Lefty said. "Useless bitch deserved it, really."

Some of the mouths offered sympathy.

Others said it was for the best.

A couple laughed.

James was surprised by how little he felt at the sight of the corpse, numb as he was to the pain that writhed beneath the heckling voices. Had it ever been about her?

He looked at the red footprints he had traipsed through the house, and the smears across the door handles and wall. He lifted his shirt. More mouths had opened across his chest and stomach, whispering and hissing and singing their opinions. Blood and foamy mucus ran from his ruptured flesh.

He pressed a finger against one mouth that had appeared beneath his navel. It had sharp, uneven white teeth, and kissed him with a moist smack. James pushed against its incisors. They opened, releasing a gobbet of black filth, and snapped through the large knuckle of James's ring finger. He noticed dully that instead of leaving a bony stump, the wound revealed yet another mouth that nipped and whispered with miniature jaws no larger than a rat's.

James laid his arms against his torso: mouths against skin, flesh against fangs. None spoke, but wherever the teeth gnawed into him more appeared, blood-streaked and voracious, until lips bordered lips without a trace of flesh between, only lightless voids hidden by dripping jaws.

The feast continued as James settled into his father's

armchair. It was a good chair, he thought, as he chewed through the fat of his own lips.

New mouths bred new mouths, spreading and biting into his chin, devouring the birthmark from his cheek and multiplying across his forehead and scalp. They chomped and swallowed and his skin vanished into a cold black nothingness before fading away entirely.

And the mouths ate their fill.

JONATHAN BUTCHER

Jonathan Butcher lives and writes in Birmingham, UK.

From the day he was able to transcribe ideas onto paper, he has been writing strange stories. He hopes he never stops.

If you want to stay updated with his fiction writing, follow him here:

www.facebook.com/jonathanbutcherauthor

Let's keep things weird.

GEORGE

DARYL DUNCAN

I gazed through the glass out over the estate. It was still the same shithole it had been when I was growing up here. Nothing ever changed. People got older, people died, and others, like my wife, just seemed to live forever.

I could hear her singing in the living room; the drink had finally kicked home. I knew, without seeing her, that she would be dancing in front of the little stereo system near the window. We had had it for years. I think it was a wedding gift from one of her asshole brothers, obviously nicked from a neighbour. I had one vinyl in all that time, 'The Best of Madness', but Doreen had thrown it at the cat one time and it had broken in two. I can remember every Christmas, opening the sock-shaped parcel and praying for a replacement. It never happened.

These days I spent all my time in the kitchen, looking out the window mostly and watching the world go by. Doreen would come in now and again when her bottle was empty and grab another. It was awful to watch someone you once loved kill themselves slowly with the drink. If I could, I would have stopped her, but I couldn't. I could only watch. And those rare times that we actually got close, I could never find the words.

There was a knock at the door and Doreen killed the music. Her bare feet padded up the tiled hall and I could hear the clicking of the many locks as she opened them. Doreen trusted nobody.

It was a male voice. Selling something, most probably.

Laughter, a few words exchanged and the slamming of the front door. Doreen walked into the kitchen. I adjusted myself and stared at her. She ignored me and went straight to the cupboard. The strains of Charlie Rich singing, 'Behind Closed Doors', burst into life.

That bloody song again.

The glass banged hard on the worktop beside me. I turned away. The vodka splashed all the way up to halfway and the dash of coke hardly coloured it at all. I felt some pity for her habit, but not that much. It would be better for both of us if she just choked to death on her own vomit one of these nights. The thing was, my wife just wasn't that rock and roll.

I held my breath as she turned to stare at me. Her eyes were barely visible, sunken so deep into her troubled skull. She left the kitchen without speaking. I breathed a sigh of relief. At least I think I did.

It got dark pretty quick and the music still played from the living room. I guessed she had passed out on the couch. The record would play to finish, the needle would lift up and return home. Just one more song and then I could get some sleep. I changed position and looked back out over the estate. Darkness had fallen. The street lamps— or at least those that worked—came on. Hooded creatures lurked in the shadows, young ones with beer and glue, getting wasted and breaking into houses. It's just how things worked around here. I closed my eyes and hoped Doreen would sleep through.

The postman woke me the next morning. The wave of bills and adverts fell upon the hallway carpet. I listened, could hear snoring from the living room. It was asleep, sound asleep. I looked at the little clock on the windowsill and it read 10.30am, Wednesday. It was Doreen's signing on day. She would be gone for most of the morning. She didn't drive and, since I was incapable these days, she had to take a bus from the estate and a taxi when she got to town. I didn't envy the poor guy or girl who would take care of her at the dole office. Her breath in the morning was enough to cut through glass. I had until just after lunchtime to do what I wanted. I could relax in those few hours. I could tidy myself up a little without the constant fear of criticism on my appearance. I was what I was. Nothing could change that.

I closed my eyes as she entered the kitchen. She never spoke. I was glad. I knew by the amount she had downed last night that her head would be in pieces, and by the sounds coming from underneath her gown that she was moments away from shitting herself. She filled half a glass, drunk most of it, and then ran—or staggered quickly—to the stairs. It was one habit I could not abide. How could people use the toilet and not have the decency to lock or at least close the door behind them? I sat there and heard the whole thing, every splash, groan, and fart. It sounded like a slaughterhouse. I waited for the flush that never came. She was off to get ready and make herself presentable. I was tired. My eyelids fell heavy over my eyes and I tried to get some sleep. I made myself as comfortable as I could in a bed that was well overdue a change of sheets. I couldn't do it myself, and Doreen had obviously forgotten about it. I had to make do with lying in my own mess and filth in a room that was far too small. Sometimes I thought of death and the comfort it would bring. I eventually fell into a deep slumber.

I was dreaming of gentle walks in the countryside with our old dog Ben—a collie type, all tan and black—when I felt something prodding me. The dream disappeared and I opened my eyes. Doreen was inches away from me with a stupid grin on her wrinkled face. The years were definitely not being kind to her. I was glad. At least, incapacitated like I was, it meant I wouldn't have to endure watching her or hearing her with other men. All through our marriage, and most likely because I worked shifts at the factory, she had many affairs and one-night-stands all under my nose. I'm sure even our neighbours around the estate knew of her sexual exploits and had had a good laugh at my expense. If they could see me now I wonder would they laugh. Knowing the people of this estate, they probably would.

"Have you been sleeping all this time, you lazy fucker?" she said as she went about putting the groceries in the various cupboards, slamming each door in turn. I didn't respond, just licked my lips and hoped she would leave as soon as possible.

"Well, while you were lying around on your fat arse all day, I have been busy. You remember busy, don't you, George?" she said, smirking. Her last bag contained several bottles of wine. She lifted them out one by one, inspecting the labels as she did. Who was she kidding? She knew fuck all about wine. I have to admit I would have killed for even one sip of Chardonnay, but my drinking days were long gone.

Her stash was under the sink. For years she had used the place to hide her booze behind the various unopened bottles and sprays of cleaning materials.

She left one bottle on the kitchen table, took off her coat, and threw it out into the hall in the hope of reaching the bannister. It fell short and landed on the floor. I watched as she unscrewed the bottle of wine and tossed the top into the sink. She grabbed a fresh glass and filled it to the brim, took a sip and sat at the table. I had that sinking feeling in my ample belly that it was going to be a really long night.

"So, Georgie boy, as I was saying, I have been busy today. Don't you want to know how I got on uptown? Shit, that reminds me, I picked up a few things for you as well. Aren't I so good to you?" she said, sipping from the glass and plundering in her handbag.

She pulled out a few small bags. I adjusted myself. I had been too concerned with her comings and goings that I had forgotten about eating. I wasn't able to eat on my own and I needed Doreen's help for that. I actually felt a tinge of guilt about running her down so much. I was still alive. She fed me. She talked with me when I was feeling up to it. I suppose in her own strange way she still loved me.

She held the food between her nicotine-stained fingers, not far from my face, and it was my cue to open my mouth. She dropped it in and I swallowed as quick as I could. I wasn't allowed cooked food anymore, and the stuff that had been recommended was tasteless and cold, but who was I to complain? Doreen kept feeding me with one hand and tipping her glass with the other. It was always a nice moment. I preferred the kind Doreen to the one that would surely make an appearance later on when the wine kicked in. I closed my mouth and blinked my eyes. It was my way of telling her that I was done. I had had my fill. I belched and she actually cracked a smile.

"Greedy big bastard, aren't you, George? Now, I'll let you digest that before I clean up your mess. In the meantime, I have to make myself presentable. Old Doreen has a date tonight." With that, she went upstairs. I was hoping she would keep her promise of cleaning me up. I had been sitting in my own piss and shit for a few days now. I was beyond caring about my own cleanliness, but I'm sure she wouldn't want her new boyfriend having to stick the smell. Although, usually when she had 'friends' over, she would shut the door and keep me out of sight. I would busy myself with life out on the estate while she busied herself in the bedroom upstairs. I would try my best to drown the sounds out, but she was loud when she was in the mood. Thankfully she hadn't shown any sexual interest in me lately. I wasn't the man she had married. I was just an ugly, deformed creature, more a burden than anything else. I hated her for letting me live like this. I had nothing left to offer the world. I closed my eyes and tried to sleep off the mood.

There she stood in an old flowery dress, the one I had bought her one day in the city, back when things were different and money was really not a problem. "What you think, George, the old lady still got it?"

I tried to nod, but the way my neck and spine were these days, I couldn't manage it. I blinked instead.

She looked at the clock and smiled. "Time for a wee drink before he arrives. Don't worry, I'll clean you up when I get back. Okay, Georgie?" She reached down and stroked my face. "Oh dear! Your skin's all dried up. I'll have to Google that and see what's up. Remind me in the morning, but not too early," she said with a wink.

A car horn blared outside in the street. She went to the window and waved, drank straight from the wine bottle, wiped her mouth and blew me a kiss. She was gone. I had peace. I actually hoped she would find me dead when she got back. A car engine revved as it sped off. I was alone.

A few hours passed and something woke me. A strange tickling sensation around the top of my head. I opened my sticky eyes. I saw a leg dangling down, trying to find its footing. I licked my lips. I knew who it was. It was the damned spider that had been torturing me for days now. Doreen was petrified by them. I didn't mind them at all. I sat still and waited. He was mine this time.

His thin legs crawled all over my face, and still I waited. Further down he climbed until several of his legs actually rested on my closed mouth. I took a breath, opened wide, and with one gulp I took him in my mouth.

He wriggled and crawled around, trying desperately to escape. There was no escape, not this time. I let him suffer in the darkness, making up for the many nights he had spun webs upon me as I slept. When I finally got bored, I swallowed once and he was gone.

The front door crashed open and I heard a heavy thud on the hall floor. I adjusted myself and watched. A hand appeared around the edge of the doorframe, followed by the rest of Doreen. She was a mess. It took her a few minutes to actually make it to her feet. It was a scene I had had to endure many times, but tonight she looked different. She actually looked scared. Her long hair was wet and plastered to her face. Her makeup was a mess and her mouth was bleeding. Blood splashed on the tiles as she spat. She cursed and mumbled as she finally got to her feet and staggered towards the kitchen worktop.

It was times like this I wish I was human. I just wanted to cry out and ask her what was wrong and what had happened? Regardless of what I was, she was still my wife. She lifted the bottle she had opened hours before and drank from it, washing the stale wine around her mouth and spitting down into the sink. Something small and yellow rolled about the sink like a roulette ball before stopping.

It was a front tooth.

"Fuck," she screamed and picked it up. She caught me watching. "The fuck are you looking at?" I moved back into the corner of my tank.

"Yeah, you know what happened, George. You want to know how my date went?" she said, ripping the front of her dress down.

There were bitemarks and bruises all around her neck and chest. She stood there swaying in front of me. Her eyes burned right through the glass tank and into me. I was frightened. I had been wary of drunk Doreen before; even when I was human she was a fearful drunk, but now I was shaking in my lumpy green skin.

The chair scraped along the floor as she sat down, grabbed the bottle, and drank from it. She hadn't adjusted herself and her tits hung out from the ripped dress, sagging mounds of dead flesh. But who was I to judge appearances? I was a dirty fat toad with skin problems and bad eyes.

Doreen sat in silence, playing with the top of her wine bottles. Her yellow finger circled the top, peeled the label from it, leaving the bits in the ashtray beside the cigarette that was almost burnt to the butt. I would have killed for the last few drags from that cigarette, or any cigarette for that matter. I really thought the cravings and human feelings would have long since vanished, but it seemed whatever had happened to me, whatever Doreen had done to me, hadn't been a complete transformation. It was times like this that I wish it had been.

A thump on the door stirred me from my thoughts. Doreen's head shot up from its slump.

"Hey, Doreen, let me talk to you, please?" said a male voice from out on the balcony. I watched as she pulled on an old cardigan, which had been hanging over the radiator, and covered herself up. I knew exactly who it was.

Her date.

I stuck my big tongue out and licked my lips. It was the only way I had of expressing myself. Fuck, it was frustrating. She glanced over at me. Her eyes were wide and bloodshot. She looked old and vulnerable. Her hands shook as she clung to the front of the cardigan. The door really rattled this time. I thought it might crash open with the force of the guy behind it.

"Open the fucking door. I won't let you do this to me. I have my wife and kids to think about. OPEN THIS FUCKING DOOR."

Doreen walked to the window, leaning over my tank as she did. I turned.

The guy's face appeared at the window. He saw her and raised his hand, as if threatening to break the window. Doreen stepped back, her face pale. The guy's fist just stopped short of the glass. I hoped he would leave. He didn't. He moved away from the window, and then I heard our rusty letterbox open.

"Doreen, just talk to me. You owe me that, at least?" He spoke in a softer tone. Doreen moved towards the kitchen door and hung around it. I didn't like where this was going.

"Just leave me alone, what's done is done. I won't tell anyone. Just go, please?" she said. Her voice was strong, at least. I didn't want her to cry in front of this bastard.

"I won't take the blame for this. I mean, who are they gonna believe? I'm a respected shop owner and, well, you're... you're *you*?" I could tell by his voice he was smiling. My blood boiled.

"You fucking attacked me. I have the marks all over my body to prove it. How about I call the police now and show them? How would that suit you and your wife and kids? They'd like that, wouldn't they?" she screamed out into the hall.

The door banged three, maybe four times really hard. This was it. He was coming in to finish what he had started.

Doreen jumped back and ran to the rack of knives on the wall. My heart sunk when I saw that she had picked the smallest one available. She wasn't thinking straight. Two more thumps at the door and then silence. He was gone, for now. Doreen was breathing heavily, but moved to the window and gazed out. She sighed before looking down at me. She smiled at me.

It was over.

"I think we need a drink, George. You fancy a wee drink? Like the old days?" she whispered. I did, but that wasn't going to happen. She left the kitchen, switched on lights all over the house, and made her way to the living room.

A few moments later, Charlie Rich was singing about a Sunday kind of woman. I knew this song, lyric by lyric, chord by chord, but after what had happened this evening, I couldn't deny the lady her guilty pleasure.

She turned it up and then appeared in the doorway. "Just going upstairs, Georgie. I want to get out of these clothes. It will help me feel better. Don't go anywhere, okay, hun?"

Okay, this was weird. She hadn't called me Georgie or hun in such a long time. I was worried. I moved to the cleanest corner of the tank and made myself comfortable. My piss and shit almost covered half the base of the glass tank. I would soon have to hop up onto the little wooden hut she had bought the other week, although I wasn't sure I could manage it. Tomorrow was another day, I would try then.

I settled down to sleep. I knew Doreen well enough to know that she had crashed on the bed and would sleep until morning. Charlie was now singing about taking it all home. He would quit soon enough.

I felt cold fingers pressing into my underbelly. Something sharp poked into my side. I tried to look but I was suddenly floating up from my filthy tank.

Doreen had me cupped in her hands, close to her face. I could smell the stale wine and bad breath warm against my cold skin. She smiled. Pieces of the meal she had had earlier were stuck between her front teeth. She began to walk backwards from the kitchen.

I have to admit it felt good to be out of the tank for a change. I can only recall being out once before, the one time she had actually cleaned my tank. She had set me down beside the dirty dishes. While she changed my bedding and popped in the new wooden hut thing, I had busied myself, licking the dry food from the plates. It wasn't much, but it made a change from the dried worms from the pet store.

Charlie was really going for it now, and Doreen set me down on the little glass table at the centre of the living room. An opened packet of fags and an overspilling ashtray sat beside me. Doreen, now wearing her best dressing gown—a black number with a cat embroidered on the sleeve—went to the stereo, lifted the needle and placed it back at the start of the record.

Charlie was off again. I didn't know what to do with myself, although the ashtray smelt really good. There were some really half-smoked healthy looking butts in there. Doreen picked me up again and began to sway gently to the sultry tones of the silver fox. I'm sure the neighbours were sick of him.

Doreen had me in her hands, facing her, about a foot from her face. Those wrinkles. I hadn't seen her this close up in months, and it wasn't pretty. It seemed the little lip hair that she was always so self-conscious of had become an afterthought. Black hairs crawled out from the caked on makeup. Her lips were dry and her cheekbones poked out with a purpose. She was so very far from the beautiful blonde I had married all those years before.

"Isn't this nice, hun? Does it feel good to be out?" she said, trying to make herself heard above the fox.

I wanted to speak. I wanted to tell her how sorry I was for what she had become. I want to apologise for not being a good husband. I wanted to speak, but all I could do was blink and roll my tongue around my mouth.

Doreen brought me slowly towards her chest. I wasn't liking what I saw. Loose, almost grey goose-pimpled skin. A fact only I knew, Doreen goose-pimpled when she got horny.

I didn't like this one bit.

She had me pressed belly down against the area just shy of her drooping tits. It felt awful. The more she danced the tighter she squeezed. She sang along softly with the record, so unaware of how uncomfortable I was.

This was it, this was how my life would end, squashed to death on her chest. Thankfully she eased up when the track finished and took a seat on the sofa.

After opening her dressing gown a little she placed me on her big milky thigh. Because of her size, I could relax without falling off. While she was lighting a cigarette, I looked around. On the opposite thigh, there were some bruises and what looked like scratches. I thought of the guy.

I bet he was at home now, drunk, snuggled up behind his wife and whispering sweet nothings.

Doreen flicked her ash onto the floor between her legs. "Did she dance as good as I do, George? You can tell me the truth. I don't care anymore."

I couldn't believe what I was hearing. I mean, after all these years, she asks me something like that. I looked up at her as she sucked hard on the cigarette, wrinkled lips almost touching together. I blinked once and hoped that she would take that as a no. She blew the smoke in my direction. I blinked again. The glowing end of the cigarette was drawing very close to me now, and I shuffled back on her thigh.

There was a look in her eyes now.

"Your silence worries me, George. I'm not liking it. It gets me thinking about what else she was good at. You can tell me anything now. It's all in the past," she said, holding the cigarette right next to my head. I could feel its heat against my face. I eased back some more and then lost my footing. I felt myself falling to the floor.

She caught me. Held me in one hand and smoked with the other, never once taking her mad drunk eyes off me until she stubbed her butt out in the ashtray. I saw a glimmer of a smile crease on her mouth. Her left hand reached down to her chest and revealed a breast. It hung flat and lifeless on her overweight stomach.

"I know you sit in that tank, George, and think of me and how things used to be. I know you watch me and have your dirty little thoughts. I'm still beautiful, I can't fault you for that." She held me up to her face and licked my head. The smell from her mouth was like shit and death. I knew something awful was happening inside that drunken stomach of hers.

"You like that, don't you?" she whispered. I didn't. I closed my eyes. I felt her dry tongue run all across the top of my head and down my back. For a moment I swore she was going to take a bite out of me. "Oh, George, you taste so good. You always did."

I felt like throwing up all the crap she had fed me earlier. My stomach gurgled. Her hand squeezed my sides. She licked me again and, as she pulled away, saliva dripped from the corner of her mouth. She groaned.

I watched as her free hand slid down her belly and disappeared.

Oh fuck, Doreen, what are you doing?

She began to writhe on the sofa and moved me towards the exposed saggy tit. I couldn't do it.

The hairs around her brown nipples were millimetres from my face. "Lick me, George, the way you used to. I don't even care if you think about her. Do it, honey, do it for Doreen."

The front door crashed opened. She dropped me onto the sofa. I landed on my back and struggled to turn over. The cushions moved back into position as she stood up.

A shadow stood swaying in the hallway. We both knew who it was. Doreen stood in the middle of the living room. I finally managed to get on my belly again. He moved into the light.

His face was bloodied. He was smiling. "Alright, Doreen, I thought I would let myself in. Let's have a drink. What you say?" he slurred.

"Get out of here. I will call the police. I will tell them what you did to me. Leave. Now."

He uttered what sounded like a laugh and rushed her. She fell back into the fireplace, and the crack of her skull on the tiles was sickening.

I crawled to the edge of the sofa. I wanted to jump down and get to her before he did, but what use would I be?

I sat there, blinking, tongue rolling out over my mouth, and watched as he rained down blow after blow into Doreen's face.

She wasn't moving by the time he spat in her face and gathered himself off her. I was waiting for him to notice me. Who wouldn't notice a toad on someone's sofa? He didn't and, after checking her pulse with a bloodied hand, he left.

When I was sure he had left for good, I took my chances.

Just below me were a bunch of old magazines and some used hankies. Hopefully, they would break my fall. If they didn't? Well, I was ready. I jumped.

With the amount of shit and rubbish on the living room floor, it took me a while to get to Doreen. Her broken face stared at me. It was pulp. I couldn't look at it and hopped around her bloodsoaked hair, out of sight of her dead eyes. I could do nothing but stay with her until someone came. They would take her to the morgue and take me to a pet shop. I hoped they would, but I didn't care.

Nobody did come. I spent my days eating anything that I could find on the floor; there were some dried up flies under the sofa and a couple of dead spiders in the hall. I was weak with hunger. The only fluids I had ingested were the drips from Doreen's wounds, but that was days ago. I had lost track of time.

The flies gathered not long after she had died. It was a pet hate of mine, how she would leave the windows open all the fucking time, but I was thankful for it now.

They had come in ones and twos to start with, but as her corpse started to smell, they came in bunches. I stayed close to the wound at the back of her head and did pretty well. I caught a couple of fat ones behind her ear, but the others were too fast. I had to give up eventually and let them have their prize.

I sat beside her—what was left of her—and watched the morning sun stream through the blinds. Something caught my eye.

It wasn't big but it was white, fresh, and crawling from the hole in Doreen's head. Another appeared, and then many more poured from the wound. My tongue darted in and out of my mouth. I snapped a couple up. They tasted glorious.

Before diving into that feast of maggots, I took a few moments and thought of Doreen, but I couldn't even picture her face. For me now, she was just a means of survival.

She would have liked that. She would have found that funny.

DARYL DUNCAN

Daryl Duncan was born in Northern Ireland sometime in the early seventies and was deemed too damn ugly to be taken outside so his mother made a nest for him in the family attic, where he was fed pages from horror novels dipped in Farley's rusks. By his mid-teens, he had taught himself to read and found it ultimately more satisfying reading the pages than devouring them. So he read horror and never looked back.

Nowadays Daryl still lives in Northern Ireland with his wife Karen and their two boys, Lewis and Scott. He is part of an amateur production group called 'Dead On Films' who made their first horror/comedy feature in 2015 entitled 'Vapours' and they plan to make some more when Daryl gets off his lazy hole and writes another script. As well as this, Daryl does occasionally try his hand at stories and wrote his first novella, 'Skud' in 2016 and it's available somewhere on Amazon. He is currently working on a novel entitled 'Keelshem' which he hopes to release sometime before his death. You can find him on Facebook but he will probably ignore you, just kidding. (No, he actually will).

THE LONELY OF THE SCHARNHORST

KEN PRESTON

Barry went first. Barry always went first. No reason, that was just the way it always was, always had been.

Barry went first in everything. First girlfriend, first pint, first time having sex, first in a job, first to get married.

First to have an affair.

Greg was a follower, not a leader.

So Barry was always, *always* the first one in the water.

Using his fins he propelled himself down. The cold of the English Channel bit him even through the wetsuit. He was used to it.

A shadow cutting briefly through the rays of sunlight streaming through the water signalled Greg's entry into the sea.

Barry was always first, but Greg was never far behind.

The two men dove deeper with practiced kicks of their fins. Bubbles streamed past their masks from the tanks strapped to their backs. As they sank deeper into the depths of the Atlantic the two men switched on their head torches. The LEDs cut through the growing gloom like lasers.

The wreck appeared abruptly in their lights. A ghost ship, a relic of the past. A WWII German battleship, jammed upside down in a crevice on the ocean floor. Just visible between the dark green fronds of seaweed waving gently in the current and seeming to bring the ship to life, the hull was encrusted in barnacles. Tiny, silver fish darted around its grey hulking mass.

Barry dutifully snapped off a few photos with his Nikon, the bright flash startling the fish.

The *Scharnhorst* had been on Barry's list of wrecks to explore for a long time. But, like everybody else in the diving community, he just never thought he would get the chance.

The problem was, with only its hull visible above the crevasse in the ocean floor, there was no way inside. No way of salvaging whatever might be left inside the battleship. You could swim over and around its hull, raised at an angle from its position on the sea bed, and you could take photographs. But nothing more.

The *Scharnhorst* had lain undisturbed here since it sank at the end of the Second World War. An ugly memorial to all the dead trapped inside.

And according to anyone you talked to who knew about these things, that was most likely the way it was going to stay.

But then Frank had got into trouble on that last dive he had done here. Barry hadn't been on that one, but Greg had. And he'd heard Frank's dying words, whispered into Greg's ear with his last breath.

Greg told Barry what the dying man had told him.

Turned out there was a way inside the *Scharnhorst* after all.

If you were brave enough.

Greg said Frank had told him he had been inside. Frank had told him that he had swum through the ship's corridors and rooms. Frank had told him he had seen the dead sailors. Frank had told him it was good that the ship was so inaccessible.

No one should go inside that monstrosity, Frank had said.

Why? Greg had said.

Because it's filled with the ghosts of the dead, Frank had said. *And they're lonely. So very lonely.*

Barry drew closer to the ship's hull, Greg at his side. Ran his hand through the fronds of seaweed, his fingers brushing the barnacled hull.

Greg swam up beside him.

Poor Greg.

Barry hadn't intended to shag Greg's wife. Lisa wasn't even that good looking. Her doughy white flesh was covered in badly inked tattoos. But, in another of Barry's firsts, his wife had divorced him. On his own, with nothing but his hand and the internet to keep him company, he couldn't be blamed really, could he?

Greg was away, at a conference. Barry and Lisa, they'd been mates forever. It was Barry who had introduced her to Greg in the first place. On that Saturday night, both of them alone with nothing to do, they'd gone out for a drink. Wound up back at his, in bed.

Turned out Lisa was down and dirty in the bedroom. Inventive. Said she'd been having these fantasies for a while now, but Greg wasn't interested. He was more of 'Wham, Bam, Thank you Ma'am' kind of guy. He got his jollies off, but she was left wanting more.

No, Barry hadn't planned on sleeping with Lisa. And once they had, he hadn't intended to continue sleeping with her. Barry, he wasn't big on morals or anything like that. Having an affair didn't bother him. But it was Greg, you know? Greg was his mate. You don't cheat on your mates.

Lisa got to him though, with her doughy, pasty flesh and her badly inked tattoos. Seemed like in bed there wasn't anything she wasn't prepared to do.

And Barry couldn't get enough of her.

The two men swam slowly around the hull of the wreck. The *Scharnhorst* had been on a daylight dash through the English Channel, away from the port in Brest in occupied France, and back to Germany. The HMS *Duke of York* had intercepted her and engaged in battle. Two torpedoes had ripped open her hull and she was sunk with all 1,600 men aboard.

And as she disappeared beneath the surface of the water she upended, sinking to the ocean floor upside down where she lodged herself into the ravine.

There was no way inside.

But Greg, he said there was a way inside the ship. That's what Frank had told him, as the nitrogen bubbles in his bloodstream killed him.

You had to swim away from the battleship. You had to follow the line of the crevasse, now a narrow rip in the ocean floor. You had to keep following it, until the wreck disappeared in the underwater gloom and you thought that maybe you should just give up and head back to the surface.

You had to follow that crack in the ocean bed until it grew wider. Wide enough that you could dive down between its walls.

And you had to go down deep enough until you could turn back on yourself because the ravine grew wider down here, forming a tunnel that allowed you access back to the battleship.

But only if you were brave enough to attempt such a thing.

Barry went first, Greg close behind. Down in the ravine the darkness was complete. Barry's LED cut dark shadows against the rocky outcrops on the crevasse's sides. Long fronds of kelp attached to the walls shifted in the current, seeming to give the walls a life of their own in the beam of light from Barry's torch. Reaching out, Barry was able to touch the sides of the ravine. His hands disappeared in between the strands of soft, waving kelp.

The crevasse began closing in on the two divers as they penetrated the gloom. Barry had to trust that Greg was still following him now as the walls were too close for him to be able to turn his head and look back. His tank scraped a rocky outcrop above him and Barry pushed himself a little deeper.

On he went as the gap grew narrower. Now, even with his torch, he could hardly see anything in front of him. He had to push his way through the fronds of kelp, waving in the current like long fingers trying to grasp hold of him. Pulling at his mask and his regulator. Trying to kill him.

Barry was suddenly aware of a pressure building in his chest. He was on the edge of panicking. The walls of the crevasse were too close, hemming him in, restricting his movement. The kelp was becoming like a solid mass he was having to fight his way through. He couldn't turn around, he couldn't go up.

He was trapped down here, and he couldn't even tell if Greg had followed him, if he was behind him still.

The only thing to do was keep pushing forward, even though the walls of the underwater ravine were still closing in.

Barry pushed harder, his tank scraping along the rocky outcrops. He had to use his hands to find handholds and pull himself along. He had to work hard to keep his breathing steady, to keep the rising panic under control.

And then he was out. The ravine opened up and he was under the *Scharnhorst*. His LED illuminated the upside down deck, a bizarre ceiling of metal covering his underwater world. The giant structure was like an inverted pyramid of jutting funnels, the command deck, the bridge, the gun turrets.

Barry hovered in the water, gazing at the wreck. It was unbelievable. Like an alien superstructure, floating in the sky.

Barry snapped off a couple of photographs.

He felt a disturbance in the water beside him and turned to see Greg emerging from the crack in the sea wall.

He'd forgotten all about his diving buddy.

Greg gave him the OK signal and Barry returned it. Greg looked up at the bizarre structure above him. Barry closed his fist and pointed his thumb upwards, the signal for ascending. Greg gave him the OK signal again.

With graceful kicks of their fins they propelled themselves up to the deck of the battleship *Scharnhorst*.

At first they simply swam around the superstructure, gazing at the anti-aircraft guns and other artillery ranged across the deck. Tiny fish darted around them and in between the rusted guns and the raised decks. The two men swam upwards, past the bridge, up to the main deck.

Barry found an open doorway and guided himself inside. His torch beam cut through the darkness, illuminating the narrow cabin he had entered.

Greg followed him.

Barry checked his air supply. It would be too easy to forget how long they had been underwater, to lose themselves in exploring the German ship, and suddenly find they had run out of air. Especially when they faced the difficult job of swimming back through the narrow crevasse again before they could return to the surface. Despite his concerns, though, Barry's insides fluttered with excitement. They were inside the *Scharnhorst*, somewhere that hardly anybody else had been.

Barry went deeper into the gloom.

Greg followed him.

Through open doorways, down cramped passageways, their sub-aqua tanks bumping against the ceilings.

That's what the dying man had told Greg. Keep going up, right into the bottom of the ship. It was dangerous to dive in there, a person could get lost in that maze of passageways. But if you wanted to see it, you had to take that risk.

It should have been Greg leading. After all, it was Greg who had heard what Frank had said.

But it was Barry who went first. Always Barry.

The narrow hall ended at a set of iron stairs. Using the upside down steps as handholds they swam up, going deeper into the belly of the ship.

Another cramped passageway, past doors and

hatchways.

They reached another set of steps and glided up along them. Past the ragged, twisted hole in the hull where the British torpedo had found its mark. The ship's hull here was wedged up against the side of the ravine, and so there was no access through the gaping wound.

Barry swam on, followed by Greg, deeper into the ship's bowels.

When it happened, it happened suddenly, shockingly.

As the beam of light from Barry's torch suddenly revealed the twisted remains of the engine room, he caught a glimmer of refracted light above him. And then his head was out of the water, above the surface. He grasped hold of something, a part of the ship's structure he didn't recognise beside him as Greg emerged from the water. The two men pulled the regulators out of their mouths and sucked in deep breaths.

Barry started laughing.

"Can you believe this?" he said. "That bloody bastard Frank, he was telling the truth!"

Greg grinned at him, blinking water from his eyes. "Did you doubt it?"

"Of course I did." Barry hauled himself out of the water and onto a ledge, slippery and cold with slime. His air tank clanged against the side of the ship's hull, a dull reverberation echoing all around them.

Greg hauled himself up beside Barry.

"I don't understand how there is still air down here," Barry said.

"When the ship sank and overturned, this pocket of air got trapped in here," Greg said.

"Duh, I know that," Barry said. "But that was over seventy years ago, there can't still possibly be air down here."

"It's got something to do with that current," Greg said, his voice echoing in the dark chamber. "As it rushes past the wreck, water rushes through tiny gaps into the ship and bubbles of air escape into here."

Barry had lost interest in what Greg was saying.

"Look over there," he said, his LED cutting through the darkness.

At first Greg couldn't see what Barry was pointing at. The maze of pipes and iron grills, the banks of walls filled with dials and levers, wheels and gang planks, all dripping with moisture and seaweed, obscured what Barry was trying to show him.

And then he saw it.

The skeleton huddled in a small corner beneath part of a huge turbine. Scraps of uniform still clung to its remains.

"Let's take a closer look," Barry said.

"Do you think we should?" Greg said.

Barry ignored him. He unstrapped the sub aqua tank and slid it off his back. He pulled the fins off his feet and laid them beside the tank. On his hands and knees, keeping his head low to avoid banging it against the pipes running overhead, he began shuffling along the iron grillwork towards the sailor's remains.

"What the hell are you doing?" Greg said.

"Come on. If we're going to explore there's no way we're going to fit through these gaps with all this kit on," Barry said, his voice echoing in the chamber.

Greg pulled his tank off too and placed it beside Barry's. He followed his friend.

Barry always went first.

They got up close to the skeleton. There wasn't a scrap of flesh left on it, and the bones were dark and covered in a scummy green. Remnants of its uniform still clung to it, but most of it had rotted away.

"Poor bastard must have starved to death down here," Barry said.

"What a horrible way to go," Greg said. "Trapped in here, in the darkness, slowly dying of starvation."

The ship creaked, a metallic groan seeming to shiver through their bodies.

"You think this thing is still shifting further down into the ravine?" Greg said.

"Can't be," Barry said. "Bloody wreck's been here since nineteen forty-five."

He shone his torch into a dark passageway behind the skeleton, the floor sloping upwards into the gloom. The steady *plink, plink, plink* of dripping water echoed down the narrow passage. Barry shone his torch up. The floor, now the ceiling, was a metal grill. He shone his torch down. The ceiling, now the floor, was also metal grillwork. There was another passageway below them, but that one was half filled with seawater.

"Come on, let's explore," Barry said.

"Are you sure?" Greg said. "If we get lost, or the wreck shifts and traps us down here—"

"Don't be a pussy," Barry said. "I know what's wrong with you, you're scared you might meet a ghost, aren't you?"

"Don't be an idiot," Greg said.

Barry dropped his voice low, and said, "The ghosts of the Dead, they're lonely, so very lonely."

"Fuck off, Barry," Greg said.

Laughing, Barry began crawling up the sloping floor. Greg followed him. At regular junctures they had to climb over girders on which the grillwork was attached. The floor was slippery with moisture and green algae.

They came to a door. Barry grabbed the wheel set into the middle of the door and pulled. It opened slowly, a rusty squeal rending the silence.

"Bloody hell," Greg whispered, and his breath billowed around his face in a cloud.

Suddenly he started to shiver. He hadn't realised how cold it was.

Barry climbed through the open doorway and Greg followed him.

Doors, many of them open, lined the passage. Barry crawled on, looking through the doorways as he passed them.

"Looks like this might be the living quarters," he said.

The beds were bolted to the floor above them. Below them on the ceiling were the remains of bedding and clothing.

Barry slipped on the algae and fell on his side. He started sliding back down the slope towards Greg until he grabbed a doorway and stopped himself.

"Oh shit," he said, looking through the doorway.

He crawled into the box-like room and Greg followed him. The ceiling was a soggy mass of rotting mattresses and bedsheets. Something scuttled out from underneath a mattress, all spiny legs and quick, darting movements. Bunk bed frames and lockers hung from the floor above their heads. Water ran down the metal edges and dripped onto the two men.

"Careful where you go," Barry said. "There are rusty springs sticking out of these mattresses. If you're not careful you'll slash open a hand or a knee."

Placing a hand against a wall, Barry carefully stood up.

Greg did the same.

The two men looked at the scattered bones and crushed skulls lying on the ceiling, along with the soggy mattresses and sheets.

"What the hell do you think happened here?" Greg said.

"Don't know," Barry said. "But it's weird, isn't it?"

"They must have gone mad with fear and hunger, attacked each other," Greg said.

"Wonder if this is what Frank saw, panicked him and sent him back out and up to the surface too fast?"

The ship groaned again, almost seeming to protest at the intrusion of these two foreign bodies in its system.

Barry bent down and took a closer look at one of the skulls. He sucked in his breath.

The skull stared back up at Barry, its empty eye sockets dark and filled with squirming life. Barry stood up and turned away. He couldn't look at it any more.

A metallic screeching echoed through the wreck and the ship shivered slightly.

The two men looked at each other wide eyed.

"I think maybe we should get out of here after all," Barry said.

Greg was over by the open door, standing with his back to it. He didn't move.

"Come on, bud," Barry said. "Let's get going."

"No," Greg said. "Not yet."

"Not yet? What the hell are you talking about?"

Greg said nothing. Stared at Barry.

"I gotta tell you mate, you're acting weird all of a sudden," Barry said. "What the hell's got into you?"

"Frank," Greg said, almost shouted at Barry.

"Yeah? What about him?"

"Frank told me everything."

"Yeah, I know he did," Barry said. "That's how we ended up down here, and now we've got to get going and get the hell out."

"No," Greg shook his head. Now that it had come to it he was having trouble getting his words out. "Not just about the wreck, he told me other stuff too."

"What are you talking about, Greg?"

The ship creaked and groaned softly. Something banged once, deep below them.

"Frank told me all about you, and Lisa," Greg said.

Barry felt like he had been punched in the gut. He tried to keep his face passive, show no emotion.

"Greg, I haven't got a bloody clue what you're talking about, mate. Can't we just get out of here first and have a chinwag when we get back on dry land?"

"Frank told me about you and Lisa, shagging each other every chance you got," Greg said. "Fucking each other's brains out, is what he said."

Barry shook his head. "Mate, come on. Frank was off his head with nitrogen poisoning. He didn't know what he was saying. I mean, think about it. Even if it were true, which it isn't, how the hell would he know?"

"Because he was shagging her too," Greg said. "And she used to tell him all about her nights with you, what the two of you got up to, because he got off on it."

Barry shook his head again. "You're having me on, right? This is a joke? Frank couldn't have told you all that, not the state he was in when they pulled him out of the water."

"No, you're right, he didn't. He told me all that shit the night before. We went out, had a skinful of beer. You know what Frank was like, always had to drink one more pint than everybody else. He got shitfaced, spilled his guts, told me everything. I didn't expect him to turn up for the dive the next day. He must have been hungover something bad. Probably why he came up too fast. Easy to make a mistake like that when you're groggy headed."

Barry kept his mouth shut.

The ship creaked and groaned.

"All right, mate, it's true," Barry said, softly. "And you're angry, I can understand that. But I suggest we get out of this bloody death-trap first, and then when we're back on the boat, then you can beat the shit out of me. All right?"

Greg said nothing.

Another groan shivered through the wreck.

"Come on, fella, we can't stay here, I don't like the way this old thing is making all those noises," Barry said.

Greg stepped backwards through the doorway. Barry's eyes widened as he realised what Greg was doing. He ran for the door, skidding on the wet, soft floor and fell over amongst the broken skeletons.

Greg slammed the door shut. He heard the latch click into place. He gripped the wheel and turned it, the rusty levers protesting at the movement. Barry was on the other side of the door now, banging his fist against it.

"Greg, for fuck's sake, stop dicking about and let me

out of here!"

Greg unsheathed his knife and jammed it into one of the metal latches holding the door closed.

"Greg!" Barry roared, pounding even harder at the door.

The lever jiggled in place as Barry tried unlocking the door.

It held.

Greg began making his way back down the passageway. Back to his tank and mask and fins.

"Greg, you shit!" Barry shouted.

Greg kept moving.

Greg thought about Barry fucking Lisa.

Greg thought about what he might do to Lisa when he got back.

By the time he got back to his air tank, and the pool of black water waiting for him to enter it, Greg could hardly hear Barry at all.

He strapped the tank on his back, slipped the fins on his feet, pulled the mask over his face.

He fitted the regulator in his mouth and bit down on it.

The wreck let out another long, anguished groan. Seemed as though Barry and Greg had disturbed it somehow. That it might move, slide deeper into the ravine.

Didn't matter.

Greg was out of here now.

He slipped into the dark, cold water, his LED lighting his way.

Greg swam down, along the cramped passageways, through doorways and down stairs. He just had to keep going down, through the wreck's maze of passageways and corridors until he reached the deck. And then swim further down, past the artillery and the bridge, until he found the sliver of a gap in the side of the ravine. Back through the narrow cave beneath the ocean floor until it opened out and he could swim up again.

Back to the surface.

Poor Barry. Greg told him not to attempt getting inside the *Scharnhorst*. He told him it was dangerous.

But that was the thing about Barry, he wouldn't listen.

He always wanted to be the first at everything.

Out of the ship's innards, Greg turned and twisted in the water, his LED cutting a beam of bright light through the darkness. He couldn't see the narrow gap in the ravine wall. He felt the urge to panic rising in his chest.

He reminded himself to keep his breathing level and calm. Didn't want to use up his air too quickly.

All he had to do was keep looking.

It was here somewhere.

He had plenty of air in his tanks, there was no rush.

Greg noticed movement beneath him. Down in the darkness of the ravine.

Just a fish of some kind, that was all.

He wondered how far it went down, what things lived in the darkness down there.

Greg swam over to the wall of rock, covered in fronds waving gently in the current.

His torchlight caught the shadow in the rocky outcrop. The entrance to the long cave which led to freedom.

He wondered what Barry was doing right now. If the lonely ghosts had found him. Frank had come down here on his own, hungover. He had always been reckless and stupid. And he had obviously seen the skeletons and imagined the ghosts, and that had sent him into a panic.

Silly bastard.

Greg wondered how long it would take Barry to start imagining things. How long it would take him to die.

Greg noticed a flash of something pale in the gloom. A disturbance on the periphery of his vision.

He turned and looked. Down into the darkness.

More movement. Much more.

Not fish.

Greg screamed when he realised what that disturbance was.

A mass of naked bodies clawing its way up to him. The flesh was dripping off these ghastly corpses, their black eyes fastened on Greg as they swam closer. Their hair drifted like seaweed, and they opened and closed their mouths like fish, lying on the deck of a fishing boat and gasping for breath.

Greg screamed again, the bubbles obscuring his vision for a second before they floated up towards the upside down wreck of the *Scharnhorst*.

The first of the dead sailors reached him, hands clawing at his legs and torso. More quickly followed and within seconds he was surrounded. They ran their hands over him, their black fingernails tearing holes in his wetsuit, in his flesh. Mouths opening and closing, revealing blackened, pointed teeth. Their skin was wrinkled and soft, some of it ripped into open sores, the rotting flesh waving in the water like the sea kelp on the rock walls.

Greg struggled to escape, but there were too many of them. A hand reached out and grasped his mask, pulling it off his face. He was plunged into darkness as his head torch drifted down into the pit of the ravine, its beam of light swirling around and around. Another one tugged at his regulator, yanking it from his mouth. The rush of air bubbles startled the dead sailors, giving Greg a moment's freedom. He used the rock face to kick off with and propel himself up to the ship. If he could get back inside, get back to Barry's kit, he would have another chance at getting out.

At escaping.

He pulled a spare torch from his belt and flicked the switch. The beam, weaker than the head torch, illuminated the upside down ship.

He swam for the wreck's deck, looming over him like an alien spaceship.

He was almost at the door when he felt the cold hand grasping hold of his ankle. Greg was pulled down with a violent jerk. The bodies enclosed him, hands running over him, open mouths drawing closer.

Greg screamed again, letting all the precious air out of his lungs.

And the crew of the *Scharnhorst* pulled him deeper and deeper with them, down into the murky depths of the ravine.

KEN PRESTON

Ken Preston lives in a cellar on the street where Jack the Ripper was born. He writes dark fiction for adults and young adults.

Go get the entire first season of Joe Coffin for free, plus more free books every month, exclusive content and competitions and giveaways, by signing up to his VIP list at kenpreston.co.uk

ALL IN THE EYES

MARK CASSELL

She was your typical old lady dressed in her finest—she always wore her finest—seated at the end of the dining-room table. Empty plates sat before us; me, my younger sister Zoe, Mum and Dad too, and Grandpa. So yeah, I'm talking about Gran. Out through the bay window, a blue sky framed her round shoulders, her frizzy hair. Somewhere near the beach the sound of seagulls resembled echoing screams.

The threadbare cushion did little for my boney arse as I sat with the taste of rabbit and vegetables clogging my mouth. As I often did every time I ate at my grandparents', I wished they would just serve a plate of fish fingers, chips and peas, and a dollop of ketchup. I still heard the clatter of a fork dropped on a plate that marked the end of dinner. I wondered if this time we'd get dessert, but of course not. Always, I hoped.

Gran reached up to her face. She tugged off her glasses, pinched in long fingers. It's weird to see someone's eyes, having removed their spectacles; the eyes seem small, the eyelids pale and somehow sunken. However, it was strange only for a moment to see Gran without them, for in the next second her eyes were larger, greyer. The pupils dark, piercing... and they further widened. She didn't blink.

A silence pressed down on me, and I was aware of my pulse drumming in my ears.

She stared, holding my gaze.

Those eyes. Those fucking eyes.

They widened still. My vision shrank, the corners darkening, and the room faded into a tunnel, the end of which filled only with those two immense eyeballs. They shifted from grey, to a weak green, to yellow. And in the very centre, that black, black core, a darkness no child should ever see. Indeed, a blackness even an adult should never see. Those eyes drilled into me, channelling, sapping my energy, my senses... I no longer felt the chair beneath me, no longer could I smell or taste roasted rabbit and soggy cabbage. All that existed were those hungry eyes.

The silence swamped me.

I've no idea what my sister was doing at the time, no idea what Mum and Dad were doing. Didn't they care? Couldn't they see what was happening? I knew that Grandpa didn't give a shit. And still Gran's eyes drilled into me, into my head, burrowing through every fibre of my body. It was like she was extracting my secrets, to see what a naughty little boy I was. Damn, I was only eight years old—we're supposed to be naughty at that age, boys *and* girls, that's what we do.

Gran. No blinking, no movement; not even a muscle twitch. Nothing. Just those eyes boring into my core, my soul. At that age I knew nothing about souls, but now I do and it was like she managed to penetrate my very being.

It probably only lasted seconds, though it felt like minutes. No, it felt like hours. My breath became short and tight, my chest rising and falling rapidly.

Inside that burning yellow, those black pupils seethed.

My vision blurred. Wracking sobs heaved up my throat like lumps of bitter fruit urgent for release. Tears flowed over hot cheeks. My palms itchy. Everyone looked at me. I knew this without seeing them. Why couldn't my parents help? Even my sister, why didn't she save me?

Still Gran stared.

And still I cried. Deflated, small.

Then her face cracked into a grin. She laughed, great shoulder-jumping bellows.

"What is it, Bobby?" she said, throwing her smile around the table. "What?"

So many tears, so much water. I drowned then. I didn't understand, I couldn't understand.

Hours afterwards, when the smell of pipe smoke replaced the stink of rabbit and cabbage, the adults would be seated on armchairs and sofas while Zoe and I sat on the floor. We'd be drawing and colouring in, but I felt detached from the black-and-white cartoons on the paper. I didn't want them; I didn't want anything. I'd changed. Again. Another piece of me stolen somehow, snatched into the void that only Gran could create. Another fragment of my young body gouged away. I found no pleasure in the colouring-in book at hand. My efforts seemed shallow and, no matter how much red and blue and yellow and green and orange I used, still those pages remained filled with black curves; dark like the centre of Gran's eyes. Gripping the felt-tip pens with clammy fingers, I felt weak. Useless. It was all I could do not to cry again, feeling my cheeks still damp, still burning. Like my insides.

Time stretched after that. Long, slow, a weight pushing down on my thin shoulders. I wished Mum would suggest going for a walk along the beach, just the two of us.

On the coffee table, through the smoky haze, a glass dish containing sweets teased me. The colourful, twisted wrappers mirrored the pages of my pathetic colouring efforts. I wanted one. Maybe a sweet would remove the bitterness from my mouth. It wasn't the rabbit that clung to my tongue, nor was it the cabbage. It was fear.

Eyeing the dish, I asked Grandpa: "Can I have a sweet?"

Chewing his pipe through that reeking cloud, he replied, "Presently."

At that age I had no idea what that word meant, but I knew I couldn't have one. I wanted to ask Mum or Dad, yet I still felt far removed from them.

The evening dragged, the TV a monotonous drone in the background: News. Never cartoons. Nothing ever fun. Still I coloured in those books, desperate to take my mind off another troubled dinnertime.

I later asked Grandpa once again if I could have a sweet. Again, his response: "Presently."

Presently. It was always presently.

As I grew up and the occasional day was filled with similar moments, in different situations, of those yellow eyes and that denial of sweets, where that stare would burn into me, digging deeper than anything ever should. And it would always end with that "What is it, Bobby?" and an amused look, a grin, that laughter, that smile, and another "What?" All as though it was natural for a granny to scare the shit out of a little boy. Eventually my tears were fewer, my sobs softer, and I've no idea when it finally stopped. I spent less time with them and, when I hit my teenage years, I all but forgot those dreaded days beneath Gran's glare, those many times Grandpa would say, "Presently."

Presently never came. Not once. At least not while they lived.

Gran and Grandpa died of old age, both within weeks of one another. How poetic, right? It's odd to see a parent cry, certainly, and that's something no one wants to witness, but... well, death comes to us all sooner or later. Indeed, to some of us it comes presently...

These days, I'm known as Robert—the name Bobby is a million miles away. I now stand with Dad in the silent husk of my grandparents' bungalow. Hollow, void of pipe smoke and the drone of TV. Now a shell, a grey abandonment of the living. Even the family portraits that line the sideboard stare through the abyss, a step aside from the gallons of tears I shed over time.

The mantel clock ticks away our intrusive seconds.

I see the glass dish, those sweets.

My feet move before I even think about it. A torrent of memories reminds me of those dinners, those countless times Gran would stare, my tears, my parents not even helping—*saving*—me, and that constant denial of being allowed a sweet.

Just as my feet had moved without command, my hand reaches out. Fingers splayed.

"Presently," I hear Grandpa whisper.

The wrapper crinkles beneath my fingertips. It is red, bold, a colour breaking the surrounding greyness, pushing back the shadows of family history. Still without thinking what I'm doing, I begin to unwrap the sweet. Smooth and round like a perfect crystal, slightly sticky. Red, such a brilliant red. The wrapper floats to the floor, gently sweeping downwards like a plastic feather, to settle on the carpet.

Again, there's Grandpa's voice: "Presently."

Dad is now beside me—I hadn't heard him. He too has a sweet in his hand. Green, another perfect crystal held so precious between finger and thumb. We glance at one another and, as though on a silent command, together we pop the sweets in our mouths. A burst of flavour, but not what I expect. Sour, foul... like rabbit, soggy cabbage, rotten, festering. Yet I do not spit it out. With my back teeth, I bite down. Hard. Dad crunches his, too. Bathed in a bleeding sunset that now soaks through smoke-yellowed net curtains, we both stand there chewing those sweets.

Seconds become minutes.

My taste buds shrivel, they tingle, recoil. Still I don't spit. A glance at Dad and I see his eyes have widened, yellowed, and their black cores now burn into my own. I know my eyes resemble his. I feel my cheeks slacken. We stare at one another, both unblinking.

I wait for the tears to come. I wait for that familiar fear as those yellow eyes bore into my soul, seeking, searching...

Nothing happens.

As before, my legs move as though with a mind of their own. Dad's, too. We walk outside, out onto the front path that winds down to the street. We tread the soggy leaves that hide uneven paving, with the chill autumn evening pressing down. Without a word, my Dad and I sit on the cracked wall between garden and pavement, facing the grey street.

Footsteps, voices approach.

Two school girls walk round the corner, both no more than eleven years old and dressed in untucked shirts over knee-high skirts. Beneath white socks, their shoes clip the tarmac. Their footfalls echo. The girls eat sweets, colourful wrappers crinkling and seeming louder than the screams of nearby seagulls.

Both now closer, and one looks at me. She jolts to a halt. So does her friend. A silence embraces the four of us. As one pair of curious eyes focuses on my own, a warmth floods through me. It soothes, refreshes, spreading out into my fingers, my toes. I shiver. I feel larger, taller. This is beautiful. Such elation, joy. Such power at hand.

So this godlike energy fills me as I sap this girl's happiness.

She cries. And her misery is sweet.

MARK CASSELL

Mark Cassell lives in a rural part of the UK with his wife and a number of animals. He often dreams of dystopian futures, peculiar creatures, and flitting shadows. Primarily a horror writer, his steampunk, dark fantasy, and SF stories have featured in numerous anthologies and ezines including Rayne Hall's *Ten Tales* series and horror zine, *Sirens Call*.

His best-selling debut novel, *The Shadow Fabric*, is closely followed by the popular short story collection, *Sinister Stitches*, and are both only a fraction of an expanding mythos. His most recent release, *Chaos Halo 1.0: Alpha Beta Gamma Kill,* is in association with Future Chronicles Photography.

For more about Mark and his work, or to contact him directly:

Free stories: http://www.markcassell.com
The Shadow Fabric mythos: www.theshadowfabric.co.uk
Twitter: twitter.com/Mark_Cassell
Facebook: www.facebook.com/AuthorMarkCassell
Blog: http://www.beneath.co.uk

BAD JOHN

ADAM HOWE

Sadie shivered in the falling snow, hands dug deep in the pockets of her mangy leopard print coat, hungrily eyeing the cars curb-crawling the Strip. Music boomed inside the titty bar behind her, the black tinted window quaking to the bass. She'd danced there herself when she first hit the Strip, before she was busted turning tricks between lap dances to feed her habit. Now she was lucky if they let her inside to slam back a shot to wash away the taste of her last john.

An ancient green station wagon tootled up to the curb, the exhaust farting fumes. It had wood-paneled sides and an I LOVE MY POODLE sticker in the rear window. A fluffy white cloud on legs scuttled back and forth, barking, inside the cage compartment at the back of the car. *Who goes whoring with their dog in the car?* Sadie thought. *And a poodle, no less.* He was a mousy little guy with a mustache and a black frizz of hair swaddling the sides of his shiny bald skull. He wore a maroon parka over a knit Christmas sweater with a smiling snowman on the front. Sadie frowned. The guy's goofy sweater was reason alone to roll him.

He popped the central lock, pushed open the passenger door. "Come in out of the cold." His voice was shrill and whiny. She climbed inside quickly before he changed his mind. He rolled the window back up, made a shivery noise: *Brr!* "Too darn cold to be standing around outside." Like she had any fucking choice. He pulled away like he was driving home from church. "Mind putting your seatbelt on?" he said. "We don't want to get pulled over, now do we?" The guy gave a little chortle that reminded her of Ned Flanders. *I'm about to fuck a* Simpsons *character,* Sadie thought. Wouldn't be the first time. Usually it was Barney the drunk or Cletus the redneck. Hell, by now she'd screwed half of Springfield.

But the guy was right; the last thing she needed was another bust. And she had plans for this dope. After she rolled him, she'd knock off early. Pay her pimp what she owed, and scrounge some more rock, head home to her flophouse and her pipe.

She buckled up and then thawed out her hands over the tepid air sputtering from the AC. She fished in her coat for her smokes, reassuring herself that her Saturday Night Special was in there too. It still amazed her she'd never pawned the gun to feed her habit. "Mind if I smoke?" The guy sucked his teeth disapprovingly. "No offence," she said, "but it smells kind of doggy in here."

She looked in the rearview at the dog in its cage. Ugly fucking thing wouldn't stop yipping at her. Maybe it suspected what she had in mind for its owner? Its coat was an unruly white hedge; its muzzle streaked with nasty brown stains like the dog spent a lot of time tossing its own salad. Its lips were snaggled back in a yellow snarl. Beady eyes glared back at Sadie. The poodle yip-yip-yipped.

The man glanced at the dog in the rearview. "Oh now, Queenie, that's quite enough of that." Smiling sheepishly, he leaned towards Sadie, giving her a whiff of his Old Spice. "She gets jealous. Fetch one of her toys off the back seat there. She won't shut up otherwise and I find it difficult to, uh... *perform.*" He grimaced apologetically, wetting his mustache with a nervous flick of his tongue.

With a sigh, Sadie leaned over the backseat, fingering through the chewed-up dog toys strewn across it. She picked up a slobbery rubber duck, holding it out towards the cage, giving it a few halfhearted squeaks. Queenie was barking furiously now, outraged that this stranger was taunting her with her own toys.

"Keep at it," the guy said, "she'll come 'round."

Squeak-squeak-squeak.

Yip-yip-yip.

"The name's Bob, by the way." And so it was; the name printed proudly (BOB!) on the key-fob dangling from the ignition. "Queenie, you've already met."

"Sadie," she said.

"Sexy Sadie," Bob chuckled, and hummed a few bars of the Beatles song.

"So listen, Bob, where'd you wanna do this?"

"Oh, I know a little out of the way place," he assured her. "Discretion's very important to me."

Fine by Sadie, thinking of the gun in her pocket.

The lights of the Strip blinked out in the rearview. Bob checked his mirrors and indicated—a real stickler for road safety—before making the turn off the highway. The station wagon puttered across a bridge above a white ribbon of frozen river, jouncing uphill along a rutted dirt track through woods. Queenie scuttled about her cage, trying to find her footing as the car rocked about, voicing her discomfort with yips and mewls. "It's all right, Queenie," Bob reassured her.

Driving through the woods, the guy hadn't stopped yapping like his yipping fucking dog. Telling Sadie how he was married. *Very happily married, thank you.* (Sadie had noticed the pale band of skin on his finger where his wedding ring usually was; that was good, a married man was unlikely to report a robbery). And that he loved his wife, but since she got sick ("The Big C") Mrs. Bob was unable to fulfill certain wifely duties. And darn it, a man has *needs*—

"This is far enough, don'tcha think, Bob?" Sadie said, interrupting his nervous chatter.

He looked around the woods in surprise. "Oh! Listen

to me, prattling away… " With another chortle, he eased his foot off the gas, pulling to the side of the road. The car crunched to a stop in the snow. "How are you and Queenie getting along?"

"Swell, Bob. We're getting along just swell." Sadie turned back to look at Queenie in her cage. She gave the squeaky toy one last honk, reaching with her other hand for the .38 inside her coat and, while her head was turned, Bob struck her a bludgeoning blow to the base of the skull, and the world went black.

She was blind, her eyes gummed shut with blood and tears. An icy wind whipped inside the car through the open driver's side door. Snow spattered the windshield. Sadie could hear the poodle skittering about its cage in the back of the car; and outside, the sound of a shovel biting into frozen earth.

She forced her eyes open, crust flaking from her lashes. She was slumped forward in the passenger seat, her blood-matted hair glued to the dash. The back of her head throbbed sickly where Bob had brained her. *What the hell had he hit her with?* Sagging back in the seat, her hair tore from the dash with a sound like Velcro. She cried out in pain as the lump on the back of her head prodded the headrest and seemed to catch fire. She thought she was seeing stars until she realized they were snowflakes, devilling inside through the open driver's door. A few swirling flakes landed on her shoulder. Melted. Skated down her bare torso. She wasn't wearing her leopard print coat anymore. Her shirt was ripped open to reveal her bra. Buttons lay scattered in the footwell. When she tried to hug her shirt around her, cover herself, she found that she couldn't; something clanked on her wrist, jewelry she'd never seen before. Her left wrist was handcuffed to the steering wheel. Instinctively, she jerked her arm back, but the cuffs were locked tight, the bracelet scraping painfully against her wrist bone.

She looked outside the station wagon, to where the sound of digging was coming from. The world seesawed as her vision blurred in and out of focus. The car was parked in a thicket of woods, propped on a grade, the hood angled up. Pine trees speared the night sky, trying to puncture the moon. Bob must have driven off-road while she was unconscious. *I know a little out of the way place...* She could see him through the windshield using a shovel to dig a hole beneath the outstretched branch of a pine tree. Bob's parka and her leopard print coat were hanging from the branch like Christmas tree decorations.

Despite Bob's mousy frame, he was wiry strong. His Christmas sweater was rolled up to the elbows. He stabbed the shovel into the frozen ground, grunting with effort as he flung snow and dirt back over his shoulder. Happy as a Disney dwarf, whistling while he worked. Completely at ease. He'd done this before.

Sadie turned in her seat, looking behind the car. The handcuffs jangled against the steering wheel, the bracelet gripping tighter to her wrist. Her panicked eyes darted about the lonely woods. Somewhere behind her, she heard the crackling flow of the iced-over river; and further downhill, the distant echo of traffic on the highway. If she honked the horn, screamed for help, would anyone hear her? Apart from Bob, that is. The last thing she wanted was to attract Bob's attention.

The car keys were gone from the ignition; she couldn't just drive out of here. She looked at her coat, hanging from the tree. Her cellphone was in the pocket. The same pocket where she'd kept her gun... the gun she saw was now stuffed in the front of Bob's chinos. Then he knew she'd meant to rob him. Not that she thought it made much difference to what he had in mind for her.

She opened the glove compartment, wincing as the

hinged door squealed. A flashlight and a spray can of de-icer rolled out and thudded into the footwell. She rooted inside the glove compartment. Maybe Bob kept a second set of car keys in here, or keys to the cuffs, or even something she could use as a weapon?

Maps, CDs, bungee cord, Kleenex—

Fighting panic, she forced herself to breathe…

Had anyone seen her leave the Strip with Bob? Another one of the working girls? They always *said* they had each other's back… but that was only to see where best to stick the knife; it was every bitch for herself out there.

How could I be so fucking stupid? She wasn't the same naïve runaway she'd been when she first started hooking. She'd learned the hard way there were guys out there who couldn't get hard without hurting, who'd rather fuck you up with their fists than with their dicks. And then there were the real Bad Johns. Sick tricks like Bob. She'd always thought she could spot them. But Bad Johns aren't always easy to spot. They don't wear hockey masks or razor-fingered gloves. They smile and wear Christmas sweaters and drive station wagons with poodles in the back.

It was that fucking poodle, Sadie thought. That's what made her lower her guard. She glared in the rearview at Bob's accomplice. Queenie was curled inside her cage, muzzle propped on her paws, watching Sadie with a snippy expression. "You fucking bitch," Sadie hissed at the dog. Queenie raised her head, snarling. Then she started to bark. Not the little yips she was making before. The kind of noise that belonged to a dog three times her size.

Bob heard the commotion and turned his head. "Hey there, Sleeping Beauty!" He planted the shovel in the ground and then hopped up out of the hole, wiping his hands on his chinos. "You about ready to have some fun? Sorry to keep you waiting, but there's nothing I hate more than digging the hole *afterwards.*"

He started ambling towards the open driver's door.

Sadie pulled hard against the handcuffs, the steel bracelet cutting into her wrist, tearing the skin. "Stay the fuck away from me!"

Bob watched her struggle in quiet amusement. "How's that working out for you?"

Sadie sagged back against the passenger door, panting for breath, her hand still cuffed to the wheel, her arm outstretched like she was beckoning Bob in.

Queenie continued to bark inside her cage.

Bob raised a finger. "That's *enough* now, Queenie," he said, "Daddy's got the filthy slut."

The dog quieted.

Sadie glared at the poodle in the rearview. She'd never seen an animal look so fucking smug.

Bob continued towards the car.

Sadie hammered the horn. *"Help! Someone help me! Please!"*

Bob indulged her. He tilted his head back, cupping a hand to his mouth and hollering over the forest. *"Help me! Please! Heeeeelp!"* His mocking voice hung in the air, the echo fading into the distance.

Then he frowned theatrically, moving his hand, still cupped, to his ear.

"Would you hush up?" he said. "I think I hear something… "

Sadie listened intently.

"My mistake." Bob gave his goofy laugh. "Nope, we're way the heck out in the willywags. No knights in shining armor out here."

She thrashed her legs, kicking and screaming and yanking on the cuffs like a trap-snared critter. Exhausted, she huddled on the passenger seat, sobbing over the footwell, breathing in ragged whoops, and through her tears, she saw the can of de-icer that had fallen from the glove compartment. Glancing at Bob from the corner of her eye, she dangled her free arm into the footwell, closing her fingers around the spray can.

Bob didn't seem to notice; he was shaking his head like an exasperated parent.

"I swear, the way you girls carry on, you'd think it was the end of the world. Now let's not make this any harder than it has to be. I need this, okay? And honestly—what's waiting for you back there on the Strip? An overdose? AIDS? I'm *saving* you from that life, honey. I'm doing you a *favor* here. Best of all you'll have plenty of company. There's little Patti and Kristen and Faye—"

He was pointing around at various trees; Sadie gave a low moan as she realized the tree where Bob had been digging was *her* tree.

"And... and I forget her name. Tall. Blonde. Butterfly tattoo on her butt." Bob frowned, looking at Sadie as if *she* might know. "Nope, it's gone. It'll come back to me." He swept an arm about the woods, like a game show host showing off tonight's prizes. "Hell, it's a regular sewing circle out here! Now let's get this show on the road, and then you gals can bitch about ole Bob when I'm gone."

He took a step towards her. Stopped suddenly. Following her gaze, he glanced down at the handle of the .38 stuffed in the front of his chinos, grunting in surprise. "I'd forgotten all about that." He pulled the gun from his waistband. "I bet you'd like this around about now?" He chuckled. "And no prizes for guessing what you planned to do with it, either. Tell me, Sexy Sadie, just how many fellers have you rolled with this cap-gun of yours?"

When she didn't answer, he said: "What I figured. You whores, you're all the same... " He raised the gun suddenly, thumbing back the hammer.

Sadie shrank back in the passenger seat. *"Please, no, don't—"*

Bob held the gun on her awhile, relishing her reaction. Then he lowered it. Gave a little snort of amusement. "Oh now, don't you worry none," he said, "I'm not gonna shoot you. Where's the fun in that?" He stuffed the gun back in his waistband. Then he reached behind him, unsheathing a hunting knife hidden beneath his sweater. The saw-backed blade was at least a foot long. He turned the knife slowly in his hand, admiring the steel, a falling snowflake shearing in two upon the guillotine blade.

"Me and Mr. Buck Skinner here—" Bob said, "Mr. *Doe* Skinner, I should say. We're gonna show you the time of your life. You ever been fucked by a Buck?"

He bent towards the open driver's door, reaching towards her—

She whipped up the can of de-icer and sprayed him a burst in the face.

Bob screeched like a scalded cat. The knife jerked from his hand and landed with a thud in the driver's side footwell. He lurched back from the car, yanking up the front of his Christmas sweater and scouring his eyes. Queenie started barking frantically. Bob staggered blindly through the snow. Sadie prayed he'd fall into that hole he'd been digging and break his fucking neck. But no such luck. He let the sweater fall from his face, his eyes slitted in pain and fury, his mouth a bestial snarl, his hair spiking from the sides of his head. He charged at the car.

Sadie scrambled into the driver's seat, reaching outside the car through the open door, her arm at full-stretch, hand clawing for the handle...

...grabbing hold of the grip and dragging the door shut—

Bob bounced off the door with a surprised grunt.

His hand found the handle. Started to pull.

Sadie slammed down the central lock.

Bob clawed at the locked door. "Open the door."

She reached in the footwell and snatched the huge hunting knife off the floor.

"Put... put that down!" Bob sputtered, a bratty kid who didn't like sharing his toys. He wrenched at the door, the car pitching and rocking. Then he prowled around it, testing the other doors, cursing and muttering to himself under his breath: "See, this is what happens when you get complacent, Robert. Was a hand-job really that important to you, you couldn't cuff *both* her hands?" As he tested the trunk—*locked*—Queenie whined and scratched her paws on the window. "Daddy's okay, baby. Everything's gonna be fine." He trudged back to the driver's side door, wrestling the gun from his waistband and raising it to the window. "Open this goddamn door!" Then a smile lit his face. He tapped the barrel of the gun against the glass. "Don't you go anywhere now."

He stuffed the gun back in his chinos, and went to the tree where he'd been digging. His parka was still hanging from the tree branch. He fished in the pockets, turning back towards Sadie like a triumphant magician, the keys with their personalized fob (BOB!) jangling in his hand. "Now we're gonna do this the hard way," he said, stomping back towards her. "It's gonna be worse for you than it was for Sherry. And she was squealing so hard she—" He stopped in his tracks. "Sherry! *That* was her name. Long-legged Sherry with the butterfly on her butt." He continued towards the car. "Well, she wasn't so high an' mighty after a little *ménage a trois* with ole Bob and Mr. Buck Skinner. No, sir! And that's nothing compared to what's coming to *you*, Sexy Sadie. I'm gonna peel you like a fucking orange, girl."

With a cry, Sadie hacked with the knife at the handcuff chain; tried to jimmy the lock on the bracelet with the tip of the blade, hardly able to see what she was doing through her tears. Bob appeared suddenly in the driver's side window and jangled his car keys. The smiling snowman on his sweater seemed to be leering at her. Bob stabbed the car key into the door slot. The central lock popped as he cranked the key.

Sadie lurched back from the door, barking her elbow on the upraised handbrake, hissing with pain as her funny-bone flared. The knife fell from her hand in the footwell. Before she could fetch it, the door swooped open with a rush of cold air. Sadie slammed down the handbrake.

The car shuddered violently, swooping down the grade like a boat being launched. The driver's side tyre crunched back over Bob's foot. He howled in pain and the car kept rolling, ripping the keys from his hands, the keys hanging from the door, the door slamming shut. Bob dropped on his ass in the snow. Clutching his foot, he watched helplessly as the car rolled away from him. He snatched the gun from his waistband, firing wildly, bullets whizzing past the moving car, grazing the hood with a flash of sparks. Sadie ducked as two shots punched holes through the windshield, splintering the Plexiglas, and embedded in the headrest behind her. Snow swirled inside through the bullet holes. The gun clicked empty and Bob tossed it away, teetering to his feet.

The car gathered speed. Sadie clung to the wheel, peering over the dash, eyes darting between Bob in the windshield, lurching after the car, and the looming pine trees in the rearview. She wrenched the wheel, left and right, the station wagon slaloming through the pine maze. A wing mirror exploded as the car clipped a tree. The rear tyres hit a pothole that shook the car like airplane turbulence, tossing Queenie about her cage. Sadie's face slammed into the steering wheel, the horn giving a startled toot. Dazed, she snuffled blood and shook her head to clear her vision—

And saw Bob hurling himself at the car. He landed with a thud, clinging to the car like a nightmare hood ornament. "Let my Queenie go, you bitch!" Hearing her name, Queenie gave a frantic yowl. "Daddy's coming, baby!"

Sadie jiggled the wheel, trying to dislodge him from the hood. Bob ducked as an overhanging tree branch whipped above his head, showering him in snow and pine needles. Glaring at Sadie through the punctured windshield, he removed a hand from the hood, snaking it through one of the bullet holes, Plexiglas crumbling around his thrusting arm as he snatched at her throat. She clawed his hand, raking it with her nails. Hissing in pain, he grabbed the wheel, trying to steer the car into a sliding stop. She hammered her fist on his fingers, but the hand didn't budge—not until she bit his thumb, blood flooding her mouth, her teeth chipping on bone. Bob let out a screech and let go of the wheel, snatching his arm back through the windshield. Sadie spat out a mouthful of gristle that spattered the Plexiglas. She stole a glance in the rearview—

And saw the frozen river behind them.

Bob saw it, too. His eyes widened in horror.

Sadie wrenched the wheel. The station wagon swerved sharply. The front end fishtailed. The car went into a wild spin, slamming sidelong into the stump of a fallen pine tree, jolting to a stop that catapulted Bob off the hood. Sadie's neck whipcracked, her teeth snapping shut on her tongue. Bob soared through the night, screaming and flailing, before he hit the ice with a meaty thud and then skated like a hockey puck to the middle of the river, skidding to a stop.

Again, she was blind. Sadie groped her way back into the cold world. The freezing wind whistled through the holes in the windshield, dusting her with snowflakes that settled in her hair and eyelashes. Twisted metal creaked and groaned. Queenie whined somewhere in the back of the car. Sadie mopped blood from her eyes, one-handed, her other hand still cuffed to the steering wheel. She pulled weakly at the cuffs, but they held tight. She reached to adjust the rearview. Ignoring her blood-streaked reflection, she peered past Queenie's crumpled cage—the dog's eyes glinting in the gloom—looking through the splintered rear window. She needed to see him; to know he was dead.

Bob was splayed on the ice like a bloody snow angel. Arms outstretched. Hands twitching like dying spiders. One leg twisted horribly beneath him. He was moaning feebly. Haloes of breath frosted above his tortured face. His eyes rolled in his skull, peering up at the wrecked station wagon upon the riverbank.

Sadie tried futilely to free her hand from the cuffs, her fingers numb, blood drizzling from her wrist. Her eyes found Bob's knife lying in the footwell. A mad thought flashed through her mind: to just cut off her hand at the wrist. She had to do *something*. If she stayed in the car she would surely freeze to death.

Then she thought of something else.

She unrolled the driver's side window, reaching outside the car to remove Bob's keys from where they were still hanging in the door. Attached to the fob was a small key. Much smaller than any other key on the fob. It turned in the cuffs with a tiny click. The bracelet snapped off her wrist and she sobbed with relief, hugging her bruised hand to her chest like an injured bird, massaging life back into the numb fingers. With both hands free, she fumbled open the driver's side door, staggered from the car, her feet crunching in the snow. She braced herself against the door until the world stopped spinning. An icy wind whipped the tails of her shirt, the sudden cold making her gasp. The right side of the station wagon was horseshoed around the tree stump. Shards of broken glass scattered the snow. Queenie peered fearfully from her crumpled cage. Seeing Sadie outside, she gave a hopeful wag of her tail.

"… help…"

Sadie blinked heavily.

For a moment, she thought it was the dog talking to her.

"… please…"

Hearing her master's voice, Queenie whined and propped her paws against the splintered rear window, cycling her legs, claws scratching the glass.

Sadie turned her head slowly towards the voice, saw Bob sprawled in the middle of the frozen river.

"… please help me…"

His face contorted in pain.

"... ice... won't hold..."

Sadie just stared at him, standing next to the station wagon with the I LOVE MY POODLE sticker in the window. A strange calm descended over her. A serenity she'd never known. A calm that not even the rock had granted her. She liked seeing Bob out there. Helpless on the ice.

She smiled at him, cupping a hand to her mouth. "*Heeeeelp!*"

A look of dread filled Bob's face.

"I think I hear something ..." She cupped a hand to her ear.

"My bad," she said. "Nope, no one's coming."

Bob started sobbing.

Queenie howled in sympathy.

Sadie rolled her eyes at Bob's theatrics.

"Let's not make this any harder than it has to be," she said, limping to the back of the station wagon. "I mean, it's not like you won't have any company out there..."

And then she opened the trunk, splintered glass raining down as she levered up the door.

"Go to daddy, bitch."

Queenie sprang from the car, down the bank and onto the river, claws clicking on the ice as she scuttled to her master. A jagged line of cracks splintered the ice in her wake. Bob's eyes widened in horror. "No! Queenie! *Stay!*"

Sadie turned her back and started limping towards the distant sound of traffic on the highway, smiling at the sharp crack of ice behind her, and then the heavy splash of water, and it was hard to separate Bob and Queenie's screams before the river swallowed them.

ADAM HOWE

Adam Howe is a British writer of fiction and screenplays. He lives in Greater London with his partner, their daughter, and a hellhound named Gino. Writing as Garrett Addams, his short story Jumper was chosen by Stephen King as the winner of the On Writing contest, and published in the paperback/Kindle versions of King's book.

His short fiction has appeared in places like Nightmare Magazine, Thuglit, Mythic Delirium, and Year's Best Hardcore Horror. He is the author of Tijuana Donkey Showdown, and two novella collections, Die Dog or Eat the Hatchet, and Black Cat Mojo. Stalk him on Facebook, Goodreads, and Twitter @Adam_G_Howe

KILLING DOG AND TIGER

GARRETT COOK

Dog and Tiger were coming through the wall. Were they going to keep him this time? Dog and Tiger were coming through the wall. They weren't there yet but he knew they were on the way. Unless this wasn't the day. Anthony turned on the TV, shunning the news for a M*A*S*H rerun. He was hoping to be calm when they arrived. If they were coming, he might as well be calm when they arrived. There was no stopping them or reasoning with them. They did not seem to understand his objections. Dog and Tiger were coming through the wall.

Unless they weren't. This might not have been the day for Dog and Tiger. They didn't talk so they couldn't tell him when they'd come to take him next. Colonel Blake had gone down over the Sea of Japan. He had seen this one before. It was not particularly funny to him. M*A*S*H was almost never all that funny to him but there was nothing on. It was still better than if Dog and Tiger showed up. M*A*S*H concluded and Dog and Tiger had not come through the wall.

His phone buzzed.

"How R U?"

"I'm good," he texted back.

Dog and Tiger had not said that he could not speak of them. Dog and Tiger did not speak. But he knew that they would hurt Becca if he didn't play along and keep their secret. He was worried Becca would make plans and they would get in the way of Dog and Tiger's plans and Dog and Tiger would make him pay for it. He kept on wanting to say no to her but he was also worried that he wouldn't say no to her because he was very lonely lately.

"Want to get a burger at the pub?"

He wanted to get a burger at the pub. He missed Becca. He wanted to ignore his bouncing heart and swimming stomach. He watched the walls. He listened at them. He could never hear Dog and Tiger when they were in the walls but it couldn't hurt to check. It hurt to check. It hurt that he knew he had to. He got a glass of ice water and sat with it. He gulped it down. He picked up the phone. All he could hope was that they would not take this night away from him and they would not decide to come and keep him up. They never came to him at work, which was nice of them and it was his day off and they hadn't come yet. He hoped they wouldn't keep him up. He wanted a burger at the pub and he wanted Becca's clear blue eyes and he wanted Becca's laughter and her company, her smile. The only thing he could do was to text back, "Yes. Sounds good."

It sounded very good to get out of the house. It sounded very good to have company. He waited for her to say what time she got off work. He hoped it would be pretty soon. He wasn't sure if they'd let him leave early. He wasn't going to chance it. He might have done good for them last time so they were being clement. He wasn't going to risk his safety or Becca's. He was not sure what Dog and Tiger were capable of and he did not wish to find out.

He crossed his hands and put them in his lap. The phone said six thirty. It was currently four o'clock. That was two and a half hours. They could come during that time. They could take him and he would be gone and he would miss her. He fired up his laptop and went to YouTube. On days when he watched the video, they were less likely to come. Watching the video was sometimes as bad as seeing them but, given the choice between the two, it was obvious which was better, so he turned on the video and he watched.

His eyes were nailed into place. His sweaty hands bound themselves together lest he be tempted to turn it off prematurely. If he turned it off, they'd be likely to get offended, if they got offended, they'd be likely to come and if they came, they would not come in a good mood. He absorbed every second. He took his medicine. He chuckled politely, barely forcing out the laugh instead of his lunch. It was funny what they did back there. Good video, guys. Great video. Three million views. It wouldn't have three million views if it didn't entertain anyone, right?

He had performed the ritual the way they liked it. Surely, they would let him go tonight. They weren't going to let him go. Dog and Tiger were coming through the wall and there was no helping it and he was going to do exactly what they told him because if he didn't do exactly what they told him there would be consequences and they wouldn't just be for him. They could do just about anything they wanted, Dog and Tiger. Who was going to stop them? Certainly not him. He watched the video a second time just to make sure. He shouldn't have done that. They'd certainly approve but his body and his mind didn't. He felt like shit again.

He felt real sick. He threw up twice, then began to cry, turning on the shower and scrubbing his skin. They didn't often come to him in the shower. This wasn't about him being naked, it wasn't about sex. They honored his privacy for the most part. They'd never film him taking a shit or anything. It could have been worse. It couldn't have possibly been worse. They'd make it worse if he fucked around with them. He never fucked around with them, he never had even the slightest temptation to do so.

He emerged from the shower, his breathing calm. He smoked a bowl then walked over to the pub. He was early but he had done much to appease them and they weren't going to punish him for having a drink before Becca showed up. He went to the bar and ordered a whiskey and coke then sat down in the booth. Even after having thrown up, he still liked the fire coming down his throat, still liked the sting and the sweet coming together in unison. He still liked the little bit of surrender to peace. He didn't get much peace since Dog and Tiger started coming around.

Becca arrived and held him tight, kissed him hello. She could feel there'd been something wrong so pressed her cheek against his a moment longer. Rubbed the top of his hand as she sat down.

"Are you good today?" she asked. That was a bit much. How was he supposed to answer a question like that?

The way almost anyone does who feels like abject shit today.

"Yeah, I'm great. Why? Do I seem tense or something?"

She clearly thought he seemed tense, though he knew that she was far too polite to say it. Becca knew that would make him feel self-conscious and she was better off not making him feel self-conscious. She clearly regretted asking. She clearly knew that he was hiding something. She was right of course because he was hiding something and he wished that he could tell her but he knew that Dog and Tiger wouldn't go for that. It was nice of them to even let him… no, fuck them. Fuck Dog and Tiger. It wasn't nice of them. He was out with her and they couldn't hear him here. He didn't think. He didn't care. But still he couldn't tell her because he couldn't bear to think of her in danger.

"A little," she said, "but maybe I can… you know, do something about that?"

She clasped his hand. She smiled.

He smiled back. He meant it. It wasn't like the laughter to the video. He was smiling. He was out at the pub and he was safe.

"I'd like that," he said and he genuinely would like it.

He ordered a burger and a beer. She ordered the same.

They ate together, enjoyed each other's company, looked into each other's eyes. Talked. About work mostly, not about the day off and not about the thing he wasn't going to think about while she was here with him because he didn't need to think about it while he was out trying to have a good time even though he might be punished tomorrow for having a good time and that would be terrible but he wasn't going to think about it even if that meant that he... he wasn't going to think about it. He was enjoying himself. He was enjoying his burger and he was enjoying Becca. And then him and Becca enjoyed a kiss. And then he asked her to come home with him. What was he thinking asking her to come home with him?

He was thinking he'd had a nice time and he was thinking he would kiss her and he was thinking they would walk back to his place, hand in hand, and push each other against wall after wall, stop under awning after awning, and they would taste each other and they would know each other and the swimming stomach would stop swimming and the bouncing heart would suddenly cease to bounce. It was nice. And it was nice when they went to bed and the bouncing heart bounced once more at the command of her tongue and her body and her passion. And it was nice to breathe even and sleep without thoughts of Dog and Tiger.

He went to work the next day calm, knowing that they never hassled him at work out of some strange covenant they'd made. The rules were clear but the purpose of them not so much so. His friend asked after him and asked how Becca was and he said that things were good and it wasn't a lie. He was relieved that things were genuinely good and he did not have to fabricate a thing that wasn't there.

He did not linger at work just to be safe. He could have done so but felt it a violation each time he tried it and he knew that such violations would only invoke their wrath. He went home and turned on the television and he sat and he waited, this time knowing what was coming next. Dog and Tiger were coming through the wall and it couldn't be stopped. They had made their choice and he would have to honor it.

Dog came first as always, a head taller than him, white fluffy mascot body covered in spots. Dog must have been a Dalmatian. His face was an eternal smile, a long, plush tongue hanging out of his mouth, salivating over life forever. It wasn't a lie. Dog took great pleasure in what he did and if one deserved joy for doing what Dog did well, then Dog had earned that widemouthed slobbertongued smile. He gestured for Anthony to come forward and Anthony did. He got up from the couch and took Dog's paw and Dog led Anthony to Tiger.

Tiger was not smiling. Though not inherently menacing, Tiger's expression was a permanent exuberant growl. His great plush mascot head was stuck in a permanent barbaric yawp of sorts, a permanent "go team". Tiger was all energy and all enthusiasm, not unlike his cousin from the cereal box. Tiger gave Anthony a gigantic hug, which Anthony returned, patting Tiger's back like the old friend he expected to be treated as. Tiger certainly considered him a friend and perhaps this was the reason the rules were so stringent. Tiger would otherwise feel betrayed.

Together, they led Anthony through the wall. He had never thought to go through the wall on days when Dog and Tiger were not there. He was certain he wouldn't be able to. And there would be no reason to go there anyway. There was nothing in the room, only the table, only the whiteness, only the "you won't get out alive" and these were things no man would seek out on his own. He was back there again in the whiteness and the nothingness and they sat him at the table.

There were cups and saucers laid out and a tea kettle. He wanted to pour the hot tea in their smug faces but he knew it wouldn't help. He sat down and he drank with them. And he thanked them. And he cried as they made him drink cup after cup. He held his bladder since one time he'd pissed himself and Tiger had smacked him around for it. He didn't want Tiger to smack him around so he was good and he drank the tea and he waited. Dog and Tiger did not drink any tea. Dog fussed with his hair and Tiger bounced up and down applauding wildly. Three million hits. He'd gotten four million the day he pissed himself. Were they hoping he'd piss himself again? He hoped not because this time he didn't.

They walked out and left him waiting and he waited and he waited until the room finally went away. He did not go back through the wall. He was never led out. It always just seemed to go away. Maybe the tea was drugged and he just didn't remember them bringing him home. Any explanation was as good as the last. What was important was that he was crying, that he was sick, that he knew they were coming back and always would come back.

He was haggard the next day at work. He was staring at the walls where Dog and Tiger seemed to still be waiting. They never came when he was at work. Still they were with him, still he was thinking of the taste of tea and the blank button eyes of his plush tormentors. He tried to make small talk with his friend but he was evasive, distracted. He answered Becca's texts monosyllabically. He had wanted to think about her body and her kisses and being beside her and feeling at peace but he was thinking of the tea party again. He was thinking of them and all the time they had taken and were going to take.

He came home, sat down and watched the walls. He did not turn on the TV but went straight for the laptop. He watched himself drinking tea until he pissed himself, then watched as Tiger struck him again and again as Dog applauded. Three million hits. Three million people on the internet had seen him. That was funny, right? He laughed for Dog and Tiger. He turned on the video a second time. The phone buzzed. He watched it a third time. He wasn't going to make them mad again.

Becca. He picked up the phone.

"R u ok?"

"Something seems wrong."

Dog and Tiger were coming through the wall. His fingers were ready to reply but Dog and Tiger were coming through the wall. Dog was already there beckoning. He didn't want to come. He wanted to answer the text. He wanted to stay. Dog made no gesture but he knew what Dog was thinking. Dog had a way of showing what he was thinking without words or movements. Becca could get hurt. He didn't want Becca hurt. He followed Dog and Tiger back into the wall and he followed them back into the room with just the table.

And a tea service. A porcelain cup. A kettle full of scalding hot tea. They had taken two days in a row. They had taken him away from Becca. They had taken his comfort, his dignity, his life. Tiger did not expect him to snatch away the kettle as he was pouring. Tiger did not expect to be struck with the kettle, splashed with scalding hot tea. Tiger did not expect him to shatter the tea cup against the table and jam a shard of it as hard as he could into the plush guts. And though the suit was padded something fierce, after a few hard stabs, plush and skin were broken and Tiger was bleeding.

Dog was upon him trying to pull him off but with a swift kick to the knee, he pushed Dog back, then slid off of the chair and picked it up, smacking Dog in his fuzzy, padded testicles. Tiger was reeling, Dog was doubled over. Another smack with the chair, another stab with another shard of teacup. A series of kicks, stomp and stomp and stomp to the reddening plush face of the monster. Anthony saw only red, only what they'd taken and his need to get the fuck out. Soon, Tiger was on the floor, bleeding, soon the chair was broken over Dog's head. Soon, splinters and shards had made short work of his padded tormentors. Soon Anthony was alone.

The white soon faded. He was surrounded by boxes, nothing but boxes. This room had become a warehouse. Maybe it was always a warehouse. Soon, Anthony was no longer alone, illuminated by a flashlight. He looked up into the weathered face of the security guard wielding it, who turned white as a sheet.

"You gotta get outta here, man," said the guard, "you of all people, man. Why would you come back?"

Anthony was confused. Had this man seen him before?

"They had kept you here two weeks, put you in all those videos. And then you decide to come back. Of all the places in the world, why would you choose this one?"

Anthony looked down, finding no Dog or Tiger at his feet. He wondered if they still stirred in the walls. The man had been right. He had been free five years, five years since the cops had found him and taken the two captors in. He rolled the man's question around his mind and, try as he might, he could not find an answer.

GARRETT COOK

Garrett Cook is the author of Time Pimp and A God of Hungry Walls. He is the editor in chief of Eraserhead Press' New Bizarro Author Series.

Q&A

DUNCAN P. BRADSHAW

Is that really my face?

It could be. It looks familiar. But who really knows what we look like? We snatch glimpses, echoes, snapshots, but we aren't able to take in the twitches, nuances, tiny muscular tics, that to us are nothing, but to others, identify us as an individual.

I think it's the same as our voices. We only hear ourselves when recorded on drunken videos, or tapes. We then wonder: if that is what we sound like, utterly different than how we sound in our own head, what else is different?

Where did these questions come from?

This interrogation.

Am I mad?

Is this madness?

Do you think a madman knows? Or do they arrive at that realisation as they study their own reflection, or question their true voice?

I remember being told when I was younger, in jest I think, that the first sign of madness is talking to yourself.

How odd, I thought.

I always believed that the first sign of madness would be to talk back.

Is this what madness *feels* like?

I have no idea. What *is* madness? To those afflicted, they would view it as normality, surely? So how does one chart the descent from a balanced disposition, into something which is deemed to be so very different.

I feel different.

But then so many things have changed in the last few days that I am not sure whether this is real, or a dream I am yet to wake from.

What is real?

Define it.

Your description would vary from mine. Like the difference in how your voice sounds to me, as it does to you.

One thing I do know. A guarantee that you could use as collateral. That in life, we encounter far more questions than answers.

It is as if we seek to collect them, use them to test our mental acuity. And it seems as though there are some which fold in on themselves, into an intangible feedback loop. No sooner do you think you have unravelled one section than, on closer inspection, you find you have done nought, save for revealing a fresh conundrum.

There is one of late which taxes me.

If love is the answer, what is the question?

What nebulous, impalpable string of thought coalesced into something which I possess, but do not know how I obtained it? It is as if I climbed up to the heavens, to suspend the most beautiful painting in the night sky, just to break up the monotony of the null void. Yet upon arrival back on the ground, I am now unable to appreciate it from such distance.

Indeed, one does not beg to ask this very question until one has lost love.

I sit here on the floor of the kitchen, debris scattered around me. This concrete shell we turned from a list of measurements into a home, a nest for our love, now nothing more than a tomb for it. Memorials arrive in the form of envelopes, bills, statements, anniversary cards, made out to the former state, which no longer exists.

For although the love within her has turned tepid,

brackish, it lays barely changed within me. How can that be? I realise that the choice was not mine to make, but why do I pry within the fresh wound when I know that there is no outcome that will return it to its previous form.

It is a completed crossword without any clues.

Then it started.

I became aware of the sound this morning, as I awoke from interrupted dreams. Yet I believe it has been going on for some time.

It is a buzzing.

Not of insects, or electrical appliance.

It is distant, yet constant.

I stalked the house, removing everything I could from its socket, turning over objects which rested on unstable furniture. Yet still the sound remained.

I walked the streets to the town centre and back; it did nothing to alter its pitch or volume.

Has it always been there?

How did I not detect it?

More questions.

Questions. Questions.

Enquiry and examination.

I returned home and sat amongst the things that we shared. I lay in the bed that we put together from its constituent parts. Nestled myself between the sheets that were dried in the stale air that we both breathed. The clothes I wear upon my alien body, laundered amongst hers. They tumbled and intertwined within the same water in the same machine. But I do not feel her touch on them, nor feel her touch on me.

I go through photos, music, book and film, of the things that we enjoyed. Laughed at. Fought over. Broke. Mended.

I thought that we had chosen each other to be the one with whom we would decay with.

Was that the problem? Had we allowed the fire which engulfed our lives at the beginning, gut and die to embers?

Why did she see it and not me?

Am I blind?

I know that although I am not blessed with her vision, I am certainly not deaf. For the noise is still there. Even the sound of destruction did not mask it. Plates smashing, wood snapping, metal being warped out of shape. It remained throughout.

Like a kettle left on the hob, undiscovered.

Like our love.

There it is.

Listen.

Just below the wailing of the world.

It is a comforting sound. Like hearing your mother's heartbeat within the womb. Knowing that no matter what happens, no matter how long you live, you will never know anything which will touch you, soothe you, as deeply as that moment right there and then.

I have to do something, for inaction leads to focussing on the noise. On the loss. On the knowledge that everything is different now, yet I remain.

The air smelt different this morning. Not inside this mausoleum. But outside.

Whilst seasons have their own musk, which alters depending on the weather, there was something else. Was it emotion manifest? If so, why not take physical form? Why so ethereal? Why does it hide? Slink from view? You think you have tracked it down but, upon turning the corner, it is gone. Vanished into the never.

Validate it.

I have to do something.

This sound. It presses against my skull. I can feel the point of the bit, pushing against the skin of my temple. Like a concept made real, itching to escape the cage of its own construction.

I stand up, for there has to be something left to ruin.

To help transform. From its old state to the new.

To replace its existence. To make it like me.

Broken.

Am I broken?

What *is* broken?

I do not feel like the person I was.

Is that what the sound is?

More questions! Every time I arrive at an answer, I do not get respite, I get more to discover. Unravel.

Debunk and root out. Why?

Again!

Can I not just let it be? This investigation, what will it yield? It will not return me to how things were. It will not turn this house back into a home. Some fractures are wide, becoming chasms. Huge rent gouges. Impossible to hide. They run under oceans, and hold continents apart. But even they are destined to crack yet further. What then? Quake. Waves. Destruction.

Other fissures, though, are so thin that they continue, even when you think they end. They worm beneath the fabric. To the core. They are the most dangerous. Not because of their reach, but because you can't see them. You think your walls are built sufficiently high enough to keep the cracks from undermining them. But they have already burrowed far and wide. They are the insurrection in waiting. Ready to undermine any attempt at salvation.

When enough pressure is applied. Either in one blow, or over time. Those cracks. Those spidery wisps of air, held between the layers, open like trenches. Only then do you realise how deep they went. Only then do you realise that no defense, nothing, can ever stop them.

We all have them, you know?

All of us.

I know mine are at their limit. I guess I will soon discover the damage it will wreak. I slam the kitchen drawer shut, nothing in there left to destroy. Yet pain. Searing agony. I look down to see that I had left my hand in the space. Looking at it, my thumb nail is swelling. There is a mound forming beneath the skin and nail.

It's trying to get out.

What is?

Why?

Where does it think it is going?

What does it think is out there?

Something better?

Something worse?

The pain gives me focus, though. Something to direct the questions at. These are easier. Simpler. The answers are finite. Aren't they? Wouldn't that fit snug, if this pain were to provide me a question without answer.

It has to escape, though. It has to go somewhere. The nail is bulging, like a roof sodden with autumnal water. The drawer has bounced open, I look into its guts and see a wooden-handled corkscrew.

It does not belong where it is going, but I have no choice. Lest I get more questions. Open it up into a pointless debate, one that would serve as a distraction, maybe, but I am sick of that.

I want answers.

I press the point against the welt of thumbnail. I am assailed by the times I have used it previously. Birthdays. Anniversaries. Christmases. The aftermath of revelation. Now nothing more than footnotes in time.

My time.

I rest my thumb against the worktop, push the point into the tough pink hill. It fights. At first. Resists me. Like the answers I seek. But I prevail, and breach the shell. It cracks, like the plates, glasses and trinkets we adorned our cell with. Like everything does under pressure.

Like me.

I twist the metal.

Too much. Too much.

It bites into the skin. As I wrench it out, it removes the nail. Amidst the blood and pus pouring from the wound, something overrides even my sense of self-preservation. The sound has grown louder. I swear it. Not by much.

Someone else would dismiss it as coincidence. But when it has surrounded you with its endlessness, you know.

It can't be. Can it?

I put my thumb to my ear, and listen.

There it is.

The whistling aria.

A singular note melody.

Persistent.

True.

Louder.

There is no doubt there. Not now. I feel wise, yet foolish. Divided, yet whole. Then it hits me. I have an answer, yet more questions.

Is that the nature of how it always is? That knowledge is infinite? Always, there are things to ponder?

That even if we were immortal, there would always be another question to be asked?

So be it. If that is the way, then I should embrace it.

I have *an* answer for now, but who is to say that it is correct? If you ask two people what colour happiness is, would you not receive two different answers? Therefore, are my answers valid? Why do I seek them out?

Validate me.

Assure me that I'm right, about this, about anything.

I did know one thing for certain. That this sound, it is in *me*. Its source or purpose, I do not know. But I want to find out. Of all the things I can answer, about why my love had to end, even though it endures within me, this is something that I can discover. I will see it through, leave no trail to go cold. If I can do but one thing, it will be this.

Will it make things better?

Will it bring me peace?

NO MORE QUESTIONS.

Begin.

Segregate thought.

Concentrate on the noise.

That damn noise.

The drone that aches, yet soothes me.

Keeps me awake at night, yet beats my name.

My name.

Mine alone.

Alone.

It's the echo that only I can hear in this cavern. This construct I find myself deposited in. It has sides which I cannot see. Bars I cannot feel. An end that I cannot accept. Not yet. Though I know that I must. In time. But not now. Now I must excavate. Reveal a truth. Any truth. Even if it's a lie to someone else, it would be true to me, wouldn't it?

Why wouldn't it?

Enough.

Concentrate.

The noise.

The expulsion from within.

It *is* within me.

Me.

Inside.

That's where I must go. Not a metaphorical journey, but a real one.

Dig deep.

Refine.

Pore over and analyse, isn't that the way of things? Perhaps I stopped; I think I must've. Become too set in my ways to warrant examination. Was that her reason for leaving? If you cease asking, pushing, demanding more, does that kill the root? Starve the stem? Wring the goodness out, and blanch it?

I put an ear to my arm, the part that aches the most. Why?

NO.

Enough.

I said no more, didn't I?

Again.

I listen. It is there. But when I listen to my knee, I hear

it too. It is everywhere. And nowhere. I don't hear it from others. Do we only hear our own then? It doesn't make a difference. As before, two sides there are to most things.

Black.

White.

Some look for the grey. It is there, I suppose, but it is lazy. We need an absolute.

I swear the bones in my arm are oscillating. They lie restrained within a jacket of skin and sinew. I can help. Both them and me. The drawer is still open; most of the contents are not fit for purpose. Though the potato peeler was something I took for my own when I left to make my mark on this world.

She never used it. Preferred her own. We had two objects in the same drawer. Both accomplish the same task. Yet one is preferred over the other. Do they both not deserve a chance? Or was its purpose waiting for this moment all along?

I pick it up and sit back on the floor. The tiles are cold, and I can feel the shards of pottery beneath me, a poor substitute for a cushion. They ground me more than comfort, for that I am grateful. I place the blade against the bone on my wrist and, for a moment, I ask myself the question.

Why?

For answers! Damn you! Don't pretend like you have just arrived late to this point. You were there the entire time. You cannot pick and choose when to show up.

I pull the peeler towards me. The pain is excruciating. The skin catches under the metal, but still I draw it back. It comes off unevenly. Patchy. In clumps of hair and blood. I pick out lumps from the blade where it has snagged on the metal, and continue.

I must.

For the sound, that strange herald, it has grown louder still. And whilst it remains a monotonal hum, it is constant and true. Neverending.

The second stroke is easier and, whether through practice or luck, the skin comes off neater. Revealing the meat and muscle underneath. The crude machine exposed at last. Its frailties. Its weakness. Hiding away like a coward.

Blood oozes in irregular ways. From pierced veins, and from shaved tissue. Sometimes it drips, sometimes it pools.

I consider it.

There are cells within my flesh, blood and bone, that remember a time before her.

There are poor wretches that know only of her.

They are joined, in the minority, by those that know only of this pain.

Yet they live together. Unaware or unconcerned with the heritage of their fellows. Why can they co-exist, when we could not? I guess that as they are made from me, they are bound to support each other, irrespective of the time period from which they originated. To spurn one another would be folly. Counter-productive.

They sing to me.

Taunt me.

Encourage me.

How can they do everything at once? How can they share the same passageways, sired in different times, yet not give me that same courtesy?

Then I remember. This is just the surface. You do not judge things by their appearance.

You delve.

They nearly convinced me then to stop. To accept, blindly, their judgement. They offered me a shallow lie, a diversion. To keep me out. To protect the truth. They know.

But are they protecting me, or are they fooling me?

What humble tools can start, only tactile interaction can achieve true understanding from. I drop the peeler, and press my fingers into my feeble flesh. I wrap my slick digits around the muscle, and tug on it. The sound! It grows louder. Just for the briefest of times. It changes pitch, too. I pull again, and get the same result.

Perhaps.

Perhaps the problem lies within me?

How far has the rot seeped?

Are the lines on my hands physical fractures from my failings?

Why did I not see?

I tap my bones. Nothing. They emit no note or tone. The vibrations I felt before are from something else. My muscle and sinew, too, are mute. I pull on ligament, turning my hand into a claw, a monstrous instrument. I show my machine that it is nothing but a puppet. There is more than the fleeting sensations it bombards me with. They are nothing but symptoms of mechanical failure, or mental anguish, atrophy of the spirit.

I release the slick strings, allowing my fingers to unfurl. The demonstration complete. More of an affirmation than anything.

Wait.

That was an answer.

I feel validated, sure that I have taken a step closer. The buzzing remains. It is louder now that I have exposed within, but its source remains a mystery.

If it's not in my flesh or bone, where is it?

I dab a finger into the slowly coagulating blood, from its crude reveal. It tastes as it always has: coppery, tangy, rich, strangely appealing. But when I rub it between my fingers, the sound changes, splits into individual beats.

Of course. What else runs through this entire machine? What feeds it, sustains it, carries infection to where it will do the most damage? It keeps me on the edge of the knife. One slip, and it would end me.

I run my hand up my arm, I know now. I trace the veins, the arteries, the highways of this liquid, and rap on my chest with pale knuckles.

I have found you.

Home.

I stand, but nearly topple over. My head is light and I can see pulsing globules in my vision. They are adorned with suckers which contract and expand in time with my heartbeat. Are they connected? Do they know what I plan?

Surely they must, for I am one.

I steady myself on the worktop and rummage through the drawer once more. With the items procured, I concede this round, and sink back to the floor. I do not envisage that I will need to stand again. My legs will not be required. The many miles they have transported me are at an end.

Pulling off my t-shirt, I notice that I can see my ribs. The point at which they join, a concave hollow, pale, shorn of hair, I can see my skin flex as my heart pumps.

I am unsure if I will be allowed to reach the terminus. If the high castle will shut down before I discover what is emanating from me. This message it is sending out. Is it being received? Is there anyone but I, capable of receiving it? Surely they must need to be dialled in. Wired to the correct frequency.

Receptive.

For all of my stubborn posturing, I cannot detect anything else.

Alone.

Am I alone?

I am.

Is that what started it?

Is this signal nothing more than a distress signal?

Mayday.

Mayday.

This vessel is broken.

Send for help.

Repair.

Reset.

Ignore its plaintive call. Push it away. Attain the peace that brought you these discoveries.

Do it before it makes you change your mind.

Can it do that?

I don't know.

I don't think we should take the chance.

I run the blade across my rib from breastbone, until I catch my bicep with the keen edge. Already the blood is evacuating. Seeking a lifeboat. Solace. A way to find something its secret can be concealed in.

I push on, and place the spatula into the breach, under my rib.

I do not know if I will get a second chance at this before it realises what I intend to do.

I pull the wooden handle towards me. Quickly. Cleanly.

The pain cuts through me.

Not just my body.

Through *me*.

The rib has broken through the skin; my crudeness has worked. With trembling hands I pull the rib across my body, snapping it off, leaving it hanging as if it were a broken spine from a book.

I can feel my eyes pulsing. On the outward movement, I fear that they will burst free from my sockets and abandon me. Terrified of what they are witnessing.

I must act quickly.

The sound.

I can hear it now.

It's changed once more.

It's...

... beautiful.

Haunting.

Melodic.

I close my fist around the blood courier organ, and pull. It makes me gasp and wince, but I cannot stop now. I am sinking, both physically downwards and into myself. It is like my eyes are in retreat, looking out through windows growing more and more distant.

With one more pull I remove my heart from its mooring. It is still connected via its thick meaty pipes to the rest of my body.

I just want to know.

That's all.

I have to know.

What is that sound?

I bring the beating lump of gristle to my tiny eyes. Now looking down the wrong end of two black-lined telescopes.

Don't trust them.

So I place it to my ear.

My god.

It's divine.

There is a melody of impossible construction. It soars then wanes, carrying me aloft on an impossible wave, before delivering me into freefall, swooping through canyon and over a lush landscape.

But there is more.

Two voices.

One sounds like me.

As if it were a recording from a time I cannot recall.

But I sound happy.

Content.

I cannot discern what I am saying, but I know what the emotion tells me.

Who does the other voice belong to?

I squeeze my heart tighter, making the aorta burst free.

In that moment, my blood gushes out. I am the conductor in the final climactic movement. The pinnacle of my hopes, dreams… and questions.

I worry for the briefest of moments that I will be unable to see it through. To ensure that every note is perfect. To see that the tumultuous crescendo is worth every drop of the admittance fee.

It is then that I hear her.

Calling my name.

Over and over again.

As I peer into the rent organ, I see two shadows within the high chambered cathedral of blood.

They pirouette and move around each other with a grace that I didn't think was possible. There is fluidity, purpose and intent.

And nothing but love.

Her voice rises above the crashing strings, so crisp, so distinct, I wonder why I didn't hear it before.

How could I?

These secrets that lay hidden within.

And in that instant, this final breath between life and death, I realise that I have no more questions. It is so clear to me now. For all those moments where we think that we are alone, desperate and uncared for, there are so many others which are filled with joy, happiness and understanding. Those moments, they are the ones that stay within the heart. The place which keeps you alive, and keeps those alive that we loved. Even when they're gone.

That is the most important thing.

We hold onto it like these two figures within, who now, as the final notes stretch out and begin to fade, turn to me and bow.

As they stand, her voice—trembling, scared—says but one word before all I know turns to darkness.

The orchestra, which had played so gamely, ceases for this litany.

"Why?"

DUNCAN P. BRADSHAW

There is no finer sight in the world than Duncan P. Bradshaw brandishing the holy ukulele of fun, which he found in a two pence grabbing machine, whilst on holiday in the south of France. Despite his inability to play it, the way the light reflects off the polished fretboard, is really rather magnificent.

When he isn't making up bios to make him sound majestic and amazing, he types words into the magical machine of letters and numbers, forming them into sentences, and in turn, stories. Best known for his zombie fiction, Duncan just wants to write down the events which run around his head, and refuse to die.

Have a look at his website,

www.duncanpbradshaw.co.uk

for information on his work, or, better yet, give him a Like on Facebook,

https://www.facebook.com/duncanpbradshaw/

SCARAB

DAVID OWAIN HUGHES

Jason picked up the framed photo from his mantelpiece and looked at the happy snap beyond the plastic glass. Tears welled in his eyes and eventually dripped down his face and onto the false pane and cheap pine casing.

The picture was captured at a pleasing point in his life; a time almost forgotten—a period that was nothing more than a cheery, distant and warming glow found in the depths of his mind. The only time he could recall the happy moments from yesteryear was when he was sober and not crawling around inside a bottle of gin.

"I've been dry for thirty-two-days-and-a-half!" he uttered, tracing the frozen faces with his thumbs. "I should have kicked it, but I wasn't strong enough to stop…"

"*It's always* one *more fucking job with you, Jason!*" he often heard his ex-wife's voice say. "*The kids need a father who's going to be around to watch them grow up. To have a dad they can play with and take them to the park. What they don't need is a drunken, good-for-nothing thief!*"

"It kept you living your airs-and-graces lifestyle. You were quite happy to gobble my cock for a new handbag or a fistful of fifties!" he'd yell back. The whisky and mother's ruin and rum and brandy and beers made it all go away, but not for the last thirty-two-days-and-a-half. All the angry, slurred voices and the screams and tears of his children were there.

They were gin-clear.

Jason could see the pained expression on his children's

faces whenever he and Tina argued in front of them—they rarely had glowing, teeth-exposing grins on their chops like they did in the photo he now held. He dragged the forming snots in his nose and throat and swallowed the jelly-like muck.

"Daddy's going to make things right, kids. *One* final job and I'm out. Done! That's a promise. No more." Jason wiped the tears from his eyes so he could see the images of his children with clarity. The palm trees in the background suggested the photo had been taken on one of their numerous family holidays.

When the bank, mulling and gun-running jobs were coming in thick and fast for Jason and his posse, he lived a lifestyle that rivalled Tony Montana's—the world was his. But a few stints in prison put paid to his activities, and soon he was a number-one target on the police's radar. He couldn't fart without a copper knocking his door.

This job's different, he thought, continuing to look at the photo. *It's fool-proof and worth over ten-million fat ones each! Enough cash to get me and the kids out of the country and away from this shit-hole for good…*

A plan to snatch his children during the raid was in place: a member of Jason's crew, Juice, was to go to Tina's house and take them by brute force, if necessary, but not deadly force. Once the kiddos were in his care, he was to drive to the airport and meet Jason and the rest of the outfit there, where they would board a plane to Hawaii.

The tickets were in place; so too was his crew and scheme. All Jason had to do was put the whole thing into gear and get the job done. Before he knew it, he would be drinking beer in the sun and enjoying his lolly with his children.

Nothing can go wrong… me and the boys have been through the arrangements a hundred fucking times. It's taken us two years to get to this point—no stone has been left unturned. Hopkins and Sons Jewellery won't know what's fucking hit it!

The small, family-owned, family-operated shop was a

goldmine; a target waiting to be hit; a grape ready to be plucked from the vine. Hopkins and Sons was a little different than your ordinary jewellers, as it stocked the unusual—ancient artifacts and special items that should only be displayed in a museum—along with the usual: watches, necklaces, rings, and so forth.

It was a shop built for the rich, a place where they could splash their cash on rare items like the materialistic whores they were. It had been a splendid find by Jason, who had stumbled across the shop while doing honest work with a road crew a little over two years ago.

Whilst digging the road to lay new pipes and lines opposite the shop on the busy high street, Jason had spotted it; he'd watched as highfalutin wretches came and went with pound signs dancing in his vision. The sound of cashing tills rang in his ears and caused him to salivate.

On his lunch break that day, Jason had meandered over to the shop and nosed outside like a flunky—he'd already had it planted in his mind that he was going to knock the joint over, so he didn't want to go inside and show his face. Even though he knew it would be a long time before he hit the place.

The golden Lynx-engraved tiaras looked as though they hailed from darkest Africa, and had him rubbing his whiskery chin with excitement. The need to steal had him shaking, much like the horn makes a pervert tremble with the need to climax. Not only were there tiaras on display, but rings from Congo, diamonds from Peru, necklaces from Serbia, pearls from Persia, prehistoric Welsh love spoons studded with twinkling gems, and a whole host of other treasures.

Every day for the following six months Jason visited the shop, but only stepped inside once, when temptation got the better of him. Security was at a minimum: one fat guard leaning on his baton and CS Spray and three cameras dotted around the shop. When he told the elderly man behind the counter he was looking for a special ring for his fiancée, Jason was led right to the vaults below.

Underneath the shop, in the warren-like chambers, Jason found there to be another lazy guard and four more cameras. He also saw some rare items, such as a scarab belonging to an entombed mummy god from ancient Egypt.

"That, my boy, is one of the rarest, most expensive items on the planet! It is owned and stored here by a descendent of the sun god Ra... In ancient Egyptian religion, the sun god Ra was seen to roll across the sky each day, transforming bodies and souls. Beetles of the Scarabaeidae family dung beetle rolled their dung into balls as a source of food and an offspring chamber in which to lay their eggs; when the larvae hatched it was immediately surrounded by food. For these reasons the scarab was seen as a symbol of this heavenly cycle and of the idea of rebirth or regeneration. The Egyptian goa Khepri, Ra as the rising sun, was often depicted as a scarab beetle or as a scarab beetle-headed man. The ancient Egyptians believed that Khepri renewed the sun every day before rolling it above the horizon, and then carried it through the other world after sunset, only to renew it the next day. A golden scarab oj Nefertiti was discovered in the Uluburun wreck..." Old git Hopkins had informed him, but Jason had mostly tuned out after the words 'rare' and 'expensive'.

Funny, it doesn't look like much! he'd thought at the time. *Still, if it's as rare as the old man says...* The drool returned to his chin.

The pound signs again jumped up and down in his vision.

Before the discovery of the jewellers, Jason had been clean for almost three years after spending six behind bars for armed robbery; he should have served ten-to-twelve, but his sentence was cut for giving up the loot and keeping his nose clean whilst inside.

He never gave his gang members away, and felt no resentment over the course of his porridge for them not serving time. He'd told the people of the high court that he'd acted alone and took full responsibility, even though witnesses had informed the police that there were indeed five involved in the heist.

Once released, Jason had made a promise to go straight, especially after finding Tina had left him and taken the children to live in the city. He cleaned his act up and got a job with the council, becoming a highway maintenance assistant.

As hard as he tried, Jason couldn't quite conquer the demons. And as soon as he'd stumbled across the Hopkins' goldmine, he was quick to cave. The old lusting for fortune returned.

Within weeks Jason had reassembled his crew—most of whom were still working small jobs, whilst others had gone straight and were begging for the opportunity to break the law in a huge, bank-account-busting way. When Jason went a knockin', they rolled up to go a rockin'.

He replaced the photo and dried his eyes.

I can't meet the guys with tears running down my cheeks like an old dear! He sniffed, snorted, and shook his head until the girlie, wimpy thoughts and ideas were banished from his hardened criminal mind. Jason looked into the mirror hanging over the mantelpiece. *How in the hell did I ever get a job in the first place?* he wondered. His head was shaved bald, and jailbird ink decorated his left cheek and the underside of his right eyelid. He also had a scar running the length of his jawline to the top of his shoulder, which had been inflicted upon him with a bottle during a fight in a nightclub when he was nineteen.

Almost twenty-five years ago to the day!

He could still recall the bouncers who pried him off the lad who had struck him with the glass. If Jason hadn't been stopped from pummelling the lad, he would have killed him.

"Fucking bouncers..." he uttered, running his fingertips down the purpley-pink tramline. The rest of his six-foot-four, nineteen-stone frame fared the same: scars from knife attacks, bites and dents all over from punches and kicks, not to mention the grotty ink comprising flaming ace cards and naked women.

He was a product of his business and the underworld he'd grown up in, which in turn had stemmed from Jason being a victim of his youth—a casualty to the anarchy that had stormed within his guts throughout his teenage years.

"Ah well, fuck it! I was never destined to be the next brains of fucking Britain," he told his reflection. "I'm destined to be fucking rich. To have all the wonga in the world and to be able to spoil my children and give them the life I never had."

Jason pulled the cuff of his black jumper back to check his watch and noticed it was almost midday. "Time's kicking on!" He'd arranged to meet the gang at an abandoned airstrip outside the city by one o'clock. Once gathered, they would go through the plan a final time before putting it into action.

Before heading out the door, Jason checked his gear, which was located in a bag by his side: balaclava, flashlight, sawn-off shotgun, tape, rope, explosives, ammo, passport, spare clothes, and a few other bits and pieces.

He zipped the sports bag up, flung it over his shoulder, and headed out the door.

At precisely five-to-one, Jason was at the meet zone. Big Bobby Briggs, explosives expert and getaway driver, was leaning against his Transit van smoking a fag. He kindly informed Jason that the others were in the back, ready to rock-and-roll.

The 'Big' part of Bobby's name was a slight faux-pas

on one of the other gang members' behalf. He'd been told Bobby was a giant of a man when enlisting a fresh face into the team. When Bobby turned up for his 'interview', Jason had told him that he was not applying for a job as a Christmas elf. Bobby had seen the funny side and was called Big Bob from that moment on.

Jason entered the back of the van and greeted his boys—it had been a while. There was Juice: all-round scout, weapons merchant and safe-cracker. His job would be to get Jason's children to the airport. A car was awaiting him across the street from the jewellers.

Harry 'Wires' Peterson was the man to knock out electrics. He would be taking care of the cameras and whatnot within Hopkins from the safety of the sewer system, which he possessed the blueprints to. Before Jason stepped foot out of the van, Wires would be sent under the street to kill everything before returning, enabling the gang to simply march into the shop.

Bosco, hard man of the crew, was not much of a thief but was a cracking streetfighter who'd rolled with Jason and his team for years. His body and fists had come in handy many a time when they'd been looking to make a quick buck. He would be Jason's support on the inside, along with Wires, while Bobby waited in the van.

After greeting his lads, Jason told Bobby to get behind the wheel and wait for his command. Jason laid out photos, plans and blueprints on the van floor for them all to see.

"Bosco, as soon as we get inside make sure you take all the guards down. Without panic buttons, cameras, and silent alarms to worry about, we should be fine. Once they're taken care of, and we have the keys to the vault, I'll take Hopkins down there and clean the place out. The scarab is the most important piece! Do we all know what we're doing?" The crew nodded and murmured amongst themselves. "Good. I don't want fuck-ups. We pull this off, we're set for life. Bobby, get this piece of shit rolling!"

By twenty-to-three, the Transit was parked opposite the Hopkins and Sons jewellery store. The street was bustling with shoppers, which was perfect—the throng of people would provide the perfect cover. Jason and his boys would be lost faces in a sea of consumers.

"Right, Wires, off you go, there's a good lad! We're slightly behind schedule, so don't go pissing about down there, playing with the rats. Get your job done and your arse back here pronto. Capiche?"

The bespectacled fella nodded, grabbed his bag, and exited the van without a word.

Jason poked his head between the driver and passenger seats and watched as Wires jogged across the road before slipping down an alley. He looked at his watch and gave his man thirty minutes, even though it had only taken between eighteen and twenty-two on their trial runs.

He turned back to his boys and looked at Juice. "Okay, Juicy. Your turn!"

"I'm ready, boss man."

"Come here," Jason said, leaning between the front seats again. "See that Ford Fiesta over there?"

"The black one?"

"That's it. Here's the keys." He placed them in Juice's hand. "Take good care of my children, and make sure you get them to the airport in one piece. Got it?"

"Of course, boss. You can trust me. We're like brothers."

"I know," Jason said, throwing his arms around the man and pulling him close to his chest. "When this is over, we're going to be stinking rich!" The others cheered. "Now, off you go."

Just like he'd done with Wires, Jason watched his man through the window before sitting beside Bosco. He looked at his watch—eight minutes had passed. A tightness knotted Jason's guts as he listened to the seconds thunder down. *Not much longer,* he thought. He always got tense before a raid.

Jason closed his eyes and willed his stomach to stop flip-flopping. Bosco and Bobby were talking, but he couldn't hear what they were saying. Everything seemed muffled, distorted almost.

"Looks like he's on his way back, boss!" Bosco said, giving Jason's arm a tap.

Jason opened his eyes and stood. He saw Wires running across the street. "Open the doors for him, Bos." The muscleman did as instructed, allowing Wires entry to the van. He jumped in. "Everything run smooth?"

"Yeah…" Wires gasped. "Fucking simple! Nobody suspected a thing."

"Right, let's fucking roll!" Jason said, removing his balaclava from the holdall and placing it on his head, so that it looked like a woolly hat. He zipped the bag back up and put it over his shoulder. The others did the same.

Jason moved across the street with Bosco breathing down his neck. When he looked over his shoulder, he saw Wires was a few steps behind. In the van, Bobby nodded at him. Jason returned it.

Nobody seemed to notice the darkly-dressed, slightly conspicuous men. People were too busy rushing around; shoppers mixed with business types, who were eating on the go.

Just after they entered the jewellers, they dropped their balaclavas and removed their sawn-offs from their bags.

"Everybody get down on the fucking ground! *Now!*" Jason yelled, firing a warning shot into the ceiling. Glass and plaster exploded and cascaded down around him. Customers yelled and screamed. Before anyone could escape, Wires had the main door locked, the blinds drawn, with Bosco manhandling the guard on the top floor. When Bosco had the man to ground and cuffed, he went and sought out the others.

Within ten minutes, Jason and his boys had everything under control: all the guards were on the floor, cuffed and rendered useless, with the customers lined up against the window. Bosco and Wires had their guns on them.

"Anyone fucking cracks a fart, let alone moves, gets a cunting round to the back of their skull!" Bosco said. He had one sole foot placed on top of the guard at his feet. The women wept and grizzled, but the men tried to look tough by keeping their shit together.

"Now, Mr. Hopkins," Jason said, walking around the counter and grabbing the old, frail-looking man by the collars of his jacket and yanking him close to his face. "This nastiness can be over and done with in the next few minutes, if you'd be so kind to give us what we want!"

"Yea… Yeah, anything! Just don't hurt anyone…"

"Give me the keys to your vaults downstairs!" Hopkins shot his son a nervous glance, who shook his head in return. Sweat broke across the old man's forehead. "Are you telling me no?" Jason asked, stuffing the barrel of his sawn-off under the father's chin. "I'll blow your fucking brains out all over your fucking ceiling, cunt!"

"Nothing from below can be taken…" the son said.

Jason looked at him. "Oh, is that so?"

The boy nodded. He couldn't have been much older than thirty.

"It's true, sir," the father said. "Many sacred items. They can't be tampered with. Please, take everything from up here!"

"That's very kind of you, but I want what's in your basement. The rare, priceless stuff. Now, give me the *fucking* keys… I won't ask again."

"I… I can't…" Hopkins said.

Jason pushed the old man away from him and cracked him across the bridge of his nose with his sawn-off. Bone cracked; blood squirted up Jason's balaclava and splashed across one of the glass display cabinets.

"*Now*, motherfucker!"

"Dad!"

"Back the fuck off, junior!" Jason said, levelling his gun at the younger man's chest.

"Here, take the keys!" He removed them from around his neck and tossed them at Jason.

"Thanks." Jason snatched the keys from out of the air and grabbed Hopkins. "Come on, son. You're coming with me. Boys, keep an eye on the lad."

"Will do, boss," Wires said.

"*Up!*" Jason told the old man, helping him to his feet by yanking him unceremoniously up off the floor. He then pushed him towards the entry leading to the back room, where Jason knew there was a set of steps leading to the vaults. "Move!" he bellowed, giving Hopkins another push.

The man rushed forward, tripped, and fell headlong down the stairs. He yelped and screamed as he tumbled with a crash. When his body hit the wall at the bottom, Jason laughed, especially as he could see the man had not seriously hurt himself—he was still moving.

Jason casually walked down the steps and clutched Hopkins by his jacket. He then dragged him along the floor behind him. When he got to the room with the vault he was looking for, he forced Hopkins to open the door. Once inside, Jason demanded the vault be opened, much to Hopkins' protests.

Upstairs, he could hear his boys clearing the glass cabinets of their goodies. A smile stretched across his face.

"I beg you, don't take these possessions!" Hopkins pleaded.

Jason didn't have time for this. He had a schedule to keep and a plane to catch. He snatched the keys out of the man's hand, levelled his sawn-off, and pulled both triggers. But only one barrel roared with gunfire.

Because of the shortness of range, the cartridge ploughed through the man's chest, and the ferocity of impact took Hopkins off his feet and propelled him backwards. His back hit the vault, and he slid down, leaving behind a bloody, slug-like trail. The spray of ball bearings peppered the walls and floor and burst certain objects within the room, such as framed photos and glassware. A thick, cloying smoke filled with the stench of gun oil permeated the air.

Jason coughed and looked at Hopkins. The man's mouth was flapping like he was a fish out of water. Blood trails snaked down either side of his mouth; bubbles of crimson burst as he tried to speak. Jason was shocked the man was still breathing, because Hopkins had a crater the size of a fist in his chest.

"Get out of my fucking way!" Jason raged, grabbing Hopkins' ankles and dragging him to one side.

It took Jason a little longer to gain access to the vault because he had to sort through the keys until he found the ones he needed to 'open sesame'. Once he gained access, he drained the secure safes and dumped everything into his bag.

Before leaving the room, he removed the precious scarab and pocketed it. He then made his way upstairs, reloading his sawn-off as he went. He thought he might start feeling guilty about blowing the old cunt away, but no. *It was rather pleasing, actually!* It was the first time he had killed anyone, even though he had been offered hits for jobs before. *I've hurt enough people in my time, so who knows— one or two of them may have died on a hospital gurney somewhere.*

He shrugged and continued walking. When he got upstairs, he turned right and walked the length of the corridor until he was back in the main room. Wires was standing over a woman with a bleeding mouth.

"She was giving cheek, so I shut her the fuck up!"

"Fair enough," Jason said. "Have you two cleaned everything out?"

"Yeah," Bosco and Wires said in unison.

"Where's my *father*?!" Hopkins Jr. asked.

"Dead, *motherfucker*. Just like you will be if you don't get down on your hands and fucking knees, cunt!" Jason spat. "Boys, get the door."

He heard the locks clack. Outside, Bobby pulled up, the tyres of the Transit screeching to a halt. Slowly, Jason backed out the door, keeping his gun trained on Hopkins' son, who was crying. When he got to the threshold, he noticed Bosco and Wires were holding the door for him.

When he stepped outside, the floor started to shake violently—car alarms blared, people ran off screaming and crying while others took cover in doorways, bus-shelters, and under parked cars. The concrete in the road split and widened by a good forty feet, revealing a blinding array of red and orange.

Jason watched as people fell into holes and crevices that were starting to appear—mothers, children, business people, the homeless. Mass hysteria kicked in as herds of people began stampeding. Buildings around them vibrated with such force that they collapsed into clouds of thick white dust and twisted metal.

Water pipes burst.

Telegraph poles snapped their wires—the live cables skipped across the pavements and roads like snakes from a sci-fi novel. People were either scorched, electrocuted, or blown off their feet as the downed lines cut destructive paths through the mobs.

The air filled with a dense smoke. From behind, Jason heard the customers inside the jewellery store screaming. Some of them fled, seemingly no longer caring if Jason and his gang shot them down.

"What the *fuck*?!" Bobby screamed out the driver's side window. They were his last words, as the ground beneath the van burst apart and devoured the Transit.

"*Jesus*! Get back!" Jason told Bosco and Wires. Before heeding his own advice, he braved a look into the cavern. At the bottom of the ravine was a lake of molten lava. He watched as Bobby screamed his way down and plunged into the red-hot river. "This can't be happening..." he muttered.

"Oh, but I'm afraid it is, sir!" Young Hopkins said. Jason turned to see a huge grin on the man's face. "We're all going to hell," he bellowed.

"What the fuck is happening?" Bosco raged.

"We told you not to take artifacts from downstairs. They belong to the ever-powerful gods from worlds long forgotten."

"Fuck you!" Jason screamed, lowering his gun and firing both barrels into Hopkins Jr.'s chest. The impact threw him through a glass case.

"What the hell did you do that for, boss?!" Wires said. "He was the only one who knows what's going on here."

"You don't believe in all that mumbo-fucking-jumbo, do you? What we have here is an earthquake, gentlemen. As soon as it blows over, we're out of here!"

"Try telling that to Bob..." Wires muttered.

"Do you want to fucking join him down that hole?!" Jason raised his voice to be heard over the screaming, charging people and blaring alarms. The gang had the entry to the shop completely blocked, as they stood huddled in the doorway.

"Like something out of a Spielberg film!" Bosco muttered.

All around them, concrete, mucky water, and earth were tossed into the air. Smoke belched out of storm drains. Jason could hear sirens somewhere in the distance. *We need to make a move. The last thing we need is the boys in fucking blue turning up.*

"Not like the UK to get an earthquake, especially one of this magnitude," Wires thought aloud as the ground stopped shaking.

"See," Jason said. "Right, let's get—"

"What in all that's holy?!" Bosco yelled. "Look!" He pointed. "Over there! Are they what I think they are... No, surely not!"

Jason poked his head around the doorway to see what Bosco was pointing at. All the people in the street had stopped and were standing around, perhaps discussing the event and helping each other.

But they should have continued running.

In the near distance, not too far from the section of road Jason and his maintenance crew had been digging up a few years back, arms and heads started emerging from the ground. The limbs appeared to be rotten, the faces missing chunks of flesh.

"No. Fucking. *Way!*" Jason screamed.

"It's whatever you took from downstairs. Maybe if you put it back, we can reverse this?" Bosco suggested.

Before Jason could answer, his attention was drawn back to the streets—the crowds were now running and screaming once more, as more limbs and heads pushed up from the ground, followed by decayed bodies. This new threat pounced upon the terrified populace and ripped the flesh from their bodies and drank their blood.

Jason witnessed one woman getting flanked by what could only be described as the walking dead. They pinned her to the floor and ripped her blouse open and tore her skirt from her body. The dead clawed her torso open and snacked on her innards, then chewed through her naked tits and face.

Children were easily picked off, as their parents left them behind to run for the hills. Soon, the avenue was overrun by the rotten, groaning dead; their stench wafted down the street.

"*Inside!*" Jason screamed. They backtracked and slammed the door behind them. Wires was quick to engage the locks.

"What's going on out there?!" a nervous teenage girl

asked.

"You fucks are responsible for this!" a suited and booted man snapped.

"Fuck you!" Jason bit back, stepping up to the man and upper-cutting him. The blow sent the scrawny businessman to his arse.

"Calm down," the teen said. "Arguing and fighting amongst ourselves isn't going to help."

A scream and hard thump from behind caused them all to turn. A young man was pressed up against the shop's window by three undead fucks. His throat was chewed out, sending blood geysering across the glass. As the dying man bucked, his weight thumped against the window, causing spiderweb cracks to develop. The undead left behind bits of their own flaky, bloody skin as they dragged their prey to the floor and out of Jason's view.

"We have to get the fuck out of here," Wires said.

"Stop getting hysterical, man," Bosco told him.

"Maybe you should try replacing what you took?" the teen offered, raising her voice. Some of the undead had now gathered their emaciated frames at the door to beat their fists against its glass. One of them only had half a tongue. It rubbed its stump of an organ against the window.

Jason looked away as cherry-coloured clots dropped off the creatures' faces, arms, and hands and glued to the glass. His guts somersaulted. "*Jesus!*" he muttered.

The shop's main window started to crack further, causing the blonde teen to whimper and shriek as particles of glass fell away.

"We need to get downstairs," Bosco said. "We'll be safe behind the thick doors down there."

"But we'll be trapped!" the suit said, getting up off his arse.

"I don't hear *your* suggestions," Wires said, jumping to Bosco's defence and getting between the men.

Probably worried Bos will level the cunt into an early grave,

Jason thought.

"Let's keep calm, okay? What about up?" Wires suggested. "Boss, when you were casing the joint, did you happen to notice if there was a second floor or attic?"

Jason shook his head, unable to take his eyes off the main window; the cracks were getting bigger as more undead bodies piled in behind their comrades. Splits raced up, down, vertical and horizontal. The centre of the pane resembled a huge spider web; the sound of splintering glass became deafening, rising above the noise caused by the few undead hammering at the door.

"We need to head down!" Jason said. "There is no upper level." His eyes flicked back to the door; it was rattling in its jamb. The lock shook as flocks of the undead engulfed the outside. In the background, Jason could see more vehicles and people being lost to the cracks in the ground.

The world was ending.

Maybe there's a chance I can fix this!

"Come on, move!" Jason yelled, pushing the girl onwards. Wires and Bosco followed behind. As they headed through the door leading to the back, the businessman screamed. Jason looked back and saw hands reaching up through the floor, grabbing the businessman around his ankles—the dirty, chipped and broken nails of the dozen or so hands were raking the man's flesh.

When he fell, Jason made to go back for him, but was stopped by Bosco and Wires.

"He's a goner!" Bosco said. "Let's keep moving."

Jason's eyes fixed onto the businessman's face; the sheer terror that was etched on it was the stuff of nightmares. Dirty digits were forced into the man's mouth and relieved him of his tongue, which stretched until its cord snapped. Blood pooled from his mouth. More hands came through the floor. Their roaming fingers stabbed through his eyeballs, whilst other talons grabbed, slashed, yanked and ripped. Before Jason turned away, he saw the man's privates being torn free; the bollocks and cock were pulled through the floor.

Probably being stuffed into a hungry, greedy and waiting mouth! Jason shivered at the thought. From below, he thought he heard the slurping and smacking of chops. Another shiver cut down his back.

The window and door exploded simultaneously. The undead flopped through the shattered glass and shredded their taut yet weak flesh on the jagged shards left in the frame. Blood pumped and squirted across the floor, which now resembled the inside of an abattoir.

"Shift your bloody arse!" Wires grabbed Jason and pulled him down the corridor. Whilst being dragged by his scruff, Jason watched as the army of darkness flooded the shop and meandered, stumbled, shuffled, and pin-balled in his direction.

They groaned, snarled and snapped their decayed teeth together in a lust-hungry way. The horde bottle-necked their way into the corridor and staggered after Jason, who was wrenched down the stairs to the vault area.

He shoved Wires' hand off him. "It's okay, I'm cool now! Turn right and head through the door. We'll be able to lock that motherfucker."

When they reached the bottom of the stairs, Jason heard thuds from behind, which sounded like bowling balls being tossed down the steps after him. He glanced over his shoulder and saw the first few undead had literally launched themselves after him.

They can't take the steps, but it won't stop them!

Bones broke, necks snapped, shoulders were jerked from sockets and legs were twisted into various unnatural positions.

But still the undead came.

Their groans intensified which, in turn, breathed forth a rotten, wet earth stench that caused Jason to gag. The putrid, skinless faces on some he'd seen pushed against the windows upstairs had had maggots and beasties scurrying around inside their mouths and skulls.

The images would stay with him until his dying day.

When Jason and the others got through the door leading into the vaults and the rooms beyond, they closed and locked it behind them with just seconds to spare. Soon, rotten dead fists began pounding at it, to no avail.

"It'll take a tank to get through that!" Bosco said. "We're safe for the time being."

"But we're trapped down here—what do we do?" the teen asked.

"I have explosives in my bag. Enough to blow a hole in a wall down here," Jason said. "I'm sure I can get us out of here, don't worry. Let's take five, regroup, and plan our next move. If the streets are crawling with those things, then maybe going out there isn't such a hot idea!"

"But we can't sit here, either," Wires said. "We have no food or water."

"Fucking chill, *princess*!" Bosco winked. "We can go a few hours without either of those. Besides, I have some snacks and a few cold drinks in my bag. I don't go anywhere without a small ration of refreshments."

The hammering on the door reverberated around the vault-like corridor/room they stood in. Either side of them were various rooms filled with numerous treasures.

"You could have taken all this, too!" Wires told Jason.

"Nah, the scarab is *priceless*."

"Put it back!" the girl snapped.

"Maybe you should put a fucking sock in it, or I'll ram my fist into your mouth," Bosco threatened.

She crossed her arms and poked her tongue out at him. Jason couldn't help but smile. Her attitude matched her jumper, which had a big anarchy symbol on it—the sign was made to look as though it had been painted on, as the dye had a running look to it. On her feet, he could see she was wearing Doc Martins—*Beetle Crushers is what Mum used to call them.*

"Putting it back might not be such a bad idea. With the

score we've got, we can still piss off out of the country and never look back," Jason informed his gang.

"*Dude*! Wake up! The world has gone to tits. Money is no good, especially if you can't rectify your mistake."

Jason poked his head into the room he had cold-bloodedly mown Hopkins down in. The man lay in a lake of coagulated blood, his face ashen. *At least he ain't up and walking the fuck around like something out of Living Dead at the Manchester Morgue!*

A rumble underfoot caused him to snap his head downwards. Jason half expected to see the ground cracking beneath his feet, but the hard, marble floor was intact. "What the hell was that?!" he asked.

"I can't see them coming through this floor," Wires said. "It's blast-proof."

The earth below shook and groaned again, but the marble remained solid. A collectively held breath was released. The three men placed their bags on the floor and looked around. Jason went to the last room on the left and entered. He made his way to the corner and tapped on the wall.

What is beyond them? How far down are we? If we blast and let a fuck ton of dirt in, it may bury us alive! And if it doesn't, it could take us months to dig our way out. We'd never survive… Fuck!

"These walls are probably the weakest, guys!" Jason yelled, giving the brickwork a few more taps. "Some explosives by here and… *Boom*!" he muttered to himself.

Jason set his bag down and removed enough C4 to level a handful of walls. He also took out extra shotgun ammo and reloaded his sawn-off. He placed his gun by his side and rigged the explosives to the detonator.

We might need a quick getaway!

Jason walked back to where the others were.

"Are you replacing that stone or not?" The girl glared, crossing her arms once more and shooting him an unimpressed look.

Full of sass, ain't ya?! he thought. "Yes, I'm going to

replace it." He dug the scarab from his pocket and showed her. "Here it—"

She snatched it from his hand before he could finish his sentence and ran into the room containing the body of Hopkins.

"*Hey!*" he yelled, watching her go.

"Which drawer did you pilfer it from?" She stood in the jelly-like blood, her back to the vaults.

"If you give me a—" Again his words were cut short, as the floor started to groan and protest once more. "Shit…"

"I'm not liking *that* noise one bit, guys!" Wires admitted. "Sounds like girders are being twisted."

They stood and listened as the sound continued. Soon the floor did start to crack, but not like it had outside. Splits developed, but the ground didn't part like the red sea. As the marble broke, particles were tossed into the air along with a thick, cement-like dust.

"We need to go! This place isn't going to be safe for much longer," Jason said. "Replace the stone. Top drawer."

He watched as the teen ripped the right compartment open and dropped the stone inside. She let out an "*Oops*" as she did so.

"What?"

"I broke it!"

More cracking. Only this time it wasn't the floor; it was the wall in front of the girl. Jason could only watch as she stood frozen to the spot, her body trembling.

"What… what's happening?!"

"Get out of there!" Jason screamed, but it was too late. Mummified arms smashed through the wall and grabbed her shoulders. The huge arms pulled, ripping the youngest in two like a piece of paper. Her guts and innards smashed against the floor, causing a crimson explosion. Her head popped off her shoulders and into the air like a bottle cap.

Then the mass pushed through the wall. Bricks, plaster

and dust flew everywhere; the powder from the stonework was that thick, Jason felt as though he was lost in fog.

Through the clouds he could see jade-coloured emeralds glowing, which were the mummy's eyes. Its bandages were an ancient yellow, all tattered and moth-eaten.

Only its piercing eyes could be seen—bandages covered everything else. The thing's massive frame appeared to ripple with muscle beneath its wrap. Bricks disintegrated under its footing.

Behind it, more of the undead spewed from the shattered wall.

"Oh, fuck!" Wires screamed as he fled the room and ran down the corridor.

Jason raised his gun and fired both barrels. The shells drilled into the eight-foot mummy's chest, but did nothing but disturb dust and singe bandage. However, the ball-bearing spray tore through some of the undead, sending a couple to ground.

Flesh and gore splashed the walls.

"Run!" Jason yelled, and turned to bolt out the door. As he ran past Bosco, he could see the man was taking aim with his shotgun. "There's no point!"

"Die, bastards!" Bosco screamed. His sawn-off roared.

Jason left him to it and rushed down the corridor to his detonator. When he got there, he saw Wires had it in his hands. "Get back, you're too close! I've set the lot—" Jason was blown off his feet and sent back along the corridor. As he floated through the air, he saw Wires turn into a liquid cloud of red nothingness.

When he hit the deck, he heard Bosco scream from behind, which carried over the horrendous sound of the walls and ceiling caving in. Bosco's cries were followed by that of wet, sloppy sounds.

Jason couldn't think about it.

He pushed off the floor with his palms and stood on shaking legs. He detected a faint ringing in his ears. He tried to walk towards the mound of earth before him. Above, daylight could be seen peeking through.

I'm saved! He stumbled forward, unaware of how close behind the mummy was.

He looked over his shoulder and screamed. His legs tangled and he was sent backwards. He landed on the earth with a hard smack. The bricks and jagged slabs of concrete hidden in the dirt dug into him. He pushed his heels into the soil and boosted himself up until his fingers were through the gap.

"Just a few more inches..." he grunted, and then he was being pulled. "*No*" Jason looked down to see the undead were clutching his ankles and lethargically yanking on his legs. He stabbed his fingers into the dirt and tried to stop himself from sliding.

Below, the mummy waited.

Jason felt hot piss shoot down his leg. He clenched his anus.

"*Please...* You have it back... We didn't mean to!"

His grip on the earth weakened and he started to slide towards his demise.

All he could do was buck his body and try to kick out with his legs, but more of the undead had gathered and were reaching up for his legs. Dirty hands and fingers clawed his shins, calves and thighs, causing him to pull his fingers out of the dirt and grab his hurt. He lost his grip.

When he hit the floor they huddled around him.

Manic laughter escaped him as hands punched through his stomach. His guts were torn free and devoured, his face was clawed to ribbons, and an eyeball was plucked out.

The mummy stood over him and looked down. "I am Ra, the ever powerful sun god!" he roared

"Fu... Fuc... Fuck *you*!" Jason managed with his final breath.

DAVID OWAIN HUGHES

David Owain Hughes is a horror freak! He grew up on ninja, pirate and horror movies from the age of five, which helped rapidly install in him a vivid imagination. When he grows up, he wishes to be a serial killer with a part-time job in women's lingerie…

He's had several short stories published in various online magazines and anthologies, along with articles, reviews and interviews. He's written for This Is Horror, Blood Magazine and Horror Geeks Magazine. He's the author of the popular novel "Walled In" (2014) & "Wind-Up Toy" (2016), along with his short story collections "White Walls and Straitjackets" (2015) and "Choice Cuts" (2015).

https://www.facebook.com/DOHughesAuthor/

https://www.amazon.co.uk/David-Owain-Hughes/e/B00L708P2M/

http://david-owain-hughes.wix.com/horrorwriter

https://www.goodreads.com/author/show/4877205.David_Owain_Hughes

https://twitter.com/DOHUGHES32

GHOST STORY

ANDREW LENNON

Night painted the room grey. The moonlight shining through the window was the only thing that kept darkness from consuming it entirely in its blackness. Adrian stirred in his bed. Any minute now his bladder would wake him for an urgent toilet trip. A pleasant reminder of the six cans of beer he'd drunk before bed.

The cold breeze swirled around the room and wound its way through the gaps in the quilt, wrapping itself like a serpent around Adrian's body.

Groaning, he threw his quilt off, climbed out of bed and walked to the bathroom to relieve himself. A whisper of cold air tickled the back of his neck, causing him to shiver; urine sloshed from side to side, covering the toilet seat and the floor around it.

With a sigh, he tore paper from the roll and proceeded to wipe up the mess. The sound of a child's laughter came from outside the bathroom. He stood upright and quickly turned to face the door.

Living on his own, he was used to an almost silent household. Besides the sound of the cats outside having sex each night, meowing their, "I love you's," there was never any noise. Unless he left the TV on to listen to while going to sleep. Perhaps that was it. Wouldn't be the first time that it had scared him. He'd often woke to the sound of a woman's screams. A suitable punishment for going to sleep while listening to The Horror Channel, one could say.

Still feeling slightly unconvinced, Adrian slowly opened the bathroom door and peeped through the crack. The hairs on the back of his neck stood upright. Any minute now something would jump out at him, but nothing came. Shaking his head at his own stupidity, and lack of bravery, he flicked the bathroom light off and walked back to his room.

The greyish blue tint that the night sky had gifted the room surrounded the bedroom door. This wasn't an uncommon sight. He often slept with the curtains open, as he liked to wake with the sunrise. The light of the night made it easy for him to see where he was going without crashing into his bedside furniture.

He entered the room and closed the door behind him, pausing for a moment to peer out the window. He looked to the moon and admired the beautiful glow it gave to the clouds as they passed by. Lowering his gaze to the back garden, he gave a visual inspection to check that everything looked okay. Satisfied, he turned to go back to bed.

Adrian froze still with fear. Stood before him was a small boy, perhaps six or seven years old. A white glow surrounded the figure. There was no question in Adrian's mind that he was face to face with a ghost. The boy wore a flat cap, a brown shirt with an open waistcoat, and knee-length shorts which appeared to be torn at the end.

The boy looked as though he was laughing, but no sound came from his mouth. The room remained silent.

Adrian's legs gave way beneath him, and he dropped to the bedroom floor. Slowly he pushed himself backward until he was sat against the wall. Trembling uncontrollably, he tried to stand up, but he couldn't; all strength had left him. He crawled to the bed and pulled himself up, terrified that the spectre was going to be inches away from his face, waiting for him. When the rest of the room came into view, there was nothing there. No boy, no glow. Just the bluish grey room, as it always was.

Still shaking, he turned the bedroom light on. Although

he was still terrified, he had to inspect the room. He felt like a child again, going through the wardrobe and checking under the bed with his father to prove that there was no monster. The only difference was that this time, there was. Wasn't there? He was sure that he had seen the ghost.

Before long, Adrian began to question himself. He had been drinking before bed, he had been watching horror films before bed. He reminded himself that this wasn't the first time he'd scared himself in the middle of the night. Eventually he concluded that his overactive imagination had been playing tricks on him again, and he went back to sleep with the light and sound of the TV playing to comfort him.

Sunrise eventually came and Adrian awoke to its bright gaze. He grabbed the bottle of water from his bedside table and proceeded to gulp until the contents were empty. He wiped his mouth, rolled out of bed, and went to the bathroom. He turned on the shower and stood outside the curtain, his hands reaching inside, the cold water pouring over his arm. As he waited for it to warm, he began pulling his boxers down with his free hand. Suddenly, something behind the shower curtain grabbed his hand.

Screaming, he jumped away from the curtain. His boxers caught around his ankles and he fell backward. Quickly he got back to his feet and pulled the curtain aside. The shower was empty.

You are really starting to lose your mind, Adrian.

He kicked his boxers to the floor and climbed into the shower.

The hot stream of water on his back felt good. He stood idle for a moment, just savouring the sensation. Closing his eyes, Adrian leaned his head back and allowed the water to run through his hair and down his face. After a moment, he stepped away from the stream, wiped the water out of his eyes, and reached for the shampoo bottle at the end of the bath. He squirted the thick blue liquid into his hand and turned back toward the shower.

A face stared at him through the flow of the water. A young boy, not quite as young as the visitor from last night. This one looked as though it was in its teens. The hot shower suddenly felt as though it had turned to ice. Adrian broke out into an uncontrollable shiver. The face moved closer to him, leaving the water untouched, the stream maintaining its constant flow. The figure reached for Adrian's face. He screamed. The figure disappeared.

Too afraid to shower any longer, Adrian rinsed the shampoo from his hands and hurried to his bedroom to get dressed.

He prayed that he didn't get any more visions, ghosts, or whatever the hell they were. Even putting his t-shirt on was a rushed task, as he was scared something would appear before him in the split second his eyes were covered by material. He couldn't help but feel stupid at these thoughts. The fact remained, though, he had seen something in his house. And he didn't want to be surprised by anything else.

Grabbing his keys, he walked out the front door and dialled a number on his phone. It only rang once before it was answered.

"Hello, Bro. How's it goin'?"

"Craig, what are you up to? Fancy meeting up?" Adrian asked.

"Sure thing. When?"

"Now."

"Now?"

"Yes."

"Are you sure you're okay?" Craig asked.

"Yeah, I just…" Adrian paused for a moment. "I just need to get out of the house for a little bit. Fancy meeting at the coffee shop in town?"

"Yeah, no worries, man. I've just got to get a quick shower and I'll be on my way. Gimme half an hour."

"Great. See you in a bit."

When Craig arrived at the coffee shop, Adrian was already sat at a table, caressing a mug. The pair exchanged a curt nod and Craig walked to the counter to order his own drink. He then walked to the table to join his brother.

"You sure you're okay, bro? You don't look good at all," Craig asked.

Adrian gave a thin smile and took a sip from his coffee. He placed the cup back on the table, hoping that Craig hadn't noticed the nervous quiver in his hands.

"I just didn't sleep very well last night, that's all. How's Mum?"

Craig straightened his posture. A subconscious movement that he did each time he was about to give his younger brother a lecture.

"Well," he started, "you know, if you came around more..."

"Coffee?" an old woman wearing a dirty apron asked.

"Here please," Craig gestured.

The woman placed the cup on the table, gave both men a smile, and then disappeared back through the door behind the till.

"She misses you, you know," Craig said.

"I know." Adrian stared into his coffee mug.

"And I know that you miss her, so why don't you just come round and see her?"

"It's not that simple."

"It really is that simple."

"I can't. I just... I can't."

"Okay, so tell me then. What is the matter with you? You look as though you haven't slept for a week, and I can't remember the last time you asked me to meet anywhere other than a pub."

"I just had a bit of a weird night, and... " He hesitated.

"I don't know. I just felt like we should meet up, you know?"

"Adrian, are you in some kind of trouble?" Craig asked with what seemed like genuine concern.

"No, nothing like that. I just got a bit scared. I saw things last night."

"Saw things?"

"Yeah," Adrian continued. "I think I saw ghosts."

Craig began to laugh, but the look on his brother's face seemed to stop it. Adrian proceeded to tell Craig about what he'd seen, looked to him for some kind of explanation. After reaching various wild theories, the pair arrived at the conclusion that Adrian had perhaps hallucinated through a lack of proper sleep. Too many nights of drunken unconsciousness doesn't give you the proper rest that the body requires.

Neither of them really bought the theory, but just having a long talk about it made Adrian feel better. As though he'd gotten something off his chest.

"So do you think you're going to be alright now, ghost whisperer?" Craig smirked.

"Shut up," Adrian smiled back.

"Do you want to come back for a bit. See Mum?"

Adrian shook his head.

"Bye, Craig." He reached out and hugged his brother. It felt strange. It wasn't something they would normally do, but he just did it without thinking.

Craig pulled back and gave his brother another concerned look.

"I'm fine." Adrian laughed. "Go on, you get going. Give Mum that hug for me."

The pair left the coffee shop together and then went their separate ways.

Standing outside his house, Adrian stared at the front door. Although he did feel better after meeting his brother for a chat, he still felt a little bit uncomfortable about going back into the house right now. After a few minutes of deliberation, he decided that the pub sounded like a much better option. He turned away and walked back down the road, completely unaware of the face in his bedroom window that watched his exit.

Several hours and several beers passed before Adrian eventually returned home. He unlocked the front door and stumbled into the living room. Before he had a chance to stop himself, he tripped over the coffee table and fell to the floor.

From his fallen, drunken state, he stared at the table in bemusement.

"Well, how the hell did that get there?"

A loud crash came from the kitchen. He climbed to his feet and ran toward the source of the sound, grabbing a vase on the way to use as a weapon.

When he reached the kitchen, it was empty, but there was a broken glass on the floor.

"Hello?" he called.

The house remained silent.

"Listen, if there's anyone there, then your chance to come out is now. Don't make me come looking for you."

A glass flew toward his face. He managed to move out of the way just in time before it exploded on the wall behind him. When he turned back he was faced by a young man. He looked familiar, but Adrian couldn't place where he knew him from. The man, who appeared to be in his early twenties, was screaming, but no sound emerged from his mouth. He shared the same faint glow that the earlier visitors had.

"Who are you?" Adrian screamed. "What do you want?"

The figure answered with another silent scream. Not knowing what else to do, Adrian repeated his question.

The figure seemed frustrated at this and grabbed another glass from the side of the sink.

"No, no wait!" he pleaded. "Please tell me, who are you?"

The glass was launched at his head again. He turned to run and smacked his face into the corner or the door frame. A red gush of blood exploded from his nose. He fell backwards, his head hitting the marble kitchen floor with a loud crack.

Adrian fell unconscious.

Adrian woke with a thumping at the back of his head, and his face throbbed. Lying on his back, he glanced around his kitchen.

What the hell?

He pressed his hands to the floor to push himself up; small shards of glass pierced his palms. He cursed in pain and rolled onto his side. When he eventually got to his feet, he stood and looked at the mess in the kitchen. Blood and broken glass all over the floor, blood on the door and the wall.

Jesus Christ. What happened here? How much did I drink?

After pulling as much of the glass as he could from his hands, he leaned over the sink and gulped water directly from the tap.

The phone began to ring from the living room. Adrian walked into the room to answer it. He noticed the coffee table had been pushed across to the other side of the room and was now positioned in front of the other door. A vague memory of falling over that table entered his mind.

He was reaching for the ringing phone when something stopped him. An overwhelming feeling that he was being watched took hold of him.

Slowly, he turned around. He was met with a glowing

face. A face he knew very well.

The lips of the face moved, but no sound came.

"I don't understand," Adrian said.

The figure's mouth mimed its message again. Tears filled Adrian's eyes. Through blurred vision he watched the figure come closer to him. It wrapped its arms around him and turned his whole body to ice. A second later it was gone.

Adrian stood alone, staring into the empty room. The ringing of the phone still filled his ears. He retrieved the phone from the table and looked at the display.

"Craig!"

He began to tremble. With shaking hands he slid the green icon on the screen and placed the phone to his ear.

"Hello?"

"Adrian, is that you?"

"Mum?"

"Adrian, there's been an accident. It's Craig."

"I know, Mum," Adrian whispered, and hung up the phone. "I know."

ANDREW LENNON

Andrew Lennon is the bestselling author of Every Twisted Thought and several other horror/thriller books. He has featured in various bestselling anthologies, and is successfully becoming a recognised name in horror and thriller writing. Andrew is a happily married man living in the North West of England with his wife Hazel & their children.

Having always been a big horror fan, Andrew spent a lot of his time watching scary movies or playing scary games, but it wasn't until his mid-twenties that he developed a taste for reading. His wife, also being a big horror fan, had a very large Stephen King collection which Andrew began to consume. Once hooked into reading horror, he started to discover new authors like Thomas Ligotti & Ryan C Thomas. It was while reading work from these authors that he decided to try writing something himself and there came the idea for "A Life to Waste"

He enjoys spending his time with his family and watching or reading new horror. For more information please go to www.andrewlennon.co.uk

MY OWN WORST ENEMY

L. DE CLIFFORD

"Sir, we believe you have Schizophrenia."

... those words, those dreaded words every person hopes they will never hear. How I wished I could hear those words. I could only hear his words, though. No, my words. My words?

Everyone has thoughts, right? The ones that just come to you when you are daydreaming. Or conversations with yourself:

* Hot girl walks into pub *

You #1: "Go for it, what's the worst that can happen?"

You #2: "Pal, seriously? Punching above your weight, move on."

But not many of us have another voice, or voices, with differing opinions. It is just that one voice, your voice, saying your thoughts. You pretty much agree with yourself, because, well, it's *you* and you wouldn't have that opinion if you didn't agree with it. Okay, so you may have had times when you have talked yourself into or out of something, but it was still only you, talking to you. Right? I guess it's complicated.

Despite it all, though, I never heard those words. I was told I had a form of OCD or Borderline Personality Disorder or Tourette's; that I was in shock or had PTSD (although they could never offer an explanation when I asked why the diagnosis), but no, that wasn't it. It just didn't fit. I was asked if I was taking drugs by every doctor I saw. None of them appeared to believe me when I told them I had never touched drugs. I was eventually diagnosed with depression, given a prescription, and sent on my way. I think they had me down as a bit of a weirdo, a socially inept guy who had just spent too much time in his bedroom on his own playing console games for a whole decade in the "Noughties".

It started after an accident. A horrible, stupid accident. My own fault, of course. I'm my own worst enemy in life and this was no different. I shouldn't have been surprised, really; it's what happens when your nose is in a social media app on your phone and you walk into a road. Don't judge me, we've all done it; played that match 3 game on the bus, or on your coffee break. Inviting everyone you can to get more 'lives'. Even me... when I was about 20. These days it's all work, overtime, deadline, weekend, rinse, repeat. I had kept the social media account and kept in general contact with people, but was unceasingly annoyed with each *buzz-buzz* I felt in my hand. And, having suffered a whole week of false alarms thinking I had missed texts or calls from work, I decided, mid-march to my next meeting, to open the app and try to disable the notifications.

SMASH

They say life is full of surprises, and I concede this point. I have had, what I would consider, my fair share of these 'surprises', some good and some bad. Some I would happily re-experience over and over, others not so much. Surprises are, I suppose as the definition suggests, unexpected, and that day's surprise was fully on form in this department. The lorry came out of nowhere. Well, I say 'out of nowhere', but various witnesses would disagree and tell the police that the lorry had been waiting at the red light, dutifully awaiting his turn to shift. And shift he did, when the red light disappeared and the amber light signalled its brief role in my near demise. The lorry pulled off and I had stepped out into its path.

When I awoke the first thing I did was squeeze my hand and try to raise my arm to look at my damned phone. *What is this thing on my face?* I thought as I pulled at something on my nose that resisted and pinged back on my forehead with a soft thud. Then I realised I wasn't dressed, and followed that thought up with the fact that I also wasn't at home in my own bed. *Is this a hospital? And, OWWWW—why does everything hurt?!*

"Oh, try not to move," cooed a soothing voice from somewhere to my right and behind me. My eyes focussed on the ceiling tiles, and my mind made face patterns out of the random holes and peaks of the textured material. A chubby hand appeared over my head, reached down, and adjusted the thing on my face. I became aware it was blowing cool air onto my nose and mouth, which made my lungs feel like they were being slowly dried. I wriggled in resistance.

"Now, now." The hand came back but this time was followed by a chubby arm and the warm-smiled face... of a nurse. Yes, definitely hospital. Shit. I tried to sit up and resumed my attempted removal of the oxygen mask.

"I don't have time for this," I grunted. It wasn't meant to be a grunt, but I had assumed that I would be able to speak properly. Instead my throat crisped up and my voice box suddenly regained consciousness to produce a noise that sounded much like I had smoked for 50 years of my 30-year life... And that I needed a drink of water, badly. I did actually. I looked around the room. The cloudy water in a vase of flowers nearby suddenly looked appealing.

"Back into bed, I'll get the doctor." I put up zero resistance to the hands pushing me back down by my shoulders into crunchy plastic pillows. It hurt too, and I took a few seconds to groan quietly and quickly regrow my bollocks to grimace through the pain. My sides ached and my head pounded. "Broken ribs tend to hurt for a while, dear," she said as she tucked the blanket under my arms. "Lie still."

She wrote something on a chart that she hooked back onto my end of my bed, and smiled at me before she left, drawing the curtain slightly and pulling it closed after she had stepped out. I must have been in a ward, but none of the noises had really registered until she left and I was on my own. The doctor wasn't quick in getting to me and, as I lay piecing my last few waking moments together with my last conscious memories, I started to feel like a complete idiot.

WHY THE HELL DID YOU JUST WALK OUT INTO THE ROAD? JUST MY LUCK. BLOODY IDIOT.

I shook myself and told myself it could have happened to anyone, at any time. It was just one of those things. No point dwelling on the negative, got to deal with it and move on.

After a while the doctor came in, pulling the curtains back in a parental 'MORNING!' sort of way. And like a teenager with their first hangover I winced at the bright light that had been rudely let in. My head felt like it was almost split in half with pain, and every waking moment seemed to make it worse. Like someone had sliced the top of it clean off and prodded my exposed, soft brain matter with their chewed finger nails. It was almost indescribable. I guess the doc noticed.

"Mr Barr, I see you're awake."

NO SHIT.

"Yes, the sore head. You had a very nasty knock to it when you hit the road." He explained that I had concussion and possible brain swelling, so waking up was obviously a good thing. He said I would probably have a sore head for a week or so, and experience dizziness and loss of balance for a week or more, once the pain subsided. They were going to keep me in a couple of days and I needed to rest. Great.

"Oh, and we have called your girlfriend. She is on her way in."

"My gir...?" The words trailed off as a picture of her

pink-cheeked face filled my memories.

NOT THAT BITCH. AS IF THIS ISN'T ENOUGH.

The voice caught me by surprise and I jerked my head left, looking around as far as I could. It hurt, but I just had to look behind me. Who the hell just said that?!

"Mr Barr, are you alright?" The doctor looked concerned. "Do you remember your girlfriend, Chess? You know, Francesca?" He motioned to the nurse to move towards me, but she had already second guessed his request before he had thought it, and had started to take my pulse and count on her watch in an overly dramatic fashion.

"Yes of course I remember Chess! My head just... I swear I just heard someone..." I tried to point behind me, not realising there was just a wall with sockets and buttons and an overhead lamp and TV. The doctor and nurse both looked blankly at the wall and then back to me, concern written on their faces.

"Half hourly obs," the doctor muttered to the nurse, who nodded a reply. "I will be back in later, Mr Barr. Try to get some rest." And he left, leaving the curtain wide open. I hated hospitals.

WELL AT LEAST I CAN MAKE THE MOST OF THE FREE MORPHINE.

Realising that was not my voice, or the nurse's, but a voice of someone who seemed to be happy to provide sarcastic commentary in my head, I demanded, "Who?! Who said that?!" The nurse, who had finished taking my pulse and was busy recording it on the chart, looked up at me again and squinted.

"Maybe I'll come back in 15 minutes." She finished scrawling, hooked the chart onto the bed and left, thankfully pulling the curtains. I watched her go and waited for the voice to speak again.

It was silent. Well, when I say silent, anyone who is sound of mind that has spent any time in a general hospital ward will tell you that silence is not a luxury afforded anyone in hospital. After a few moments on my own, for the first time since being properly conscious, I became aware of a distant wailing, random beeping noises and, in the cubicle to my right, a patient feebly shouting, "Nurse, nurse! Help me! Nurse!" I wondered how long he had been calling out for; it had been going on for as long as I had been awake.

SHUT. UP!

Shit, did I just say that? I wondered to myself. *Okay, so that wasn't my voice, but did I think that... did those words just come out of my mouth? No. No, I'm pretty sure they didn't. It must have been another patient, maybe the guy in the cubicle to my left.* I sniffed a laugh and smiled to myself. I was in hospital, after all. Most of the patients in the ward were probably over ninety and had no clue where they were. I decided it must be the bump on my head making my thinking go wrong. Some scientific explanation about concussion, maybe bruising of the brain. Maybe they would tell me when I was more compos mentis and not shouting at imaginary people stood behind me.

My mind drifted back over the day, starting with breakfast and trying to remember what I had. Orange juice and toast with butter. I was quite pleased I could remember that. Short term memory: check. I'd had breakfast with Chess at seven in the morning. (*Eyes heavy. Drifting. Ugh my head.*) Chess; we had been together for four years. I met her in the office we worked in at the time. I was an arse and made her cry, but my apology was the beginning of something special and there we were years later. (*Drifting. Is the room getting warmer?*) Long term memory: check.

I gave in and, falling back into sleep, I relaxed a little. I was going to be just fine I told myself.

YEAH, I WILL BE.

I slept for almost a day and when I awoke Chess was there. She immediately stood and held my hand, telling me she was so glad she stayed, that she knew I would wake up, et cetera, et cetera. She could definitely talk, that girl, but it was one of the things I loved about her.

DOZY COW, I WOKE UP YESTERDAY. YOU WEREN'T THERE.

"Chess," I interrupted her joyous rhetoric abruptly. "Did you hear that?" Chess froze mid-sentence and listened intently, eyes looking around, trying to source what I had heard.

"The beeping? The guy next door crying?" she ventured.

"No, the voice." I cringed saying it out loud.

"The... nurse? The man next door?" Chess was trying to be as helpful as possible, which annoyed me a little.

"He's not talking at the moment," I admitted. It, or 'He' as I had just referred to it by, had gone silent. It wasn't a he, it didn't have a form. Not one I had seen yet anyway. It had an opinion, voiced it, and that was it. I didn't answer, because then I was talking to it. Talking to it would be admitting it exists. This was starting to become a routine in my mind and I decided to believe the concussion I had suffered was more like a proper head injury. Yes, that must have been what was causing this... anomaly.

"Well, baby, if he isn't talking at the moment, how can I hear him? You really took a bang to the head, didn't you?" Her concern seeped out of every tiny detail of her kind face, another reason I loved her so much; she really cared. She was a great girl. She'd never get into Mensa, but was still a great girl.

"Well clearly you won't hear him when he isn't talking," I snapped. I was a little irritated at this statement of the obvious, "**I** don't hear him when he isn't talking. It... it. Not him. This conversation is getting annoying." I actually said the last bit out loud, which I had not intended. Chess looked hurt but decided to steer the conversation in a different direction.

"Okaaay. So the doctor said that I can take you home first thing in the morning. I'll come in after breakfast tomorrow to pick you up. Do you want me to bring your jogging trousers to wear? You do realise all your clothes were cut off, right?" My face must have dropped; No, I hadn't realised. "Yes, well, I will bring those and a t-shirt. Or how about your dressing gown? Would that be comfier for you? Should I bring slippers or your Converse? Do you know what happened to your shoes? I'm guessing they didn't cut those off, right? Where do they put someone's things when they come into hospital, is there a locker? Do you want something to eat or drink, you look like you've lost weight?"

WHATEVER, LOVE, STOP WITH THE 20 QUESTIONS! IT'S ENOUGH TO DRIVE A PERSON INSANE. PAUSE FOR BREATH, COME UP FOR AIR, FUCK!

"Whatever," I muttered, stopping myself from repeating the rest of the sarcastic spitting of the voice in my head, its annoyance obvious. Realising what I had said, I looked to Chess's face—no reaction. I figured she didn't hear it or she was being nice to me in my incapable, and clearly confused, state.

Chess kissed me on the forehead and left to get coffee, returning to sit with me for the rest of visiting hours. They both did. I floated from conscious to semi-conscious, the morphine melting and reforming the room around me. Chess talking, me trying to answer, the voice always answering. My mind trying to piece together reality from shards of fuzzy snapshots taken by my eyes, opening and closing straight away, unable to stay open. Although I was so grateful for her company, it was hard work not asking her every time the voice said something if she had heard it. It was even harder work not repeating what was being said. The voice favoured bad language, a lot, and the overwhelming desire to simply allow myself to vocalise the voice was almost impossible to resist. I was exhausted by the time she left.

THANK FUCK FOR THAT... Was the last thing I heard before I gave in to a deep, deep sleep.

Having slept solidly again, I felt better the next day. My head was clearer and the voice seemed to have disappeared. My ribs still hurt and the bump on my head was still there and throbbed if I touched it, but that was to be expected... the important thing was the voice had gone.

My journey home, in dressing gown and Chess's pink slippers (because I forgot that I didn't own a pair of slippers when agreeing to wear them) was uneventful and brief. Chess helped me into the house and sat me in the lounge, tucked up with a blanket on the sofa and freshly fluffed cushions that usually only the guests were allowed to use. After a small amount of faffing, she went into to kitchen to make a cup of tea.

WELL, THIS IS THE BLOODY LIFE, INNIT? HUGE SATELLITE TELLY, BIG SETTEE, BET YOU GOT AN EN-SUITE AND ONE OF THOSE BIDET THINGS, TOO; LOOKING FORWARD TO THAT. YOU GOT A DOG, MATE?

Startled, I looked at the TV—it was definitely switched off. The radio too. I could hear Chess in the kitchen, the kettle beginning to boil and a tap running. Our front garden was at least three metres back from the road and it was a quiet little cul-de-sac, but I still looked out the window. No-one. I was feeling better. My head didn't pound, I had slept a LOT over the last couple of days, I wasn't taking any pain relief; so where the hell was this voice coming from?

DON'T QUESTION IT, JUST ACCEPT IT. "RESISTANCE IS FUTILE" HAHAHA.

The voice laughed at its own joke. "Seriously?!" I blurted out, annoyed at the presence of the voice still and its intrusion into my thoughts. "Piss off!"

"What?" Chess was walking towards me, a cup of tea in each hand. "Are you okay?"

"Yes. Sorry." Stammering to think of an excuse for my

apparently random outburst. "It's my headache, still there a little." That would do, I figured, even if it was a lie. I could play on the whole head injury thing for now.

"Oh, baby. You want me to get anything?" She placed the tea down and sat next to me, resting her warm hand on my blanketed knee.

YEAH, IF YOU COULD GET OUT OF MY FACE, THAT WOULD BE FUCKING GREAT.

"No, no." I tried to hide a smirk; it was only funny in a rebellious and sarcastic teenager kind of way, but it completely was not funny of course. "I'll be okay, just gotta tough it out." I felt like an idiot for saying that last bit, like I was reconfirming my manhood by gritting my teeth through a little headache and some well-placed bruises.

TOUGH MAN. IMPRESSIVE STUFF.

After Chess read out the 'Get Well Soon' cards—all two of them—she decided she would get out my hair and let me rest, but to call her if I needed anything. The front door closed. Relief. Right—I was going to sort this 'thing' out once and for all. 'We' were alone. Time to evict this squatter.

"So." I decided I may as well speak out loud; no-one was in the house now, no doctors judging me, no concerned girlfriend. Just me... sort of. "I'm not really sure how to converse with you, actually. This isn't something I have had a lot of experience of in my life, you know; talking to the voice in your head." I paused, hoping that I would receive nothing but silence in response, as usual.

NOT THAT I CARE, BUT WHAT DO YOU WANT TO TALK TO ME FOR ANYWAY? I'M PRETTY MUCH NOT INTERESTED IN YOU, OTHER THAN WHEN YOU ARE GONNA DRINK THAT TEA.

Why did that make a difference? I wondered to myself.

AND I CAN STILL HEAR YOU, EVEN IF YOU ARE ONLY PUTTING YOUR BRAIN IN GEAR AND NOT YOUR BIG MOUTH.

I jumped to my feet at this revelation but quickly

lowered myself back to a more rib-pleasing sitting position.

I don't know why but I simply did not expect the voice to hear what I had not actually spoken out loud.

"I can talk to you without talking?"

IF YOU MUST, BUT I'D PREFER IT IF YOU DIDN'T. I'M NOT HERE FOR CONVERSATION.

"Well I may continue the traditional form of conversation for now, being that I actually have a mouth I can use, and want to… and why the hell do you want to know if I'm going to drink the tea?" The question was ridiculous, considering all questions I could have asked at that point, but still.

I PREFER SUGAR. IF THERE'S NO SUGAR IN IT, I DON'T WANT IT.

"Well it's my bloody body. I will drink what I damn well like!" My point had gone out the window with aghastness; how dare he! I asserted myself with a confident hand reaching out, grabbing the mug and slurping the scolding hot tea—no sugar.

YOU MAY LIVE TO REGRET THAT.

The voice sounded like a big brother who had just discovered his most prized possession in the hands of a younger sibling, totally destroyed. I recalled my older brother, Robby, who had died when we were kids—he sometimes caught me in his stuff and there was always hell to pay. I missed him. Hang on…

"Robby?" I asked.

WHO? OH. FUCK NO, I'M NOT YOUR DEAD BROTHER. YOU DO REALISE THAT WHEN YOU'RE DEAD, YOU'RE DEAD, RIGHT?

"Great. Thanks for that." I paused. We were getting off topic. What was the topic anyway, tea?

What do you talk about with a voice whose origin appears to be your very own head? The weather? Current affairs? I guessed that if I thought something, words or images, the voice was aware of them. "I take it you could tell there was no sugar?" I decided that the question was reasonable, considering the situation.

YEAH, AS SOON AS IT TOUCHED YOUR FAT LIPS.

"There's no need to be rude." I was getting antsy now and I decided to just come out with it, although the voice probably already knew what I was going to ask a split second before the words formed and floated through the air of my empty living room. "What exactly do you want with me?"

I DON'T FUCKING KNOW, I'VE ONLY JUST GOT HERE. IT'S BEEN THREE DAYS NOW AND YOU HAVE BEEN IN BED ASLEEP FOR MOST OF IT. WHAT I WOULD REALLY LIKE IS A STEAK. RARE SIRLOIN WITH A PEPPERCORN SAUCE AND CHIPS. AND TO BE ABLE TO GO FOR A WALK.

This was the most the voice had said to me so far, I felt I had made an inch of progress. "So, you know what steak tastes like?" I ventured conversationally.

IF YOU DO, I DO. I THINK... I DUNNO, I'M LIMITED TO WHAT YOU DO OR THINK... FOR NOW. CAN WE GO OUTSIDE?

"Why?" I asked in absence of any other sensible question.

BECAUSE I HAVEN'T BEEN OUTSIDE YET. I DON'T COUNT BEING WHEELED FROM THE WAITING AREA TO THE CAR BEING OUTSIDE. I NEED TO BREATHE THE AIR.

"You breathe?"

DUH. YOU BREATHING RIGHT NOW?

"Yes, for me!" The cheek of the voice—who else would I be breathing for?

LOOK, WHAT YOU DO, I DO. CAN YOU JUST GET OVER THAT NOW? STAND UP AND GO TO THE BACK GARDEN, COME ON MAN.

"So, you can't do anything but talk to, no, *at* me?" I triumphed as the realisation started to set in, and I felt suddenly a lot more in control. "Basically, unless I do something, you are just a voice, sitting and talking to me, trying to get me to do things or being generally rude and sarcastic."

WHAT THE FUCK IS YOUR POINT?!

Ah-ha, I had cracked it. It really was just a voice in my head! It must be the concussion! Great! I will just ignore the voice, hopefully it will go away over the next few days and life will be back to normal. I may even find myself telling the story of the 'voice in my head' as a pretty cool campfire tale and making out I totally made the whole story up. At the end I could even start pretending to talk to myself and telling myself out loud to kill everyone, grabbing at them all in a pretend maniacal way, shouting 'RAH' to make them all jump, you know, for dramatic effect like they do in films. Not that I ever get invited to outdoorsy events; it's all office parties, cocktail and black tie events and meeting clients. This wasn't the sort of small talk I could use whilst trying to win a contract.

DRAMATIC WOULD BE RIGHT. ESPECIALLY IF I STOOD UP AND ACTUALLY HACKED EVERYONE TO DEATH. THEY WOULD NEVER SUSPECT THAT WAS COMING. HA!

Deciding that I must be a little bit warped somewhere in the recesses of my mind, to create a murder-intent voice that only I can hear, I decided it would be better for my mental health if I just ignored it and not have any further conversations with it. It, not him. It.

GOOD LUCK WITH THAT.

For the first week after the accident it was there, but it was easy to ignore. Almost like office air-conditioning, you get used to certain background noises, and that is what I decided to treat the voice as, background noise. But background noise can get louder and louder until it is no longer background, and the voice soon moved itself to the very front of my mind. To start off with, I had the TV or radio on wherever I went. Chess would come home to find me asleep on the sofa (as I was always tired) and the first thing she would do is walk around the house turning everything off. I couldn't have silence. That's when the voice could be heard.

After a week or so, I decided to go back into the office. It was too much staying at home, being awake and alone with 'it', and I couldn't sleep forever. The effort of trying to drown out the voice was ridiculous, and I figured I would start feeling better if I didn't have all this time on my hands to do nothing but try not to listen. I was greeted by my manager, who shook me by the hand vigorously, spluttering something about how he couldn't believe I was back and so soon; I winced a little and pulled back. My shoulders still hurt from the bruising and the shaking made my broken ribs rattle in their own cage.

Quickly letting go, my boss started some dreary rhetoric about how pleased he was to see me, how the office had not been the same without me and how so many clients had asked after me, blah, blah. It felt nice, weirdly. I almost believed it. But the nice feeling didn't last as I opened my email inbox. 300+ emails, all unread and all needing attention last week. I wasn't surprised; this is why I never took holiday.

Needing a break after reading the first 50 emails, headache creeping in, I decided to go get a coffee from the vending machine and stretch my legs. As I stood in the break-out area I sipped my coffee and read the bulletin board to see if I had missed anything. Incoming calls had doubled the week I was off—I sarcastically wondered why to myself. *Could it be that's because I take 20 calls a day on my own? Could be!*

LAZY FUCKS, THAT'S WHY. WHY THE HELL ARE WE HERE ANYWAY? LIFE IS TOO SHORT TO BE COOPED UP IN A STUFFY OFFICE TAKING SHIT FROM PEOPLE WHO THINK THEY ARE BETTER THAN YOU. TELL THEM ALL TO GO FUCK THEMSELVES. JACK IT IN. I CAN'T STAND THIS PLACE ALREADY.

Oh, for goodness' sake. Can't I have just one day with you shutting up? I thought, knowing the voice would hear me. *It's just never ending. When are going to just fade away? Bugger off?* My chest became tight.

FEEL THAT? I'M WORKING ON IT.

I clutched at my chest, screwing up my shirt into my fist. I wasn't in pain, exactly, but I couldn't breathe or talk, and it was not a pleasant feeling.

AND THERE'S MORE.

As the tightness subsided the back door to the smoking area opened and a group of people who worked on our customer service hub all walked in, talking loudly and making their way back to their desks.

"Stinky fucks, go do some work for a change." All five people turned around angrily to see who had said it and, finding no-one else in the room, they glared at me.

"What did you just say?" growled one of the larger blokes, walking up to me. I was dumbfounded. It had not been MY voice that had said the words, but the sound had come out of MY mouth. I opened and closed my, apparently uncontrollable, mouth like a goldfish—open, close, open, close—trying to form the syllables of an excuse.

"I'm so sorry, I have a head injury!" It WAS my voice this time, but I couldn't believe the excuse I had just come out with.

"That's the guy that got run over last week, walked straight out into the road," mumbled one of the large man's colleagues from somewhere behind his massive frame. I saw a little head peep round him to catch a glimpse of me—possibly before I met my inevitable end.

"Just keep your opinions to yourself, *mate*, brain-dead or not." The 'mate' was definitely said with a lemony acid that melted the air around it as the word formed. I didn't get the feeling we would laugh about this over a pint at lunchtime.

"Yes, yes. I'm so sorry," I mumbled, scurrying past the staring eyes of five people, who now believed I had actual brain damage. This will be fun to live down at the Summer party. Still, at least it wasn't my boss.

I turned the corner into my office. My boss was in my office, leafing through the ton of post that had been dumped on my desk whilst I had diced with death for a second time in as many weeks. He looked up as I walked in, a concerned look on his face. I was starting to recognise this look.

"I farmed your cases off to Gerrard and Andy in Ops." I died a little inside. *Why those guys? It would have been better if they had just been left to fester for a week until I came back.*

"It would have been better if they had just been left to fester for a week until I came back." I almost slapped my hand across my mouth, but it was too late. That was my voice again, but not my words! Bloody hell, what was going on?

"What?" My boss rose up immediately at my insolence "We rescued a million-pound deal for you!" I goldfished again. What the hell had happened to how glad he was to see me back?

"Look, I think you should go home. Maybe you came back a little soon. We appreciate it but take some time. Rest yourself…"

"Okay!" I snapped, one hand truly bitten off. Within five minutes I was on the number 86 heading back to the safety of isolation.

On the bus the voice persisted, talking, whinging, bitching, putting me down; my sense of dress, my crappy suburban bungalow, my choice of transport. In my fragile state of mind, I couldn't tell who it was that was talking to me. My head jerked from left to right, behind and in front of me; *where did that voice come from?* No-one on the bus was talking, but all who caught my eye gave me nervous smiles or annoyed what-are-you-looking-at glares. They must have all thought I was an escaped patient from St. Anne's.

JEEZ, OF ALL THE MINDS IN ALL THE WORLD, I GET STUCK IN THIS ONE.

I had no idea what that meant, and I didn't want to. I was one bus stop away and then I could hide in my bungalow retreat, cowering from reality… and call a bloody doctor, because this was NOT right. The bus had barely made it past the end of my cul-de-sac as I frantically scraped my front door key all over the door aiming for the lock, like a frustrated noob trying to putt a golf ball into the hole just two inches away, and failing every time. Once in, I reached for the address book next to the phone, found the number for the surgery and dialled. When the old receptionist lady picked up the phone she began to introduce herself and was cut short by my interjection. "I think I've gone mad! I had a hit to the head, you see? Can I see someone today?!"

An hour later I was in the waiting room. The duty doctor saw me very quickly. I imagined that the poor old receptionist lady had highlighted my plight to him in advance, i.e. I was mad, but an hour-long chat later and I was on my way home with a prescription for sleeping pills, some patronising 'You have to allow yourself time to recover fully' wisdom, and a sick note for a few more weeks.

I went home and popped two pills, swilling them down with some left-over wine I found in place of the milk in the fridge door, and went to bed.

WHERE THE FUCK ARE YOU GOING? WHY THE FUCK HAVE YOU TAKEN THOSE? I DON'T WANT TO SLEEP. I DON'T WANT...

The words faded as the effect of the drugs took hold. Sleep was peaceful, deep and uninterrupted. When Chess came home, she brought me a glass of water and smoothed my forehead until I was awake. I told her what had happened; she didn't believe me. Just like the doc, she thought I just needed sleep and time.

NO MORE FUCKING SLEEP!

My life went on like this. I woke up in the morning, said goodbye to Chess. The voice would start the moment I awoke. It hated Chess, it hated me, it especially did not like to sleep. I would drink a glass of water, take some more pills, fall asleep and wake up when Chess came home. The voice would start its rhetoric of hate, I would eat a little, drink a little, make my excuses to Chess and go back to bed, pills already slipping chemically down my throat. I visited the doctor again, and he referred me to a specialist. The specialist referred me back to the doctor who, in turn, referred me to another specialist. They all had their theories, but most revolved around the hit to the head I had sustained in the accident, the stress from my job, my past, or a massive combination of all of it that would require years of therapy in one form or another. I eventually agreed with the depression diagnosis and let them all believe that I was another case solved. It just wasn't worth it and the more I tried to explain myself the crazier even *I* thought I sounded.

The voice continued to wear me down, berating and insulting me. Frustrated at its lack of control, the mental pressure increased. Psychologically, I was breaking. I began to lose weight. The voice became angrier, stronger and louder. The doctors continued to treat the symptoms and sign me off from work. I festered in my house day-to-day, alone but never alone.

Six weeks or so after the accident, I had taken my usual two pills and slunk back into bed, waiting for the peaceful darkness to take me once again—but nothing. I looked at the clock: 8.30am. I was usually feeling drowsy by now. I shifted myself back up to a sitting position, adjusting my pillows, and grabbed the sleeping pills from the bedside table, retrieved the leaflet inside and started to skim-read the side-effects section, musing that if insomnia was a rare side-effect, it would be just my luck that I would suffer from it.

YOU CAN'T KEEP ME DOWN? THINK I CAN BE CONTAINED, THAT YOU ARE WINNING?!

Why? Why are you still here? The words filled my mind like a child shouting 'echo' into a void. The word 'why' repeating over and over. I scrutinised the leaflet a little harder, "Does it say I can't take more than two at a time?"

DON'T YOU DARE.

Hmmm, no, I don't think it does. Let's try shall we? I squeezed another two tablets from their foil pouches and chucked them back dry; I meant business. I gagged a little at the metallic, unnatural taste they left in my mouth and throat, but I didn't care. Five minutes later, all of them filled with swearing and a story about how I was going to 'be sorry', I plummeted into my desired silent slumber.

"Baby, what happened?" I was woken with a gentle shake of my shoulder… and the dog licking my face. Chess was kneeling next to me, her hand on my forehead in a way that almost made her look like she knew what she was doing. She may have found an actual temperature if she knew that's why people did it. I looked around me. The clock on the wall, gently ticking away, declared the time to be 18.25.

'Hang on—that's the lounge clock, isn't it?' I focussed. The realisation of lying on the floor of the lounge crept up on me like a child playing peek-a-boo. I knew where I was, but the surprise of being there was no less than if I had remembered being in the hospital last, or work, but I hadn't been there… had I?

"Er…" the sound of sheer intelligence must have dripped from the syllable of confusion. "I… must have walked down here in my sleep. I guess." It was the best I could do on the spot. Chess was still looking at me intently. she may not have blinked for a full minute.

"Sleep-walking? That's new." She didn't sound convinced but I guess, for lack of any better, common-sense-filled reason, she had to believe me. She was probably wondering why I didn't just fess up to falling asleep on the lounge floor. Perhaps I should have said that instead of being slow witted.

HAHAHA. HA. HA. HA. HA. HA.

The first peal of laughter from the voice was almost uncontrollable, but the proceeding 'ha's' were slow and deliberate.

I DID SAY THAT I WAS WORKING ON IT, THAT THERE WAS MORE. YOU LIKE? I'M PRETTY HAPPY WITH MY EFFORTS SO FAR. YOU WALKING AROUND HELPS, THINGS LIGHT UP IN HERE. I CAN SEE WHERE I NEED TO INTERFERE WITH THESE ELECTRIC PULSE THINGIES, AND I JUST COPY THAT. SEEMS TO WORK PRETTY WELL.

"You fucking…" I stopped myself again. No, no… not out loud this time.

"What?" Chess was helping me onto the sofa when I blurted out the swears. She was the only person in the room, of course she was going to think I was talking to her.

"You fucking amazing woman!" I was going to get at least one sentence right today, quickly finishing the proclamation. Chess didn't look impressed; she hated swearing.

"Language! What is wrong with you? Ever since you hit your head. Seriously, baby, please, tone it down." She plumped up the pillow. "Right, do you have a headache? Should I call the doctor? Did they say anything about sleep walking? Do you want to go back to bed? Can I get you anything? Do you want tea? I saw Terry today, he looks well doesn't he, being married suits him…" The questions continued as she walked out of the room. I could still hear her, though. There was no pause for breath.

SHUT UP! SHUT THE FUCK UP WOMAN. SHUT. UP. IT'S ENOUGH TO TIP YOU OVER THE EDGE, INCESSANT DRIVEL. BLAH, FUCKING, BLAH. TELL HER TO SHUT UP, MAN.

No, I responded in my head, *why would I be deliberately rude to her*, and why the hell should he tell me what to do anyway. Although I didn't speak the last thought in my mind, I suddenly got the distinct impression he had heard me anyway. It. Not he. It, dammit.

IF YOU DON'T SHUT HER UP, I WILL.

This was too much. *You shut up. How about you just shut up for a change.* I wasn't usually an out-with-it sort of guy, but this was rapidly changing in my mind. My mind? This was becoming an interesting subject for debate.

RIGHT. FINE, HAVE IT YOUR WAY.

I have heard this line before—in movies. Bad things usually follow that were blatantly anticipated by the viewer but, for some strange and unknown reason, do not seem to be considered by the person rejecting whatever thing or resisting whatever change is upon them. I think I may also have heard Chess say it once at the start of our relationship, and, as I recall, the outcome was not in my favour.

I proceeded to stand up. Only, *I* didn't. At least, what I mean is, it wasn't ME that stood myself up. As I rose the gravity of what was happening began hitting me like a Luton Truck hitting a butterfly at 70mph—much faster than it should have been, yet I should have seen it coming a mile off. I had never, in my apparently sheltered and easy life, experienced such a sensation; it was like that feeling you get in your stomach when you are on a rollercoaster that does a 'gravity' drop from a spectacular height, twinned with the weird unconnected, and almost outer-body, feeling you get when you have been sat down for too long and your foot goes numb. You know it's your foot because it's connected to your leg, but when you touch your foot you can't feel the sensation. Your brain does a 'WHAT?' and makes you believe you are touching someone else's foot, but then the feeling comes back and reality, and pins and needles, bite! That numbness of 'whose body is this?' with the weird stomach thing… that was how it felt.

For a brief moment, I lost myself in the feeling. The weightlessness, the sense of calm and peace. I had no cares in the world, I had no body, no real life—no work. Ah, no work. No boss, no Gerrard and Andy. However, this brief moment didn't last and only worked against me. My guard was down, I was musing an alternative existence, and all I remember was, what I can only describe as a pop. A bit like when you pop your ears when you get to the top of a hill, or when a plane takes off. I, no, my body began to walk towards the kitchen, where Chess was humming away to herself whilst whirl-pooling a teabag and daydreaming out the kitchen window to the garden. It was in full spring bloom and, to this day, I am grateful it was one of the last things she saw. My hand reached towards her neck, her back still to me, and as I watched my fingers stretch out to grab her the sunlight caught the edge of a knife sat next to the sink. I suddenly changed my mind—ugh, no—my mind suddenly changed itself, and my hand darted towards the knife.

No! No, god no!

Holy shit! That was my voice, but it hadn't come out of my mouth. My own voice box had not screamed the pleas of a desperate man, howling like a wild animal caged for the very first time. That was my voice, in my mind. My mind? His mind?

IT'S NOT THE BEST FEELING, IS IT? he taunted inwardly as my fingers curled around the hilt of the knife. No, his fingers. Good god, this body was no longer mine!

I tried to regain control of my limbs; I had no idea what to do, of course, I just 'closed' my eyes, even though I had none, and tensed. But nothing. No! No, come on. Try again. My weak pulse of energy became a little more intense, but the moment was fleeting and gone. I tried to hold my breath, but I couldn't; it wasn't mine to hold any longer. I was weak, I was less than weak. I was purely spirit. Consciousness only.

"What are you trying to do? You are nothing, you are useless. I get to live, you get to exist, for now." His now familiar voice ripped my vocal cords, detuning them to his own gravelly tones. His laughter was a roar of victorious glee and murderous delight. I knew what he intended to do in that same moment. I was powerless to stop it and powerless to turn away from it.

Chess had pivoted around on her heel at his words, a little startled. I imagine she had thought there was an intruder; the voice was a lot deeper than mine and it had a strange accent, not my local accent.

"Wha...? Oh it's you! What the heck are you doing, you scar..." she said as she looked up at me/him. "Baby?" Her beautiful eyes gazed into mine. We had done this so many times, but I had never realised the different hazels and browns in her eyes. Her beautiful eyes that were always so kind. Her deep, loving, naïve eyes that were now wide and consumed with terror as he raised the knife, in slow motion, above her head. She raised her hands, glancing towards her steely demise and then looking back at me. Those beautiful eyes now empty, tear-filled tunnels that I looked into. Her soul crying, her heart had already begun to break, my own soul tried to reach out to hers, to tell her it wasn't me.

Please, no. Chess, it's not me, please believe me! Please hear me. I love you, Chess, dear God, I love you. NO!

"She can't hear you... yet!"

"Nooo, baby, plea..." The words gargled in her throat, blood pouring from her gasping mouth as he plunged and turned the blade, pushing it deep into her neck. As he withdrew the knife, licking his lips, her body lifelessly fell to his feet, her right arm awkwardly bent underneath her unnaturally arched back, her left hand still clutching at her ripped throat. And they were his feet now, not mine. He shuffled them to nudge her off.

"I've wanted to do that for years." He gave a coarse 'Ha' and let go of the knife, which dropped onto her chest and slid down to rest on the floor next to her, where a crimson pool was rapidly forming around and in-between his toes. I could feel the warmth and wanted to feel sick, but it was no longer possible. He looked down at her. She was still.

I tried to sob. I was enraged. How could I possibly let this happen? I wanted to kill him, like he had killer her. I wanted him to suffer. How, how could I do it?! Why years? No, fucking just no. Fuck. The anger was like nothing I had ever felt before and it was stirring me.

You fucking wanker. I'll fucking kill you.

"Whatever," he said, and, kicking Chess's body out his way, he turned and walked out the kitchen into the hallway, bloody footprints tracking his slow and confident pace. I could feel him, his thoughts and feelings. I couldn't feel his soul, I couldn't feel his conscience. All I could feel was black; darkness. And the hottest anger I had ever known.

I reached out as he passed the phone in the hallway. It was one of those stupid 1950's rotary jobs, with the big dial on the front that you would have to use to choose one number at a time. Chess loved this kinda stuff, saying it was 'cute' and that 'kitsch is all the rage, you know'. It's funny the things that go through your head at times like this. I never would have imagined when she bought this telephone how it would be put to its final use.

I tensed, summoning all the energy as my consciousness could. Much to my surprise my arm, momentarily MY arm, responded and reached out, my hand grabbing the heavy square black object. 'They sure made things to last in those days,' was another thought that crossed my mind, right before I swung the phone swiftly up and, as hard as I could, smacked myself on the forehead.

"What the fuc...?!"

ARGH, SHIT!

It hadn't worked how I intended, but he was shocked enough that I still had use of my arm and my hand was firmly gripping the cold plastic. Staggering around, dizzy from the first impact, I swung again, bending my elbow and circling my arm in a cack-handed bowling move, striking my temple. It went black; I couldn't move, talk or see. All I could do was think.

SHIT.

How I wish I could have heard those words. Words are all I am left with now. Even now, her last words echo in my mind. Her eyes as they turned from colourful annoyance to blackest horror. Sometimes I think I can hear her speaking, softly asking me how I am and a million other questions, all asked with one motivation in mind; to make sure I am okay. I tell her I am okay, nothing of me to worry about. He shuts me up, again.

Now I sit here, existing. Day-to-day, hour-by-hour, seeing and hearing everything, but not being able to experience it. A prison within a prison. Living, but not living. Existing, but only in the recesses of my own mind.

Since that day when I found my last physical strength, I have had no control, no place in this world or my own world. I have plenty of time to think. I can do this much at least. I think about the life I will never have with Chess. I think about revenge.

I get stronger every day, but so does he; you find yourself with a lot of time in prison. And now I sit and talk to myself, but now I am the voice. He no longer talks to me; he no longer responds but I talk to him. I tease him, curse him, chip away at him, no, at me. Me? I know he hears me, I feel it. The depth of despair being reached and then the floor bottoming out on him as he realises, all over again, that I will never go away. One day he will kill me— us. If he doesn't, I will. I am now my own worst enemy.

L. DE CLIFFORD

Louise de Clifford currently lives somewhere in the vast plains of south Wiltshire and often talks about living everywhere else one day, when she wins the lottery of course. When asked she will tell you that the most interesting thing about herself is her three cats, Jambi, Fraggle and Nermal, which may actually be true as they have their own Instagram page and have more followers than she does.

As well as writing, Louise loves anything creative and arty, especially singing and has been in a band with her wannabe rock god husband who plays drums. She recently decided that, as she hasn't played her violin for a decade, that she is going to stop telling people that she can play violin...so maybe you should just forget anything about the violin...unless you want to buy a violin?

Not that she has any spare time with all the amazing ideas she is always coming up with, but in her spare time she likes to read, draw, go camping, swim, walk and other things that you generally put into the 'hobbies' section of a CV and regret during each interview. Oh, and procrastinate – she's really good at that.

THE MIRROR AND THE CHAIR

CRAIG SAUNDERS

There's blood on the chair. A dot, drawn down, like a fat exclamation, one a girl might draw. A teenager with new stationary; a gold pen, one with sparkles, and one lurid and red. It's not dry, that ungainly spot, so it gets longer all the while I look at it. Maybe it's just that I can't not look at it, and imagination and time make it more than it is. The policeman in that chair doesn't notice. He's laconic. He's got this slow way of doing everything, from talking and moving, to the way his eyes occasionally slide down to look at the few notes he takes. He looks down for a while, I look at the blood. He writes, that exclamation gets longer. Or, it's just imagination. He moves and thinks and speaks slow and leaves plenty of room for fancy.

"My wife…"

He watches me with heavy, lazy eyes. I mean languid, perhaps. Deep, blue, watchful. Water in an old quarry. He nods but says nothing. What does he have to say? Why does he have to say anything at all? He doesn't. Not a thing.

"… I don't know. The phone. I thought… her mother. I called. She's not there."

"She's somewhere."

That worries me. Such a simple sentence, but the open kind. Room to fall in that sentence. An open elevation. He watches, blinks—everything—slow.

I nod, hang my head. Worried. Not guilty. Not tears, or drama, because I'm a guy and he's a guy. If he'd been a woman, maybe I'd have welled up. Not over the top. Just wet eyes. Watery.

His eyes shift downward and he writes something. I don't say anything. I worry what it is he's writing. I don't think I said anything at all. I didn't leave anything behind, and now it's time to make sure my words are tidy, too. The wood's dry now.

There's blood, though. I thought it would be clean. No mess, no fuss. Just… slipping away.

I thought about this. This guilt. I knew I could kill but not if I could bear it.

It's not as heavy as I thought. More. Crushing. Sinking.

Sinking under water. Everything's about water. I hear drips. Splashes. Lapping waves. Trickles. I feel it on my skin when I wake, like evaporation happening right next to me. Like I sleep beside a lake, the quarry, and she's mouthing something as she goes down. It was dark. The water still dark in the morning. Had it been misty? I can't honestly remember. The feel of it, I do remember. Damp on my skin and in my hair.

I stayed that way, by the edge of the water, for hours. She didn't come up.

Heavier than the water, this guilt.

"Can't think of anywhere?"

I shake my head. Shake. Nod. I planned this. Rehearsed. Spoke to myself. Placed a chair there, in our kitchen. It's where we sat, so it's a natural place, for me. The living room wasn't. A couch, you sit back or forward, it just looks wrong, or contrived.

His head goes down. He writes something. The spot, dark and wet on the dry wood backrest of the chair is longer. I hear drips. I glance, quick, so he won't notice. By the rear legs of the chair, blood drips. Blood, not water. The chair, bleeding. Drip.

Scratching—the sound of his pencil on the pad. Maybe

the point of the pencil's worn low, and it's the sound of the wood against the rough notepaper I hear.

The scratching slows. He looks up, mouths something, but no questions come out. There's question in his eyes, though. Mine, too. I don't know what my expression is. It's not one I've seen in the mirror I watched myself in while I sat in this chair, the mirror in the policeman's chair so I would see what he would see.

The drips are music. Fast, quick. A lullaby. A verse, a chorus.

He slumps, like he's fainting, light-headed. Maybe he is. The blood turns from a spot, to a drip, to a puddle, to a pool, to a lake.

He closes and opens those deep eyes and I stare. I stare, wide-eyed—I wasn't expecting surprise—I haven't practised this. She's there, next to the blood. The policeman's eyes open and close and my mouth does the same.

My wife is wet through, and wan. Pale clothes and hair and skin and eyes milky like dead, drowned women. She seems thin. Not blown and bloated or even eaten, but just like a shade, like things looks with sunglasses on in the dark, looking into the shadow. Just a dim, thin thing. She's not there, but I'm here, the policeman is in her chair and he slides to one side, sees the blood all around him and sighs, says something that sounds like hugs.

That's why, he's thinking. *That's why I'm dying.*

He doesn't fall. She can't push him because surely, she's no more than a shade. She stands in the blood pooled around the chair. The wood's dry now. It was wet when I pulled it back from the quarry. Wet when I cut her loose so she could sink again. I can see the marks where tape pulled some of the colour, a stain like ages oak, from the legs.

Everything seems pale. Her, the dying man. Me, too. I should have let her sink in the chair. I brought it back. People have four chairs. Three's not right. They'd ask,

"Why three chairs?" I'd say one broke. They'd think.

She walks, her feet wet and the blood wet, so she spreads the mess across the kitchen floor. She still drips and leaks water like she brought the quarry with her and if she stood in the man's blood long enough she'd wash it all away.

I think her feet look normal, but pale. Her veins are almost black. Tendons, bones, skin, all hard and white. There's a corkscrew in her hand and she puts the corkscrew on my lap before she moves around, and then behind me. She kneels and winds tape round my ankles, my calves. I look up. I'm sitting where the policeman would sit as I watch myself and practise my lies in the mirror. In the mirror, she's behind me. Below is a pool of blood so deep and dark I can't see where it ends.

CRAIG SAUNDERS

Craig Saunders is the author of over a hundred novels, novellas and short stories including 'Masters of Blood and Bone', 'RAIN' and 'Deadlift'. He writes in many genres, but horror is his favourite.

Craig lives in Norfolk, England, with his wife and children, likes nice people and good coffee. Find out more on Amazon, or visit:

www.craigrsaunders.blogspot.com

www.facebook.com/craigrsaundersauthor

Twitter: @Grumblesprout

THE DARKLING

J.R. PARK

The front door slowly creaked open disturbing a stillness that had claimed hold of the house for days. Its inertia was so thick as to be almost palatable, like the bland taste of stale water, and when Darren closed the door behind him as carefully as he had opened it, he swallowed back the strange sensations that tingled on his tongue. Placing his rucksack on the carpet, it kicked up dirt that had lain undisturbed for days, making his throat tickle as he breathed in a lungful of air, thick with dancing dust particles.

Is this what death tastes like?

He shivered as he looked down the hallway, berating himself for such careless and unsympathetic thoughts. Now wasn't the time to spook himself with morbid whimsies.

Shaking his shoulders in an attempt to dislodge his mind's macabre meanderings, Darren took cautious steps into his Grandmother's house. It seemed like nothing had changed since he'd last been there as child. The wallpaper still had the same green, floral rosettes arranged in vertical columns and separated by borders of rose heads and daffodil petals. Even now, at twenty-four, he still found himself seeing the dragon faces his mind made from the botanical patterns.

Darren smiled at the tooth-filled mouths and the nostrils that billowed smoke. He never understood why others couldn't see this image. To him it was as plain as day.

What a delightful imagination you've got, Grandma Flo used to say before ruffing his hair and offering him another toffee.

He sighed as he walked into the kitchen and took a seat by the dining table. On the side lay a pile of unopened letters. He flicked through them, reading the printed name on the front of each.

Florence Hannam.

Mrs Florence Hannam.

He'd always thought it was an old fashioned name, but it and others like it had seen a resurgence in the last few years.

Grandma Flo had become trendy again.

Darren smiled at this thought and relaxed back into the chair, placing the letters back on the table and taking in his surroundings. The place wasn't a mess, but it wasn't really clean. The sides were thick with dust and insects had taken to calling the windowsill home. It was a little unkempt, but only through recent neglect.

Of course that made sense; she'd been dead for a good few days before anyone found her. That's what his mother had told him, anyway. Fell to the floor and cracked her head. Unable to get up, and with no one around, all she could do was patiently wait for death to take her.

A tear collected around the edge of Darren's eye as he thought of his Grandma, helpless and vulnerable. The air grew colder and pricked his skin as her final moments played out in his mind

The call of a magpie, outside, brought him from his reverie, but the sound of something else made him shiver; footsteps from upstairs.

Darren held his breath and listened. Had the others already arrived? His parents were driving back from Scotland and had messaged this morning to say they'd be delayed. Their solicitor was due any moment, but what would she be doing skulking around upstairs?

He called out and waited for a response, but none came.

He should be alone in the house, and yet the noise above him suggested otherwise. The creaking of the floorboards across the ceiling...

Rising to his feet, Darren crept towards the stairs and tried to ascend without treading too hard on each step, lest the boards creak beneath him.

It could be a burglar. Someone in the street that had watched the ambulance take a dead body away. Perhaps they thought they'd seize the opportunity and hunt for any valuables. Old dears like Grandma Flo were notorious for hiding their savings under mattresses.

Clenching his fists as he prepared for a fight, Darren's mind raced with possibilities.

He hoped it was a burglar.

Anything but...

Following the sounds, he traced the direction, but he already knew which room they'd be coming from. When his senses confirmed his fears he felt his stomach contract and his jaw clench.

At the far end of the landing, next to Grandma Flo's bedroom, stood a door that looked the same as the rest. But the magnolia panels and metallic-black door handle held the resonance of a nightmare, one Darren had spent his life trying to shake.

Childhood fears had been circling his thoughts since he walked through the front door, and now at last they were ready to infiltrate his conscious mind. Darren felt his scrotum tighten as those fears took hold. His throat dried and his heart pounded in his ears.

Come on now, he told himself. You're not a little kid anymore.

The dragon faces on the wallpaper watched his cheeks fade white, showering him with a wave of patronising grins, sinister in their friendliness towards his growing terror.

He laughed at himself; at the preposterousness of his reaction. But it was a forced laugh, and a smile that quickly disintegrated with disingenuity. Darren's steps grew smaller, his footsteps lighter, as he approached the innocuous looking door. His eyes scanned the woodwork, picking out the scratches that had been painted over; an attempt to conceal them, but failing to completely fill the ragged grooves that scored across its width. Placing his hand on the door handle, he felt the cold metal throb with evil. He placed his other hand on the key sitting in the lock and felt the resistance as he went to turn it.

A bang from behind made him jump away from the door, spinning around to confront its source. He saw nothing, but the noise came again. Then a gurgling slurp. A sloshing of liquid.

His face relaxed as he recognised the sounds and stomped across the hallway with purpose. Entering the bathroom, he opened a cupboard door, only to be blasted with a wave of dry air and the musty smell of an arid atmosphere; the kind that can only be produced by a boiler kept in a confined space.

Pressing a button on a control panel, Darren turned the central heating off.

Must have been left on timer, he thought. *The pipes had been warming up, causing them and the floorboards to expand.*

On the floor was a growing patch of damp; its influence spreading across the carpet and up the wall. Following the trail of mould, Darren got to his knees and peered underneath the wash basin. A pipe running vertically up to the tap was slowly dripping water onto the floor. He touched the lino below, itself swollen with moisture, and was not surprised to feel the softening effects of rot. This kind of deterioration must have taken weeks, maybe months.

Downstairs a phone bellowed with the cry of an old fashioned ringer.

With adult eyes, and the power of reason, he looked

back at the door across the hallway. Its air of menace had rescinded but the haunting memory of his Grandma's words echoed in his mind.

Stay out of the Darkling room, Darren. It's dangerous in there.

It took thirty minutes to reassure his mother that he had everything under control and it didn't matter that they weren't due back for another couple of hours. Yes, he was sorry he didn't check his mobile phone, and yes he'd charge it up as soon as their conversation was over. The solicitor would be here any moment and he was perfectly capable of taking instruction and receiving the will. Everything was going to be fine.

Their relationship had been fractious in the past, and the ten minute telephone call was a reminder that he'd made the right decision to move far away at an early age in his adult life.

Darren marvelled over the plastic receiver as he placed it back on the cradle. A home phone. He hadn't seen one in a while. Especially one that looked so antiquated. It didn't take long in this modern world for things to quickly become outdated. Even his Samsung was struggling to keep up with the demands of Instagram, Facebook, and all the other apps that ran automatically in the background. He was lucky if the battery lasted to the end of the day.

Above him came a clunk and patter as the heating cooled, causing the pipes and floorboards to contract under the lowering temperatures.

It really did sound like footsteps.

Heading out to the hallway, Darren retrieved his phone charger and torch from his bag then headed further into the house. He searched around the kitchen, through the cobwebs under the sink, and eventually found the stopcock. Pulling the lever, and satisfied the water was shut off, he stepped back out of the cubby-hole and straightened his back, groaning at the strain his muscles had endured in such an unnatural angle.

Turning a tap, he allowed the water to run until the flow died down; reducing to a trickle and then eventually fading away.

Darren smiled to himself, proud he'd picked up some useful knowledge from his father over the years. He made his living as an actor, treading the boards every night in the West End of London, but he was just as capable as the next man. A point he'd been determined to prove ever since he came out as gay, three days before his twentieth birthday.

It had taken a while for his parents to come to terms with his sexuality. They had outwardly appeared fine with the announcement, but Darren could sense a frosty unease with the situation; especially from his dad. Over the years, though, they had seemingly grown used to the idea, and the initial shock of their son questioning a moral code they didn't even know they possessed had gradually subsided. Although things had never been quite right since.

A certain level of friction existed, and he found it uncomfortable to talk about his boyfriend. It was clearly best left unspoken, which eventually drove a wedge between them. Unable to truly relax around his parents, he found the relationship difficult to maintain, finding excuses not to visit, until, over time, he saw them only at Christmas.

His Grandma on the other hand seemed oblivious to it all. It was unclear if she had actually understood what they'd told her. To her 'gay' meant happy. Queer meant strange. They didn't want to labour the point, especially his parents, and so the conversation was left with an air of uncertainty as to whether Grandma Flo had truly grasped what was being conveyed.

The world changes, he mused. Language changes. Back when he started out at drama school the term actress was a common saying, but slowly it had died off; an unnecessary gender division.

In today's theatrical world a performer was simply called an actor, regardless of sex.

Grandma could go on believing he was happy. On the whole, she'd be right.

Walking into the sitting room, Darren took a seat in a stiff-backed armchair, and played with his phone as he patiently waited for the solicitor to arrive.

What was in the will? Would there be anything for him?

Being the only grandchild, Darren was sure of some inheritance.

He wouldn't be here for any other reason.

As the minutes became an hour he grew bored of his friend's tedious status updates and found his gaze drawn to the wall to his left, full of framed photographs. Standing up to get a better view, he admired the portraits and scenes; the split-second moments from his family's history spanning three generations. He saw a photograph of his Grandma, maybe as old as he was now. They had the same eyes. The same cheeky smile. And, judging by her lavish headscarf, the same taste for flamboyant fashion; certainly the elaborate pendant around her neck was an elegant design of geometrical craftsmanship. Above her portrait was a picture of his parents stood outside a church; his mother dressed in the finest white wedding-gown and his father looking like the happiest man on earth as the pair posed in front of the monasteries congregation of choral monks.

Beside that picture was a photograph of him as a child; a face full of youthful exuberance and joy. His hair was light blonde and ruffled by the gentle wind that blew across the beach. With a spade in hand he stood beside a half-fallen sandcastle, pleased with his handiwork and eager to show it off to his proud parents.

Standswick Sands... he muttered, remembering his childhood holidays at the caravan park on the coast.

The windows began to rattle, bringing him from his recollection, as a train hurtled by on the nearby tracks, passing through the local station. It was a sound and sensation he'd forgotten, but now he was experiencing them again, it was something that was intrinsically linked to his Grandma; to this house. Like banana sandwiches and staying up late to watch horror films on a Friday night.

He smiled. He used to love visiting his Grandma. That was until he first ventured into that room.

The vibrations began to gently fade as the train passed by. Of course it was the train's doing, but back when he was seven he would have blamed something else...

Where was that solicitor? She said two o'clock. It was now nearly four.

His mind latched onto the adult world. To a world of rules and legality. Grown up things. But it did no good. With every rattle of a window, every clunk from the heating, every shriek from a passing bird, he felt his thoughts being pulled back to the nightmares of his youth.

A bang sounded from upstairs again. This time so loud it made him jump.

It was the pipes.

And again.

The pipes.

And again.

Fluctuations in temperature causes molecules to alter speed resulting in changes in density. As the density changes, the objects adjust in size, banging against each other as they settle against their surroundings.

And again.

Enough!

This was ridiculous. Darren tried his best to fight the creeping dread that clawed up his spine and made his shoulders stiffen. He could no longer fight the memories. He had to prove to himself that these dark fantasies he'd tried his best to bury did not exist in the adult world. He had to confront them.

Walking back up the stairs he felt a chill creep over him. Attempting to ignore its influence, he looked across the hallway and stared at the door, daring for it to do something, to prove the impossible; to show him that all those nightmares he'd suffered, those visions he swore for years were true, *did* exist.

Of course they didn't.

But they'd seemed so damn real.

It had all started one evening when high winds blew a storm across the country. He was seven years old and staying at his Grandma's that day. With the worsening weather causing floods and upturning trees, his parents were unable to collect him, meaning he'd have to sleep over. The prospect wasn't terrible; in fact it was one he was overjoyed to hear at the time. Told to run upstairs and fetch his Grandma's reading glasses from her bedroom whilst she spoke to his parents on the phone, Darren was lost in a daydream about dinosaurs when he realised he'd turned the handle of the wrong door.

Stepping back for a moment, he scratched his head. This door was normally locked, but the excitement of new discoveries overcame his trepidation of the unknown. A strange smell, overpowering yet intoxicating, ignited his nostrils.

What was that?

As the door eased open, he saw long shadows fill the room. They moved and writhed in the darkest corners, curling together like a pit of snakes. Darren stepped forward, trying to make sense of this vision. He struggled to see outlines, as black on black, a twisting figure with long spindly limbs reached across the room and aimed its claws towards his soft, delicate flesh.

The boy was rooted to the spot as he glimpsed a row of

teeth, exposed by a grimace; a mixture of hunger and desire. Eyes flickered in the dark, long and narrow, with shifting cat-like slits that scanned the child's form. Darren's skin peppered with goose bumps as the air turned arctic. His own eyes widened, but the form remained nothing more than a murky impression within the dwindling light; its presence growing ever closer to its prey.

"Darren Benjamin Prince!" his Grandma shouted, scolding him with wrath unwitnessed until that moment. "Come away from there this instant."

Turning, he saw his Grandma, already behind him and pulling him from the room, slamming the door shut and twisting the key in the lock.

"Stay out of the Darkling room, Darren," she continued as she led him back down the stairs. "It's dangerous in there."

The Darkling room.

The Darkling room.

The Darkling.

What was the Darkling?

Of course years later he finally understood what she meant. Darkling was an old term to mean something growing darker. A word that had fallen out of fashion with the changing times, like the word actress, or gay meaning happy.

She must have been concerned that he'd hurt himself in an unfamiliar environment and the light rapidly fading. But to seven-year-old him it perfectly described the vision he'd witnessed; the shadowy wisp that spilled across the room with an eagerness to feast on his meat.

This recollection had haunted him ever since, and he'd found himself replaying it over and over again, trying to make sense of what he'd seen.

Did he really see a monster?

Of course not?

He had a wild imagination, and always carried a sensitive soul. The discovery of the strange room and the sudden unusual outburst of his Grandma must have coloured his memory, painting it with the imagery of those Hammer horror films she used to let him watch. The more he thought about it the more ghoulish the nightmare became.

And that was all it was.

A nightmare.

A fantasy brought about by an overactive imagination.

However, the tendrils of that event defied all reason and continued to grip at his thoughts, refusing to unravel and release its stranglehold. Darren was traumatised. After that night, he hated going upstairs in his Grandma's house, nervously creeping up the steps only to run back down as quickly as he could, picking up speed as he ran past the door to the Darkling room and refusing to even glance at its scratched surface.

Even when sitting in the relative safety of her living room, he'd be able to hear banging through the ceiling. Turning the television up did nothing to mask the noise and only served to annoy his parents.

The banging became screams, and eventually he caused so much fuss he never visited his Grandma's house again.

Until today.

For the last seventeen years, that night and its aftermath had never been far from his mind. Over the years, the memories had faded, dulled and been confined to the fantastical imagination of a scared little boy. But without any answers, without any rational explanation, he could never truly let it go.

What had he seen?

What were those noises?

Why did no one else react to the loud thumps and terrifying shrieks that shook the house?

Oh, it's the just wind, they used to say. But their explanations did not satisfy their sceptical son.

What was in that room?

Another train hurtled by, reminding him of the world

outside these walls. A world which he understood. Of engines and timetables, of bank accounts and taxes, of parking tickets and takeaway coffee.

He knew better now. The rattling of the windows, the doors shaking in their frames, these were the sources of the banging. The screeching of the brakes as an old train pulled into the station. This was the cause of the screams he'd heard.

Darren understood all this, but it still took a great effort to move his legs across the landing; still he felt his palms moisten with sweat; still he felt himself grow dizzy as he approached the hated doorway.

Tracing his fingers over the scratched grooves, he tried to focus on a distant memory, a time when he was even younger, maybe four.

A cat. He remembered a cat.

Grandma's cat.

Willow.

Black, with pure green eyes. It must have caused this damage.

Darren touched the cold metal of the key and went to twist it, only to find it already fully turned. It was unlocked, just like that fateful night.

His heart raced, thumping against his rib cage and filling his ears with the rhythmic sprint of his erratic pulse. Swallowing back the fear that dried his throat, Darren once again recounted the logic that he desperately needed to galvanise his resolve; to drive him forward to this confrontation.

The train.

The screeching of the brakes.

The cat.

The fear.

All just fear.

Holding his breath, as if in preparation for an impact, Darren pulled the handle. The mechanism turned, its click echoing around the landing, and slowly he opened the door.

The room was long with wooden floorboards, exposed from the lack of carpet, but not smoothed or varnished, but flecked with paint, with remnants of underlay stuck to the panels and carpet tacks still embedded and crudely bent.

Aged and crumbled cardboard boxes were stacked in towers, obscuring the back of the room, and tall wardrobes lined the walls, their doors open a crack, allowing a menacing line of black to border each one.

Darren flicked the light switch, but no illumination spilled from the blown bulb, allowing the continual creep of darkness as the evening drew in. His limbs grew light as he stepped through the doorway and adrenalin flooded his body. The shadows behind the towers of boxes lay motionless, but throbbed with intention as he tried his best to stare them down.

Heading deeper into the room, he scanned all around, looking for a threat, waiting for the darkness to creep towards him like it had done all those years ago.

As the room remained still, Darren's confidence increased.

Stopping at the first wardrobe, he glanced over its ornate carvings of lattice weaves and four-legged beasts. Slowly opening the door, he breathed a sigh of relief when he discovered its contents to be free from would-be attackers. His interest held by the lavish clothes that hung from wooden hangers, he began to look through them; ball gowns of the finest silk and feathered hats with plumage so striking he knew not of any bird that could carry such exotic markings. Noticing something by his knees, Darren crouched down, and pulled out a large package wrapped in cloth. Removing the outer layer, he revealed an intricate portrait of a beautiful young woman. The twinkle in her eye and delightful smile reminded him of the photograph he had studied downstairs. A warmth radiated through him as he realised he was gazing upon the image of Grandma Flo in her youth. How beautiful she was and how adored she must have been by the artist. Every brushstroke was an act of worship, hailing the perfection of the painting's subject; and how exquisite she was! Darren stood back to admire the portrait from afar, noticing the same elegant pendant, looking even more stunning with the vibrancy of colour captured by the artist's palette.

The light dimmed further as the evening lay claim to the world outside. His vision struggled with the fading light, but as he turned and looked around the room he saw it with new eyes. His terror had subsided, been replaced with an affection for the elder relation he hadn't felt since he was a small child.

No wonder his Grandma had been so angry with him. She must have been afraid. Afraid he'd hurt himself and in the process break some valuable artefact from her mysterious but glamorous past. The boxes were stacked in precarious piles, the floor littered with the sharp protrusion of carpet tacks, the wardrobes overloaded and wobbling on their age-warped bases.

With the fading light, this place was a minefield of hazards for a small boy, clumsy with inexperience and a desire to explore. This Darkling room could certainly be dangerous.

A smile spread across his face. Her actions had not been born out of anger, but of love.

Darren closed his eyes and opened his arms, allowing the world of this room to be at one with him. He sent forgiveness into the ether and hoped that the spirit of his Grandma, if such a thing existed, might sense his penance and grant him pardon.

What a wonderful woman, he thought, marvelled by

her old clothes and curious of the life she had once lived. Why didn't I get to know her?

The light was little more than a silvery sheen through the window when a train thundered past. Only this time it sounded clearer. Closer.

"Darren," a faint voice called out.

Shocked by the barely perceptible sound, Darren stumbled backwards, knocking into a stack of boxes and sending them crashing to the ground. He followed suit and hit the floor, sending dust flying into the air.

Attempting to climb back to his feet he reached out, grabbing hold of a box flap and accidentally opening it, spilling the contents across the floor. A velvet robe fell across his chest, unfolding to reveal a bag of chalk pieces, a set of candlesticks, and a wooden board.

Scrambling to his feet, he caught sight of the board, recognising the shape of his Grandma's pendant carefully etched in to it.

"Darren," the voice called again, much louder.

He looked across the room, but was rooted to the spot through fear and confusion.

The darkness began to bend and warp, to writhe over itself as a bloodied hand emerged from the shadows.

"Darren," the voice called once more, this time with a resonance that chilled his blood.

A woman's face appeared from the gloom. Her eyes were wide with terror and blood smeared her cheek.

"Mr Prince. Please. Help me."

Darren held his head in disbelief.

"Who are you?"

"My name is Sarah Miller," she wheezed, too scared to talk at any volume. "I'm Mrs Hannam's solicitor."

The solicitor?

Had she been up here the whole time?

Had the banging above him not been the heating after all, but the solicitor all along?

She crawled towards him, pulling herself along with

one hand whilst the other arm hung uselessly by her side. Blood poured from her suit jacket, suggesting a grisly injury, and as her face became clearer he noticed a six-inch gash running down her cheek.

"What happened?" he asked, rushing towards her.

"I came here to meet you and your parents," she half whispered with a weakened voice. "I looked around the house, but when I came in here, someone attacked me"

"Who...?"

The solicitor looked towards him with pleading eyes as she reached for his hand, but collapsed to the floor before she could take it. The shadows unravelled from the corners of the room and rolled over her like a thick, black ooze, engulfing every inch of her body. Sarah Miller fought back, trying desperately to claw her way out of the stygian substance holding her captive.

Wrestling her head free, Darren watched in disbelief as she opened her mouth in an attempt to scream, only to see the darkness climb up her neck and force its way down her throat.

A pair of eyes blinked behind her, somewhere in the black; training their feline pupils on the man standing before them. Darren took a step back, but was entranced by the indescribable entity before him. As it slipped ever closer, the outline of its spindly limbs grew nearer, fading in and out to suggest the shape of a tall, slender humanoid, bending and twisting with a refusal to hold form.

An arm stretched out, taking a meandering path that reached across the room towards the frightened young man.

Darren's fugue state finally broke and he turned, sprinting towards the door.

But it was too late.

The creature had caught his leg, tripping him up and began pulling him back. He screamed as he fought against its grip, but to no avail. He watched as a set of razor teeth appeared from the grin of this unnatural monstrosity. The

Darkling was real. And it was hungry.

Downstairs he heard the front door open and the muffled voices of his parents. He tried to scream, to warn them of the danger, but his throat had already been opened.

The dragons on the wallpaper held their unflinching grin as they watched the Darkling pull at its prey, dividing Darren's flesh as it wrapped its midnight skin around his body.

J.R. PARK

J. R. Park is horror author based in Bristol, UK. Using pulp horror as his base palette, Park has been experimenting with the genre since his first book Terror Byte was released; a techno-noir-horror with a nod to Shaun Hutson. The bleak brutality of his third book Upon Waking was coupled with an unusual narrative that both confused and received critical praise.

As well as his full length books, he has had short stories published in collections by Knight Watch Press, Sinister Horror Company and Matt Shaw Publications.

His influences are cited as cheese before bed, misheard conversations and the pregnant emptiness of darkened rooms.

Find out more at www.JRPark.co.uk

BURY ALL YOUR SECRETS IN MY SKIN

ALICE J. BLACK

"Bless me father, for I have sinned." A low, female voice talks to me through the screen at my right. I resist the urge to look.

"I am listening." My voice sounds gravelly. I sit quietly and wait for her to continue.

"This week I have committed two sins. I have taken the Lord's name in vain."

I continue to sit quietly. This is her time, her confession is what will absolve her of her sins.

"I have also lied to those that love me. They believe that I am sober and have been for a month. Last week I had a drink. I had so much that I got very drunk. I am ashamed of my actions." She sighs and I picture her shoulders sagging, her head drooping. She is done.

"Are you remorseful for the sins you have committed?"

"Yes, father, of course." Her voice takes a higher lilt, almost like she is trying to make me believe. It is not my place to judge but I know that her story will come full circle again next week.

"Then your penance has been granted. Speak to your family and take the truth with you. Lies do not hold in God's eyes."

"Thank you, father."

There is relief in her voice and I know that she is a clean slate. I hear the soft shuffle as she gathers her belongings and then the door to the confessional is opened. She is gone and I am left to my thoughts.

As a priest, my role in confessional is to sit and listen to other people's slip-ups in society. Over the years this is a skill I have honed until I feel I can give sound advice and offer true penance. However, I also find that it becomes an effort. Each time I am due to the confessional my feet slow and my mind wanders. The taking of other people's sins, no matter that Christ is the one offering absolution of their fallen moments, is draining to me. I feel that each sin I take slips inside my skin, adding a little darkness each time.

Pushing up the sleeve of my robe, I bare my forearm to the meagre light filtering through the wooden screen. The razor I remove from inside my clothing is sharp and nicks my fingers as it glances the skin. I press it to the soft flesh of my forearm and slice the blade across the skin, feeling an immediate release as blood trickles from the wound.

I have made space for more of the darkness.

Kelly Treply stared up at the huge, monstrous figure of the church. It was the only building in town that still retained some of its original history, the rest having been knocked down for redevelopment. It was beautiful and foreboding at the same time and, as she stared from across the street at the stained glass windows and huge, wooden doors leading to the sanctuary, she almost got lost in it.

"Don't tell me you hate church as well?" Kelly turned to look at her colleague, Richard Jones. A well-built man, he stood a head taller than her and wore it well with broad shoulders and a handsome face. His wife was one lucky woman. Kelly knew she could allow herself those thoughts now. Though born and raised a Catholic, it had been a long time since she considered herself true to her religion.

"I hate church," she told him with a deadpan glare. She wasn't afraid to admit it either. After years of being dragged to this very church by her parents, and raised in such a strict fashion that she had no childhood, she had grown to hate the church and everything it stood for. "But we have to go in."

"Do you really think the father will know anything? And if he does, is he obliged to tell us?" Richard swept his shirt tails back as he stuck his hands in his pocket and Kelly got a view of his hardened chest as his shirt pulled taut. She averted her eyes.

"No. And no. But we have to try. Come on." Without further resistance, Kelly stepped off the pavement and strode across the road. Richard was quick to follow and she couldn't help but wonder if he chased after his wife like that.

She made it to the steps and trotted up the base concrete without looking up at the building. Stopping at the huge, oak doors she took a deep breath. It was open, as she expected it to be, an invitation for anyone who wished to step in to make themselves at home. Kelly did not want to be at home in that place. Not now, not ever.

Stepping over the threshold, her skin tightened and goose bumps rose on every inch of her flesh as the darkness surrounded her. She wanted to turn around, to step back outside into the strong glare of the sun and forget about this place, but she couldn't. A shuffle behind her indicated that Richard wasn't far behind and she took comfort in that fact.

Words ran through her head like a mantra. *I am not going to confession. I am not going to confession.* It kept her moving.

Inside, she was hit with a sense of nostalgia as she saw the church she had attended as a child. Rows of wooden pews stretched out either side and the flooring was the original stone flags that caused her footsteps to echo with each step she took forward. Sticking to the very centre of the aisle, she made her way forward towards the altar, the huge shrine taking up much of the space beyond in ornate gold hues.

"Officers," a man in robes stepped into sight. "Can I help you?"

Kelly repressed the shudder that threatened to run through her at the sight of the man. She could not hold him accountable for her wish to leave the religion. What he chose to do with his life was his choice. Kelly stopped and assessed him mentally. He held his hands together in a tight steeple at chest-level, the white of his skin stark against the black robes. His hair was white and thinning and his face was beginning to droop as age began to prey on his skin.

"I'm PC Treply and—"

"Treply. I know your parents." He smiled and his thin lips stretched out wide and pale. "And you, I believe, for some time."

"Yes." She smiled. "And this is PC Jones. We're here to ask a few questions."

"What is this regarding?"

"A crime that was committed last night."

"Then you must come to my office." He dipped his head and turned. Kelly glanced across the way at Richard and followed, glad once again that she wasn't alone.

"You never told me you're Catholic," Richard whispered, leaning close. His voice left a sweet trail of goose bumps on her neck.

"I'm not," she mumbled back. Normally, questions about her personal preferences would have been shut down but she didn't mind keeping him right on this one.

They made their way to the left of the pews and, as she took in the whole church, she caught sight of the confessionals at the far right corner. Two little wooden booths, now vacant, but used readily in the confession of sin. She shook her head. Confession of sin, the act of making a person pure again. She averted her gaze and instead watched the priest in front, the black robes swirling around his feet.

It wasn't long before they were in a little office. The walls were wood panelling, the only decoration there. They were ushered into chairs at the opposite side of the desk and he took a seat facing them.

"What can I do for you, officers?" he asked, all business now.

"We've had recent reports about a gang of youths causing trouble outside on the grounds of the church," Kelly began.

"Inside as much as outside," the priest corrected her.

"Nothing in the reports mentions that."

"It's a more recent thing." He shook his head. "Night before last they came in just as I was closing. Ran about the place like hoodlums. It took a whole hour to get them all out."

"And did you ring the police at this time?"

"No. I was too busy herding children."

Kelly sighed. "Our job is to stop nuisance and protect people. You should have called. We also would have had it on record."

"Did they break anything? Take anything?" Richard asked.

"Not that I know of." He shook his head and leaned forward on the desk. The sleeve of his robe rolled up and Kelly caught sight of a large gash on his arm.

"Did they hurt you?" she asked, pointing to the wound.

"No." He shook his head with a quick smile, fighting with the garment to pull it down. "That was a gardening accident."

"Right."

"Father, if you should have any more trouble with these youths please have no hesitation in contacting the force. We are here to protect so let us do that. And I do believe the same group of young men is causing havoc at other places in town. If we can pin them down then maybe it will stop altogether," Richard told him.

"I will. Thank you, officers."

"Thank you for your time. We'll see ourselves out." Kelly stood and opened the office door, striding out and down the long corridors towards the front of the church.

"How do you know where you're going?" Richard asked.

"Good memory." She shrugged. But it was more than just a good memory. This was the family church. When Kelly was too young to fight against the religion shoved down her throat she had been here as much as them. She knew every inch of this church.

They made it outside into the high-noon sun and Kelly took in a deep breath where she paused on the steps. It felt good to be outside. Inside that church everything felt claustrophobic, trapped.

"So what do you think?" Richard asked as they crossed the road towards his car.

"I think he's hiding something."

"About the kids?"

"No. Something else."

"Bless me father, for I have sinned." A man begins his confession and I sense guilt in his voice.

"I am listening," I tell him.

There is a shuffle as he makes himself comfortable and a sigh as he tries to find the right words. "Father, my sins feel like they are mounting up. I am becoming a Godless man."

"Tell me your sins."

"At Mass, I was not there. My mind wandered and I did not give God my full attention that day."

"Go on."

"My mind, father, is on another. I am having sinful thoughts about a woman who isn't my wife." A pause. "I

231

cannot stop myself thinking about her. I want to be cleansed of this sin."

"Do you love your wife?"

"Of course." The answer comes a little too quick.

"Then the thoughts will dissipate. True love conquers and your wife is testament to that. You have not committed adultery."

"No. But I am worried that I might."

"You must put your trust in faith. You will be guided through this hard time and your thoughts will become pure once more."

"Thank you, father."

"Go now and be with your wife. Make your mind resolute in its thoughts and remember to worship your Lord."

"Of course, father. Blessed be."

The other side of the confessional opens and then closes with a soft bang. The man is gone and the booth is empty. I sigh. I can already feel his sins trying to worm their way into my skin, dark and malicious. I have taken the intent of sin from this man so his thoughts are pure but the evil that resonates from it must go somewhere. I must take his sin, carry his secret.

I take the blade from my robes and lift my sleeve. I become witness to a dozen or more red gashes across the length of my arm. Some are worse than others, some are healing. It doesn't matter, there will always be more. Pressing the razor to my skin, I drag the blade across the flesh and watch as the skin splits so easily, blood pooling in the wound and then dripping down my arm.

I breathe in deep and allow the secrets to be buried in my skin.

Kelly had been sitting at her desk for hours, the mug in

front of the computer ringed with stale coffee and the dregs at the bottom drifting up to catch her nose. With a grimace she pushed it away and leaned further into the screen. She had tried a million different databases, internet searches and God-knows-what to try and find something, anything, on Father Collarhan. Nothing had come up. Not a stitch. But it didn't stop the gut feeling that Kelly had; something was definitely up with him and she was determined to find out what.

"Treply, don't you think you've spent enough time trying to dig up dirt?" Richard asked, setting a fresh cup in front of her.

"Thanks." She picked it up and took a sip. "And no. There's something going on there."

"I think your senses are off on this one." He shook his head.

She rubbed her eyes and looked up. Richard was perched on the end of her desk, leg hitched up and hands crossed over his knee, staring down at her.

"I don't." She finally shook her head. "I just can't put my finger on it yet."

"Well listen, it's late. I'm going home. You should too." He pushed himself up and spun on his polished shoes.

"Night," she called after him. watching him leave. He was going home to his wife. There was nothing for her to go home for. No reason to leave work behind. Instead, she turned her attention back to the screen and continued scrolling.

After another hour and another cup of coffee gone cold, Kelly finally stretched. Her muscles were aching and her back was arched. Standing, she looked up. The office was quiet, the bank of computer screens all black except for hers. The overhead lights were dimmed as she sighed and glanced at her watch. It had just gone nine. Nine in the evening, she should have been at home relaxing or doing something nice. Yet here she was, still at work. Shaking her head, she grabbed her bag. Kelly knew she was too work-focused but when it came to catching bad guys, that's what she was good at. All she had to do now was pin something on the priest and she would sleep a little better.

Her eyes slid back to the screen as she switched it off and a small smile tugged at her lips. That's what she had been doing all wrong. An internet search would only show something that had already been done. Maybe he hadn't been caught yet. Well that's just what she intended to do—catch him in the act.

Her smile grew as a renewed energy coursed through her. It wasn't time for home, not yet.

Outside, night had fallen and the streetlights lit the wet pavement in a slick, yellow glow. A quick glance showed she was alone in the street. Hurrying across to her car, Kelly jumped in, slung her bag onto the passenger seat and started it up. Instead of driving in the direction for home, she took the same route as she had earlier that day and it wasn't long before she was at the church. Everything was quiet and, as she parked across the street, turning off the headlights, her attention turned to the huge stone building with the door still standing open.

Kelly sat back in the car, her neck craned to the right and waited.

She waited a whole two hours and in that time she saw nothing. No movement, no sound, no indication that anybody was in the church. With a sigh, she started up the engine. She hadn't found anything tonight but there would be other days and she had plenty of free nights.

Driving down the road, Kelly finally made for home, ready to rest and let the exhaustion seep from her body.

I sit in the dark in my office, the sting of the day's confessions wearing hard on my skin. In the meagre light cast by the window, I glance at the welts on my arm. The angry wounds stretch across my skin, the redness and swelling from each blending with the others. There is no distinction between them anymore. But I can distinguish. I know each and every sin. I know the confession of every person and the secrets they have buried within me.

Each one of the cuts is a marker, a sign of sin and reclaimed penance. For me there is no penance. I feel the darkness growing inside me. It festers there like something old and rotten, lingering in some unforgotten place, but it is there and it is growing. It surges through me like a power threatening to release, and I am afraid. I know that the darkness will come soon. My body cannot hold such evil for much longer and I am afraid of how it will manifest.

I am weary. Beyond weary. My life is beginning to drain. It sucks me dry from the inside and there is nothing I can do to hold my head above water. There is nowhere to turn. I have my God but he does not want this sin in the world. I know he would have me carry the darkness within in order to free the world but I cannot do it for much longer.

In the dim light, I watch as something ripples beneath my skin. It is not the settling of flesh or weeping of wounds; this is something more, something deadly. Something that grows.

"Richard," Kelly called him over to the desk as soon as he walked through the door. He wore a brown suit today and it clung to his shoulders like nothing else. She quickly averted her gaze, not wanting to be seen ogling her partner, and waited for him to approach.

"You look like shit," he greeted her.

"Good morning to you too." She plastered on a smile.

"Did you sleep at all?" He perched on the side of her

desk again.

"Listen, we're going to the church again."

"Now?"

"Tonight."

"Jeez, Kelly. What's going on with you? The guy is harmless."

"He's not. There's something going on there, Jones. I was there last night and—"

"You went on a stakeout?" His face dropped.

"Yes. And this time I think we need to go in."

"You realise that we can't. We're the police, we can't break and enter."

She shrugged. "So call it something else. Are you with me?"

He shook his head and stood up. "I hate this but you're not going in alone. I'm there."

She nodded and smiled grimly. This was their chance. They would catch him tonight and it would put her unrest to bed once and for all.

"Bless me father, for I have sinned." Another man. I draw in a breath and let it out slowly. I can feel a surge in my chest and I swallow hard. I cannot let it out. Not yet. Not ever.

"I am listening," I tell him and clasp my hands together.

"It's getting worse, father. I am struggling to control myself, my behaviour." A sigh.

"Go on." The thing inside me pulsates and tries to climb up my throat. I swallow it back down like gorge and hope that I have not been heard.

"I can't stop hurting her. My wife. Every time I raise my fist I know it's wrong. There's something inside of me that tells me to stop. But I can't. It's like I'm not myself anymore. And then when it's over, and I see what I've done, I'm full of so much remorse I think about ending my own life."

"Your behaviour is yours to control, should you wish it." I sense the anger permeating deep within his skin. It throbs with raw energy, waiting to get out. The darkness leans towards it.

Movement, like he's shaking his head. "I can't. She just makes me so... mad! Everything she does, everything she says. I want to punish her for being so foolish."

"Punishment is only the Lord's to give out, not his servants."

Another sigh. "I know. I'm worried that next time I might not be able to stop, father. I'm worried I might kill her."

"Listen to me," I tell him, the darkness surging in my chest roils towards him. "You are in control of your actions and your behaviour. Nobody else. You must seek self-control and wield it like a shield."

"Yes, father."

"Go now and make amends with your wife. Seek the sanctity of self-control and you will prosper."

"Thank you, father." The door opens and shuts closed with a muffled bang. I take a deep breath and roll up my sleeve. The darkness is already anticipating the next sin. It waits at the utmost layer of skin waiting to breach, like a bird looking for a tasty morsel. I must feed it.

I take the blade from my robe and at the bottom of my wrist—the only space left on my arms—I draw it across the soft flesh. I wince at the sharp pain and then the blood begins to flow and I feel the darkness lapping up the evil of sin as it pours into my skin.

The day dragged as she worked through stacks of

paperwork. Police work had seemed like such a good idea when she first signed up. The thought of being out there, helping society and doing the right thing was part of it, but of course the attractive pay packet had helped. Now it seemed that, after passing her probation and moving out of the normal beat duties of a cop, becoming a detective meant so much more paperwork than she had ever anticipated. Sometimes she wanted to throw it all up in the air and forget everything.

All she could focus on was the priest. Tonight they would go and they would find whatever was going on inside that church. She was determined and she was sure.

"Trebly, how's the Dorcile case coming?" Trevor Carter, her superior, appeared at her desk. An older man, his grey hair was beginning to recede and he had spent one too many years behind a desk judging by the pot belly he was sporting beneath his white shirt.

"It's coming, sir," she told him, patting a stack of paperwork. "But listen, I wanted to ask you about Father Collarhan."

"What about him?" The man frowned, his eyebrows knitting together in display of a caterpillar.

"I think there's something strange going on at that church."

"Aside from the youths?"

"Yes. He's hiding something."

"And what makes you think that?"

"Call it a hunch."

Carter sighed audibly and his grip on the door frame tightened. "How many times do we have to go through this? We can't work on hunches."

"But—"

"No buts and no subordination this time either." He held up his finger in chastisement. "You almost got both of us fired the last time and I won't cover for you again."

Her shoulders sagged as the words sunk in. "Yes, sir."

"I mean it. I want movements on the Dorcile case

today, got it?"

"Yes, sir."

He disappeared from sight, the sound of his heavy footfalls reaching her eyes right until he entered his office. Her stare lingered as her mind wandered. There was no way she could forget about this. She always trusted her instinct and it had bagged her a lot of perps in the past. Tonight would be no different. She caught sight of Richard crossing the floor plate and decided not to tell him Carter had called time on the church. What he didn't know wouldn't hurt him.

"Bless me Father, for I have sinned." The voice is familiar. I clear my throat and take a moment to try and place it. Then something looms in my mind and I realise it is the man from earlier. He is back. I frown but give my usual response.

"I am listening."

There is a sigh and then something deeper, primal almost. A sob. Then the man is crying. I see his figure lean forward like he's resting his head in his hands and his shoulders heave. A knot forms in my stomach.

"I was here earlier," he finally starts after managing to calm himself.

"I recognise your voice. How can I help?"

Another deep sigh as if he is trying to find the words.

"I took your advice and I went home to my wife. I apologised. I tried my best, father, I really did." A pause and another sob. "But then she got mad. She said she was going to leave me."

The knot tightens in my stomach and a shiver runs down my spine. I feel as if I already know what is coming, though the words have yet to be spoken.

"There was a bag packed on the bed and she picked it

up and tried to get past me. I grabbed her arm and held her there. We struggled and I threw her. I meant to throw her back into the bedroom. I just wanted her to see. But she fell, father. She fell down the stairs." He breaks down, his voice cracking and the tears flowing as he lurches forward. His words ooze into the air around me, filtering through the booth and encapsulating me within its grasp. Inside me, the thing pulses beneath my skin, reaching forward, grasping for the evil that feeds the dark soul.

I do something I have never done before. While the man in the booth beside me cries, his guilt ripping him apart, I take the blade from my robes. I slice the last remaining free piece of skin on my wrist and watch as the blood oozes out and wince as the darkness forces its way inside, sucked up like a babe at the teat. I feel it filling me, the evil act flowing through my veins like it's a part of me. Almost as if my lifeblood has been changed to some black, viscous fuel.

"Father," the man starts again, finding his voice. "There is no penance left for me here, or anywhere. But I can't stay."

I force myself back into the present. "Where will you go?"

A movement catches my eyes and I see he is shaking his head. "I don't know. Anywhere. Anywhere but here."

He has shed his evil and left it with me where it buries deep under my skin and he plans to leave. Red hot rage flashes through me as I realise his ignorance. He has forced his crime—his sin—upon me and now he plans to leave while it festers in the dark. All of them the same. The sins of others have become as much a part of me as anything I already am, if not more. Why should I be the one to carry the burden? Why should a person come to confess their sins to me and then leave free and light while I must endure the ongoing darkness they have put me under? Equality is surely lost in this relationship and it is something I cannot continue. I must remedy this. Now.

"Come on," Kelly hurried across the road. The church loomed up in front of her, tall and daunting against the night sky. There was a light coming from inside and as it hit the huge stained glass window, colour refracted into the night. If it wasn't so eerie, it would have been a beautiful sight.

Behind her, the soft thud of Richard's shoes hit the pavement as he kept up. They took the stairs together, almost racing to the top where she stopped at the door, taking a moment to draw breath.

"Remind me what it is we're doing here?" he whispered, glancing at her then back at the street.

Her heart pounded in her chest and her stomach was in knots. She glanced at Richard, momentary guilt clawing to the surface.

"Carter told you not to come, didn't he?" Richard straightened up and his lips pulled together in a tight frown.

There was no point in lying to him now. "Yes."

"Jesus, Kelly. Do you live, just so you can defy orders?"

"There's something going on in there."

"And this is based on a hunch."

"Listen, I trust my instincts every day and they never steer me wrong. Why would this be any different?"

He sighed, glancing at her. In the dark she saw his eyes were dark and his brow furrowed, but it began to loosen and he relented. "Fine. But we get in and get out. Got it?"

She nodded once, "Got it," then her eyes were on the huge door that stood in front of them. This would technically be the make or break point. If this wasn't open then the whole operation was a bust. She held her breath as she grabbed the huge handle and pulled it to the right. She felt it give underneath her weight and the mechanism

241

opened, the door immediately swinging inwards. Turning towards Jones she grinned and stepped into the darkness.

I am me. I am different. I am stronger. The darkness courses through me like a train wreck, smashing everything inside and promising to make me a better man. I revel in the warmth as the viscous darkness flows through my veins, replacing my blood and becoming a part of me. My fingers stretch and I feel the air around me. My mind is working faster than it ever has and my body feels like it could withstand anything. I am immune. I am invincible.

Opening my mouth, I let out a roar of triumph as the darkness takes hold.

"What was that?" Richard whispered, his back ramrod straight as he stared at Kelly. She shook her head.

"I don't like this," Richard went on.

Kelly didn't like to admit it, but neither did she. She was right to trust her gut when she thought about this place. There was definitely something going on within these walls but she couldn't put her finger on it. If the roar was anything to judge by, this was way out of their league. Still, there was no way she was backing down. As an officer of the law it was her job to protect the innocent and if that meant putting herself in harm's way, then so be it. She threw another glance at her partner. His brow was cut in deep lines and his lips were puckered as he peered into the church from the shadow of the porch.

"Go home. I'll handle this," she told him. She meant it as an instruction. She wanted him to walk away. He had so much more to lose. She couldn't have that on her conscious.

With a deep breath, Kelly pushed forward, stepping into the church. Behind her she heard the loyal footsteps of Richard in close pursuit. A grim smile flicked the corner of her mouth before subsiding. She needed her wits about her if she was going to stay alive.

Everything is varying shades of grey and black. It feels like home and, as I step from the booth, I realise I am home. This darkness that is coursing through my body is like home. This is what I have been missing all along. The cuts were a means to an end and they let me become who I was meant to be.

Around me the church begins to fill with a shadow so dark it's like the sun being blotted out. I have never known a darkness so complete, or felt so right. I grin and feel my mouth split. But there is no pain. There will never be pain again. My grin grows and my cheeks crack open, skin flaking. I feel it falling to my feet. My grin erupts into peals of laughter as I hold up my hands and surrender myself to complete evil.

Her eyes flicked to Richard on the other side of the aisle as laughter filled the air around them. It wasn't the laughter itself but the intent it held. As a cop, she had seen plenty of different responses to crime and nervous laughter could be one of them, but this wasn't nervous. This was dark, malicious, bordering on the side of unhinged.

Swallowing, she reached for the gun on her belt and drew it, clicking the safety off. In her peripheral vision she saw Richard do the same. Suddenly she was glad he had stayed. Her partner's skills were a match for her own and she would have it no other way.

Taking the lead, she stepped further into the church, scanning every possible space for the person she expected to see. The laughter died off, the echoes retaining their semblance against the cold stone walls before dying. Silence ensued and that was worse than the laughter.

The breath she held in her chest escaped slowly through her nose, a technique she had taught herself for stealth, but also to calm her nerves. Every one of her senses was lit up and she was running on it.

They crept up the centre aisle, Kelly scanning the left pews, Richard the right, for any sign of movement. Everything was dark and the only sound was her partner's shoes on the flagged floor. She crept onwards, making her way towards the altar of the church. She saw the gold of the shrine glinting in the dim light.

Something to her left caught her eye and her body swung in automatic response, arms coming up, holding the gun out as her eye tried to pick out the detail. At first she saw nothing but the darkness that shrouded the church, and then she saw it again. It looked like a man walking towards them only, this was no man. His limbs impossibly extended as if he had grown five feet in a matter of a minutes. His arms waved out at his sides and it put her in mind of tentacles. His legs were the same, bending in the middle at the knee and disjointed as if there were no bones left. As he moved forward, gliding soundlessly across the floor, his head came into view.

Her jaw dropped. It was the priest. His head attached to his neck which had rescinded all signs of skin. Instead she saw a black mass writhing within, like black putty stretching, stringy in places and thick in others.

"What the fuck?" Richard muttered beside her.

Kelly pulled herself back into the present. She saw her partner standing tall, shoulders firm and legs planted apart, his gun raised as the thing stalked nearer.

"Stay where you are!" she yelled, her voice echoing around the church.

Laughter greeted her and a shiver ran down her spine. This was the cause of the laughter. The priest. Only she didn't think he was a priest anymore—or human for that matter. He kept gliding on tentacled legs towards her, no effort expended to stay upright. It was almost like a creature from the black lagoon—from her worst nightmares—had surfaced, only this was somehow different. He felt dark, his malicious intent palpable.

"I knew you would come." His voice was a deep hiss, a venomous snake waiting to attack.

"I said stay where you are." She squeezed the gun.

He kept advancing. "Don't be afraid. I have simply become a higher entity."

"You need to stay where you are, or I'll shoot." It was the first and only warning she would give. Beside her she sensed Richard tense like a coil ready to spring.

He laughed and continued gliding towards them. "I am the darkness I have been forced to endure. Everyone has sinned, Kelly. Even you."

She swallowed hard and shoved the thought away. She couldn't let him get into her mind.

"I warned you," she growled, dropping her arms and pulling the trigger. The bullet hit the place where his thigh would have been but it passed through the black oily substance like it was thin air. Father Collarhan stared at the spot for a moment, a little incredulous that she had dared to shoot. When he looked up his dark brown eyes were gone, replaced with black discs. Anything that had been left of the man was gone.

The thing kept advancing towards them, tentacles licking the air as if testing the water. It wouldn't be long before it was on them.

"What do we do?" Richard asked, taking an involuntary step back.

Kelly's eyes flicked to the front of the church where the

altar stood, the gold shining like a beacon. The font. She had to get to it. "Distract him."

Kelly ran towards the creature as Richard sprang into action, firing off another bullet to direct its attention towards him. The creature was drawn to the sound and Kelly took the opportunity to duck beneath its flailing limbs. As she passed its body, a sense of dread cut through her so deep she thought she might collapse with grief and die right there. Then she was past and the dread subsided. Shaking herself up, she sprinted towards the altar and the font that stood beside it. She needed to get the creature up there.

Kelly spun just in time to see the creature's dark arms circling Richard. It seemed almost tender but as her partner began to wilt beneath the dark, oily arms, she screamed.

The priest turned towards her, the spin almost like a dancer's pirouette as his arms went wide. Richard forgotten, it made its way up the aisle, shuffling forward on extra tentacles of darkness that had sprouted from within. Kelly drew in a breath. She had to wait until exactly the right moment. Further and further he moved, closer to her. Behind him, she saw her partner prone on the floor. She shifted her gaze back to the creature. It was almost on her.

"Hey!" she shouted and Collarhan paused, head cocking to the side on top of its long stalk. "Time to cleanse."

With a pounding thrust, she picked her leg out and connected with the font. It wobbled and then toppled, sending the holy water gushing down into the aisle. It hit the creature and it screeched, the sound so high-pitched she had to clamp her hands over her ears. She watched as it began to crumple, the tentacles that held it up melting into the water beneath.

It was working.

But the decomposition began to slow. It was beginning

to take strides towards her. She had to act.

With an animalistic roar, Kelly lunged from the top step onto the creature. She felt her hands flow deep into the oily darkness and realised that it felt dry and cold at the same time as that feeling of dread began to permeate her skin. The creature tumbled backwards beneath her weight and they dropped to the floor. Its head hit the water and she held it there, ignoring the stench of decay and the immeasurable unhappiness that swept across her. She had to hold on just a bit longer.

She watched as, beneath her, the darkness began to fizzle within the holy water, the oily substance poured through every orifice in his skull. And then beneath her, she felt the bone began to crack, its whole head caved and dropped into the water. What remained of the priest became still.

Kelly watched for a long time as the black substance oozed across the floor, dissipating into nothing.

Kelly pushed herself up on weary limbs. She stumbled across to Richard and dropped to her knees on the floor. "Jones." She patted his cheek gently.

He roused slightly, eyes opening a tiny slit and then peeling open as he sat bolt upright.

"Woah, take it easy." Kelly held out her hand. "We don't know what that thing did."

His head snapped to the left. "What *was* that thing?"

Kelly shrugged. She had no idea, but suspected that he had been evil incarnate.

"Come on." She held out her hand and hoisted him to his feet where the pair of them stood, staring down at the priest's body.

"So what's the official story?"

"Homicidal priest. We had to take him down." His

body had returned to normal as if nothing had been out of order at all. The only thing visible to show any sign of deterioration in his mental health were the cuts on his arms.

"He was crazy," Richard added with a nod.

"Thanks for sticking with me." Kelly turned to her partner. "Without you I'd be toast."

"Anytime." He waved his hand.

"Come on. I'm sure your wife is wondering where you are."

He nodded and turned. "Yeah I reckon so."

"By the way,"

"Yeah?"

"Have you always had that streak of grey in your hair?"

ALICE J. BLACK

Alice lives and works in the North East of England with her partner and slightly ferocious cats! Alice has always enjoyed writing from being a child when she used to carry notebooks and write stories no matter where she went. She would be the girl in the corner scribbling away while everything went on around her. She writes all manner of fiction with a tendency to lean towards the dark side.

Dreams and sleep-talking are currently a big source of inspiration and her debut novel, The Doors, is a young adult novel which originally came from a dream several years ago. Several of her short stories have been included in anthologies with Burning Willow Press, Dark Chapter Press and JEA and she is always working on more. When she's not writing, she always has a book attached to her hand and will read from whatever genre suits her that day.

www.facebook.com/alice.j.black.doors

@alicejblack

https://alicejblack.wordpress.com/

JUST EVENTIDE

DAN WEATHERER

One second Joel was there, the next he wasn't. It makes no more sense twenty-nine years later than it did back then, and I was there: I saw the whole thing unfold before me. Pity then the multitude of police officers, doctors and psychiatrists, who tried (and failed) to understand that which falls outside the realms of conventional wisdom. I told no lies that day, and I'll tell none now. Facts are facts, no matter their origin, and the truth behind the disappearance of Joel, despite how fanciful my tale, needs to be told—if not for your benefit, then mine.

My hometown Chellton hides a wealth of secrets and not all of them pleasant. This is an uncomfortable though necessary truth; one that I came to grasp many years later, having finally broken free of her grasp, free to put down fresh roots elsewhere. Only now am I able to shrug aside the naivety of childhood, and revisit those times free from nostalgia's taint.

I need not try hard to recall, for there it was, laid bare before me, the grotesque truth of it all, plain as day to relive, yet impossible to fully comprehend.

I saw what was, as it was. Free from the fancy of imagination, free from the power of suggestion by those authority figures that *thought* they had understood the events of that day.

It's almost laughable; how could they ever truly understand?

For years, the memory of that day just wasn't a part of

my life or a part of my thinking. It lay boxed, dormant, almost hidden away, like the gun in the attic of my grandfather's house; he knows it's there, and I know it's there, but if we don't mention it, if we don't think about it, then it's not there at all.

Denial can be a wonderful thing. How I long for those days now.

Stripped of its mental camouflage, there are truths that I can no longer ignore. Memories of a childhood spent in the small market town are, despite my best efforts, invariably tainted. Their innocence, long swallowed by the shadows cast by an unending misery that continuously blighted the town, and of which we only vaguely acknowledged in passing. The forces at play within the town demanded respect that we were unwilling (or unable) to show.

Perhaps that is why we suffered so?

You might argue that it was up to our parents to shield us from its reach? That they ought to have done more? That they ought to have done *something?*

Easier said than done, for to understand the truths that haunt Chellton, they first need to be feared.

Before I delve into the meat of my story, I think it only proper that I introduce myself. My name is Matthew Barnes. I'm a chartered accountant who has done moderately well for himself, in that I am comfortably well-off, own my home, drive a decent car, and can look forward to a couple of holidays a year. I've a wife, Charlotte, who has weathered my storm for nigh on twenty years, and we've raised a daughter together, Ellie, who left for university last September. I'm not worried about her, she's a bright, well- adapted young woman. She'll do well; as a family, we have all achieved in our chosen fields.

So, with the tedium of middle age looming (I've already purchased the sports car and had designs on an affair), I find my mind is preoccupied with my past, and the occurrences that shaped both it (and me). For the purposes of this story, think of me not as the man who devoted his adult life to the study of numbers and the ingratitude of his clients; think of me as a boy of eleven, who still believes that there is such a thing as magic, and that the world is ripe with adventure. This is how I think of myself when the grind of daily life becomes a burden, and the shadows of Chellton's truth threaten to overwhelm me. This is how I cope with his memory.

It is important that I begin by describing the geography of the town in which I grew up, and the surrounding countryside, for I believe the environment may have been somehow conducive to the unfortunate events that blighted our small community. Now, that might seem an odd assumption to make, but you will see that Chellton was a unique town in many ways; ways that only became apparent to me after I had left.

If Chellton were to be viewed from above (as is possible nowadays via drones and satellites etc.) it would appear to resemble a teardrop in shape, in that the layout of the town is somewhat dictated by the mass of woodland which surrounds it. At its thinnest point, it takes forty-five minutes to walk from one side to the other. The trees (I'm not an expert on Dendrology!) grow tall here; they grow thick too: thicker than any forest I've visited since, and as my wife is a keen walker, we've visited many. It could be the sunniest day of the year; the rest of the county might be recording record high temperatures, but if you are in the forests that surround Chellton, you'll see little of the sun and feel its heat even less.

The forests were a magical place to a boy like me; filled with untold promise, mystery and danger.

Danger—that word never bothered me then.

We heard it said all of the time. The teachers at school would lecture us on things not to do, a lecture to be repeated later that same night by parents. They, having read the letter sent by the school but weary from the day's chores, would then launch into their version, the message largely the same, only delivered half-heartedly. We were often warned that the woods were dangerous and that we weren't to go there, but to me, therein lay the appeal.

There is only one road into and out of Chellton. The A672 dissects the forest at its thickest part and carves its way into the heart of town. In the winter, when the snow is particularly bad, the road was often closed, and we'd be isolated from the outside world for days at a time. This was ideal for the older kids, who, as there was no High School in town, needed to be bussed out to various schools in neighbouring villages. A closed road meant a day off school. I don't ever remember completing a full winter term at St. Benedicts such was the severity of winter back then.

Anyway, one road in and out can't be good for a town for a number of different reasons, never mind England's temperamental climate. It's clear now that the town suffered in terms of growth and rejuvenation. We had few in the way of small businesses, but we got by, mostly ignorant as to what we were missing out on with regards to the rest of the country. Looking back, it was almost as though time had passed Chellton by.

Case in point: The estate that I grew up on was the first and only new build that I can recall in twenty years. There was talk of a second build, and they did get as far as clearing land, but nothing else happened. Heavy machinery came and went. Piles of bricks lay shrink-wrapped for weeks before it became apparent that the builders were not coming back, and the houses were not going to get built. (I think almost everyone in town took away at least a wheelbarrow full of bricks after that; I recall building a modest sized fort in the back garden with the ones my father liberated).

I do remember that there was a sense of trepidation hanging over the entire project, and the feel was that the people of Chellton didn't want it to go ahead. The friction that the creation of our estate had caused was felt throughout most of my childhood (for reasons I will touch upon later). There were many times I fell asleep *willing* the new build to happen, so that attention might be drawn away from our estate, and we might be accepted by the community as a whole, joining as one in the face of this new, outside threat.

Outside threat? What outside threat?

Reading that back, it seems ridiculous to say now, let alone think, but that was how we (and the rest of the estate) were seen when we moved into *The Willows*.

It was a stigma that I unknowingly battled against the entire time I lived in Chellton. Granted, I did little to help my case (in some respects), but I was a child, and as a child, I should be afforded the right to make mistakes.

Back to describing Chellton and its quirks: the town had two churches, one ornate, the other not. One boasted a highly decorated spire that reached for heavens; it was the tallest structure I'd see until I visited London many years later. The other, a modest tower, flat and unassuming, content to meet God half way. Both shared the same name. That always struck me as odd, and I could never fathom as to why two churches, both of which lay directly opposite one another and were built at around the same time, would share a name. I can only assume there was a severe case of one-upmanship at play between the two religions; you only need to look at their delivery of the Lord's Prayer: one congregation going to the length of adding an extra line of praise, intending to appease God more than *those* across the road.

So silly.

I'm sure he/she hasn't the time nor the inclination to get involved in such trivialities. If he/she were to, they'd be no God of mine.

As a historical market town, the town square remained as the hub, meaning that on every Wednesday and Saturday, no matter the weather, stalls would be set. There would be an assortment of meats, fruits, cheeses and homewares on offer, all modestly priced. If I passed the square on market day, I'd see the same procession of villagers, each purchasing more or less the same thing they did the week before, recycling similar pleasantries beneath a sky that threatened rain.

The town had two primary schools: the Catholic school St. Luke's, and the Church of England school, Springbank. Much like their respective religions, the two were almost continually at war. It was harmless stuff, mostly; stone throwing, name calling, the occasional organised scrap. Just your general roughhousing, or so our parents called it. I'll admit to enjoying my fair share of fights; nothing feels better to a young boy than the comradery of a cause worth raising a fist for.

At eleven, as mentioned earlier, we were bussed out to high schools in the surrounding area. This meant that a lot of childhood friendships were broken, when, tired of the wars of old, parents would send their children to schools further away, where it was believed the battles of the past would be forgotten. Of course, this was not so, and they resumed as furious as ever, only this time with a different school. (Children, much as their adult counterparts, will always find something to disagree over, whether it be territory or the colour of your blazer).

Chellton also played host to the last of the doomed *Save and Shop* chain of supermarkets that went bust in the early nineties, though I swear our branch somehow stayed open until ninety-eight. It might be that it was privately bought out, and continued to trade under the same name, but it's also possible that it was overlooked during the closure process, and was subsequently forgotten about.

I remember it sold little other than the most basic of household supplies. The brand packaging was a plain white with bold, military-type font detailing in as few words as possible, the contents within. It didn't matter if you were eating *Save and Shop* bread or cornflakes—it was highly likely that the packaging tasted better.

As for local industry, most of the men farmed or worked at the Terbutt's Tractors factory on the edge of town. The women cooked, cleaned and gossiped. The days of gender equality was still several years from reaching Chellton.

There was little else of note: a Pharmacy, which I remember as a haven of hush and folded cardboard packets. Then there was the video shop, stocked with the latest three-year-old releases (that were new to us), the Doctor's surgery with its ever-packed waiting room and constant whiff of Elastoplast. The town had three public houses (that were good for a pint and a fight), two public parks (with broken play equipment) and a winding, muddied brook which wove between *The Willows* and the rest of the town, a natural incision (though easily jumpable), further separating us on the estate from the regular residents of Chellton.

All the pieces that comprise a town were present, only ours were grossly outdated, or warped in such a peculiar way as to appear odd to those passing through, yet perfectly normal to those who chose to call Chellton their home.

My friend, Joel, hadn't had the best of times during his ten years of life. His family were known locally as one of the poorest; his home one of the more rundown properties on the already unkempt *Brookfall Estate*. When he was three, his mother had left him and his brother to the care of his father. At the age of six, his father, under the strain of mounting debt, had committed suicide, choosing to hang himself from a beam in a neighbour's shed. Under a cloud of animosity, Joel's mother had returned home to look after him and his brother. His brother drowned a year later, falling through the ice at *Dilling's Lake*.

Perpetually malnourished, and afflicted with long-sightedness (which I believed to be a super-power, and would constantly call upon him to use), Joel soon caught the attention of the town's bullies. Marcus and I did all we could to take him under our wing, but we couldn't be with him 24/7. Though he was a quiet sort, he had a sharp sense of humour and was fiercely intelligent; it's a shame that few outside of our friendship ever got to see it.

Looking back, it's clear to me now, that I saw Joel as the little brother I never had. I often wonder how our friendship would have developed through high school and beyond, had it ever have been given a chance to do so.

Marcus, on the other hand, had everything that I ever wanted as a child. Doting parents pandered to his every whim, and he could be counted on to own the latest must-have toy. More than that, they encouraged him to dare to dream, and regardless of the trouble he often found himself in (and led us into), he'd rarely be punished to the degree that Joel and I would inevitably suffer at the hands of our parents.

Marcus was a born leader. He was boundlessly enthusiastic and charismatic. He could convince you to march into the depths of Hell, that lad, and you'd know without needing to look, that he'd be stood right at your side, regardless of the adversity before you. It was his childhood wish to join the army, and often our games would be centred around his interest. He'd take us out on patrols of the neighbourhood, instruct us in the ways of guerrilla warfare (his version) and have us build a variety of bases around the town, each stocked with an array of sticks and a large pile of rocks, *'just in case'*. I can't remember a time (save for school) where his face wasn't caked in mud (or camoed up, as he referred to it).

We lost touch shortly after I left Chellton and, despite several attempts to contact him since, I've received no response. Lord only knows what he is doing with himself these days; Joel's disappearance hit him hard. His last words to me, slurred by the effects of our marathon drinking session, were that *'he should have done more'*.

More of what?

That question has haunted me on many a sleepless night. I'd tried to make him see Joel's disappearance as a senseless tragedy, one which we could never hope to understand fully, yet no amount of reasoning would get him to see otherwise. He blamed himself, and for a long time, I let him do so. I maintain that nothing he or I could have done differently would have prevented what happened to Joel, save for us venturing into the woods in the first place.

It was the height of summer, though it always seemed to be so whenever I recall a happy childhood memory. Logic dictates that we spend most of our time as children, holed up in the classroom, bored and restless, our attention wandering from the topic of the day, to thoughts of how best to spend the evening or weekend. It is the time spent free of authority that I recall most fondly, as I suspect, do you.

The summer holidays then; six weeks of unbridled freedom, surely the best times of our young lives! Father was at work (Father was always at work, and even when he came home, he shut himself away in the backroom occupying himself with yet more work), and Mother, well her domain was the kitchen, meaning I was free to pass the days however I saw fit. That is by no means meant as a sexist remark; my mother seemed to live her life in that cramped kitchen. If she wasn't cooking, she was cleaning, and if she wasn't cleaning she was sharing a pot of tea with Mrs Flannwell from next door. My activities were the least of my parents' concern, and I admit that I preferred it that way: I didn't want to end up like Miles Wolloughy.

Miles Wolloughy was a boy from my class, and his parents interfered in every aspect of his life. Every morning he'd present our teacher with a fresh note, detailing the how's and why's of something or other that he wasn't allowed to do that day. The poor lad had to observe childhood from the sidelines. He *wanted* to play, and we asked him to join us several times, but the one and only time he did, his parents found out, and he received such a beating that he never dared risk a game with us again.

It's a strange way to parent; that's for sure. I'm almost certain they did him more harm than any of our childhood japes may have.

I digress. It was a Tuesday, and the holidays were drawing to a close. September was on the horizon and with it the dread of a return to school. We'd exhausted most of our favourite pastimes, having partaken in numerous games of football, manhunt, and *British Bulldog*. Boredom threatened, and this was something I was adamant I would not allow; holidays were for holidaying. There was enough time for boredom when we returned to the monotony of the classroom.

There'd been a murder-suicide on our estate, the

previous weekend. A middle-aged couple, long-time married, polite and unassuming, had been found dead, their throats slashed. The town had pointed the finger at him when it ought to have pointed at her. Again, these sorts of events happened frequently in Chellton, and while we weren't in any way shocked by what had happened, we were all too aware, having gone to see the house for ourselves. Expecting to see police tape stretched over the doors and windows, we had left disappointed; the house appeared ordinary in every way. The only thing that might have hinted at anything untoward was that the curtains remained closed during the day. (Marcus later accused me several times of leading them to the wrong house).

We were sat, Joel, Marcus and I, in a semi-circle on a patch of wasteland at the bottom of my street that we had named *The Green*. It was here we played most our games, and though it was little more than a snatch of uneven, mismatched turf, it was (or so we liked to think) ours.

It was I who suggested the idea: "How about we go into the woods?"

Joel's face immediately displayed his distaste. "I'm not allowed into the woods," he lied.

Marcus: "Why do you wanna go in there anyway?"

At least I had Marcus hooked. I knew it would be easy to get Joel onside, should Marcus swallow my story. If Marcus and I went, then Joel would surely follow.

"I wanna go hunting tree sprites," I replied.

Joel groaned.

"What the hell are tree sprites?" asked Marcus, his face twisting in confusion.

Now, I can't lay claim as to the origins of the tree sprite story; this is yet another of those tales heard in passing. The identity of the storyteller whom I heard it from is long forgotten, only the details of the tale remain.

From their reactions to my suggestion, it was clear that Joel knew what was coming (having heard me discuss tree sprites before), but Marcus did not.

"Tree sprites! You mean to say you never heard of tree sprites?" I toyed.

"No!" shouted Marcus, his patience wearing thin. "So are you gonna stop dicking about and tell me?"

I leant inwards, Marcus and Joel did likewise, and with my voice barely a whisper, I began to recite the tale as once told to me.

'There were once three children; two brothers and one sister, who lived in a farmhouse on the land that Chellton would later be built upon. The brothers were aged twelve and ten; the sister much younger at four years of age. It might seem cruel now, but with their parents barely able to feed their children, never mind themselves, they were all set to work in the fields.

'One year, they encountered an unseasonably hot summer, and their crops withered and died. Then, in mocking contrast, came a winter like no other; cold beyond cold, with snowfall several feet deep, making travel impossible, isolating the family from the nearest village.

'Supplies soon ran out, and with both food and money scarce, the father (at the mother's bequest, might I add) led their three children into the woods, with promises of rabbit broth that night, still ringing in their ears. When the eldest boy questioned as to why his father carried an axe and an empty sack, the father merely replied: "So that I may slay, and eat."

'Four figures entered the forest that day.

'Only one returned.

'The father, with his axe slung over one shoulder, crying tears of remorse that froze upon his wind-beat cheeks, dragged behind him the sack, no longer empty, leaving a bloodied trail that enticed all manner of woodland creatures from their burrows, with its warm, coppery scent.

'It is said that the spirits of the slain children haunt the woods and that, if you listen carefully, you can sometimes catch the laughter *of the little girl, carrying on the breeze.'*

"It's not true," said Joel, his voice hoarse, his throat tight with fear. "My mum said it's all just a load of bull-crap."

"I never said it was true," I replied. "I'm just telling you what I heard."

Now, Joel might have appeared dismissive, but I knew that he feared the forest, and not only because of the story I had just shared. Truth is, a couple of kids older than us had gone missing a few years ago; one of them was Joel's cousin.

"The forest is dangerous; it's riddled with caves and potholes. There's no such thing as tree sprites." He said, desperately trying to convince us that we ought to share his fear.

"What else do they do then?" asked Marcus, his interest piqued. "I mean apart from laugh? Laughing isn't scary; not to me, anyway."

"Ah, there's more," I began, my confidence growing as I began to relish in my role as storyteller. "You know that feeling when you are being watched in the woods, but there's no one else around?"

"Yeah?" nodded Marcus, his eyes wide, his attention, mine.

"That's them watching you. Deciding whether they want to play with you," I whispered.

"No way?" gasped Marcus.

"He's making it up!" shouted Joel, pulling his knees into his chest. "It's all bull-crap, my mum said so."

"And then what?" asked Marcus.

I knew then that I had him, hook, line and sinker. I couldn't stop. I couldn't help myself, I kept on with the story, creating fiction and passing it off as truth.

Perhaps I ought to have left it be.

Perhaps then we wouldn't have gone so gamely into the woods.

But I didn't leave it be.

"And then… well, if they want to play with you, they do. But you can't ever leave them. Not ever. Because they are trapped in the woods, and so are you. For all eternity."

"Bull-crap," mumbled Joel, from behind his knees. "Stop it, now."

"How do you know if they want to play with you?" asked Marcus, intrigued.

"They call your name," I replied, my imagination working overtime. "But only you can hear it, nobody else. They'll look at you like you are mad if you tell them what you can hear. They'll call you a liar, but to you, it's as clear as day."

"Can you see them?"

Joel is sobbing. His shoulders heave. His face is buried in his knees. We both ignore him.

"No, no one ever has. They can disguise themselves as tree bark, or leaves, or sticks and mud." I'm excited now, talking fast and gesticulating with my hands. "You could be right next to one, and you'd never even know. One could be leaning against a tree right next to you; you'd not even see him. And he'd reach out and yank on your hood, or cause you to trip, and you'd never know what happened, but you'd hear them laughing."

"Really?" asked Marcus, blinking profusely.

"Really," I replied, satisfied with my performance. Marcus had believed every detail, even the ones I'd added on the fly. I'd sold him an adventure for the day, and even if we went into the forest and found nothing (which, of course, is precisely what we *would* find), the day would still be charged with anticipation. That, to me, was a day well spent.

"Right. We're going then," began Marcus, standing as he spoke. "And we're going to make a night of it."

I stood, excited at the possibilities ahead, and then

paused, a sudden lump in my throat. "What do you mean by '*make a night of it*'?"

"Exactly that! I've a tent I've been dying to try out. I used it in the garden a couple of times, but it's not the same as a real camp out. It'll fit us all in, no problem. I'll go and fetch it, along with a few supplies: water, chocolate, a torch, things like that." He pointed at Joel and I. "You two go and get what you need: crisps, something to drink, sleeping bags or a blanket. Oh, and bring a couple of comics in case we get bored."

I stared at him, my mouth agog.

"Now, please. I wanna get up there as soon as possible. The sooner we start looking for the tree sprites, the sooner we'll find them!"

He turned away and headed towards his house; his parting words carried on the breeze: "Man, can you just imagine what the others at school will say when we tell them that we saw tree sprites?"

I looked at Joel, who was sat on the ground with his face still hidden behind his knees. Now, I'll be the first to admit that I was desperate to go into the woods that day, just for something to do, and when my mind was set on something, it was set for good. What I hadn't considered during my fantastical rendition of the tale of the tree sprites, was that Marcus would want to stay the night. Nobody ever stayed the night in those woods, at least I'd never heard of such a feat, and I was reluctant to do so. However, if I voiced my concern to Marcus, it was highly probable he'd never take on board any idea of mine, ever again, and I was beginning to grow sick and tired of his army games. I admit that it felt good to wield a degree of influence over our group, and I didn't wish to undermine my position by admitting how afraid I was over spending the night camped in the forest.

So, what did I do?

It shames me to admit, but I turned to Joel, ignored his pleas, and projected my cowardice onto him, just like all weak-minded boys do.

You know by now that Joel accompanied us into the woods. Reluctant though he was, I privately assured him that there was nothing to fear, even going so far as to admit to adding my own dose of fiction to the story and that I'd look after him, never letting him out of my sight.

It'll be fun, I said. *An adventure to tell the other kids at school about. Just think, they'll think you are cool and brave, staying out here for the night. Maybe they'll go easy on you at playtime?*

Of course, to keep up the pretence with Marcus, I hammered home the truth of my fiction at every given opportunity, cruelly shooting down Joel whenever he'd try to convince Marcus that I was lying—belittling him, just like all the other children did to him at school.

Each of us had fed our parents a lie as to where we would be spending the night. I said I'd be camping at Marcus's, and Marcus said he'd be watching videos at my house. Joel didn't say anything; he didn't need too: his mother barely noticed his absence as it was.

And so later that afternoon, the three of us hiked into the heart of the woods with the intention of staying until the following morning, hoping to capture the sight of a fictional tree sprite or two.

We'd made camp. How deep into the woods were we? I couldn't possibly say. It was the first clearing we'd found after a grueling thirty minutes' walk—here was as good a place as any. Though there existed a few, well-worn tracks used by ramblers and dog walkers, Marcus opted to steer clear of them, citing that *'tree sprites would no doubt lurk deeper*

in the forest, away from noise and dog shit'.

The tent was eventually pitched after much arguing. We even had a fire, started courtesy of Marcus having stolen a bottle of lighter fluid and a half-empty box of *England's Glory* matches. It was up to me to collect the twigs for the fire, a task that I delegated to Joel, hoping it would tire him enough to forget about his complaining.

"Well, would you rather be here, or home with your mother?" I'd asked, having pulled him to one side, spite lacing my words. I'll never forget the look on his face; one of complete surrender. He didn't want to admit to me that he didn't want to go home. How awful must it have been for him, that the forest was the lesser of two evils?

I felt for him at that moment, as I do now, but, young and foolish that I was, I refused to act on my instinct to pack up camp, and head back to my house. I genuinely would have preferred us all to stay there, safe in my back garden, safe to make up more bull-crap ghost stories without fear of reprisal, but I was a stubborn so 'n so, and I didn't want to seem weak in front of Marcus.

Now I'm not saying that I ever believed the stories of the tree sprites to be true, but being in the forest where they were set after dark—that puts a whole new perspective on your beliefs, and things that appear ludicrous in the light of day, seem entirely plausible in the dark of night.

It was late. Darkness weighed upon us; the air chilled us to our cores as we sat huddled around the fire, each lost in thought, our minds wandering from one deliberation to the next.

Marcus, buoyed by my earlier attempt at storytelling, had endeavoured to recite a ghost story of his own making. Joel had pleaded with him to stop, before retreating deep into his sleeping bag, pulling the drawstrings tight, thereby sealing him into his polyester tomb, save for a tiny air hole where the string would tighten no further.

Marcus, fuelled by Joel's reaction, continued unabated.

I yelled at him to stop.

Whether it was the shock of my outburst that silenced him, or the glint of fear in my eyes, I'll likely never know. Marcus never did finish his story.

And so, we sat, absorbed by the dance of the flames, neither boy speaking to the other, wishing for the break of dawn.

The sound of snapping branches was enough to rouse us from our thoughts. We exchanged furtive glances, before standing, and turning our attention to the shadows that haunted the perimeter of our camp.

For a time, there was no sound; no rustle of trees, nor moan of the wind, and all was still.

Then, a cacophony of yells, sudden and angry; followed by the sounds of more branches snapping, and Craig Humphries and Darren Worthing, thundered from the shadows and into our camp, frightening the life out of us.

Craig and Darren were teenagers. They attended one of the out of town high schools; I wasn't sure which, but both were known locally as troublemakers and bullies. Craig was the only black kid in Chellton, and he'd had it tough growing up, suffering regular beatings until he grew big and confident enough to start handing them out himself. Darren was his constant companion. At nearly six feet tall (and almost as wide, at least to my eyes) he was an imposing sight. Together, the two of them were near-on untouchable. Having them gate-crash our camp meant that we were to become the target of their amusement for however long they deemed fit, and there was absolutely nothing we could say or do to change that.

In the chaos, Marcus had fled into the woods (a reaction that took me by surprise) with Craig giving chase half-heartedly, disappearing into the murk, only to return empty-handed seconds later.

"Let the fucker run," spat Craig, picking his way back through the tangle of tree roots and grasses. "He'll not get far. Likely piss his pants and come back here, begging for us to go easy on him." His eyes narrowed on Joel and I. "Besides, we've these two pussies to play with."

Darren snorted, and shoved me hard in the back. I fell to my knees, my face inches from the fire.

Craig laughed.

Darren did likewise.

Joel began to cry.

"Aww. Does the lil' babby want his mommy?" cooed Craig. "Do you want your dum-dums?"

Darren laughed again.

From my place in the dirt, I watched Joel ball his fists. His breath came quicker, and his torso stiffened. He became larger somehow, his physique disregarding the malnourished form it was supposed to represent. He reached past me, reached *into* the fire and grabbed hold of one of the thicker logs we'd thrown onto the pile. In one fluid motion (and with a scream of rage that I'd never heard uttered by a person before, nor since), Joel withdrew the log from the fire and brought it crashing down onto Craig's right arm.

The *SNAP* was almost deafening. To this day, I'm not sure whether it was the sound of the branch breaking, Craig's shattered Radius, or both.

Craig cried out in surprise and pain, clutching his arm instinctively, withdrawing it to his body, as Joel drew back and prepared to strike his other arm. Darren, though slow to react at first, took a step towards Joel, just as Marcus dove from the bushes, his war cry lost among the furore, and tackled Darren mid-step, forcing him to the ground.

Joel, shaken by events, dropped the burning log, and backed away from the melee. I rushed towards Marcus eager to help, as he was struggling to keep Darren pinned.

Craig sat. His mouth hung open and tears streamed down his cheeks. He watched motionlessly as the two of us wrestled Darren back to the ground. Joel, stood opposite, slowly backed towards the gloom of the camp's perimeter. He was trying to say something to me; his lips were moving rapidly, but I couldn't hear his voice over the sound of my pulse thumping in my ears.

He was crying again, pointing towards something behind me.

And then the laughter surrounded us, insistent and churlish. I stopped trying to contain Darren, who shrugged me aside as if I was a leaf caught on his coat. Marcus tumbled quickly after. Craig stopped sobbing, as did Joel. Everyone scanned the surrounding trees for signs of life.

There was no snapping of branches, no sounds of movement, but still the laughter came, growing in chorus, raising in volume. Marcus looked at me, and I at him. Darren clambered to his feet and began to back towards Craig, who, in turn, climbed gingerly to his feet, his injured arm hanging limply by his side.

The fire flickered momentarily before extinguishing completely.

Joel cried out my name. It hung in the air for an impossible length of time, before fading into silence, becoming one with the stillness of the night.

With the help of a couple of torches, the four of us stumbled through the darkness as best we were able, hoping to find a trace of Joel. Even Craig, injured and in pain, joined the search, and though neither of us dared venture far, for fear of befalling a similar fate to Joel, of him we found no sign.

When we recounted our story back in town, we were labelled as liars. Joel's mother accused us of being in cahoots; saying that we'd somehow devised a plot to kill her boy, and then concocted a *'cock and bull story'* to make sure that no one took the fall.

I told her that Joel was better off away from her.

She slapped my face.

I feel the sting of her open palm whenever I think back to that day.

I wasn't allowed to play with Marcus after that. Darren and Craig were also split up. Last I heard, Craig moved away, and Darren was put into a Young Offenders Unit for assaulting a girl of ten.

The provocation for the attack? She had laughed at him.

There's not a day goes by that I don't think about Joel. I often wonder if we'd have made it out of Chellton together, and remained friends thereafter? I like to think that would have been the case. But whatever happened to him that night, boy or not, I know that I failed him.

And I'm sorry, Joel.

DAN WEATHERER

Dan lives in Staffordshire, where is married to his wife Jenni and is a (proud) full-time dad to his daughter Bethany, and his son Nathan.

Although an award-winning film-maker and an accomplished playwright, Dan's passion for books is evident in his output.

Completed novels *The Underclass* and *The Tainted Isle* are currently with his agent. Expect to see *The Dead Stage*, a book detailing Dan's experiences as a novice playwright appear via Crystal Lake Publishing in 2018.

Visit www.danweatherer.com for more information about Dan and his work.

AN EYE FOR AN EYE

DAWN CANO

Say what you want about me, but before you pass judgement, know that my heart was in the right place, despite my methods being a little, how should I say this— unorthodox.

My name is Christa, and I killed two people. Surprisingly, I still have a few friends, which is strange, considering what I used to do in my spare time. By day, I am, well, I was, a veterinarian. I saved the lives of animals, all day, every day. I had patients ranging from newborn puppies and kittens to a parrot that is almost seventy-five-years-old. Everything I did was for the animals and I put so much time, effort, and money into my career, that I never bothered starting a family. Besides, given my current situation, no man would ever want me.

You see, I'm currently sitting in a Texas women's prison, serving out a life sentence for murder. Before you stop reading, let me explain.

Two years into my career as a vet, I realized, more than ever before, that animal cruelty was on the rise. Texas, true to form, never seemed to strengthen its animal cruelty laws, and more often than not, offenders would get off with nothing more than a slap on the wrist. With each case of unpunished animal abuse I heard on the news or read about on the internet, I became more disgusted and outraged.

I remember it like it was yesterday. Halloween night, 2014. Sitting at home after a long and complicated surgery on a female English bulldog that was having a tough labor.

She started haemorrhaging and her heart rate fell sharply, so I had no choice but to operate before it was time. All of her puppies died, except for one, but I saved her. After a long and gruelling day, I picked up some Chinese takeout and headed home to unwind.

As was the norm for me, I dropped my keys off on the table next to the front door and switched on the television, setting my food on the coffee table. I kicked off my shoes and walked to the fridge to grab a cold beer. I sat in silence on the couch, eating and sipping my beer, numbly watching the weatherman drone on about how an approaching cold front brought with it a slight chance of snow the following week. The weatherman issued a warning to all residents of north-central Texas to bring in their plants and animals, as the temperature was expected to dip into the twenties with the cold front—a rare occurrence in Texas in late-October.

When the weather concluded, I ignored the following commercials as I finished my dinner, still thinking about Bella, the English bulldog. The final news story of the evening was about keeping pets safe on Halloween.

It's a little late for that, I thought, as it was already ten-thirty on Halloween night, but I listened to the story, just the same.

"Veterinarians and the Dallas Humane Society recommend keeping all pets indoors this Halloween. Black cats are especially vulnerable tonight, so if you have a cat, or any pet, keep it safe by keeping it inside," the perky news anchor finished.

I shut off the TV and made my way into the bedroom, where I undressed and climbed into bed. I remember nothing else until the next morning.

The next day, Friday, I awoke to my alarm buzzing at the usual five-thirty am. I wiped the sleep from my eyes and stumbled my way into the kitchen to start a pot of coffee. Once I turned on the coffee maker, I went into the bathroom to take a shower.

I dressed, made my way back to the kitchen, and poured myself the first of three cups of coffee. I switched on my tablet and headed over to Facebook, where I was immediately hit with a story of a black cat found dead a couple of miles from my home. Apparently, the cat died when a couple of teenagers filled its anus with firecrackers and lit them, essentially blowing up its insides. The teens were arrested and held at the Tarrant County Jail in Ft. Worth, awaiting arraignment.

At that time, I could do nothing but shake my head at the complete lack of respect for life. Even if it was *just* a cat, so what? That cat could have been a child's favorite pet. Maybe it was the only pet an old woman could have in her retirement community. Even if it were a stray or feral cat, animals have feelings. They feel pain. They don't understand things the way you or I do.

After looking at my newsfeed for a little while longer, I shut down my tablet, grabbed my keys, and headed out the door, on my way to the clinic. I had a feeling it was going to be a long day, and I was right.

The minute I got to work, I was informed by one of the vet techs that my partner, Dr. Jerry Goldman, had been called out. He had a death in the family and I was to take on his workload, or reschedule his appointments. Not wanting to make any worried pet parents more stressed out by having to reschedule their pets' appointments, I saw the sick pets, and rescheduled those who only needed immunizations or check-ups.

As the day wore on, one of my patients was Witchy, a sweet and adorable two-year-old black cat. Her parents loved her, but she truly belonged to the couple's four-year-old daughter, Layla. Layla was autistic and took the cat's illness harder than the rest of the family.

With a little digging, I found out that Witchy caught and ate part of a bird the day before. Witchy's problems began later that night and I ended up performing surgery on Witchy to remove a bone that had become lodged in her throat. When I took Witchy away, Layla sobbed and repeatedly called her name as she tried to follow me to the back of the clinic. I promised the little girl that Witchy would be okay and that she could visit as soon as her "friend" was out of surgery.

As I operated on Layla's pet, I imagined the damage done to the cat killed the previous night by the ruthless teens. The fear in the cat's eyes, the thoughts racing through its head as it tried to get away. The more I thought about it, the angrier I became.

Fucking little cowards have to prey on an innocent animal that can't fight back.

I hope they spend years in jail for this shit.

Yeah, right. Their parents will go into court and strike up a deal with the judge. They'll probably not even get community service.

How would those little fuckheads like to have firecrackers shoved in their asses…

That's when it hit me.

If there is serious injury, you are to take life for life, eye for eye, tooth for tooth, hand for hand, foot for foot, burn for burn, wound for wound, bruise for bruise. Exodus 21:23-25

Before that day, I was a firm believer that violence should not be used to solve any problem. I don't know what made that Friday any different, but I think I felt something in my mind snap. If the criminal justice system wouldn't do anything about animal abusers, I would.

I finished the day at the clinic at around nine, and stopped by a convenience store to pick up a sandwich and some chips. I wasn't hungry, but I had planning to do and I needed to keep my strength up to figure out what needed to be done.

I went home and threw my food on the kitchen table,

grabbed my tablet, a piece of paper and a pen, and sat down next to the sandwich. With a little digging, and since arrest records are public record in Texas, it wasn't hard to find out the identities of the teens who had killed the cat. As I suspected would be the case, they were both out of jail, awaiting trial.

The teens, brothers, lived just three blocks from me, so getting to them wasn't a problem. I just needed a way to get them away from their house. Lucky for me, there was a park right across the street from where they lived, and that would do nicely.

I did some research on the internet to find a place that sold fireworks. Once that was done, I called my partner and told him I would be running a little late in the morning. I had to check out the park.

Once I had a game plan in mind, the sandwich and chips laying on the table looked a whole lot more appealing. I devoured both in under ten minutes, washed it down with a couple of beers, and went to bed. As I lay there, waiting for sleep to come for me, I realized I hadn't felt this good in a long time. Justice was about to be served.

The next morning was cold, sunny and windy. I put on my winter coat and gloves and walked the three blocks to the park. It was deserted, as I hoped it would be, and as long as the weather stayed cold, it would remain relatively deserted, save for a few brave dog walkers. I walked into the park, and ventured deeper, into the area surrounded by trees. I found two trees close enough together to serve my purpose. All I needed to work out was how to lure the kids away from their home.

I realize the above text makes it seem like I enjoyed doing what I did, and part of me did. The other part wondered how I had become so callous and uncaring as to take two boys away from their parents. As I was about to give up the ridiculous notion of getting revenge for the animal that was killed, images flashed through my mind of how incredibly terrified the cat must have been, and my anger returned.

I went to work and spent the whole day figuring out how to get the kids to the park. After the clinic closed, I made up an excuse about not feeling well and went home to gather my supplies. Once in the house, I went to the closet and pulled out some rope, a box cutter, an old bandanna, my gloves, a hammer, and a knife.

Since I left the clinic early, I had plenty of time to head over to the fireworks stand and purchase a package of fifty firecrackers. With my "tools" gathered, it was time to go to the park and set up.

I tied two long pieces of rope to each tree, a few inches off the ground, and set the rest of the supplies down a few feet away, behind another tree. I slowly made my way out of the park, trying to look as casual as possible, even though my heart felt like it would beat right out of my chest. My breathing increased and sweat formed on my forehead, but I think I managed to pull it off, as nobody looked at me in an odd or alarmed way.

I rounded the corner that would take me out of the wooded area, into the open field, and I couldn't believe my luck. There, in the park, kicking a soccer ball around, were the two boys. I immediately recognized them from the news reports and, in that instant, came up with a game plan. I approached the teens with a smile on my face.

"Hey, I know you guys. You're the ones on the news! The ones who killed that cat, right?"

The boys stopped playing and looked at me with trepidation in their eyes. They were expecting me to berate them for what they had done, but I had other ideas. Just as I approached, a cell phone started ringing. One of the boys reached into his pocket, pulled out his phone, and walked away from me. I continued my charade with the remaining teen.

"Dude! What you did to that fucking cat was awesome. I've hated those fuckers since I was a kid and one scratched the hell out of me. I wish I had the balls to do what you did!"

The kid smiled, and I knew then that I had him.

"Yeah, man. You should have heard him scream right before he died. It was fucking amazing. I've never heard an animal make those kinds of sounds before."

"What's your name, kid? I'm Marie."

"Brandon."

"Brandon, just between you and me, you inspired me to do something I've never done before. You should see what I've got tied up to a tree over there."

"Where?

"Over there, in that group of trees. I wish I could show you, but if you wander off, you'll probably get in trouble, huh? I don't want to get you into trouble with your folks, but this is so awesome! Ah, well, I guess I'll finish the job myself. It's been nice talking to you, but I guess I should be going. It'll be dark soon."

At that moment, I felt like a creepy paedophile trying to pick up little kids, but I didn't care. It was obvious that Brandon really wanted to see what I had done.

"Hey, I do what I want, so let's go. One thing though, if the cat is still alive, you have to let me help you."

I laughed. "Sure thing, man. It'll only take a few minutes, since I've done a number on it already. Dude, I ripped its fucking skin off."

Brandon looked shocked. "Seriously?"

"Yeah, come on! We don't have much time left before it dies, and I still have a couple of things planned."

I started walking, hearing Brandon's footsteps right behind me. I turned back to determine the whereabouts of his brother, and discovered he was nowhere to be seen.

As we got closer to the trees I set up, I slowed down, giving Brandon the opportunity to get ahead of me.

"Sorry, man. Keep going. I'm right behind you."

Brandon moved far enough ahead that he never saw me remove the hammer from the inside pocket of my coat. He never saw me raise it above my head and swing it to where it connected with the top of his skull. The next thing Brandon saw was black.

I'm not proud of what happened next, but in the end, I achieved my goal. After knocking Brandon unconscious, I dragged him a few feet further into the woods where I had the rope tied to the trees. I took off his shoes and pulled his pants and underwear around his ankles. Then, I tied him to the tree, face down. One rope around each wrist, and one around each ankle, giving me perfect access to his asshole. I shoved my bandanna in his mouth to keep him quiet.

I spread his ass cheeks and began inserting the firecrackers I bought, one at a time, packing as many in there as I could, fuses pointed out. His ass leaked blood and stretched out as I crammed in more than forty firecrackers, and when I was finished, I sat down against a tree and waited for him to wake up. The sun set, and there was a biting cold wind that helped speed up the process.

Brandon awoke with a start and immediately began struggling. It didn't take him long to realize that he wasn't going anywhere, so he stopped fighting and began to cry. For a moment, I felt sorry for him, and wondered if I should walk away and forget the whole thing. Then, he released a shriek that reminded me of what that poor cat must have sounded like at the end of its life.

There was Brandon, six inches off the ground, half naked and crying. Suddenly, I felt nothing.

"Did you ever think, for one fucking second, how that cat felt when you were torturing it? Do you understand that you might have taken the life of someone's pet? Does the phrase, 'an eye for an eye' mean anything to you?"

Brandon began fighting again, and as he stopped to

catch his breath, pissed himself. Since he was lying face down, a steady stream of urine splashed the dead grass beneath him. I can't explain why, but the sight made me laugh. Maybe now, he was feeling a little of the terror the cat felt right before this idiot killed it.

"Not so funny, is it, asshole?"

As I spoke, I heard another voice coming from the other side of the trees, calling Brandon's name. I had to act fast, or risk getting caught.

"This is the end of the line, son. I'm sorry it has to end this way for you, but since you showed no remorse for your actions, I took it upon myself to invoke your punishment. See you in hell."

Brandon began struggling against the ropes as I lit one of the firecrackers with a disposable lighter, and since they were packed so tightly together, it didn't take long for them all to catch. Each one exploded, sending the teen into a frantic frenzy to try to escape the pain. By the time the last one went off, Brandon was unconscious.

My attack made it on the ten o'clock news, but since I was careful and left no evidence behind, the authorities had no idea who could have committed such a heinous crime.

What I've failed to mention is that Brandon didn't die—at least not right away. When the firecrackers went off, they ruptured his colon, sending bacteria-filled shit coursing through his body. Although the doctors pumped him full of antibiotics to try to prevent an infection, Brandon died a few days later.

What a shame.

After that, life for me returned to normal, and I kept an eye open for other crimes against animals that took place around my neighborhood. All was quiet for a while, until one day, in early January, I saw a news report about a man who threw hot bacon grease on his pit bull because the dog wouldn't stop barking. The man was arrested for animal cruelty, but because he had no previous record, he was released on bail while he awaited trial. The dog survived, but lost both eyes in the attack.

I got especially excited when I heard this report, because the dog, Max, was a patient of mine. He was owned by an older man, Thomas Johnson, and I knew exactly where the piece of shit lived, since I'd made many house calls to the Johnson home in recent years. Johnson lived alone in a small, two-room house on the edge of town. Within seconds, I knew what I was going to do, and I knew it would be a lot of fun.

I went into the clinic early the next day before anyone else reported for work, and made my way to the back, where we kept the drugs and surgical equipment. I filled four large syringes with pancuronium, a neuromuscular paralytic, and grabbed a scalpel, putting everything in the computer bag I took with me every day to work. Having a firm plan in mind, I went on with my day, seeing patients as usual, but as the day wore on, my excitement grew.

I left the clinic at 6:15 and made my way to Johnson's house, on the other side of town. By the time I got there, it was dark, which made things a lot easier for me. I walked up to the front door and knocked. After a minute or so, the door slowly opened.

"Hi, doc." Thomas said to me, staring at the floor in front of him. At least he was ashamed of what he had done. If he expected to open the door to a friendly face, he was sadly mistaken, as he would soon discover.

"Thomas," I greeted coldly. "Let's talk. May I come in?"

"I... I'm not feeling real good, doc. Can we talk some other time. I just want to lay down."

"We need to talk now, Thomas. Let's go inside," I said as I pushed my way into his house.

I sat on the dingy tan sofa sitting against the left wall in the room. As usual, I sat on the right and Thomas sat on my left, which is exactly where he usually sits when I come over. It put him in the perfect position for me to carry out my plan.

"What happened, Thomas? You loved Max, didn't you? How could you do something so awful?"

Thomas continued crying, tears and snot running down his weathered face. "I don't know. He wouldn't shut up! He kept me awake the night before and every time I told him to be quiet, he just seemed to bark more. I was in the kitchen, making breakfast, and I was gonna share with him, like I always do, but—"

"But instead, you blinded a twelve-year-old dog with bacon grease? Did it ever occur to you that he might have been trying to tell you something? Maybe he was sick or in pain. Maybe he just wanted your attention!"

The old man sobbed. He leaned away from me to take a tissue out of the box on the end table, when I reached into my own pocket for one of the syringes. The drug I was about to give Thomas was a paralytic, meaning he would be awake and aware, but unable to move. That's exactly what I wanted. I wanted this scum to see everything that was about to happen to him.

As he sat up and turned to face me again, I stabbed the needle deep into the right side of his neck and pushed down the plunger. Thomas screamed, but shut up when I began speaking.

"How do you think Max felt when the one person he loved hurt him? How do you think his life will be now that he's blind? Not only has he lost his eyesight, he's lost the person who was supposed to always love him!"

The drug started working as I reached into my pocket for another syringe. This time, I stood in front of Thomas and stabbed the needle into the left side of his neck. I had given him enough to paralyze a two-hundred-pound mastiff, yet, this small man was still moving.

You have to be patient. If you rush this, you'll get careless, I thought. I took a deep breath as I stared into Thomas' face. I watched his muscles relax as the medicine took effect.

"Thomas, have you ever heard the expression, 'an eye for an eye'? I think it fits here, don't you? You took Max's eyesight from him as he's nearing the end of his life, and I think it's only fair that someone take yours."

I removed the scalpel from my pocket and watched Thomas for a reaction. Of course, the drugs had taken hold, so he couldn't do anything but stare at me with horror in his eyes. The fact that he felt remorse for what he had done didn't matter at all to me.

Scalpel in hand, I straddled Thomas, putting one knee on each side of his thighs. I'm not a large woman, but I seemed to easily contain the man in front of me. I pushed his head back and whispered in his ear, "This is for Max and all the other animals who are injured and killed by assholes like you."

I sat up and stabbed the tip of the scalpel into Max's left eyeball. It surprised me when the eyeball made a slight popping sound, similar to the noise a grape might make when stepped on. Pink fluid ran down the old man's face as I hacked away at his left eye, pulling it out in pieces. Thomas was fading fast, so once I was satisfied that he'd never see out of that eye again, I started on the right eye.

As I climbed off Thomas' lap, there was a knock at the door, and then a man's voice boomed, "Mr. Johnson, this is the police. Open up!"

I stayed silent, rooted to the spot in front of Thomas when the voice spoke again.

"Mr. Johnson, your neighbor called us and reported hearing a scream from this address. Open the door and let us know you're okay."

Silence.

"Mr. Johnson, you have until the count of three to open this door or we're coming in!"

I looked around the small house, and soon realized there was no way out. No back door, no basement or attic. I was stuck.

"One…"

I looked at the scalpel still in my hand and thought about using it to slice my own throat.

Death isn't pleasant. I can't do that, I thought.

"Two…"

It's better than spending the rest of my life in a prison cell, isn't it?

I raised the scalpel to my throat as the officer outside the door finished his countdown.

"Three!"

On three, the front door came crashing in. The officer used so much force that half the frame came in with it. A large, black man wearing a police uniform had his gun raised and pointed at my chest.

"Drop the weapon, ma'am! This is your only warning."

I allowed the scalpel to hit the floor and slowly fell with it, as sobs took over my body. Within seconds, I was lying face down on the floor with the officer straddling me, placing handcuffs around my wrists.

Mr. Johnson died that night. The shock to his system was too much for him, and his heart gave out. In March, I was tried for murder. The judge claimed that he understood why I did what I did, but that 'premeditated, vigilante justice' wouldn't be tolerated on his watch. Since the old man died, I was tried and found guilty of murder. The jury sentenced me to life in prison without the possibility of parole.

Unlike some other criminals, I don't regret what I did. I regret getting caught, and with better planning, I'd still be a free woman.

My hope is that whoever reads this takes up where I left off. Abused and neglected animals need people like me to defend them when the justice system fails.

Unfortunately, I can't allow myself to grow old in this hell hole. I had to bide my time while I had a cellmate, but now that I occupy this tiny space by myself, I can end my self-induced misery.

As I sit here finishing my notes, staring at the sheet I have tied around the ceiling beam, I beg you... please make my death worth something.

DAWN CANO

Author of stories such as Sleep Deprived, Bucket List and Cash Out, Dawn Cano gets a kick out of making people sick. Often referred to as the 'Queen of Extreme,' when she's not thinking of gruesome ways to kill those around her, Dawn frequently roams the Pennsylvania countryside, staring at Amish people and trying to pet cows.

Check out her books here:

https://www.amazon.com/Dawn-Cano/e/B01C80B12U/

And find her on Facebook here:

https://www.facebook.com/dawn.cummings.716

HE AND SHE IN HEAVEN AND HELL

ANDREW FREUDENBERG

He found her in a supermarket parking lot, crying and trying to hide the bleeding stumps where her wings had been. Her once lustrous white dress was streaked with blood. She snarled as he approached. He smiled.

"Relax. I'm here to help."

He held his palms up to show he meant no harm.

"I fell."

"I know."

As he wrapped a blanket around her shoulders, she looked up at him with the bluest eyes that he had ever seen. They were as cold as the ice and snow that covered the ground around them.

"How did you know where to find me?"

"Oh, I just got a phone call. Someone somewhere else does the finding. Come and sit in the car. It's freezing out here. Here, just let me clear this garbage off the seat. There you go. I'll come round."

Once both doors were shut, he rubbed his hands together before turning the key in the ignition. The engine coughed a couple of times before reluctantly starting. He turned towards her.

"We won't go anywhere for a minute. I just wanted to get the heating going. I've got a bottle of Scotch somewhere."

Who are you?"

"Nobody special. Just a guy who does odd jobs."

"So I'm an odd job?"

"So to speak, yes. Here, have a swig of this."

"What is it?"

"Whiskey; to heat you up."

Her eyes glowed as the fiery drink washed down her throat.

"See? Feeling better already."

"Thank you."

"It's my pleasure."

'So, what happens now?"

"Another drink?"

She almost smiled.

"No. I mean what happens to me?"

"Ah."

"Ah?"

"I don't know yet. I expect someone will want to look after you."

"Not you?"

"Oh, I'm not really the mothering type. There are... places... people."

"You mean Churches don't you? Worshippers..."

"Well..."

She took another swig from the bottle and sat up in her chair.

"Have you any idea about the Kingdom of Heaven?"

"Well, I..."

This time she smiled widely enough for him to see the pointed ends of her teeth. She licked the alcohol off her lips before wiping them with her arm.

"Do you think I'm stupid?"

"Stupid? Why would I..."

She leant across towards him so that her face was just inches from his.

"Do you think I don't know who you are? I can smell you..."

He shrugged.

"Well, it was worth a try. I thought maybe I'd get lucky and avoid all the usual unpleasantness."

"I heard that you people were lazy. What are you going to do with me? Eat me? Rape me?"

She squinted at him.

"You look more like the monkey than the organ grinder though. I'm guessing you wouldn't even get a taste. What am I? A present? What happens if you don't do your job properly? Slit your throat? Take out their... frustrations... on you?"

"Oh I always do my job properly. I've been doing this for a long..."

He stopped short as she grasped his collar and smashed him through the windscreen. He rolled over the hood and disappeared. She laughed, took another swig of whiskey and got out of the car.

When he stood up smoke was already starting to rise from his suit. He stood with his fists clenched, any pretence at decorum now abandoned. The air around him glistened with drops of moisture and he phased in and out of focus.

"Oh, it's like that is it? What a shame."

She watched as he grew, limbs swelling and twisting into grotesquery. His feet were becoming hooves and thick hair sprouted from his legs. His chest widened and darkened, the skin turning leathery and scarred. With a sigh she threw the bottle aside and got out of the car.

"What a show, what a show."

She clasped her hands together and intertwined her fingers, looking towards the sky and gathering strength. Words not fit for human hearing spilled faster and faster from her lips in dry whispers. A web of cracks ran out across the concrete with her at their centre, as her weight multiplied.

He was now about five times his original size. His jaw had extended and it hung open, pink drool pouring from between enormous fangs. He kicked the car and it flew backwards twenty feet before smashing into a parked truck. The sound of wailing alarms filled the air.

Her metamorphosis was moving quickly now. Serpentine tentacles of light writhed around her, wrapping her in a cocoon of dazzling luminescence. She rapidly caught up with and overtook his growth and was soon more than ten times her original height. Utterly obscured by illumination she blazed like a small sun in the dim winter evening.

With a groan and a physical effort that rippled across his body, he grew again too, expanding to a height of some sixty feet. He roared in triumph, his spittle hitting her and hissing as it turned to steam. There was no mistaking the dog-like nature of his face now, despite the gnarled horns sitting atop his head.

As the light covering her began to dim, what lay beneath was revealed. Soft human skin had been replaced by diamond shaped scales that gleamed even in the darkness. Her face, now bereft of hair, lips or nose, had become reptilian. Green eyes stared out malevolently from lidless sockets, a dark membrane occasionally flickering across them. Huge wings formed from the ruins of her own, now spread out behind her, were as pale as the rest of her. She had become the white lizard.

"Look! What the hell is that?"

"Oh Jesus…"

A small crowd, either finished with their shopping or attracted by the noise, had filed out into the parking lot. They stared up at the scene unfolding in front of them, their minds struggling to deal with what they saw.

"Are they making a movie?"

"I don't see any cameras."

He lunged for her, swiping with gnarled claws. She sidestepped him and smashed an arm into his back, sending him sprawling into the side of the supermarket. Brickwork crumbled and fell, revealing the inside of the building. Shoppers stared up through the gap in horror.

The group outside the building looked at each other in hope of understanding but found none in each other's faces. Then they turned to the uniformed security guard that stood with them, desperate for him to assert his authority. He looked back at them with the hang-dog expression of one who knew his duty but not how to enforce it.

"What? You think I'm going to restrain them? Come on…"

"Shoot them!"

The guard craned his neck up at the creatures that towered above them.

"Are you crazy? What's that going to do? Let them deal with it."

A trio of police cars, lights blazing and sirens screaming, roared into the car park and skidded to a halt. After a few seconds' hesitation their crews clambered out and hid behind the vehicles. They looked less than confident, despite the guns in their hands. Whether it was deliberate or simply a shaking hand, a single shot rang out.

The demonic beast turned towards the source of irritation and growled. It was a low rumbling sound that shook windows and loosened the bowels of those who heard it. He took a step towards the patrol cars before reaching down and commencing to fling them as if they were toys. The first flew out of the parking lot, across the adjoining street, over the row of residential housing on the other side and into a shop on the other side. The second slammed into the side of the supermarket, narrowly missing the crowd of gawkers at its corner. They turned and ran. With the third he raised it above his head before throwing it down at the cowering cops. Two were crushed instantly and another was struck as the car scraped along the tarmac. The others fled screaming into the night.

Taking advantage of his momentary distraction, she stepped up behind him and bit into his neck. At a glance it could have been mistaken for an act of affection, but as soon as she tore her teeth free, along with a chunk of flesh, the illusion passed. He span around, landing a clawed fist into the side of her head, before backing away. She staggered but stood straight, sneering at his retreat. Gore smeared her teeth and face. Her eyes burned a terrible black.

Something in her expression must have concerned him because he ran. She gave chase. As she ran her wings extended and she took flight. When she caught up with him she grabbed him by the head, lifting him up into the air. They passed over the adjoining street and two rows of houses before she could hold him no longer and let go, sending him crashing into the side of a nightclub emblazoned with neon signs. Dust and sparks flew all around as he bounced off it and crashed into the ground, crushing cars and bystanders alike. She alighted a little way off, causing chaos and confusion amongst those fleeing from the scene.

Around the city the presence of two battling beasts was starting to be noticed. Panicked conversations between emergency services crackled back and forth as they tried to make sense of the information they were getting.

"Dispatch, there is a giant lizard and a giant dog fighting in the northern part of the city."

"Please repeat. Is this a situation for animal control?"

"We're not talking someone's escaped pets here. These things are sixty feet high goddamn it."

"So when you said giant…"

"I meant it. Yes. We need… I don't know… missiles or something here."

"Missiles? Please hold."

As heated conversations were held and emergency vehicles dispatched, the two giants clashed once more. They wrestled each other down the road exchanging punches, the sound of crushing metal and breaking glass following them as they squashed cars and smashed shop windows. On the corner they found themselves outside a church, its gothic design and cumbersome size at odds with the thoughtlessly designed buildings it co-existed with. From within came the sound of Christmas hymns, a rehearsal for the festive season. He and she both paused.

He turned towards her and cocked his head, a ridiculous parody of a normal sized canine. For a moment their eyes met and then he was off, leaping over the ironwork fence and up to a stain glass window depicting the ascension. He leant down and thrust his head through it, sending shards of colored glass flying. Singing turned into screaming as he reached in and plucked out a member of the choir. Standing to face her, he bit the head from the hapless vocalist and then threw the corpse at her. Before she could react he reached back in and took another and again, decapitated them and swallowed the head. A geyser of blood bloomed from the now bereft neck of his victim.

There was no sorrow or pain apparent in her expression. Instead there was just a darkening of her eyes and a chilling of the air that hung around her. Again she began to grow, stretching and contorting into something twice the size. He grew too, discarding the spent life in his grip, and howling as his body extended to over a hundred feet tall.

With a single swipe he sent the bricks of the clock tower showering over her. The bell within fell onto the roof with a terrible clanging, before rolling onto the ground. Batting away the cascade she ripped a huge section of the wrought iron fence from the ground and swung it at him. He roared as the sharpened tips penetrated his skin. It was little more than a minor annoyance though.

Several helicopters had arrived and were circling the battling pair. Two were from local television stations and the other belonged to the city police department. One of the news crews was flying dangerously close, determined to get better footage than their rivals. A producer on board encouraged the pilot in his foolishness. His exhortations crackled through the chopper's communications system and out into the ether, washing over he and she along with the chatter from the rest of the city. The maelstrom of panic passed over them and they listened without interest.

"Get in closer, this is going to be the making of us. Come on, they're only interested in each other."

The craft swooped in, a cameraman framed in the open side door. It was the act of a moment to reach out and grab it by the tail. The engine screeched in protest. Seconds later it was spinning towards her. She hopped to one side and it missed her by inches. It ploughed through the building behind her before exploding into a fireball. Aviation fuel and burning metal was strewn in all directions. Cars detonated one after the other, igniting a chain reaction both up and down the street. Howls of pain filled the night.

With a sprightly leap that belied her enormous size she leapt up and pushed herself off the church roof. It evaporated beneath her. With a thrust from her wings she reached the Police helicopter's dangling skids and grabbed them with both hands. She and it crashed to the ground with a thud. Ignoring the human sardines rattling around within, she held the whirring blades out towards him and ran. Metal bent and twisted as it struck the leathery torso, gouging out small chunks of flesh before grinding to a halt. He pushed back in fury and she did the same. Between them metal and meat screeched in protest as they were forced together. A shower of sparks met gasoline fumes and a fire erupted between them.

As the tattered remains of the craft and its crew fell to the ground he shoved her back through the walls of the church, sending her sprawling. She lay there for a moment, catching her breath. When she turned her head to survey her landing place her gaze met that of a priest. The cleric was covered in grime from head to toe. She wondered if he saw anything holy in her. From the way he turned tail and left, it seemed unlikely.

Her rival ran off down the road, flames licking at his fur as he went. Cars and citizens were crushed alike underfoot. Now that he was so large he simply trampled everything before him, rather than consider where he was going.

The city was now awash with the sound of sirens. The conflagration caused by the initial exploding helicopter was spreading. A gas main exploded spreading the flames still further. Ambulances and fire engines rushed back and forth in confusion, battling against the growing tide of panicked citizens flooding out from their homes and heading for their cars. Police vehicles circled nervously, absolutely out of their depth and unable to think of anything constructive to do. Few slept now. High overhead a pair of fighter jets circled.

"Control, this is Gator. We have eyes on target, requesting permission to engage."

"Negative, Gator, negative. We need to move them away from the city."

"I don't think anyone is going to move them anywhere they don't want to go, Control."

"Hang tight, Gator. Your time may come."

"Roger that, Control."

She pulled herself up from the rubble and looked out over the blazing chaos. She felt no pity or qualms about the destruction or empathy for those killed by their quarrel. Such thoughts were not for one such as her now. Now was a time for killing and ensuring her victory. Base instincts ruled the day. As she scanned the horizon, she wondered where her foe was heading or if he even knew that himself. With a sigh she set off in pursuit.

He had no particular destination in mind. He just wanted to find a little breathing space, regroup for another round. Although he too was primarily focused on the demise of his rival, he wanted to be sure that whoever triumphed there would be an abundance of collateral damage. Although his masters had tendrils snaking through much of this world, he considered it to belong to her people. The onus had always been on him to darken and bring down all that was around him.

She moved considerably faster than him, half jumping, half flying. She left no less destruction in her wake. As he realized that she was gaining ground on him he turned and gathered up his energy. The wounds from the helicopter were no more than scratches to him, but they had angered him and he wanted to see her bleed. As she landed, destroying a cross-town bus and a beleaguered ambulance as she did so, he took the advantage and charged her. He clasped both of her arms before attempting to sink his teeth into her neck. She writhed and fought to free herself, her wings fluttering behind her. His fangs struggled to penetrate her scales with only the tips actually piercing them. Her blood was sour and foul, not what he had expected at all. Worse, it only trickled from the wound and not gushed, as he had hoped. He stepped back to look for a softer spot.

Her forked tongue flicked out and scraped over an exposed eyeball before gouging itself deep into its centre. Instinctively he pulled back, putting both hands over the ruined eye. She had no lips to smile but her nostrils twitched in pleasure at his pain. Without looking up he charged her. His horns were more effective than his teeth at piercing her defences, and this time gore spurted from the holes he had made. Snuffling and snorting he shook his great head from side to side, tearing her open.

The scream that echoed out across the city shattered windows and burst eardrums. He pulled back and admired his work with his one remaining eye. His face dripped with her juices and viscera.

"You are finished" he hissed.

"Not yet."

Once more she began to glow and disembodied tentacles swirled and danced around her. They wrapped themselves around her body and her outstretched arms, crackling with electricity.

"No…"

Red embers glowed in her eyes as the field of energy around her grew. With one stamp of her foot a tsunami of devastation rolled out in all directions. Skyscrapers turned to dust and fell in its path, everything else it touched simply lost cohesion and ceased to be. When it struck him he proved that he, too, was capable of expressing extreme pain. His howl cracked the earth. A mile above them the fighter pilots decided to take matters into their own hands.

"Control, Control… engaging targets."

Eight missiles roared towards Earth, falling in a semi-circle around he and she. A bilious mushroom of combustion engulfed them both, scorching the earth and ruins that lay around them. Gradually the flames that obscured them faded away, leaving two blackened figures of normal size. He lay on the floor, thrashing and moaning, while she stood over him, blackened but still alive. She wiped the soot from her face with the back of her hands and blinked. Her eyes had returned to their former stunning blue.

"I think I might pass on that help, if that's alright with you."

She put her foot on his neck and slowly put all her weight behind it until she heard the crunch of bone and he stopped moving. She looked at him sadly and shook her head.

"I fell you know. You could have just helped."

She turned and walked away, alone once more.

ANDREW FREUDENBERG

Andrew Freudenberg is a writer of dark and speculative fiction. Although he has always loved to write, he is also easily distracted. In the late 20th and early 21st centuries he was distracted by music, both making it and running clubs and a record label.

In about 2010 he remembered his love of writing. Since then his short stories have appeared in multiple anthologies. He currently lives in the English West Country, where he and his Ninja wife are raising an army of sons.

HABEAS CORPUS

KITTY KANE

Sighing and putting on her hot and itchy court wig, Justice Judge Judy James steeled herself for yet another day sitting in the stifling courtroom, listening to the dregs of society attempt to defend the heinous actions they perpetrated upon one another. A ten year veteran of The Old Bailey in London, she often nowadays found herself despairing more and more of her fellow human beings.

Forty seven years old, Judy had been a high court judge for twenty of those years, working her way up the career ladder having spent six long years at Cambridge university, and then a further six high flying years as one of the finest prosecutors the country had ever seen. Working for the crown prosecution service, plus one year as an assistant district attorney, had seen her become one of the most respected women practicing law in the country, and perhaps even the world at that time.

Many high profile and disturbing cases had been laid out for dissection in her courtroom. Many great young upcoming law practitioners had made impressions upon her, and one of those was a man she would once more see today.

Jonathan Jester, nicknamed The Court Jester, was an amazingly accomplished defence lawyer. His clients were always high profile, and always very rich. Jester charged handsomely for his time and expertise, but in Judy's experience of him it paid off. Only twice had she ever seen him lose a case, and both times as a result of his clients in-court stupidity rather than any ineptitude on his part. She respected him totally, but she certainly didn't like him.

Smug and partial to flaunting just how successful he was, he wound her up. From the fact he drove a beautiful, but rather loud penis extension in his Maclaren Mercedes—limited to only ten in the country—sports car, to other smaller irritations she had found in him, one of which was insistence out of the court room of referring to her as Judge Judy. Certainly over time she had become accustomed to being teased for sharing a name with the American TV judge Judith Shiendlin, her name being Judy and all, but most knew to stop when she turned her withering glare upon them. Jester had never stopped, and indeed seemed to revel in her ire.

The case she was presiding over today was a heart breaking one and a little close to Judy's own heart. An eight year old girl that had been a high profile misper (missing person) for three torturously long days, had been found carved up and her body pieces scattered around an old Victoria cemetery in North London. The case had been covered extensively by all the newspapers, tabloid and broadsheet alike, and the choosing of the jury had been a difficult matter, firstly finding somebody that hadn't heard much about the case, or finding people that when questioned about their thoughts on such perpetrators did not give answers that showed they could not be classed as impartial. No, jury selection had been difficult, and Judy knew this particular case was going to be very hard for her.

There was one reason, and one only, that prompted the young Judy to seek desperately to succeed in the field of criminal law, and to give it everything she had: she was doing it for Jamie. As a child Judy had a sister. Two years younger than herself and named Jamie-Ann, Judy had doted on the cherubic child that was her baby sister. The moment her mother brought Jamie home from the hospital Judy had adored her. Always wishing to help her mother do anything for the baby, the girls had become very close as they grew, with Judy fiercely protective of her sibling. However that changed one fateful day.

The girls had been playing out in the back garden as usual, when they decided they wanted to build a fort. Having done so many times before, the girls' mother kept some old blankets, sheets and pillows for exactly this purpose, and kept them stored in a box in the shed. But on this day, the fort-making items were not in their box as they had been taken in for washing after yesterday's fort had fallen to enemy fire, and collapsed into the mud. Telling her sister to wait there, Judy pulled back with great effort the ever-stiffening bolt of the heavy garden gate, stepped up upon the gate itself to take a ride with it to its open position, and ducked indoors and upstairs to the laundry room.

Down in the back garden, the young Jamie had thought what her sister had done on the big wooden gate looked like great fun, and as a slight breeze brought it back to its closed position, but not locked, the child ran along and jumped upon the gate, emulating the big sister she adored.

What happened next nobody was ever certain of, but Jamie-Ann vanished.

Judy struggled back down the stairs, trailing the fort sheets behind her, and the pile of linen in her arms obscuring her vision to begin with delayed her discovery of her sister's disappearance. Calling for her sister to come start building, Judy had dropped her burden upon the concrete driveway and turned, expecting Jamie to be running towards her, but she wasn't. Jamie would never run anywhere again. They found her body four days later in an old disused churchyard; she had been beaten and abused repeatedly, and they never located her missing head, and still had not until this day.

Nobody had ever been prosecuted for Jamie-Ann's rape, torture, murder and mutilation, but Judy still lived in hope every single day that one day, somehow justice would be served for the sister she always felt she let down.

Having glanced over the charge sheet of the man accused today of another despicable child murder and defilement, her heart had skipped when she saw that, like Jaimie's, Jessie Jones's head had not been recovered, despite searches in every graveyard for miles around.

For a few moments when the case landed in her inbox she had wondered if she should speak up and perhaps not preside over a case that could be classed as a little too close to home, but she had faith in her own ability to maintain an impartial mind set, and so had allowed it on the rota for her court room. Always as she prepared to turn the large ornate door handle that opened the door between her chambers and the courtroom proper, Judy would take several very deep breaths to prepare herself for what was coming. On this day she took several more, and then she stepped over the threshold into her raised Judge's box, and the entire courtroom rose in respect to her.

As Judy settled down into the familiar and worn leather covered seat, she glanced over at the box where the defendant sat between two rather beefy guards, and found herself staring briefly into a pair of eyes that emanated evil so strongly that a shiver ran down her spine. She hadn't felt so unnerved from looking at a defendant in years. As if reading her thoughts, the defendant Joseph Jedidiah Judge, who she though rather aptly named, given the circumstances, curled his cruel mouth into a devilish smirk, raised his eyebrows, further showing his piercing green eyes, and ran his tongue across his lips in a seductive manner. Looking quickly away she called the court to order and settled to hear the case.

The details as laid out by the crown prosecution service were awful to hear. The service had given the case to one of their most accomplished and long standing prosecutors, a kindly man known as Jazz. His real name was Jazwygicit Jozygert, of Polish descent but English born. He was well respected but none attempted to call him by his real name for fear of pronunciation difficulties. Judy found it hard enough calling him Mr Jozygert, (sounds a little like yoghurt) in court, let alone attempting the even more difficult Christian name.

Judy found herself calling recessions a little more often than usual, as the details of the child's suffering were hard to hear for both public gallery and court to hear. Even Harvey, the elderly court clerk, was raising his bushy grey eyebrows and he had certainly heard many vile things over his years as clerk.

The Crown was laying out the facts of its case. Jessie had vanished from a McDonald's toilet in town. Her mother had allowed Jessie to just run in to use the toilet while she stayed outside with the pushchair containing her young twin sons. She had watched Jessie skip up the stairs to the toilets, but both boys had begun fussing, so she turned her attention to them. Having rearranged their sitting positions, and stopped their whinging, she had waited and waited and waited for her daughter to return. Her anger beginning to grow after ten minutes or so, she had struggled her way into the packed out McDonald's to seek her errant daughter.

She made her way to the stand where the sauces were kept, knowing how well Jessie loved to play with the plungers on the sauce bottles, but Jessie wasn't there. Nor was she in the toilets, or indeed the building. Jessie had gone, vanished without a trace.

The police had been swift to arrive in large numbers, bringing with them a trained family liaison officer. While of course they hoped the child had simply wandered off and was safe somewhere, they knew by experience that children of this age disappeared usually as a result of foul play, and the outcome was often bleak.

The search had been massive, with thousands of volunteers searching day and night for the child, finding nothing. Finally it had come to an end when four teenagers, having gone in search of a place to get high, had stumbled first across a human hand, and then a thigh, in the old and abandoned graveyard of the crumbled church of St John.

The police and forensic teams scoured the churchyard, and recovered Jessie in twenty different pieces. Bagging up the grim discoveries, they soon had accounted for everything, apart from the poor child's head. That was nowhere to be found. A search of records showed where any previously convicted or charged child-molesters lived had thrown up a large amount of such offenders in the area, and the police began the disgusting task of visiting them all and asking questions.

As the pair of officers that had been sent to the house of Jedidiah Judge entered the property, a feeling of unease had taken hold of them. Police officers often developed almost a sixth sense, and PC Jennifer Harlow was no exception to this. While her colleague asked some routine questions of the convicted child-rapist, she cast her specially trained eye around his house.

Disturbing images were framed on the walls; not paintings, or arty photos, or even the ridiculous canvas prints that were all the rage right now. No, adorning the walls here were posters of the kind that come at the centrefolds of magazines for children. *Peppa Pig, Teletubbies, Tweenies, Rosie and Jim, In The Night Garden* were all there. On the shelves there were no ordinary ornaments. Instead there were items generally found in homes with small children.

The items he had on display sent shivers down PC Harlow's spine. Baby bottles containing what looked to be blood. A plastic potty with real faecal matter, floating in what appeared to be real urine. An assortment of dummies, all with either razor blades or huge nails inserted into the rubber teats. Threaded onto a string, and fastened on each end to allow it to hang from the shelf front, were countless human teeth, all small enough to be from a child. And just when she thought she could not get anymore disgusted, she spotted some strange, leathery brown objects upon one of the shelves. Stepping closer, she couldn't quite contain her small scream as she realised what she was looking at.

Hearing his colleague make her muffled scream, PC Justin Tilly rushed in, finding his normally hard as nails partner with her hand clapped across her mouth, and tears in her eyes. He followed her gaze to the shelf. He too took a sharp intake of breath as he realised what he was seeing. Dried and almost mummified, spaced neatly on the shelf, were ten sets of human—but clearly juvenile—penises and testicles.

Realising they had stumbled across a really bad case, they quickly turned their attention back to the nonce in the other room. He had not moved; he still sat in his stinking armchair, and as they arrested him on suspicion of murder, he showed exactly what he thought of being arrested by both defecating and urinating in his trousers as the marched him outside to their car. The stench on the way to the cells had been unbearable.

The interview process had consisted solely of the defendant answering every question with 'no fucking comment'. The case had been brought solely on forensic and testimonial evidence, and what they found in his house and out-buildings.

Having secured the correct warrants to search the property, the forensic teams had begun to make grim discoveries. In an out-building, which had shelves lining its interior walls, they found the first five children. All aged between five and ten years old, laid on the shelves with their hands and arms across their chests, were the completely skeletal but headless remains. Protruding from each skeleton were tools, mostly wedged in amongst the rib cages, a bizarre and macabre tool organiser.

Further down the large and wild garden, among the bluebells that swayed so prettily in the breeze, sat a small, child's-size picnic table. Hidden from any prying eyes, but still exposed to the elements, around the table sat another three headless yet skeletal corpses. Upon the once gaudy coloured, but now sun-faded table, lay a child's tea service. Insects crawled over the tiny plates and cups, and the same insects then crawled over the headless remains of the children.

Making their way through this voyage of macabre discovery, the forensic teams stopped often. They shook their heads and each had pain in his or her eyes, for these poor little angels must have suffered so very much. There was just no let up from the gruesome finds. More bodies were turning up with alarming recurrence. Down the very bottom of the garden, amongst what looked like a compost heap, they found a further two skeletons. Both headless, one of a child around six years old, but the other clearly a baby.

The entire force working on the investigation were stunned by the sheer number of child corpses they were finding. How could this amount of children have been murdered on their patch over the years and them not have any idea. Sure children went missing often, but more often than not it was a result of parental snatching. The area had a high concentration of folk of other ethnic descent living in it, and the police often found cases of parents splitting up, and then the children being stolen off, usually by the father, and secreted in their home countries.

Carbon dating would of course tell them just how old the bones were, but with a body count of nine and rising, questions would indeed arise. However, the biggest question was: where were the heads? Not a single skull had been recovered.

The team inside the house were sifting through the detritus. They found many items of children's clothing, some for children as young as six months. The vile owner of the house had more of his gruesome 'ornaments' on shelves all throughout the house, and when the officers went upstairs, they were stunned to find all three bedrooms decorated just as children would have them.

One bedroom was all in pink, frills abounded in the small room. Laying under the covers of the princess bed was yet another pair of bodies. One completely skeletal, one in the latter stages of decomposition. The smell in the room was a cloying odour of decaying flesh, mixed with the countless pink tree-shaped car air fresheners that hung all around the room. The two pitiful bodies laid upon the bed had their hands intertwined as they lay nestled in a putrid mess of viscera. The suffering of the two could only be guessed at. And, of course, no heads were present.

The team inside started to bring out the grim finds. First came the bodies, and the team did what they could to protect against the now huge gathering of media that had descended upon the property. In the blue bedroom they had not found any corpses, but they had found both a video camera and many recordable VHS tapes, lined lovingly on primary-coloured shelves, which so many parents would lovingly attach to walls of children's bedrooms throughout the land. They carefully tagged, bagged and loaded each one with heavy hearts, as they realised that viewing those tapes would probably be awful.

The third bedroom made the hair on the necks of the investigators stand up. Walls adorned with childish murals, there stood in the centre of the room an oversized cot. Laid upon the unusual sized bed was a sleeping bag with a picture of Elsa and Olaf from Disney's *Frozen*, and at the bottom of this sleeping bag was where they found the final corpse the horror house had to offer.

The almost mummified remains of a prepubescent child was scrunched up in there, its skin leathery and a hole where the genitals had been. Tears streamed down even the most hardened face as they realised just what abuse this child's body had taken, the only comfort being that it was likely to have been posthumous, and the child had probably only suffered the once.

One evidence find from the hook in the kitchen had caused some excitement: a wrought iron key hung there amongst a large number of other keys. One of the forensic technical team kept looking back at the key. Jason Kellaway thought he had seen it before, but his mind wouldn't quite give up the piece of information he needed straight away. Once a morgue assistant, and also a gravedigger for the local authority, Jason was one of the most respected team members. He had worked the two depressing jobs to support his wife and son, whilst taking his forensic degree at night school to ultimately do the job he was doing today. Accurate and fastidious, he had worked his way into a mid-seniority position with the forensic team and was happy at his level.

As the team wrapped up the gruesome stripping of the house of untold horrors, the key was placed in an evidence bag and taken off to the station. Jason was still bugged by the thing. Just where had he seen it?

The team delegated the horrendous duties of this investigation that needed to be done. Of course the most important evidence was likely to be the plain-sheathed VHS tapes found in the bedroom of the house, but none wanted to see them. All knew they were going to be depraved and disgusting, but the viewing had to be done.

The first tape actually threw up no information at all. It was footage from a CCTV camera that was attached over the front door of the monster's house. The grainy footage was many hours of simply what was happening in the road, but several evenings on the tape showed many young children playing happily outside, blissfully unaware they were being watched.

Several tapes like this were viewed, and the team began to wonder if they had misjudged the possible content. On the fifth tape viewed however, a different setting came into view. The camera was shaky and the subject much darker than the CCTV footage. It was evident that the filmmaker was walking, and swimming into view came part of what looked to be a large pair of gates. Huge metal gates, and the team saw a hand enter the frame holding a key. As one the team became more alert, for the key in the hand was the key they had discovered hanging from the hook in the kitchen. The key turned and the filmmaker walked through the gates, shutting them quietly behind.

As the man walked up a darkened driveway, Jason Kellaway suddenly jumped up and paused it. Looking at his colleagues, he said, "I knew I recognised that key. I've used it myself many times. Sonofabitch. Asshole. Cocksucker!" As he spewed this uncharacteristically vehement angry statement, he made the entire room jump as he punched the wall next to where the footage was being played. "That is the key to St Joanna's churchyard, home to the crematorium! Also home to the morgue! I used it myself back when I was studying. I was the morgue assistant and I also dug graves. There is a shed. Only the gravediggers use it. We need to go to it."

The DCI agreed with him and dispatched Jason and a team to St Joanna's straight away. The unlucky ones got to remain and view more of the vile tapes. Soon the tapes took a turn for the worse, and what they began to see on the screen violated the eyes of even the most seasoned police officer.

The team recognised the view of the bottom of the garden, and sitting around the plastic table were the corpses. But, in this shot, the corpses were not skeletal. The skin was greying, and slippage of the skin was occurring. Rigor and liver mortis appeared to both be long past; a sheen of light mould adorned the skin and maggots crawled in the neck wounds where the heads had been removed. The camera was placed upon the table, but the view did not let up its disturbing vistarama. The lap of the man came into view, as did his hand, opening the fly of his trousers, fumbling around inside and drawing out a tiny but erect penis.

If they hadn't known this was a grown man they looked upon, the team would have taken the organ for that of a child, so small and immature was it. Out of frame, a hand must have taken a hold of the China teapot, for it floated into view, and the tip of the exposed penis was inserted into it. After thirty seconds or so, liquid spilled from the spout of the teapot as the vile man urinated into the plaything. Still not putting his penis away, the man's hands disappeared above the table, and began to serve his decapitated 'guests' his tea of urine. For two hours the process was repeated over and over. The only sounds to be heard were birds singing and occasional grunts from the man. Eventually the bizarre film was over, the strangely malformed organ zipped back into stained trousers, and the picture faded to black.

Many more disturbing tapes were viewed, taken all around the macabre and childish house, progressing in severity of disgust, but not a single act of actual violence appeared. The films always showed the children as corpses; not a single frame showed them alive. Frustrated, the team knew they were missing something important. But what? It wasn't long before the tapes gave up the worst of all the secrets they held.

The shaky camera focused once more upon the crotch of the man's trousers, shook a little as he again removed his underdeveloped member from his stupid underwear. The officers in the room watching suddenly took a renewed interest as the camera panned out and showed a room they had not seen before. This room was strangely silver in colour, and they realised this was because the walls were covered with kitchen foil. The surface of the walls was uneven, and looked as if some sort of DIY soundproofing had been performed upon them.

The camera swung once more and the room gasped as several large jars came into view. Each jar contained a semi clear liquid and, within, a roundish object. The hands of the filmmaker grabbed one of the jars. Opening it, he pulled out the soaking wet but fully preserved head of a child. A young girl of around six or seven years old, by the looks of it. As he shook the wet substance from the decapitated child, the monster on screen forced open the dead jaws of the head, and lowered it slowly to his waiting lap.

The sound of a chair scraping furiously caused all present to turn just in time to see one of their most seasoned colleagues lose his lunch onto the floor. His vomiting may have been the first, but it certainly wasn't the last. Even the veterans of the team couldn't bear to watch this violation of a dead angelic sweetheart. All present in that room wanted to vow vengeance upon this monstrous perpetrator; nothing could be too bad to happen to this vile creature.

The team, pretty much resigned to what they were going to find in the gravedigger's shed, traipsed there slowly, forensic guys first, dusting for fingerprints as they went, collecting any tiny strand of hair, fiber, or even out of place plant matter that they came across. Kellaway had been correct. The large ornate key slipped into every lock they had found barring their way throughout the crematorium and morgue, and it did indeed open this shed.

The team were still disgusted by what they found there in neat rows on the shelves of the foil-covered shed. Jar after jar of children's heads stared at them, and they began the grotesque process of collecting, tagging and bagging the macabre finds to take back to be matched with the remains found at the house of horrors. The monster in custody at the station was still refusing to answer a single question, and even with the glut of grim finds, no hard evidence that he was responsible for the murders had been found.

The DNA testing and matching had been a long one, and while the heads indeed matched the corpses found, two remained unmatched to bodies. Both female, both with perfectly preserved features, both with mouths containing semen, but no bodies. They knew one was likely to be the missing head of Jessie, the poor angel found in twenty pieces, but the other remained a mystery throughout the investigation and still was to this day.

The efforts of the police team and Crown prosecution team to put this monster away forever had been seriously hampered by surprise findings that nobody expected. The DNA of the mummified penises did not match any of the heads, or bodies, or even any missing person reports. Receipts of shipping had been found that seemed to show these strange ornaments had been purchased, and not taken from victims.

Upon a strip search of the suspect, it had been discovered that he could not have been the owner of the genitalia on the films, for there was no malformation there. Worse still, the semen found inside the mouths of the heads had been destroyed by the formaldehyde to the point it was non-identifiable. The horrific case was tumbling down, and the police could not charge for the many murders that had been committed.

The case in fact rested only upon a small amount of blood found on the vile man's shoe that matched the scattered remains of Jessie. On this they had charged him, and on that charge this case now hinged. The jurors did not get to see the many hours of taped evidence, but Judy saw it. Judy saw it all.

Time surged on, and Judy declared it time to adjourn for the day. The prosecution had laid out their sketchy case, and defence had begun. The courtroom was sombre as the jury and congregated public filed out. The guards told the defendant to get up to be taken once more to the holding cells below, and Judy herself wearily went to her chambers, where she collapsed into her chair, disgusted once more with humanity and its deprivations.

As she sat and contemplated these horrors that were

placed in front of her time and time again, she reached into her bottom drawer where she kept a bottle of black label vodka. Once upon a time she would have mixed it with large amounts of coke, but nowadays she drank it neat. After three large triple shots, her head began to run over the events of the day, and suddenly something came to the fore of her mind. Jumping up, she grabbed the evidence envelopes and, firing up the VCR, she found the tape of the police entering the shed at the crematorium.

Once more the careful processes of the forensic officers swam into view, but Judy fast-forwarded; this wasn't what she wanted to see. As she saw the shelves containing the jars come onto the screen, she allowed the tape to run once more. The quality wasn't great, and the almost cloudy liquid of the formaldehyde obscured the view into the jars properly, but she soon found what she was looking for. Third from the end, although the jar was grimy, the viewer could see a ribbon pushed up against the top of the glass. Feeling her heart leap, Judy downed another triple shot and snagged her glasses from the desk.

She managed finally to get the scene to pause so that the line of VCR atmospherics did not obscure that which she aimed to see. Putting on her glasses she peered closely at the screen, then gasping to herself fell back into her chair, tears threatening to tumble from her already tired eyes. The ribbon which she saw in the jar, she knew she had seen it before. In fact, she had made it.

Judy and her sister had spent a lot of time with their maternal grandmother as young girls, and crafting had been a popular activity for them all. Judy had excelled at embroidery, and had embroidered a length of ribbon for her little sister. The embroidery had been clumsy and childish, but she had put on all of Jamie's favourite things, and also her name, sewn in bright green thread. It had been many years, but Judy saw and recognised that special ribbon. The vodka burned as it came back up, and Judy wretched as she realised this jar contained the missing severed head of her little sister.

The burn of the vodka's return did not stop Judy swigging more and more of the spirit, bypassing the glass now and glugging it down as she fought within her mind to deal with the horror of the realisation that she was looking at her dead sister in a jar on a film. Playing her mind over the proceedings so far in the case, and her legal brain told her that the case was frail. The case was frail and the defence lawyer was the best goddamn lawyer money could buy. That defendant was going to walk, she felt it in her blood. She was never ever wrong with these gut feelings. But this was different. This was personal.

Taking one last and very long pull at the vodka bottle, Judy began to collect items from her chamber. The pencil sharpener, the letter opener that was a small facsimile of Excalibur, the poker from the fire place, some keys from a secure drawer in her desk, and her lighter. She placed them all into her hand bag, and set off shakily from her office to the stairs that would lead her down to the holding cells.

The officer assigned to cell watch had fallen asleep at his post, but to ensure she would not be disturbed, Judy hit him across the back of the head with the iron poker. She cringed at the crunch and hoped she hadn't hit the poor guy too hard. Reaching for his belt, she took the keys he held there, in case he should come to and interfere with her intended actions. The cells only contained the defendant from Judy's case, and a Romanian accused of fraud. Smoothly opening the door to her defendant's cell, Judy slid in and locked it behind her silently.

The man didn't stir as Judy secured his hands with the guard's cuffs. He did begin to stir when she tied his feet together with her silk scarf, tightly tying the safety knot she remembered learning in Guides. He awoke properly when she pulled down his police issue prison trousers and pants, and when he saw the judge sat there with a very sharp letter opener held at the base of his penis, his eyes widened and he began to open his mouth to talk.

"Don't say a fucking word you piece of shit. I have some specific questions you will answer, understood?" The man looked shocked but nodded.

"What did you do to my sister? Don't tell me it wasn't you. If not you, then you know and have enjoyed whatever happened to her. She is in the jar they could not match with one of your gruesome damn trophies. I loved her, I needed her, I've been so alone. What did you do, you piece of shit?"

Taking hold of his pinkie finger, Judy inserted it into the desk pencil sharpener she had brought with her and began to turn the handle. Nail shavings plinked into the clear case on the sharpener, followed quickly by increasingly thickening gnarled and nicotine-yellowed skin. As the blood exploded into view, the cuffed man's eyes widened in pain and he began to whimper. The resistance on the sharpener handle increased as Judy reached the thin layer of muscle, then white and shining bone appeared. Judy felt strangely invigorated at the sight, and moved to the opposite pinky, repeating the torturous process.

"Dammit, you crazy-ass woman! What do you want?" he howled, eyes taking in the newly sharpened point of his little fingers. "T'wernt me what took the children, you know... not all of 'em... not even most of 'em. T'was my brother. Ya'll ain't found eee yet and ya won't, not from me."

Judy attempted to insert his ring finger into the sharpening hole, but it was too wide. In disgust she threw down the sharpener. The case that had collected the gristly shavings fell off and a pool of blood spilled upon the cell floor. Grabbing her letter opener, she moved down to his feet. Inserting the tip of the blade under the nail of his big toe, she pushed down with all her strength, the sharp blade easily penetrating the softer nailbed. The man cried out once more, a pitiful wail, but Judy was not satiated.

Repeating the process nine more times, and then taking the point of the fireplace poker and bludgeoning the man's shrivelled scrotum, Judge Judy finally got the information she required. Her head span. She was transported back to those idyllic days of playing fort with the sister she adored. Many times over the years had she come up against the phrase 'red mist descended'. Judy now experienced a red mist of her own. Blindly she went about that last bit of business that day. As she had done so many times before, she hung her judicial wig upon the hook on her door, closed the chamber, and stepped into the empty and echoing corridor.

They found her the next morning. People arriving for work at the courthouse spotted an unusual black item hanging from the stone sword of the statue of lady justice. On closer inspection, they were shocked to find the dead body of Judge Judith. Hanging in full view of all entering the Old Bailey. Gruesome though this find was, it was nothing compared with the other discoveries they would make in the famous courthouse that day.

Down in the holding cells, they found one very concussed guard, blood crusted upon his swelling and beaten head. In the cells themselves, they found what remained of the suspect. His body had been mutilated beyond recognition. His fingers and toes were a mass of blood and bone. His penis and testicles had been removed, and sat atop a fireside poker that was leaning against the holding cell cot. His body was a mass of bruised weals and, where his head should have been, there was just a blood-soaked pillow. The court guards did not see much viscera themselves, and one vomited, while the other fainted away.

At approximately the same time as this was happening, the elderly court clerk arrived for the day. Entering the back way into the court house, he had missed all the action. He went as he always did to the judge's chamber, to ensure everything was straight, and to remove any vodka bottles that might give away the trapped torment of his esteemed colleague. He knew she drank to hide from her torment. He understood. He knew.

As he entered the room, his heart sank. Even he could not help this time. This time her torment was going to be clear for all to see, for sitting on top of the beautiful walnut desk was a large jar. The sides of the jar were filled with blood, but as the clerk stepped closer he saw a decapitated head. It was a head he had spent a lot of time staring at just yesterday. The head of the defendant, the aptly named Joseph Jedidiah Judge, sat in the jar, and protruding from one eye was a letter opener that looked rather like Excalibur, the letter opener belonging to his great friend, Judge Judy.

The clerk sat in the worn leather chair, put his head in his arms and cried. He cried not from grief, but from the gladness that his friend had finally been able to release herself from the emotional prison she had built around her all these years.

Yes, he was happy she was no longer tormented by being trapped within.

KITTY KANE

Kitty Kane aka Becky Brown hails from the south of England where she lives surrounded by squirrels. She is also one half of writing duo Matthew Wolf Kane, and has been published both in collaborations and stand alone stories. Kitty is the author of stories that have appeared in Full Moon Slaughter and Down The Rabbit Hole Tales Of insanity from J Ellington Ashton Press, and has several more stories in forthcoming releases from JEA. She also was part of the first V's charity anthology battle challenge from Shadow Work Publications, in which she won her battle, and made some life long friends. She has also has her work in a Christmas anthology from BURDIZZO BOOKS which was called twelve days in which Kitty cheerfully roasted babies in front of the open fire.

Kitty is currently editing her first solo anthology, The ABC of murder coming soon from Anthology House. She has lots of exciting projects lined up this year including her own novella, a MWK collaboration novella, many short stories and lots of general madness.

Kitty says of her writing style that it errs on the side of bizarro, but she enjoys writing classic horror also. A lifelong fan of all things horror, you will find her generally up to no good. Her eyes are brown, her hair is subject to change...one steadfast thing with her though, she can never be accused of being sane.

LOVE, EAT, PREY

ASH HARTWELL

Holding Hudson's hand, Craig almost skipped across the road towards the invitingly lit village pub. If he had had the choice he wouldn't have selected to have their first romantic meal away together in a pub sporting the name *The Slaughtered Lamb*. But, as Craig noticed on the drive down, pubs were scarce in this part of the West Country and this one was within walking distance of their rented holiday cottage. As far as Craig was concerned, the only name that mattered was *Hudson*. His beautiful girlfriend and—he hoped—soon-to-be fiancée, danced across the road beside him, giggling in that childlike way he found so endearing.

The pub itself was small, no more than an old two-room cottage, converted to a one-room bar. Several tables occupied the middle of the room and an old couch faced the fireplace. The fire crackling in the hearth was a welcome sight to the two lovers as they shook off the dampness of the night before approaching the bar. The few locals supping pints fell silent, watching Craig and Hudson approach with detached interest, but offered no form of welcome.

Craig smiled as the barman—an elderly, overweight man with a bushy, greying beard—stepped forward with a quizzical look. The other men gathered at the bar turned away but didn't continue their conversation. The crackling hisses and pops from the fire was the only sound in the room.

"Good evening." Craig's voice sounded loud in the hushed room.

"Good evening, Sir. What can I get for you and the good lady?" The barman was well-spoken but with a thick country accent. His lips curled in what Craig took to be a smile, although his eyes preserved their questioning look. He looked Craig, then Hudson, up and down with a slow, deliberate gaze that lingered on Hudson's chest a little too long for Craig's liking.

"I'll have a pint, please, and..." Craig looked at Hudson questioningly.

"Orange juice, please." She spoke direct to the barkeep, saving Craig from repeating her order. As the man moved away to prepare their drinks she pulled a face at Craig which reflected her feelings on the weirdness of the silent pub, before wandering away to a nearby table.

Craig waited for their drinks, only joining her at the table once he had paid the socially retentive barman. The men at the bar began talking quietly to one another as he moved away. He could feel their gaze on his back as he took his seat but, when he turned around, they just looked away, continuing their conversation, which was obviously about him and Hudson.

"I know you wanted to do the whole romantic meal thing but I think I'd feel happier eating those supermarket pizzas we brought with us. I feel like an exhibit here," Hudson whispered with a smile Craig hoped would never lose its sexiness. "Besides, I have plans too." She winked at him over the rim of her glass.

"Better drink up then," Craig replied hastily, before downing half his pint.

Hudson threw her head back and laughed aloud, attracting the attention of the locals, who stared over at the two lovers with open annoyance, bordering on hostility. "Alright, calm down, Romeo, we've got all weekend."

"Ssshhhh. We may have angered the locals." Craig's voice was no more than a whisper as he stole a quick glance over his shoulder at the men propping up the bar. "So much for the warm West Country welcome they mentioned in the brochure."

"I know. Did you see that guy stare at my tits? It gives me the fuckin' creeps." Hudson downed her drink, slamming the empty glass down on the table with obvious anger. "You ready, babe?"

"Two seconds." Craig drained the last of his beer, standing up as he did so. He returned his glass to the table and extended his hand towards Hudson, a broad, almost defiant smile on his face. "Shall we find a more private establishment to while away the evening?"

Hudson took his hand and together they left *The Slaughtered Lamb* having spent barely five minutes in the hostelry. As they walked around the village green, heading for the lane leading to their rented cottage, Craig had an uneasy feeling, like someone was watching him. Glancing back, he noticed two of the men stood in the pub's doorway. They were openly staring at him and Hudson.

"This place is like something from a horror movie," Craig said, increasing his pace slightly. "I'll be glad when we're snuggled up in front of the TV with a pizza."

"Who said anything about television?" giggled Hudson, seemingly unaware of the interest their visit still caused, but matching Craig's increased pace.

"I thought you said we had all weekend?"

"I've got an insatiable appetite, what can I say?" Hudson's upturned face caught the early evening moonlight, her eyes shining with excitement. "Race ya!"

Hudson ran off into the dark shadows of the unlit lane with Craig following her at a steady jog, easily keeping her in his sights. The cottage, located at the end of a short gravel drive, was about half a mile down the lane and he waited until Hudson turned into the drive with a shriek of victorious laughter before increasing his pace. Craig closed the distance quickly, wrapping his arms around her as she tried to reach for the cottage's wrought iron door handle.

The soft scent of Hudson's perfume filled his nostrils as his mouth closed in on her neck's soft skin. Giggling, she fumbled with the lock before pushing the door open. A blast of warm, pine-scented air greeted them as they stepped inside, still wrapped in one another's arms, Craig kicking the door shut with his heel. Together they stumbled towards the couch.

"Pizza?" Hudson asked as she broke away from his clutches and headed for the cottage's small kitchenette. She threw her coat over the back of a chair as Craig slumped onto the couch with a frustrated sigh. "Hey! A girl's gotta eat. I've got to keep my strength up."

"Do you have to do it now?" Craig struggled out of his coat, letting it slide to the floor as he undid the laces of his boots.

"I think it might be wise," Hudson replied, more to herself than to Craig, as she stared past her reflection in the windowpane at the dark woods beyond. She thought she had seen something moving, illuminated briefly by the moonlight as the clouds parted for a moment, but she couldn't be sure.

"Okay, I must admit I'm hungry after the drive down, but don't think your virtue will not be threatened this night, my lady." Craig lapsed into a comic medieval accent he felt was more in keeping with the cottage's dated décor.

"And I trust you will not be too presumptious to assume it will be you who threatens my virtue?" Hudson replied, following his lead with the historical accent. She didn't take her eyes off the darkened treeline as she spoke, fixing her gaze on the spot where she thought she had seen movement. The clouds had blown across the face of the moon, plunging everything beyond the rectangle of light shining out from the kitchen window into complete darkness.

"Do you suggest I will have to fight for your affection, my lady? Because frankly, I don't know if I can be arsed." Craig reclined on the couch, laughing.

"Who knows what the night will bring," Hudson replied mysteriously, still stood in front of her reflection in the kitchen window. After a brief moment she turned her attention to preparing their supper, but she still couldn't shake the thought something or someone was lurking in the woods.

She put the thought out of her mind as she prepared a simple salad to complement the supermarket-bought pizza, then opened the cheap bottle of wine she found in the welcome basket left on the kitchen table. She called Craig to collect the wine and find some glasses while she transferred the pizza to a plate. Finding some forks, she gathered the pizza and the salad together and followed Craig back through to the cottage's living room.

They ate the food then made love in the warm, romantic glow of the open log fire before lying naked on the couch to finish the last of the wine. Hudson listened to the wind blowing through the branches of the nearby trees and the fierce sound of a rainsquall lashing against the window while Craig dozed quietly beside her. She snuggled in close to her lover, the strange reactions of the villagers and the half-glimpsed shadow in the woods all but forgotten as she relaxed in his comforting arms.

Gradually, the fire died in the hearth and Hudson reluctantly stirred from the safety of Craig's sleepy embrace. Sliding from the couch, she removed a few logs from the small pile stacked neatly against the wall and placed them on the fire's glowing embers. She used the poker to gently prod the fire's smouldering remains; she had always had a healthy suspicion of fire and felt nervous being this close, especially in her naked state.

"What's the time, babe?" Craig yawned as he spoke.

"Not sure. It's late, though." Hudson could smell the warm scent of pine from the log pile, the lingering aroma of Italian herbs and garlic from the pizza, and Craig's musky scent and stale aftershave. She crawled back to the couch, a seductively wicked smile playing on her soft lips.

"It's way past your bedtime."

Craig tried to pull her onto the couch but Hudson stopped him with a firm hand on his chest. She tilted her head to one side, listening to the sounds of the woodlands outside the cottage. A new odour reached her nostrils, stale sweat, beer and the healthy stench of human fear. She pushed Craig back onto the couch with an uneasy smile.

"Hold on a moment there, Loverboy. I need a drink." She stood up and blew Craig a kiss before padding almost silently into the kitchen. She stood at the window, oblivious to her own nakedness. Several flaming torches burned in the darkness beyond the glass. The flickering lights lit up the figures standing in the treeline and cast strange, dancing shadows into the woodland's leafy canopy. Hudson knew the figures would be able to see her. She bit her lower lip as a tingle of excitement passed down her spine, the tiny hairs on her arms bristling.

Craig watched Hudson walk across the room with a contented smile then, picking up the TV remote, he scanned the channels, searching for something to watch while he waited for her to return. Finding an irreverent cartoon for adults he pressed select just as the first rock smashed through the window—showering the carpet with jagged shards of clear glass—and bounced across the coffee table. In the few seconds it took Craig to understand what had just happened, another two rocks came through the broken window. One landed on the couch next to Craig while the other clipped the edge of the television, narrowly missing his unprotected head as it tumbled through the air.

"What the fuck!" Craig spluttered, finally reacting to the danger and scrambling behind the couch.

"I can see people out in the woods," Hudson stated calmly, as if unaware of the rocks still rolling across the cottage's stone floor.

"Hudson! Get away from the window," Craig screamed at his unsuspecting girlfriend. His voice came out in a high-pitched croak, his throat felt tight and dry. Several heavy thuds resounded off the cottage's old brickwork which Craig assumed were more rocks, only these had missed their intended targets.

"They've got flaming torches, what the fuck is that all about? Don't they know it's the twenty-first century?" Hudson darted through from the kitchen, her long, dark hair trailing out behind her.

"Who has?" Craig gave her a confused look. He obviously hadn't heard her earlier comments.

"The people standing in the woods." Hudson gave him a disapproving look as if disappointed he had not hung on her every word, despite the rocks and glass that had been raining down on him at the time.

"What fucking people standing in the woods?" Craig's confusion only deepened with her explanation.

"I think they were in *The Slaughtered Lamb* earlier, but there are more of them now." Hudson didn't even flinch as another rock sailed through the window, dislodging another shard of glass, before landing in the fireplace with a loud crash.

"Why would the villagers throw rocks at the cottage?" Craig had pulled his jeans off the back of the couch and, such was his haste, was now struggling to get them over his feet.

"They're weird, superstitious folk down here," Hudson replied. Then, almost as an afterthought, added, "And it's a full moon."

"Do they know we're in here? They could kill us if one of those rocks hit us." Craig had finally pulled his jeans up and was reaching for his sweatshirt.

"They know." Hudson thought back to when she stood naked in the window, in full view of the villagers gathered in the darkness outside. "And I rather think that's the point. I don't think we're welcome here." She made no effort to find her clothes, although she felt vulnerable naked; Hudson saw little point in getting dressed.

"Why? Why would we not be welcome?" Craig pulled his sweatshirt over his head as he spoke. Hudson noticed it was inside out and was about to tell him, but then thought better of it as he continued. "What could we have possibly done to deserve being pelted with rocks?"

As if to punctuate his words, a rock smashed through the kitchen window and landed in the stainless steel sink with a loud clatter. Several more thumped into the cottage's brickwork. Then one bounced off the front door with a thunderous crash, causing it to rattle and shake within its wooden frame.

Hudson felt her anger rising, but she didn't feel scared. Frustrated maybe, annoyed undoubtedly, but not scared. Her fiercest emotion threatened to overtake her soul, threatened to unleash itself on those who chose to ruin her weekend away with Craig. He had tried several times to lure her away but she had always put him off in the past. But when he suggested this weekend it just seemed right, and she couldn't possibly put him off again, not without running the risk of damaging their relationship. This weekend she planned to tell Craig her secret, but not like this.

Another heavy impact shook the front door as Craig scrambled to his feet. "I've had enough of this. They need to know they can't scare us away, whatever their reason!" His words were full of bravado, but his actions were far more cautious as he crept towards the door.

"You can't go out there," Hudson said, a note of alarm obvious in her voice. "I don't think you can reason with them."

"So what then? We stay trapped in here all night, or at least until they decide to storm in and stone us to death? What will that achieve?" Craig had stopped in his tracks, unsure what to do next. His eyes darted nervously between the front door and Hudson, who remained huddled behind the couch.

"I don't know, but I know it's not safe out there. Why

don't you try the police?" Hudson's words had an edge to them that hadn't been present before as she hugged her knees to her chest, fighting the urges building deep within her body.

"Yes! Good idea, I'll do that," Craig muttered as he fumbled in his pocket, searching for his phone. After a few minutes of frantic, short-tempered dialling interspersed with loud curses, Craig dropped his phone on the couch. "No fucking signal! Bloody bumpkin village."

"I got nothing either." Hudson had pulled her phone from her jeans pocket which hung over the back of the couch. She swept her hair back from her face and tried to smile reassuringly. "I'm sure they just want to scare us. They'll probably go back to the pub soon and have a good laugh at our expense."

"What about the damage? Who pays for that?" Craig's practicality was one reason Hudson loved him: faced with a bloodthirsty mob, he worried about the bill. "Maybe it's all just an insurance job. We'll lose our deposit then get sued for the rest."

Hudson's theory of the villagers being out to scare them quickly collapsed as a burning torch flew through the broken window. The flaming cloth, wrapped around a broken branch, landed on the flagstone floor and slid towards the couch. Hudson scrambled away from the approaching flames, her teeth bared in anguish. Craig, seeing the danger, reacted quickly, surprising even himself as he leapt into action. Grabbing the torch's handle, he lifted it from the floor and swung it into the open-hearth in one smooth motion.

A second torch followed the first. Then a third crashed through the kitchen window, catching on the decorative curtains which quickly burst into flames as the torch swung back and forth, suspended in the material's elaborate folds. Hudson screamed as she watched the fire engulf the curtains. Craig rushed towards the danger, the primitive need to protect his lover coming to the fore.

Hudson pulled herself to her feet using the couch for support. She could not fight the urge any longer, her primal fear of fire had released her inner beast and she was no longer in control. The scream that sent Craig rushing to the burning curtains was not because of her fear of fire, but by the pain shredding her insides. While Craig beat at the flames with a damp hand towel, Hudson staggered to the bathroom. She may no longer be able to hide what she became, what she was, but she could at least protect Craig from the horror of the transformation.

Hudson had barely twisted the bathroom door's lock into place when her pelvis and shoulder blades twisted out of shape. She fell to the ground, her back arching as her bones tore apart at the joints. Another scream, deeper, more guttural than the first, ripped from her throat as her fingers and toes grew and arched into razor-sharp claws and the bones in her face ripped apart forcing her mouth open. Long pointed teeth broke through the gums in her newly formed muzzle as the top of her skull flattened and broadened. Her fine delicate skin sprouted coarse, dark hair and her long, luscious hair became a shaggy mane that covered Hudson's reformed shoulders and stretched down to her flattened breasts.

Hudson straightened to her full height, the medicine cabinet's mirror reflecting her wide, yellow eyes and slavering jaws, as she threw her head back and howled. The sound echoed back and forth off the small bathroom's country-styled, rose-tinted tiles.

"Hudson? Hudson?" He sounded out of breath, his voice distant. "There's a wolf out there. Did you hear it? Hudson? Where are you?"

Hudson's claws scraped across the tiled floor as her primal instincts took over. She felt trapped. Her flailing arms caught the shower curtain, ripping it from its plastic rings and pulling it down on top of her. The smell of fire filled the air as she clawed the door, scoring deep grooves into the softwood. She snarled, throwing her weight against the door, shaking it in its frame.

"Hudson? Is that you?" Craig almost coughed the words. "We have to get out, the fire, it's spreading." He sounded closer. There was a loud crash as another window succumbed to the barrage of rocks and torches.

Hudson turned and readied herself for another charge, her thick tail knocking her shampoo bottle and Craig's aftershave into the bathtub. She hurled herself against the door and heard the wood splinter. Above the heavy, thick smell of burning wood and paper, Hudson could detect the scent of humans. It wasn't Craig, she knew his decayed urban, artificially perfumed scent, but this was more earthy and basic. Salty sweat and stale tobacco mixed with the scent of sheep, cows, and farmyard muck and it was growing stronger. She tilted her head to one side and pricked her ears. Men's voices, raised and angry, came at her from all directions, the speakers encircling the cottage.

"Hudson!" The urgency in Craig's voice drew Hudson's attention. He was right outside the door. She snarled. She felt threatened, it was involuntary and natural, an instinct left over from the days when her ancestors lived wild.

"Hudson? Are you okay?" The door's wrought iron handle swung down and a weight hit the door. Hudson backed away. Nobody she had ever known had seen her like this and she couldn't be sure how he would react— how she would react.

"Hudson! The cottage is on fire, we have to get out!" Another loud thump shook the door. The villagers' voices were louder and more frantic. People shouted instructions as they approached the house, their obvious intention to trap Hudson and Craig inside the burning cottage.

Smoke began to find its way through the crack between the now-battered door and the damaged frame. Hudson sensed the time had come; to delay would be fatal, but to act would be a revelation she doubted Craig was prepared for. She had planned this moment so differently in her head, but those narrow-minded villagers, with their nineteenth century view of the world, had forced her clawed hand.

With a roar of frustration and anger, Hudson smashed her way through the door, sending splinters of wood in all directions as she crashed into the cottage's narrow hallway. She shoulder-barged a shocked Craig to the floor as she struggled to regain her balance on the bunched up rug and splintered fragments of the bathroom door. Hudson's lips curled back in a snarl as she stared down at him, an old world reaction to her closeness with a human, before she turned her attention to finding a way out of the burning cottage.

Craig lay on the floor in the hallway. He had thought his beloved Hudson had taken shelter in the small bathroom, a way of avoiding the flying rocks and burning torches. She had at first chosen to remain naked as they came under attack and he hoped she'd gone in search of something to cover her modesty. There was no way of telling what these villagers were after, especially after the way the barman had blatantly sized her up earlier. The burning torches may just be a way of driving him and Hudson out so the villagers could take their time with her.

He had heard a wolf howl but thought it came from the woods, never realising it was already in the cottage. But that was no ordinary wolf. And where was Hudson? He peered through the shattered door at the disarray in the bathroom beyond and felt relieved not to see her mangled body. Hudson had obviously not been in there when the wolf creature broke in and although this gave his anxiety a fleeting moment of respite, it didn't get him any closer to locating her.

A bloodcurdling scream from the kitchen area pulled Craig from his brief moment of confused inactivity, forcing him unsteadily to his feet. Fear gripped his throat. His legs felt weak and his stomach churned as he stumbled back through to the cottage's main room, fearing the creature or, possibly worse, the villagers, had attacked his future bride. A haze of dark smoke drifted across the room, stinging Craig's eyes as he squinted towards the burning kitchen.

For a second, the creature stood silhouetted against the flames, the lifeless body of a villager dangling from one of its massive paws. Then it darted into the flames, leaving the man's body slumped against the wall, before leaping through the broken kitchen window in one easy bound.

Hudson hated fire, but the villager had stood at the entrance to the kitchen brandishing a knife. With her increased turn of speed and the power of her strike she crossed the room and broke his neck before he had a chance to defend himself. He emitted one brief scream, which had died in his throat as the small bones in his neck separated from one another, alerting his friends to her attack. She had seen Craig stumble into the room and knew if she retraced her steps, returning towards the bathroom, her carnal, animalistic instincts would see him die in a similar fashion to the man hanging from her hand. Without thinking, she surged into the flames, springing onto the kitchen side, and diving headfirst into the small vegetable garden beyond the kitchen window.

Once out in the darkness and relative wilderness of the woods, Hudson felt more at ease. This was her natural environment, one in which she thrived. No longer trapped within her human skin or the confines of the burning cottage, she was free to hunt the yokel lycanophobes who still thought it acceptable to persecute her kind. She had seen the hatred in their eyes while in the pub; it was a look Hudson knew well. Some people, the uneducated and blinkered, still held on to their bigoted, outdated views so passionately they could sense the wolf lurking beneath the surface. If she were honest, Hudson expected the villagers to come, but Craig would never have understood why, so she'd just stayed naked and ready. The locals' eagerness to use fire on one of their own cottages had surprised her, but that just paid testament to the fear created by centuries of folklore.

Hudson could smell her prey. Out in the dark, she was the superior hunter. She ran through the woods in near silence, her strong leathery pads barely touching the ground, her eyes clearly picking a path between the trees, closing in on those that threatened her. She ran past a young man holding a shotgun, tearing his throat out without breaking stride, before closing in on two older men shouting instructions to those nearer the cottage. Hudson relished the brief look of terror on their faces as her strong arm and razor-like claws tore one man's face from the skull beneath while her teeth savaged his companion's throat. She moved on swiftly, not caring whether they were dead or not, her revenge extracted.

Hudson circled the cottage, killing two more men and a woman. The woman stumbled right into her in the dark and Hudson dispatched her with a lazy flick of her index claw, neatly slicing the woman's neck open. The men were happily chatting, obviously prematurely celebrating Hudson's death, unaware she had escaped the burning cottage and was stood just a few yards away. The one lewdly boasting about seeing her naked in the window died without his testicles, his friend enjoyed a quicker and far more painless death.

Leaving the bodies for the wildlife, Hudson padded towards the cottage. She stopped at the treeline, where woodland gave way to mowed lawn, and sniffed the air. She smelt Craig, *The Slaughtered Lamb*'s barkeep, and another man. The steam rose from her coat, joining the vapour swirling from her snout as she slowly advanced on the burning building. The entire kitchen side of the cottage was alight, the flames flickering high into the night sky, the smoke drifting away into the trees while the cottage's other side appeared untouched by the fire. Hudson moved round the building, avoiding the fire, looking for a way back in.

Finding a broken window, Hudson reared up and stared into the smoky interior. The thick, acrid smell of the smoke filled her nostrils, overwhelming her and blocking out her ability to smell the human's scent. With a scrabble of claws, she was over the sill and prowling across the room's thickly-quilted double-bed. Jumping down, she hooked the door wide open with her paw and crept into the hallway beyond.

Craig lay on the floor near the front door. The sound of someone moving clumsily about the room came from another nearby doorway, and it was towards the noise that Hudson crept. Rounding the frame of the doorway, she saw the barkeep rummaging through her and Craig's suitcases, holding a towel across his face to protect him from the smoke. Hudson let out a fearsome snarl as she reared up on her back legs. This time the old man's eyes lingered not on her breasts but on her teeth, his leering expression replaced by a look of sheer terror. Hudson slashed his fat, bloated abdomen open with one powerful swipe of her arm, allowing his intestines to hit the floor shortly before his knees. She stared into his eyes as he died and was back in the hallway before his chest hit the floor. She was in a hurry.

Hudson returned to Craig's prone form and licked his face until he moaned and tried pushing her away. She persisted, forcing him awake. With a start and a stifled scream, he returned to full consciousness, staring into her blood-coated face. Hudson's tail thumped against the wall in her excitement and relief at seeing Craig alive as she turned away in search of the last of her prey, leaving her lover to find his own way out.

She did not have to search far; her prey came looking for her. He appeared at the end of the corridor brandishing a large knife, and without warning charged towards her. Hudson met him head on. Her claws tore into the flesh of his shoulder. His knife tore into the flesh of her shoulder, but she hadn't finished. Her teeth ripped into his throat. Hudson ragged him hard, shaking her head from side to side, applying more and more pressure to his neck until his head separated from his shoulders. Then she limped back into the bedroom, up onto the bed and out of the window.

Craig stumbled out of the front door, coughing the smoke from his lungs as he shouted for Hudson. He wasn't sure what he had seen in the smoke but knew he was lucky to be alive. That knowledge was reinforced when he came across the savaged remains of two men on the edge of the wood as he scoured the area surrounding the blazing cottage for Hudson. He feared the worst; he hadn't seen her since the first few torches ignited the kitchen curtains, and he couldn't even be sure how long ago that was.

Then he found her. She lay curled up at the edge of the garden, her pale skin reflecting the flickering flames. At first, because of the blood covering her face, chest and arms, he thought she must be dead. Then she took a breath. She had a bloody hole in her shoulder where something had obviously stabbed her, but after a quick check that was the only wound he could find. Scooping Hudson up in his arms, Craig carried her through the garden towards his parked car.

"Am I alive, what happened?" Hudson looked up at Craig with tired eyes.

"You're alive, babe. Some creature ripped those villagers apart and we need to get out of these woods before it comes back." Craig glanced around nervously as he spoke.

"Okay! Whatever you think's best." Hudson closed her eyes with a soft smile, sure in the knowledge her secret was safe, at least for another month.

ASH HARTWELL

Ash Hartwell has had over fifty short stories published in anthologies from, JEA, Stitched Smile Publications, Nocturnicorn Books, and Open Casket Press, to name a few. JEA published his collection of shorts, Zombies, Vamps and Fiends in 2015 and his debut novel, Tip Of The Iceberg, is out mid-2017.

He was born, lives in Northamptonshire and is planning not to die for a while.

JINMENKEN

ADAM MILLARD

The fist came from nowhere; a wet slap to the side of the head which rattled his brain and bandied his legs. It was all he could do to remain on his feet as a trillion white dots danced around in the space between his eyes and eyelids. He was suddenly aware of shouts and screams, panicked interpolations laden with expletives, and though he recognised at least one of the voices—it sounded thick and vague, as if its speaker were sitting at the bottom of an ocean—there were several which he did not.

Blinking the white dots away, Michael staggered back, his hip crashing into what he could only infer to be the pool table upon which he had recently been a player. The pub—*The Mermaid's* something or other—swiftly returned to him in all its kitschy grandeur. His aggressor, a heavy-set thug with shorn head, had by now snatched up the nearest pool cue and was attempting to shake off two gentlemen, who were doing everything within their power to prevent the thug from striking again.

Michael spat a glob of blood onto the sticky pub carpet and was about to speak when—

"There was no need for that, mate." It was Alan, Michael's best friend, stepping forward to confront the thug, who was still trying to sidestep the duo blocking his path, although no longer with any real determination. "It's just a game of pool."

The pub seemed to return to normal, then. Punters ordered drinks from the bar, and the fruit-machine standing in the corner resumed its incessant chirruping and epilepsy-inducing flashing. The fight—if it could even be considered as such, what with its brevity and remarkable one-sidedness—was over before it had begun.

"I think we should leave, Michael." A hand wrapped around his upper arm, gently tugged him away from the pool table. It was Carrie, and her voice was barely a whisper, a staccato exhalation drenched with fear.

All at once a surge of defiance coursed through Michael. Why *should* they leave? Because some asshole was a bad loser? It didn't sit well with him. And besides, he had only just got the drinks in; the froth had yet to dissipate on his and Alan's pints Carrie and Lisa's drinks—some ungodly sweet cocktail the colour of pissed-on sludge—sat untouched on the table to his right.

"We're not going *anywhere*," Michael said. His jaw clicked as he spoke, and for a moment he wondered if the damage done—ostensibly superficial—would require further attention.

He turned, walked across to his beer, picked it up and took a long, solid slug. He watched as the two Samaritans led the thug across to the other side of the pub and sat him down at a table.

"Nice moves, there," Alan sighed. He picked up his own glass and took a mouthful. "On the bright side, you stayed on your feet. That was a helluva punch. Fuck, I didn't even see it coming until it was too late."

Satisfied that there would be no further skirmishes— the thug was laughing with the two men, now, seemingly over the altercation—Michael settled onto the leather bench at the back of their table. "Fucker almost punched me into the future," he said, not without humour. He was secretly glad of the two men who had bravely stepped in to block off the thug, for it was a fight Michael would not have stood much chance of winning.

Easing in beside him, Carrie said, "The guy was an asshole. I hate people like that. Out for a fight, that's all.

Makes me sick." She gently squeezed his leg and smiled. Michael adored that smile and the way it dimpled her cheeks. "Let's finish our drinks and get out of here, yeah?"

Michael turned to Alan, who was nodding in agreement. Lisa beside him said, through a heavy yawn, "I've got an early start in the morning, anyway," as if that should be the deciding factor. The truth of the matter was, as a ward nurse Lisa *always* had an early start. She was also always exhausted. Michael didn't know how Alan put up with it. Her constant fatigue and ridiculous hours must have made it almost impossible to maintain any sort of sex life.

Thankfully, Carrie was just a barista.

"We're not leaving because of that prick," Michael said, the last syllable slightly louder than the ones before it, for he was still chagrined at the sheer gall of the thug and wanted him to know it. The thug, however, was too busy rolling a cigarette and shouting unintelligibly at the big-screen and the myriad interchangeable rugby players projected upon it to notice.

"It's not because of him," Alan said. "Lisa's got an early start, and I'm not feeling it tonight. You've already hit your limit" —he motioned to the half-empty pint sitting on the table in front of Michael— "and this place is about to get rowdy as hell. I didn't even know there was a game on tonight."

"Nor me," Michael said. "Fucking rugby." If it were up to him, all rugby fans—thugs and criminals to a man— would be taken outside and shot. It was probably a good job it was not up to him.

Beneath the table, Carrie's hand ran up along the outside of his thigh before tracking inwards, fingers gently trailing over his flies. "An early night wouldn't hurt us either," she said. "That is, if you're not too tired after your tussle with Goliath over there."

"Not much of a tussle," Michael said, somewhat despondently.

"You were the bigger man," she said, and now she was applying pressure to his groin, pressing gently down, seeking out his burgeoning erection. Into his ear, she whispered, "I think you deserve a reward."

"I think I need a piss before we leave," Michael said.

The cubicle was filthy, its toilet overflowing with soiled paper and cigarette butts. Michael dropped the seat down so he didn't have to look at it, lest the pint he had just finished make a sudden and unwanted reappearance.

He took the small bundle of coke from his jacket pocket and unwrapped it, being careful not to lose any of the powder it contained to the piss- and shit-stained cubicle floor. Using the cistern at the back of the toilet, he prepared a trio of lines before snuffling them up through a rolled twenty.

Now he was ready to leave *The Mermaid's* something or other, and to hell with the thuggish prick and his stupid game of rugby.

For an August night the weather was atrocious. Rain peppered the windscreen faster than the wipers could sweep it aside. Michael could just about make out the lights of the car in front through the torrent. It was gloomy, but not yet full dark.

In the passenger seat Carrie toyed with her phone. Michael guessed she'd stumbled upon yet another addictive puzzle game of some description. He would lose her to it in those moments of silence, those breaks in conversation and activity, for several weeks or until she mastered it to the point it became monotonous, whichever came first.

He didn't mind. Those asinine cryptic apps made her happy; she often smiled like a child as she played them, and Michael would watch her as she played, would find himself smiling along as intense concentration played about her features and her tongue, upon occasion, popped out of the side of her mouth.

"Slow down."

It was Alan from the seat directly behind his own. His words were accompanied by a gentle kick halfway down the seat.

Michael glanced down at the speedometer: 52 m.p.h. "I'm hardly going *fast*," he said. "Just because you're used to riding shotgun with your mom."

"With *your* mom," Alan replied, puerilely. "And she loves it."

Michael couldn't help but laugh. Perhaps it was the three lines of coke he'd just snorted; under normal circumstances, a 'your mom' joke would barely scratch his funny-bone.

"Did you just say that you sleep with Michael's mom?" Lisa asked Alan from the back seat. It was banter, the kind of thing they all partook in when the mood was right.

"Only on nights I'm not with you," Alan said.

"Well that's never, then," Lisa said.

"And only on the nights Michael's not sleeping with her."

"A bit much, Al," Carrie said, suddenly emerging from her game. Perhaps, Michael thought, it was a change between levels. When she returned to the game a few seconds later, he knew that's what it had been.

Michael arrived on the A454 in good time. Traffic was surprisingly light, which was a good thing. He wanted to get home while Carrie was still in the mood so that they might finish what she started back at the pub. But first there would be a quick stop in Bridgnorth to unload Alan and Lisa. Lisa who didn't really like Carrie (the feeling was mutual) but tolerated her for the sake of Alan the same way Carrie put up with Lisa. It never ceased to amaze Michael how good they both were at concealing their unwarranted disinclination for one another in order to protect the sanctity of the group.

If the shoe were on the other foot, Michael knew he would not be able to make such an effort.

"How many times?" Alan suddenly said. "Slow down, dude. It's slick as all hell out there. If you have to brake—"

"Do *you* want to drive?" Michael said. "Chill the fuck out, mate. Let those of us with a license get on with it, yeah?"

It was a cheap shot—Alan had failed his test on three occasions, and was currently awaiting a date for his fourth attempt—but there was nothing Michael hated more than backseat drivers.

"You should probably slow down," Carrie said nonchalantly and without looking up from her phone.

"Don't you start," said Michael, a tension mounting inside of him. The road ahead was now clear. A little rain wasn't going to slow him down, and neither was the complaints of his passengers. He just wanted to get rid of Alan and Lisa now. Miserable pair of fuckers.

He pressed gently down on the accelerator.

"Oh, well, that's smart," Alan said, for he must have felt the car's steady quickening. "You know what? I hope the police pull us—"

"There's no police out here," Michael said. "They use this stretch for races." He didn't know if that were true; he simply wanted to unnerve Alan. "No cameras either," he went on. "In fact, I'd go so far as to say this is probably the least patrolled stretch of carriageway in the midlands."

65 m.p.h.

71 m.p.h

77 m.p.h.

"Michael," Carrie said, and when he turned to face her he saw that she was no longer interested in her game; she looked angry. "Knock it off."

"Knock *what* off?" Michael hammered at the steering wheel with open palms. It hadn't occurred to him until now, but he was still frustrated about what had happened back at *The Mermaid's* something or other. Coupled with three lines of coke off the back of a grimy toilet, he was a ball of raging fury.

And judging by the way his girlfriend was looking at him, an idiot to boot.

"You're being a dickhead," Carrie said. "Slow down—"

"Can you believe that fucking *asshole* back there?" Michael said through gritted teeth. His head snapped to the side as he relived the heavy punch the thug had connected with. He quickly snapped it back across to the road. "I should have dropped that fucker!" He knew it was the drugs speaking, but in that moment he felt as if he could take on anyone. He wanted to turn the car around, head back to the pub and lay into that sonofabitch. Keep hitting him until nothing remained but a pile of meaty flesh and grey matter. He wanted to do that before the coke wore off and he went back to being boring old Michael Sullivan, the pussy who lets people hit him and get away with it, the faggot who allows people to tell him how to drive his own car.

"Just calm down!" Carrie was frantic now, and as she lunged forward, her phone slipped down into the foot-well.

But Michael couldn't calm down. He just wanted to hurt something, to take his anger out on something other than the steering-wheel.

The car veered to the right; the rapid *thump-thump-thump* of painted lines passing beneath the tyres sounded like the ceremonial drumming of some ancient tribe. Carrie screamed, begged Michael to straighten up and reaching for the wheel herself. Her seatbelt snatched her back into place, just shy of the wheel.

"I'm going back there!" Michael was howling now, a

madman without a full moon for inspiration. He grabbed the wheel with both hands and pulled it hard to the right, his intention to squeal across into the adjacent lane and continue back in the direction from which they had just travelled. And it might have worked out that way if he'd first slowed down. As it was, the car made it just across the median strip before its wheels locked up.

At 75 m.p.h., the car flipped once, twice, a third time; a cacophony of twisting steel and shattering glass. For Michael, everything happened in slow-motion. He watched as Carrie thumped forward, momentarily ejected from her seat, her tiny frame snapping like so many broken twigs, her nose exploding like a crimson bomb upon the glove compartment. Then she was pulled back into the seat as thin slivers of glass shredded her face and neck to ribbons. As his own face planted squarely into the airbag where a moment ago there had been a steering-wheel—and as the car completed its second flip—something passed over his shoulder and slammed into the already-decimated windscreen.

A body.

*Some*body.

And over they went once more. By now Michael cursed the cocaine he'd snorted, for it was surely that which stretched this horrific scene out into perpetuity. He felt no pain, and no matter how much he prayed for unconsciousness it did not come.

He was forced to watch as the body of his girlfriend, the bodies of his friends, were bent and broken by invisible hands.

Then there was greenery in the car, whipping at Michael's face, as the car completed its fourth and final flip. He knew this road well, tried to picture the embankment they were now sliding down as the unmistakeable smell of petrol filled up the crumpled shell of his vehicle and lulled him toward obscurity.

Cars explode, he thought. *Cars explode when they flip over and this one's no different.*

But the car did not explode.

What happened next was so much worse.

Michael Sullivan survived.

This is important, Michael told himself as he locked his front door, walked down the path and climbed into his '06-plate Corsa. It was a cold night, one year to the day of the terrible accident in which his girlfriend, his friend, and his friend's girlfriend had foolishly entrusted him with their lives. The maudlin anniversary was not what made this night so important, for he knew he could drive that stretch any night of the year and still not obtain the closure he so desired. What made it important was the strange pull he had been feeling these past few days, an almost inexorable summoning.

He had dreamed, three nights prior, of Carrie, wandering along the thin strip of kerbing at the side of the A454, her clothes bloodied and torn, her face all but obliterated. Slivers of glass protruded from her pale white flesh. And yet despite her obvious trauma, she skipped incongruously along, as if this were the happiest she had been in her life. The dream had not finished there, however, for a mile or so along the road Carrie had met up with Alan and Lisa. Both were bloody, broken caricatures of their former selves, slumped against a hedge, almost like marionettes whose strings had been cut. And yet they, too, were apparently happy; their faces contorted with smiles far too wide for their heads.

Michael had wakened with a start, a thin sheet of sweat coating his entire body. What a strange and terrible dream, he had thought, and yet he could not ignore it. And that had proven to be the case in the three days that followed, when everything seemed to remind him of Carrie, of that night a year ago. Just yesterday, during a rare venture out, he had found himself face to face with a man he had not seen in twelve months.

The rugby thug.

Here he was at the newsagents purchasing a paper and tobacco, unaware that the man standing in the queue behind—heart racing, head pounding, stomach churning—had once bettered him at pool and subsequently met with his giant, tattooed fist. A year had passed in which Michael had not seen this man, but now, of course, here he was.

It *meant* something.

Michael pulled away from the kerb, drove slowly and carefully between the cars parked either side of his street, and turned right.

It was raining, as it had been on the night of the accident—

Accident?

You murdered them the moment you snorted those lines in that filthy cubicle!

"That's not *true*!" Michael screamed. "It could have happened to anyone!"

Anyone stupid enough to use coke, you selfish bastard!

"Shut up!" He slapped at the side of his head, hoping the accusatory voice—an ungodly amalgamation of Carrie, Alan, and Lisa, for they were now Legion, it seemed—ceased its cruel hecklings. They came to him every now and then, as if to remind him of his past transgressions.

As if he would ever forget.

The roads were preternaturally quiet; a few cars—cabs, mainly—dawdled along. A tractor slowed Michael for two miles before finally turning off onto a country lane, leaving the carriageway ahead wholly clear.

He kept to the speed limit, despite the urge to drive faster.

Shortly after the accident he had placed himself in rehab, a thirty-day detox designed to free him of his addiction once and for all. For thirty days he had existed on a ward in which men screamed themselves to sleep at night, the stench of sweat and vomit a constant. Two suicides and a month later he had left that infernal place feeling better than he had in years.

Newly-clean, almost reborn, he had deigned to forgive himself for what he had done.

He was still working on it.

Two roundabouts and a T-junction later, Michael joined the A454. Bound for Bridgnorth, he was less than six miles from the spot rage had got the better of him.

"Leave those ones for now," a voice had said as flashing blue lights filled the overturned husk of a car. "This one's still alive."

Michael had sobbed as they eased him gently from the smouldering wreck, his body cut and sore but no breaks and no internal bleeding. "You're very lucky to be alive," were words he heard many times during his time in hospital, words which continued to follow him though rehab and beyond.

Lucky?

Sure.

The rain drummed a thousand skeletal fingers upon the roof of the car as he drew closer to his destination; the wipers worked manically at the windscreen, fruitlessly. A distant rumble of thunder—*twisting steel, breaking glass, hissing tyres*—startled Michael, and he almost crossed the intersection.

Straightening up in his seat, he cursed himself for being so skittish. But it wasn't the weather which caused his agitation; it was the feeling that, one way or another, after tonight, things would be very different indeed.

Two miles to go, and still not a vehicle in sight. Michael glanced toward the dashboard clock which flicked over to 22:21. It was getting late, and the inclement weather was no doubt a factor, but six miles without so much as another soul was... curious.

A flash of lightning illumined the road ahead and the fields either side of the car, and when it was gone—leaving the Corsa's dim headlights to resume the mantle—the world seemed darker, somehow. Then came the inevitable crash of thunder, much closer this time, and loud enough to send sheep running across the leas in search of shelter and sanctuary.

One mile to go.

Michael hammered at the steering-wheel with open palms. "What are you doing?" he screamed, for suddenly he realised the absurdity of his actions. There was no redemption out here for him; there was no forgiveness to be found amongst the grasslands and nothingness of the A454. There was only roadkill and wheel-trims, squashed badgers and flattened hedgehogs scattered about the road with their innards stretching for miles and miles and their hopes and dreams of ever reaching the other side lying in tatters.

Like Carrie.

Like Alan and Lisa.

Just bloody roadkill.

The scream in Michael's throat caught as, suddenly, the car's headlights flashed upon something in the road ahead. Slamming his foot down on the brake, the car began to squeal as the creature—a dog? Yes, it *had* to be—stood motionless, watching the oncoming vehicle with mild indifference.

The car did not flip this time. Instead it barrelled into a wire fence, past that and into a hedge, and then onto an open field. There was no airbag fitted to this car, though, or if there was it was defective, and so Michael's face met the steering-wheel with a sickening crunch. Pain stabbed at his legs and back as his head flew back and thumped against the headrest. His eyes remained open the entire time, tear-filled and stinging.

How long he sat there, unmoving, unwilling to even try, Michael did not know. The car had stalled, had travelled only a few metres into this empty field in which he now found himself.

You're very lucky to be alive...

Hissing, the taste of blood like copper upon his tongue, Michael reached down to unclip his seatbelt. Once he'd managed that, he reached for the handle and gave it a lethargic tug. The door opened easily, for the car had come to settle upon a slight incline to the right.

Michael slowly stepped out, thankful that his legs were still working, and although they were, he struggled to remain upon them, as if his torso had suddenly gained weight. He slumped to his knees, his hands finding the cold, sodden grass; the skeletal fingers of rain now rattled upon his spine, too many to count.

He crawled for a while, unsure of which direction he was heading. Away from the car was the best he could do. Back to the road, where he would flag someone down.

The fact that he had not seen another car on the road since joining the A454 was not lost on him. But what else could he do but wait? Someone would surely be along, someone would help—

A howl from nearby derailed his current train of thought and caused him to fall still in the mud beneath his hands and knees. Breathless, he listened, trying to discern from which direction the noise had emanated, when there came another sound from his right.

A barking. As of a mad dog.

Then, to his left, a guttural growl from somewhere within the darkness. Michael snapped his head across, squinted through watery eyes in the hopes of seeing the thing standing there, but he could not, not right away.

A feral bark from the gap in the hedge ahead—the aperture created by his car—drew his attention away from the darkness to his left. And now he realised, with some dismay, that he was surrounded on three sides by wild animals of some description. The image of the dog he saw just before losing control of the car was not quite right as it played through his mind. And he didn't have to wait long to discover why.

Through the void in the hedge it came at a canter; a solid black body, muscular and sinewy all at once. But when his eyes fell upon its face an involuntary moan escaped his lips.

The creature wore Carrie's face as its own. Its teeth bared, Michael could just about make out the dimples in her cheeks and the beautiful shock of blonde hair framing her face, hanging down over thick, furry black shoulders.

Paralysed with fear as the things to his left and right stepped from the darkness—and what a lovely couple they had once made—Michael lost all control of his bodily functions, and he slumped to the dirt, sobbing and cursing the gods for allowing these things to exist.

The thing that was once his best friend barked once before leaping onto his back, and then they were all upon him, tearing at his flesh with their teeth and scratching at him with their claws. He saw their faces as they rolled about, their fur-covered rain-matted bodies as they pinned him to the ground and feasted.

And the rain came down in sheets as Michael Sullivan was finally granted the redemption he so eagerly sought.

ADAM MILLARD

Adam Millard is the author of twenty-two novels, twelve novellas, and more than two hundred short stories, which can be found in various collections and anthologies. Probably best known for his post-apocalyptic fiction, Adam also writes fantasy/horror for YA/MG, as well as bizarro fiction for several publishers. His work has recently been translated for the German market.

OIL IS THICKER THAN BLOOD

BENEDICT J. JONES

The apartment is large, airy and furnished throughout to a high standard little different to a hotel suite. A week old Premier League football match plays on the television and although a low table is covered in bottles of spirits the men in the apartment sit in relative quiet. An efficient air con unit keeps the apartment cool despite the oppressive heat outside but the air is still thick with cigarette smoke. Hale, of the Gulf Star, picks up a deck of cards and offers it to the men around him.

"Poker? Pontoon?"

There is a shaking of heads and a recharging of glasses. Svenson, of the Prestige, takes a mouthful of Johnny Walker before speaking, enjoying the taste of it on his tongue.

"I see the bloody Somalis have taken another ship."

"Which?"

"The Tara."

"Shit! That's Gemmell's ship."

Silence, once more descends over the men as they stare into their glasses, each man studying the liquor within rather than verbalising their thoughts. The man who runs the apartment for its owner appears from the other room and asks the men if there is anything else that they require. There is a general shaking of heads and the man vanishes once more with an impassive smile that hides his true feelings towards the westerners that he serves. Hale puts down the deck of cards and looks up at the others.

"I suppose you already know about Lehman?"

Heads are shaken and men look up, attentive now and eager for news. Hale lights a cigarette and leans back in his chair.

"If someone will grab me another beer then I'll tell you all about it."

Van Den Berg, of the Hellespont Giant, pulls his huge frame from his chair and grabs a fresh bottle of Heineken, so cold that the bottle sweats, from the large refrigerator. He passes the bottle to Hale who runs his finger through the moisture on the bottle and then takes a deep bite before continuing.

"Well, you all probably know that Lehman has been captaining the Panama Valdez since he left Exxon. He was carrying a load through pirate alley…"

Lehman leaned against the bridge of the Panama Valdez and stared out over the deck. Light reflected from the white-painted deck made it glow in the moonlight. He could see Martinez walking along one of the gangways; the first mate was so far from Lehman that he looked like a stick figure in a Lowry painting. Lehman took a mouthful of his coffee and waited for the man to make it up onto the bridge.

"You got it from here?"

Martinez nodded.

"Yes, Captain."

Lehman exited the bridge and made his way down to his quarters, sleep being all he wanted. He trusted his Filipino first mate to keep the ship running smoothly. As soon as Lehman lay down in his cot his mind seemed to come awake. He swore and tossed and turned but sleep finally came twenty minutes—seeming like twenty hours—later. Lehman dreamt of burning lakes of red on black and himself standing naked at the edge of it.

A hand shook him awake. He sat up immediately.

"Sorry, Captain."

Chen looked apologetic as the captain swung, fully dressed, off his cot and pulled his shoes back on.

"This had better be good."

The small Chinese passed him a cup of coffee and Lehman smiled. He took a swig and got up.

"Well?"

"Misser Martinez say he need you in radio room."

Lehman nodded and picked up his cap as he headed up to the radio room. When he arrived he saw a concerned looking Martinez standing over the radio operator, Vallacer. Vallacer, like Martinez, was from the Philippines as were several other members of the crew, the rest being made up of Sri Lankans and a few Europeans. The radio chattered and Lehman heard Arabic voices through the static. It sounded to Lehman like there were half a dozen voices speaking beneath the cloak of white noise.

"What are they saying?"

Vallacer shrugged. Lehman looked to Martinez who did likewise.

"Do the pirates ever speak in Arabic?"

Martinez nodded.

"I've heard them do it before."

"Shit. Increase speed. How long till dawn?"

"About five hours, Captain."

"Keep me updated, Vallacer. Martinez, with me on the bridge."

As Lehman checked the ship's position, Martinez stood close by at his elbow. The captain didn't look up as he spoke.

"We maintain speed. No way their little piss-ant speedboats can catch the Valdez."

Lehman's eyes were cold and Martinez nodded to his

captain.

"I'm going back to bed—do not let our speed drop, even if the engine falls out this bitch."

Martinez grinned as the captain vanished off the bridge. If there was one man he wanted to be with rolling through pirate alley then it was Captain Lehman. The first mate stared out at the clear night sky and watched the stars overhead. If there was a view to beat this then he hadn't seen it yet.

An hour later and Lehman was once more roused from his sleep. Chen looked at him with his head tilted to one side.

"They need you."

"You'd better get some coffee on. It's going to be one of those nights."

Chen handed a cup to the captain with a smile.

"I thought you need another cup, Cap'n."

Lehman took a draft and grinned; Chen made the best coffee that Lehman had ever had on board a ship. He headed up to the bridge and cast a sour look at his first mate. Martinez looked strange, as though someone had told him they had sighted an iceberg in the Gulf.

"Well?"

Martinez looked away

"Come on, man! Why've you got me up now?"

"It's Langdon, sir…"

"What about him? What illness has he contracted now?"

"No, he saw something far up the deck."

"Saw what, Martinez?"

The first mate looked the captain dead in the eyes as he spoke.

"A woman."

Lehman laughed.

"Didn't he manage to get his dick wet in port then?"

Lehman shook his head and turned away, still laughing.

"He was serious. This was no mariner's fancy. He

described her to me."

"And?"

"He said she was wearing a…"

Martinez ran his hand in front of his face.

"A veil?"

"No the whole thing. A burka. And he said she only had one arm."

"Oh, this gets better. Where is he?"

"Down in the mess."

Lehman grunted a response and left the bridge to find Langdon.

Langdon sat in the mess and looked, to Lehman, even paler than usual; Langdon was an able enough seaman but always had some complaint in regards to his health or his ship mates, something that always grated on Lehman's sense of things. The seaman ran a hand through his collar-length hair and refused to meet Lehman's eye.

"So?"

Langdon finally looked up and the captain saw that his eyes were red and raw.

"I swear I saw her, Captain."

Lehman nodded and took a seat on the bench next to Langdon.

"Tell me what you saw."

"She was down at the fo'c's'le. At first I thought it was a trick of the light. She kinda just came out of the shadows."

"And she was wearing a burka?"

Langdon nodded.

"And her arm?"

"That was the worst of it. I called out to her and she turned to face me and I saw that her arm was gone below the elbow and in her other arm she was holding…"

"Yes? What was she holding?"

Langdon looked Lehman straight in the eye.

"A dead baby."

The captain blew out a long breath and adjusted the cap on his head.

"Okay."

"You believe me?"

"Yes, Langdon, I do. You stay here and sort yourself out. I think we might have ourselves a stowaway."

Lehman left the dining room and headed back up to the bridge.

"Martinez. Organise a search. I want this woman found."

"You think he really saw her?"

Lehman nodded.

"A thorough search. Langdon thought he saw something and I don't know if it really was a person or not but we need to check."

Martinez looked doubtful but he headed off the bridge to find any of the crew that weren't engaged in essential activities. The captain leaned against a bulkhead and watched as his men moved along the decks and gangways in the too-bright glare of the overhead lights. Lehman jotted in the log as he waited. He waited for the cry of one of the searchers that would alert him to the presence of a stowaway—none came, and eventually Martinez returned to the bridge. He shrugged at the captain and slumped against the lockers.

"Nothing?"

"Nothing. If there was someone there we would've found them."

Lehman nodded.

"Okay. Send Langdon to his bunk but keep your eyes open. I'm going to have a walk around."

Before he left the bridge Lehman grabbed up a walkie-talkie and shook it at Martinez. The first mate nodded.

Beyond the glare of the lights above the deck the night

was still and Lehman could see clouds moving in from the East. The radio attached to his belt crackled before he had even moved ten metres. Lehman turned the volume up to better hear the sound on his handset. It sounded like a thousand souls screaming as one. Lehman recognised the language as Arabic, but could identify none of the words. He stopped at the rail and stared into the night. The sea seemed calm and the clouds seemed closer, lower, than they had been a moment earlier.

The handset crackled again.

"Captain? Captain?"

Lehman clicked the handset.

"Martinez, come in."

There was no response except a burst of static, and Lehman headed back towards the bridge. The ship began to tilt and sway as he moved across the deck and Lehman saw the clouds overhead now seemed close enough to touch and the sea was swelling around the vessel. Lehman grabbed at the ladder and hauled himself up. Martinez stood at the helm, beads of sweat rolling down his face like escape pods heading towards the earth.

"What in hell's name is going on?"

"Sir, you need to speak to the engine room. It's chaos!"

Lehman grabbed up the mike and called down to the engine room.

"Kessel, come in, it's Lehman."

"Captain! We're flooding! We're taking on… water."

The last word didn't ring true.

"Water?"

"Well, I don't know what to call it. It's as thick as oil and as black as blood in moonlight and Jesus! The smell… It smells like copper. Wait, Ramos has found something. My God, Captain, there are things in this stuff."

The link to the engine room cut off with a hiss and Lehman slammed the mike back down. He reached under his chair and pulled out a grey lock box. Company policy strictly prohibited the carrying of weapons on board ship but Lehman had always preferred to reduce the risk of someone sneaking a gun on board by having his own. He slipped the clip into the hand grip of the Beretta and chambered a round.

"Martinez, I'm going down to the engine room—take the bridge."

The captain vanished through the doorway and Martinez felt very alone. He picked up a heavy torch and laid it within easy reach. He looked out over the huge expanse of deck below and watched as the lights flickered. The shadows twisted and flexed along the edges of the deck and Martinez struggled to see what moved within them.

Hale stops talking and sits back in his chair to light another cigarette. The men around him are quiet and staring.

"And then?" they ask as one.

Hale shrugs and finally finds a fresh pack of Marlboros in his pocket. Van Den Berg holds out a light for him and Svenson grabs him another beer from the fridge.

"Come on, man!"

"Okay…"

Lehman ran into his chief engineer before he reached the engine room.

"There you are, Captain. I couldn't raise the bridge on the intercom."

"What the hell's going on in there?"

The engineer clapped a hand to his brow.

"We've got the pumps going to try and clear out whatever the hell it is that has flooded in."

"What did Ramos find?"

"I don't know. Something slammed against his leg. Beneath the surface you could just about see them, like birds fluttering behind frosted glass."

The captain stared at the king of the engine room; the big engineer was one of the most solid and dependable men that he had ever sailed with.

"I know how it sounds, Captain."

Kessel seemed distracted. There wasn't time to dwell on the madness, so Lehman asked the most important question.

"The engines?"

For a moment Kessel looked away.

"They've slowed down. I'm not sure if I can even raise half speed out of them."

"Do what you can. I'll have to call this in."

Lehman turned and walked away. He tucked the Beretta into the back of his waistband as he headed back to the bridge. It was quiet when Lehman walked in. Martinez stood staring out at the deck.

Lehman coughed and the first mate turned to look at him, his left eyebrow arching into a question. The captain shook his head in response.

"When does he think they'll be working again? We're as good as dead in the water here."

"Soon as he can, you know Kessel. They're going to have to pump all that crap out the engine room first. We'll have to call it in and make sure we have men on both radars. How's the weather?"

"Those swells died away as quick as they appeared."

"Okay. Get the men on those radars."

Martinez nodded and headed for the doorway.

"Captain? What are we going to do if they come?"

"Do? What can we do? We'll just have to hope that French warship is in range."

The first mate slipped away and left Lehman to his thoughts.

The sun bled into the sky as dawn approached and Lehman watched the horizon for signs of either small boats or a larger warship. He saw nothing and the sea lay still as the sun crawled slowly into view. The radio and satellite phone gave off nothing but static and the radar screens were a mass of strange shapes. Lehman had sent Martinez off to his bunk and remained alone on the bridge.

Chen stuck his head through the doorway to the bridge.

"Coffee, Cap'n?"

Lehman nodded and took the flask.

"How are you, Chen?"

Chen smiled, but then Chen always smiled.

"I be happy when we go again."

It was Lehman's turn to nod.

"We'll be underway as soon as we can."

"I know, Captain. But I worry I won't see land again. Any land."

Lehman looked at the clouds shifting in his coffee.

"I'll get us back. At worst we'll have to wait for the company to pay a ransom on us."

"A ransom for the oil maybe—how much is old Chen worth, Cap'n?"

The smile was back on his face and as he left the bridge Lehman said nothing.

Martinez reappeared. The first mate looked no better for the sleep he should have got; his hair, usually slicked down, stuck up from his scalp at odd angles and his eyes were as puffy as if he had been in a fight.

"Coffee?"

Martinez grabbed up a cup and held it out while the captain poured.

"Get much sleep?"

"No. Every time I closed my eyes I dreamed."

"Of?"

"A black sea under a red sun and terrible things in the

sea."

The first mate rubbed his face. Lehman thought of his own dreams and said nothing.

"Are you okay to stay here while I check in with Kessel?"

Martinez nodded and slipped into the chair that Lehman had just vacated.

Captain Lehman stood at the top of the ladder to the engine room and called down for Kessel. After a moment Ramos appeared.

"He's not here, Captain."

"Well where is he? I need those engines."

"He... he..."

"He *what* man? Where is Mr. Kessel?"

"He said to say he'd gone fishing..."

Ramos looked apologetic.

"Can you get the engines working?"

"We're trying, Captain, but we can't find anything wrong with them."

"Keep trying. I'll check back once I've found Kessel."

Lehman stormed through the ship and headed for Kessel's bunk. He wasn't there. He checked in the mess and found Langdon sitting alone. The man looked up as the captain entered and flinched.

"They're here, Captain. They're all around. Can you see them?"

"Shut up, Langdon."

The man looked away as Lehman glared at him.

"No more of that talk or I'll have you gagged."

Lehman slapped his hand against the bulkhead. The careful order of his ship was unravelling. Chen came down a ladder and the captain grabbed him.

"Chen, have you seen Mr. Kessel?"

"Yes, Captain."

"Where?"

"Out on the deck."

"On the deck?"

"Yes. He had a…"

Chen struggled for the word and then raised his hand above his head and shrugged.

"What? What did he have?"

"It looked like a spear, Captain."

Lehman shook his head and quickly made his way back up to the bridge.

"Everyone has gone mad, Martinez."

The first mate looked at the captain.

"I think I'm halfway there myself."

Lehman pulled his binoculars from their case and scanned the deck. He spotted Kessel near the fo'c's'le leaning out over the rail above the sea. He passed the binoculars to Martinez.

"Watch the horizon. I'm going to go and talk to Kessel."

The captain clipped a walkie-talkie to his belt and slipped the Beretta into the back of his trousers.

As Lehman made his way along the gangways, towards Kessel, Martinez scanned the horizon and watched the thick clouds moving in fast from the east. The sky seemed to burn red and the sea appeared black beneath it.

Martinez kept the glasses on the sea and his heart punched in his chest like a boxer at a speed ball as he watched the shapes that danced beneath the surface.

The spear that Kessel held was home-made; it looked as though the engineer had hammered pieces of scrap into the shape he required. It resembled a great iron harpoon. A thick cable attached it to the railing.

"Gonna be some good fishing tonight, Captain. I'm fishing in the sea of souls."

"What about my engines?"

"Fuck the engines. A man doesn't get many chances like this in his life. Better than Marlin in the Gulf of Mexico."

The engineer was staring out over the rail.

"Look at the size of them…"

Lehman slid the pistol from behind his back and pushed the safety off.

"Mr. Kessel, you're needed in the engine room."

Kessel took no notice and instead hefted the spear back onto his shoulder, all the while looking over the railing.

"In a minute," muttered the engineer.

Lehman raised the pistol and aimed it at the centre of Kessel's chest

"Kessel!"

Kessel launched the spear over the side and grinned. He grabbed the cable in his gloved hands and began to tug. Lehman noticed that he had rigged a small winch up to the cable.

"Kessel leave it. We need you. I need you!"

"Go back to the bridge, Captain. I'll reel this in and then I'll fix your goddamned engines."

"Return to your post, Mr. Kessel, or I will shoot you."

The engineer grinned and, while keeping one hand locked around the cable, reached for the knife at his waist.

"Don't do it!"

"You won't kill me, Captain."

Lehman lowered the pistol and shot the engineer through his left leg, just above the knee. Kessel sat down on the deck, hard, and howled.

"Toss the knife or I'll shoot you in the other one, you stupid bastard."

Kessel bit back his howls and then threw the knife over the rail, his other hand stayed locked to the cable. Keeping the gun aimed at Kessel, the captain took the handset from his belt and hailed the bridge. Martinez came on the line.

"Get down here. Mr. Kessel will need some help to get to the engine room."

"I can't leave the bridge, Captain. You need to get off the deck. They're everywhere!"

"What are?"

"The shadows are all around you, Captain! Get off the

deck!"

"Martinez, get down here. That's an order."

The handset crackled once and then was silent.

"Martinez!"

The cable in Kessel's hand tugged once and the engineer peered over the rail.

"My God, Captain…"

The engineer didn't finish the sentence. The cable jerked again and flipped him up over the rail. He began to scream as he disappeared over the side. Lehman rushed to the side. He could see where the cable entered the sea and his eyes followed it. Kessel burst to the surface and raised his hand, except there was no hand. It must have been sliced off by the cable. Lehman saw a shadow below the surface and watched as it moved towards Kessel. He aimed double handed and fired twice at the dark shape—it continued to move towards the stricken engineer.

"Swim, man! Swim!"

Kessel continued to bob on the surface as the shadow moved below him.

"Help me!" screamed Kessel. Then he was gone, vanished beneath the surface as though he had suddenly had lead weights attached to his legs.

For a moment Lehman considered firing again but then he looked away from the too-dark sea and stepped back from the rail. He stood and stared up the sky—it didn't look like the sky he had seen the day before; it seemed too low and had taken on an odd hue. Lehman hurried back along the deck towards the bridge.

Langdon sat in Lehman's chair on the bridge. Martinez was nowhere to be seen. The seaman was looking out of the window at the sky. The captain levelled the pistol at Langdon and moved away from the door.

"What're you doing here?"

"Someone had to hold the bridge for you. I saw Martinez heading for his quarters."

"You don't look so scared anymore, Langdon."

"Because I've accepted it, I've accepted what we are, what they are."

"And what is that?"

"Have you ever thought about those old slave ships crossing the Atlantic?"

"No, Langdon, I can't say I've dwelt on it much."

"You don't think we're doing the same thing—running through the night with a cargo of misery and lost souls?"

Lehman leaned back against the helm, making sure to keep his gun hand several feet back from Langdon.

"We're just carrying cargo, that's all."

Langdon grinned suddenly.

"I can imagine a Portuguese slave ship captain saying the same thing."

"Except he was carrying people in chains and I'm just carrying oil."

"It's the same thing."

"No, it isn't. Get off my bridge, Langdon."

Langdon stood up but kept his hands out wide from his sides, his hands open.

"I'll go, Captain, but this isn't your ship anymore."

Lehman locked the door behind Langdon and tried to check the position of the ship. The navigational devices had been smashed and the charts were gone. The captain checked the Beretta—there were nine rounds left. He checked the lockbox and found another twelve bullets. Lehman drank the last of the coffee from the flask and looked out at the sea. He could see shadows dancing beneath the surface.

The ship stopped moving. Lehman checked his watch; it was just before eleven. A few minutes later there was a soft tap at the bridge's heavy door. Lehman checked the pistol and opened the door. Chen stood in the doorway. He was clutching a flask and a sandwich wrapped in cellophane. He passed them quickly to Lehman.

"They're coming for you, Captain."

Lehman nodded.

"I thought they would. All of them?"

Chen shook his head.

"Mr. Martinez is dead. And Vallacer. They would have killed me but I hide in the freezer."

"Go back there and wait till this is over."

"Let me stand with you, Captain. You can trust Chen."

"I know I can, but I can't put a man who can make coffee as good you as you can at risk."

Lehman forced a grin.

"Are they armed?"

Chen nodded.

"Knives and tools."

The Chinaman looked away from Lehman. The captain grasped Chen's shoulder.

"Get back to your freezer and stay there. I'll come and find you."

Chen nodded.

"It is a cheese sandwich, Captain. The cheese you like."

Lehman locked the door when Chen clambered down the ladder.

Then Lehman sat down, ate his sandwich and drank a cup of Chen's coffee while he added to the log. He knew that he could hole-up in the bridge until he starved, but then he would be leaving the Panama Valdez to Langdon. He reloaded the Beretta and opened the door. The windows, roof and bulkheads were impenetrable to an assault by men armed with knives and tools—they would have to use the door. He pulled together a make-shift barricade and stood back behind his chair. He laid a hammer on the chair and put the spare bullets for the pistol in his pocket.

They came half-an-hour after noon.

"Captain, throw out the gun."

It was Langdon.

"Why don't you come to the door, I'll be happy to give it to you!"

Silence.

Something flew through the door above Lehman's point of vision; smoke trailed behind the object. Lehman scrambled back and found the smoke bomb in the corner. He grabbed it up and threw it out the door as the first crewman leapt the barricade; a scarf covered the lower portion of his face and a cleaver shone in his fist. Lehman shot him twice in the chest and as he retook his position behind the chair he put a third round into the man's head.

They were swarming at the door, now, tearing the barricade to pieces. Lehman fired into the mass of bodies and watched blood spatter and blossom against the bulkhead walls. And then they were gone. They left behind three bodies sprawled in the doorway and the one that Lehman had shot inside the room.

Lehman grabbed up the hammer and followed the retreating mutineers out. They hadn't expected him to follow and as they scrambled for cover one caught a bullet in the face and another took a round through the shoulder. Lehman moved in with the hammer.

"My ship, you bastards, my ship!"

The hammer rose and the hammer fell and Lehman was splashed red.

"Get his gun! Get his gun!"

Langdon and the last of the mutineers closed in; a swing of a hammer, the slash of a knife, a squeeze of a trigger, a body falling, a punch thrown, a blade stabbed in, another gunshot, another swing, another slash, another body falls. Langdon pressed against Lehman, a knife through the captain's flesh. The Beretta pressed against Langdon's head.

"It's my ship!"

"It's their ship now!"

Shapes all around, shades come out into the daylight; screams, whispers, shouts, guttural grunts and the cries of the lost. Lehman smiles as he feels his life leaking from his side.

"Mine."

He whispers it as he squeezes the trigger and Langdon's head comes apart like a rotten coconut thrown against the ground.

Lehman looks out to sea and sees the shadows swimming closer. He can discern the all too human shape of them now, so close to the surface that he is almost able to see the features of them now... at the end.

"There isn't any more, that's it."

Hale gets up and pours himself three fingers of Johnny Walker blue label.

"But how did you hear it?"

"They found Chen floating in a life raft the day before yesterday."

"You spoke to him?"

"He isn't speaking to anyone... no, I pieced it together from the log Lehman had given Chen and of what I know of Lehman."

Silenced reigns over the room.

"But what happened to Lehman? What about the ship?"

Hale looks away.

"You don't want to know what I think. But they still haven't located the Panama Valdez, or Lehman, and I don't think that they ever will."

He takes a deep drink from his whiskey.

"A captain stays with his ship no matter where it goes."

BENEDICT J. JONES

Benedict J Jones lives in London. He writes crime, horror and western fiction. He has had over thirty short stories published as well as the collections "Skewered; And other London cruelties" and "Ride the Dark Country", novellas "Slaughter Beach" and "Mulligan's Idol", and the novels "Pennies for Charon" and "The Devil's Brew" both featuring his ex-con turned private eye Charlie "Bars" Constantinou.

RAT-A-TAT

KAYLEIGH MARIE EDWARDS

James Walker was the first person to see the new house.

He opened the curtains that morning, expecting to see the same thing that he always saw—a plot of land that had been empty for as long as he could remember. Instead, he saw a too narrow, too tall, grey house with a tilted chimney on its slanted roof.

He stared at the house, trying to work out what was so wrong about it. The chimney was clearly askew, but for some reason it seemed straight when you looked right at it. After a moment of consideration, James realised that the whole house was askew, though the longer he stared at it, the harder it became to tell which way it was leaning.

A large '1' was carved into the centre of the front door. This struck him as odd because there was already a 'number one' house further up the street. He stared through the window at the object that hung under the carved number, squinting across the distance to make out what it was. He was looking at a very large, brass doorknocker that was hanging where the letterbox should have been. He squinted a little more and determined that there was no letterbox at all.

His hands still held the curtains; he hadn't noticed that he hadn't let them go. And now, he wasn't just holding them; he was gripping them, the colour slowly draining out of his knuckles.

Who doesn't have a letterbox? he thought, chewing the insides of his cheeks. He didn't suppose that a missing letterbox would be considered scary to most people, but this wasn't an ordinary house with an ordinary door in the first place, and it creeped him out more than anything ever had—until he noticed the next oddity. There wasn't even a door handle.

Next, he noticed that the house had no windows; no glassy eyes to look at him with, and yet he felt that it was watching him somehow anyway. Besides the engraved number on the door and the peculiar chimney, the house had no distinguishable features.

The weirdest thing about this house wasn't even in its physical construction, but in how it came to be there in the first place. It had quite literally appeared, in its entirety, overnight. Not a single brick of it had been there the previous day, but now there it was looming over Lannhill and throwing a huge, dark shadow towards James's house. If he didn't know better, he would have sworn that that shadow was reaching for him.

Lannhill was one of those tiny towns where everyone knew everyone else. You couldn't so much as sneeze without someone opening a window a few houses away to yell 'bless you!' People grew up there and had the same neighbours for their entire lives. They lived in each other's pockets, and that's how they liked it.

If ever there was a place that still had a genuine sense of community spirit, it was Lannhill. James had received over one hundred cards on his last birthday, and each of them was posted personally, and with love, by each card giver. If there was a death in the town, hundreds would turn up to the funeral, even those who hadn't known the deceased. It was just the done thing.

However, James had not heard so much as a hint of this new house—not from anyone. Not even from Old Man 'Carp' Carpenter who lived a few doors up, and he was a guy who knew everything and was happy to tell you so.

"What are you staring at?" The voice was quiet but it startled him out of his thoughts. He was suddenly aware of his aching hands and he released the curtains, shaking out his fingers.

Kelly was looking at him from their bed with a sleepy and curious expression on her face. He managed to hold her gaze for a second but then lowered his eyes to the floor. Still, that was a second longer than he'd managed to make eye contact with her for a while.

"There's a weird house across the road," he replied, and then headed towards the door.

"What?" She smiled, rubbing her eyes. He pointed over his shoulder towards the window.

"Have a look." He left, turned in the corridor, and went into the baby's room.

Things hadn't been right between them since the miscarriage, and James felt terrible for that, amongst other things. Kelly had been trying—he knew that—but he just couldn't face her. She was the love of his life, but he didn't know if he'd ever be able to look at her again without that nasty stab of guilt.

They'd been together for two years when Kelly had told him she was pregnant. He was surprised, as was she, because she'd been on the pill the whole time they were together, but they accepted the hand they were dealt.

She'd moved into his family home with him almost immediately, and a few months after that, his parents had move abroad, as per their retirement plan. They'd intended to the sell the house, but with James and Kelly's new situation, they decided to hold off and give them the house for a few years, until they had enough money to get their own place. No grandchild in their family was living in rented accommodation, thank you very much.

James and Kelly moved into his parents' old bedroom, and after the initial panic of an impending new life had subsided, they'd got to work turning James's old room into the baby's room.

They were in their mid-twenties, and James's reflex reaction to the news that he was going to be a dad was utter panic, though he would sooner have died than let Kelly see that. She was panicking too, and the last thing he wanted to do was put the idea in her head that he was going to lose it and bolt, though the thought had crossed his mind. But only for a minute.

After a firm talking to from his dad, James had realised that there were really only two options: be a bad father, or try his best to be a good, responsible one. He picked up more hours in work to save money before the baby came, and while he was working those shifts, Kelly went to her appointments alone.

The day she came home and told him that they were going to have a boy was the single happiest moment of James's life. The next time Kelly returned home from an appointment, the baby's room was painted a soft blue, and James was hard at work constructing the crib. He hadn't grown up as handy with tools as his dad had encouraged him to be, and the crib was the first thing he'd ever built. He considered it his masterpiece.

Almost halfway into the pregnancy, Kelly came home one day from work at a supermarket in the next town over, and informed James that she had quit her job. Just like that. She was pregnant and tired and didn't see why she should be on her feet anymore, especially since James was earning a decent amount, and even more especially because they didn't have to pay rent. He'd been furious. How could she make a decision like that without consulting him first? Was she aware that they had a baby on the way? Did she realise that had she kept her job, she would not only have had paid maternity leave, but a job to return to afterwards? What was she expecting, for him to take care of everything? Was this the twenties all of a sudden? Was he expected to earn the money while she stayed home and baked pies all day?

He'd called her a freeloader, and she'd cried, but she always cried when they argued, and he didn't pay attention. He told her that he was going to the pub to blow off some steam, and that's when she'd keeled over with her hands pressed to her stomach.

Her breath was coming out in shuddering, tear-filled sobs, and for a second he'd been irritated by how child-like she looked and sounded with her face scrunched up like that. And then she'd complained about the stomach pains.

James stood at the centre of the room but tried not to look up from the carpet. The crib he'd built stood by the window, the mobile with its swinging bunny rabbits hanging above it. That was the hardest thing to look at, he'd found, even though they'd suffered the miscarriage months ago. He could barely look at the walls, let alone the stuffed toys, and he had no idea why he'd entered the room in the first place.

He'd thought that he was underprepared for a child when they were expecting their son, but he had never felt worse than when Kelly had told him that was no longer the case. When she'd left for the hospital, screaming at him to leave her alone as she went, he was worried, but not *that* worried. He thought at the time that if something was really wrong, Kelly would have put their argument aside and let him go with her, but she hadn't.

Being told that she'd miscarried because of stress had hit him in a way that nothing ever had, and he thought nothing ever would again. The loss was a unique type of pain unlike anything he'd experienced before, and the guilt of knowing he could have been responsible for it had been slowly driving him into the ground ever since.

Kelly told him that it wasn't his fault; sometimes these things just happened. But he knew in his heart that he shouldn't have been shouting at his pregnant girlfriend, that perhaps he should have been more understanding about her leaving her job, and that it had been his duty to make her feel supported, and he hadn't. They'd lost their child because of him. Every time he went into his son's room, he felt like another piece of him dissolved, but sometimes the compulsion to go in there and try to pretend that everything was still fine won.

Today, however, his imagination wouldn't comply and the weight of what had happened was heavier than usual. Then, something else occurred to him—he ought to go across the road and knock on that door.

He didn't know why, but suddenly he felt a stronger draw to that unexplained house than he did to the room he currently stood in. Before he even knew he was moving, he was headed towards the stairs.

"Where are you going?" Kelly called to him as he rushed past their bedroom. He heard her but didn't feel that he had time to stop and explain. He slid his hand down the bannister as he ran down the stairs, stumbling on the last few steps in his hurry. He reached the front door, threw it open, and took off across the street without stopping to put his shoes on.

He had almost reached the heavy-looking front door of the place when he came to a sudden stop, wondering what on earth he was doing. When he'd first seen the house only ten minutes before, he hadn't wanted to go anywhere near it, and now here he was, running outside in nothing but a t-shirt and his boxer shorts, intending to bang on the door of a house that well and truly gave him the creeps.

The sun must have been moving in the sky, because the

house's long shadow drew back and seemed to disappear into the house itself. He knew it wasn't possible, but the closer he got to the house, the colder the air felt.

He was about to turn around and head back when another compulsive surge went through him, and the next thing he knew, he was so close to the door that he could smell the wood. He waited for a moment, listening, but there was nothing moving inside.

He curled his fingers around the doorknocker, expecting it to feel dry and rusty. It was smooth and— incredibly—warm. It was *inviting*. He lifted it, and then without exercising much added force, let it fall. It hit the door a lot louder than he expected and he shrank back a little. The single *thump* echoed back to him from within, as if the noise were hurtling around the house and ricocheting from every surface, somehow louder each time it came back to him. Then, it abruptly stopped, as though someone had muted it like they would mute the volume on a television.

James waited. He wiped his hands on his shirt, leaving damp prints. He was starting to feel like an idiot—he didn't know what he'd been expecting—and was about to turn back, when he heard something.

"Hello?" he asked, pressing his ear to the door. The sound came again—a voice—a hushed, serpent-like whisper that slid through the cracks in the door like a tongue. It told him something.

He was sat at the kitchen table with his head in his hands when Kelly appeared in the doorway. He was aware of her presence, but he couldn't look up at her, now for a completely different reason than usual.

"You okay, babe?" she asked. Her voice cut through him in a way he didn't expect. Suddenly, he was angrier than he had ever been, and he didn't know how to handle it. So he continued to sit there without looking up, gripping his hair until his head hurt.

"Babe?" she repeated. He raised his eyes to her, noticing the way she pressed her hand to her tummy, as she had been doing for months. He'd noticed it before, but assumed it was a subconscious gesture on her part. He'd felt sorry for her every time he'd seen her hand resting there, as if she still held on to that protective maternal instinct. Now, the gesture seemed obscene to him. Not just obscene, but sick.

She was about to say something else, and then she noticed the way his blazing eyes stared at her hand. The tired smile fell from her face as her hand fell from her tummy. He knew.

He raised his eyes to hers and they stared at each other for an expanse of time that tortured them both. James sat shaking in his chair, commanding himself not to jump up across the table and strangle her. Kelly pressed herself into the doorway as if she were trying to sink into the wood and disappear. She wracked her brain, trying to come up with an explanation that would somehow alleviate her of any responsibility.

How the hell had he found out?

Eventually, James rose from his chair. It scraped back against the tiled floor, making her wince. He walked around the table, praying that she would just move out of his way so he could leave the room. Everything in him was screaming violence. He wanted to kill her.

Kelly, as usual, was oblivious to his feelings, though they were obvious. She was inside her own head, frantically trying to figure out how to make this his fault. She only surfaced from her thoughts when he was face to face with her.

"Get out of my way," he snarled, through gritted teeth. She stared at him, not moving. He drew in a breath. "And then, get out of my house."

"Babe, you have to understand, I was afraid that you…" she started, but didn't finish. She was interrupted by the back of James's hand across her cheek. Her face burned immediately, like she'd been leaning into a fire. She stared at him, shocked. He stared back at her even more shocked by the fact that he'd hit her. He'd never put his hands on anyone, male or female, in anger before, and he didn't like how it made him feel.

He expected to feel remorse and shame. He had always hated men who hit their girlfriends. But he didn't feel anything but powerful. He despised the satisfaction that came with it. It was as though the strings that held his long-standing morals together were fraying and snapping away.

He'd loved this woman for years and had done everything he could to make her happy. He had never imagined a day that he would look at her and feel so repulsed.

"You hit me!" she screamed, breaking the silence. The old James would have cared, but the old James had been killed by the secret that the house had whispered to him. New James felt nothing but irritation that although he'd hurt her, the blow to her face didn't even register compared to the pain she had inflicted on him.

"You're a piece of shit, Kelly," he breathed. His face was now as red and as hot as hers. She shrank back out of the kitchen, realising that she wasn't looking at the James that she had known all this time. This James didn't appear to be one she could manipulate, because this James had somehow become privy to the knowledge that not only did he owe her nothing, but he had been living a lie.

"I'm sorry," she replied, with fake sincerity. She was screaming inside her head, sifting through options. Yelling at him wasn't going to work, because he didn't look at all guilty for smacking her. She had the terrible feeling that crying wasn't going to work either, and that meant that she was going to have to resort to trying to twist everything.

"Please don't kick me out. I'm sorry," she said. Tears slipped over her cheeks, but James now saw them for what they were—a control tactic, devoid of any real emotion.

"Get. Out." His fingers closed around the edge of the door, digging into the wood. He was feeling an ugly urge to hurt her a lot worse than his backhanded slap had, and was desperately trying to restrain it. He'd never felt so provoked, angry, or out of control. Even worse, he had never been so sure that he was capable of something horrible. He hadn't suspected that this side of him existed, and the mixture of feelings it brought was disorientating.

"How did you find out?" she muttered, finally lowering her eyes to her own feet. She was ashamed, which was an uncomfortable feeling, and she was beginning to resent him for inflicting it on her.

"You've got one more chance to leave, or I'm going to do something that I don't even think I'll regret," he replied.

"You don't understand," she tried. "I thought you were going to finish with me, and I didn't know what else to do."

This brought a fresh wave of rage that rippled through him. His fingers now hurt as he dug them into the door. Was she actually trying to justify lying about getting pregnant? Not only justify it, but blame *him* for it?

His mind flicked back through images of their relationship previous to the 'pregnancy'. She'd always been insecure, though he didn't understand why she'd worry about his feelings for her—he'd fallen in love with her almost instantly and she knew that. He went over his memories, remembering the odd occasion that he'd caught her out in lies. She was prone to exaggerating—he'd always known that about her. She did it so often that her friends made fun of her for it, but he'd found it sort of endearing and assumed it was tied into her insecurity. Everyone was guilty of exaggerating on occasion, if only to make whatever story they were telling a bit more interesting.

With her flair for drama and need to be liked, Kelly just did it a bit more than the average person.

Now and then, he'd get home from work to find her home already, though she was supposed to finish work later than him, and she'd explain that her shift was moved, or she'd had an early finish. He would always discover that she was lying, and that she'd called in sick because she just didn't feel like going to work that day. It perplexed him that she'd lie to him about that, but assumed she was just embarrassed because she'd been too lazy to get out of her pyjamas.

In hindsight, as he visualized the ease with which a lie would slip from her lips, he realised, for the first time, that she was just a liar. Insecurity might have been a contributing factor to her deceitful habit, but now that the rose-tinted glasses were off, he could no longer make that excuse for her.

Several other 'small' lies she'd told him came flooding back: she couldn't wash the dishes, sorry, because she'd had an allergic reaction to the washing-up liquid (but only sometimes); no, she couldn't go to the pub, because she'd been inexplicably throwing up all day (though she wasn't ill), and come to think of it, he shouldn't go out either because she needed to be looked after; she was allergic to gluten (yet she conveniently seemed to have no problem with bread, which was lucky because she absolutely loved sandwiches).

The little things that he'd been aware were probably 'untruths' seemed different now. It was an irritating habit, but her lies had always been trivial and harmless. But with the new information he had, he realised that there was no such thing as a 'little' lie from Kelly; everything she lied about was designed to incite sympathy, guilt, or get her out of things she didn't want to do. They weren't harmless fibs; they were manipulations.

Even so, he'd never thought that she was capable of going as far as pretending to be pregnant. Beyond that, he hadn't believed that anyone could be capable of being so twisted as to invest in that illusion so fully, only to fake a miscarriage to avoid being found out when the baby bump didn't start to show.

For months, he'd looked after her through bouts of 'morning sickness', listening to her retching from outside the bathroom door. For months, she'd made sure that he couldn't take her to her doctor's appointments—they were always short notice, or rearranged for times that he couldn't get out of work. On the occasions that he'd managed to change his shifts, her appointment had suddenly been cancelled, or she was too ill or tired to go.

He couldn't believe he'd been so stupid, but all of this was only occurring to him now that he was watching it in his mind, one incident after another. It was obvious, in hindsight, but not being able to go to the odd appointment here and there, at the time, hadn't struck him as odd.

The thing that was hurting him the most and that had shortened his once impossibly long temper fuse, was the fact that she'd allowed him to love and prepare for a baby that didn't exist. A *son*, she'd said. She had even sat there with him as he went through possible baby names. And then, she'd forced him to grieve. Not only that, but she had engineered the entire 'miscarriage' with the intention of making him feel responsible for it.

She had watched him break down several times. She'd held him in her arms as he sobbed, in that week that he'd had to take off work because he couldn't face leaving the house. She'd watched as he drifted and then entirely sank into a dark depression that made it difficult for him to open his eyes in the morning. She'd watched him struggle to make amends for what he'd 'done'.

And for what?

As if she'd heard him thinking, she piped up again.

"I shouldn't have said I was pregnant, but I thought that we'd stay together for sure if I was. I *wanted* to be," she said, the words tumbling from her mouth just like all her past lies had. "You weren't paying attention to me, and I was sure your feelings were changing and I panicked and it just came out."

It just came out, James repeated in his mind. He laughed out loud. Kelly didn't recognise the snorted laugh for what it was, and mistook it for encouragement.

"I stopped taking my pill, thinking that I'd get pregnant for real and you wouldn't have to know, but it just didn't happen. The longer it went on, the more I panicked. I had to end it somehow." She stopped talking and took in a breath, as though her excuse for it all was valid. When he didn't speak, she went on.

"No one's perfect, Jay. It's not like you've never lied before. Remember that night you told me you'd be straight home from work but then you went out drinking?"

James looked at her, unable to stop his mouth from dropping open. The rambling excuse for what she'd done was one thing, and the comparison she'd made was an infuriating other. But it was the lack of remorse that was boiling his blood. He glared at her, still gripping the edge of the door. It was no longer just an outlet for his aggression, something to seize in his hand in place of her throat, but a handle to cling on to. He held on tightly, knowing that if he lost his grip, he was likely to launch himself on her, and he didn't know what he'd do. That door now represented and embodied what was left of his dwindling resolve.

"I know it wasn't the best idea, but…"

"You told me I'd killed our baby!" James exploded, cutting her off before she could say anything else to trigger him. "You made me think that I was having a son! I spent weeks decorating that room, building the…" his voice broke on the word 'crib'. "I was pulling extra shifts, exhausting myself to make sure we'd have a good start with him. My parents gave us this house for him! We talked about nothing but baby names for weeks, and we went shopping—together—for all those baby toys and clothes. And then I lost him, and you as good as told me it was my fault. You made me think I'd killed him!"

There was silence between them for a while, and then Kelly had the audacity to shrug. James's fingers started slipping and he let them, because he had a feeling that the next thing she was going to say was going to be it.

"But it didn't exist in the first place, so I don't understand why you're going on about it now," she said, pursing her lips.

HE, James thought, choking back as much anger as he could. *And it wasn't real for you, because you knew it wasn't. But for me, the whole time...*

"Most men just bugger off when the baby comes anyway," she continued, oblivious to his hand coming off the door. "So don't you try and make me feel bad for..."

James lost it, and as he did, thick, black smoke poured from the chimney of the house across the road.

When all was done, and the consequence of Kelly's secret had played out, the '1' etched into the door faded into the wood until it was no longer there.

As Lannhill grew dark that night, the house faded away, until all that was left of it was that puff of black chimney smoke, dissipated many miles in the air above the town. It was no longer visible, but it hung there for a long time.

Lannhill had never known a tragedy like the murder/suicide of James and Kelly. *They were so young*, most people said, when it came up in conversation, which it did for years. No one knew why it had happened; James had always been such a wonderful boy, and he and Kelly had been a perfect couple.

Though the incident had been contained and limited to two victims, Lannhill, for a lot of people, no longer felt safe. People started to lock their doors at night again, and others moved away. The feeling of trust between them slipped away like the black smoke, and the community eventually unraveled. If a lovely, young man like James Walker was capable of something so heinous, then maybe someone else in their midst was capable of the same, or worse.

As the town of Green Fields wrapped up its Christmas celebrations, people went to their beds happy and full of the kind of quiet contentment that comes after being involved in a large town event. But as they slipped into sleep, a cold spot appeared in the town centre. As the deepest, darkest part of night crept in, a house appeared. And as the town of Green Fields stirred under the first rays of morning light the next day, a number '1' burned itself into the front door.

KAYLEIGH MARIE EDWARDS

Kayleigh Marie Edwards is a writer who can't imagine why anyone would be interested in what she writes in her bio; after all, she's not Stephen King or Dean Koontz or Anne Rice, or even Stephanie Meyer. But since we're here, there are some important things you should know:

- If you put cake near her, she'll eat it
- She loves Stephen King and if you have any way of introducing her to him then she begs that you, in the words of the brilliant Captain Picard, 'make it so'
- She has an excellent zombie apocalypse plan

K.M.E mostly writes comedy and horror fiction, stage plays, and articles. Most of her inspiration comes from real-life conversations, so be warned that if you're in close proximity to her and you say something stupid, you'll probably be used as material for an upcoming story.

She can be found scribbling away at www.spookyisles.com, or responding to requests at www.gingernutsofhorror.com, where she has a page called 'Challenge Kayleigh'. She boasts that she adores horror to the point of being capable of writing a positive review of any horror film – no matter how poor public opinion of it may be, so throw a challenge her way (there are prizes).

You're not still reading this, surely? The only reason this bio is this long is because she asked how long it had to be and was told 'exactly 256 words'. **(true story – Ed)**

The secret of life is… oh, she's hit the word-count now so there's no time for the answer, sorry.

PAPER THIN ROSES OF MAYBE

DAMIEN ANGELICA WALTERS

"Please don't be angry, Joshua," Maddie says. Her dark hair spills over her shoulders; her blue eyes gleam grey in the candlelight.

"How can I not be angry with this?" He waves a hand toward the window, his shadow playdancing on the wall. Outside, all is somber, edged in sepia tones of a forgotten age, all moving closer, a little more each day.

"Please," she says. "Let it go."

"How can *you* not be angry?" he asks. "It won't be long now. It's coming faster now. It will be here, and we will—"

"Be immortalized forever," she says. "Someone will come along one day and say yes, I remember this. I remember them."

He laughs, the sound like broken glass ground in a fist. "There won't be anyone left."

"There's always someone left. Always."

He turns toward the window, giving her his back. He doesn't understand this new calm. She threw the phone across the room when it stopped working, hard enough to gouge the plaster wall. Holding a photograph of her parents, she cried for hours, screaming it wasn't fair.

He had no one to call, no one to mourn.

"Everything will be fine," she says.

He looks out over the city. Over what's left. A handful of streets, apartments, offices, department stores, the edge of a park. The trees on this side are heavy with green, the buildings all red brick and glass and shining metal faces, but on the other side, the flat side, they are brown and tan and cream, reminiscent of a snapshot from the early 1900s. Wind pushes past the window and blows the curtains into a fabric ripple. The wind travels past the buildings into the park, and the leaves quiver. The other trees are as frozen in place and time as the rest of everything.

Above the sepia world, the sky is a shade of caramel; the clouds, buttermilk. In the real world, the sky is pale blue and threaded with wisps of white. As the clouds scuttle across the sky and enter the other world, they stop and change color so quickly his eyes can't capture the transformation. When he glances at the place where movement ceases, a wave of dizziness strikes, complete with sweaty palms and a racing heart.

He doesn't need to go to the windows offering a view from the back of the building. It's there, too, creeping closer and closer, sandwiching them between a nightmare and impossibility.

"Nothing will be fine. Look at it." He jabs his finger toward the window. "Look at it."

She pinches her bottom lip between her teeth and shakes her head. "I don't have to. I know what's there."

A tiny jingle-jingle drifts through the air as a child rides a tricycle in the street, pedaling in wide, disconsolate circles. A young mother stands off to one side with her arms wrapped around herself in a cocoon of make-believe solace.

Joshua closes the curtains and lights a cigarette, the smoke forming a halo around his head. Maddie's nostrils flare in disapproval. It doesn't matter, he almost says, but he traps the words inside. The little bell rings out again and disappears without an echo.

Maddie might not be afraid anymore, but he's afraid enough for the both of them.

"Come to bed," Maddie says.

He doesn't want to sleep (What if it comes during the night, freezing them in place in their bed?), but he slips beneath the blankets and curls his fingers around hers.

Once her breathing turns soft and even, Joshua climbs out of bed and locks the apartment door behind him out of habit, not need. The streets are deserted, the silence absolute, and the pavement swallows the sound of his passage.

He steps to the edge of the real city and gazes across the street, a once busy tangle of shoppers, cars, taxis, a choking miasma of need and want and must have now. The air smells of apples turned sour and old perfume, but underneath, it holds the musty scent of cardboard boxes filled to bursting with old paper and ancient memories. He shivers, although he isn't cold.

The sidewalk and most of the street is still real, still concrete and asphalt. In front of what used to be an office, he stares down the street, at the line where real meets unreal. The buildings, depleted of their natural colors, are all two-dimensional and flat, like paintings on a museum wall.

In his peripheral vision, he catches sight of a woman dressed in a long black coat and white gloves, with a tiny hat balanced on the back of her head. She nods in his direction and continues on. He follows her, keeping a safe distance from the other world, until she comes to a stop. "My children came here," she says. "They wanted to see. That's my daughter." She points to a woman with short hair and earrings dangling to her shoulder. "My baby girl."

"No, don't touch her," he cries, but he's too late; she's already reaching. The sepia pulls her in, expanding all the while to fit her into the tableau. In an eye blink, her coat turns mahogany and her skin a shade of parchment; her face wears sorrow mixed with expectation. Joshua backs away. The street has turned half grey, half walnut brown.

He runs all the way back, back to the apartment, back to Maddie, safe and real and warm in their bed.

They sit in the kitchen with the curtains shut and drink lukewarm tea and eat peanut butter and jelly on stale bread. After, he pretends to read while Maddie rummages around in their spare bedroom. When something crashes to the floor, he turns the book over on the table and finds her sitting on the floor surrounded by a jumble of forgotten things on her lap, an old lamp on its side behind her.

"What are you doing?"

She smiles, cheeks pink. "Remember the rose you made for me? On our first date?"

"The one I made from the napkin?"

"Yes." She lifts a battered and stained scrap of paper that resembles a squashed pumpkin with a long stem, not a rose. "I want to have it with me when it happens."

He sits on the floor and cups his hands around hers, the misshapen flower in the center of their grip. The night he gave it to her, he knew he wanted to spend his forever by her side. But not like this. Never like this.

"Maddie?"

"What?"

He tries to find the words, but a lump sits in his throat instead. When he finally chokes it down, he shakes his head, afraid he'll say everything wrong.

He goes outside again the next night and stands in the

quiet. A clock above one of the building doors stands frozen at 11:15; the watch on the wrist of the woman in the dark coat shows 2:23.

Time stopped, and the world stopped with it, he thinks.

On his own watch, the second hand ticks away. His time hasn't stopped yet, but it's close. His cheeks are wet with tears, tears he doesn't remember crying.

Two nights later, he returns and sits on the curb with his elbows on his knees and his fingers linked beneath his chin. A wave of anger coils up from the inside, all scarlet and laced with thorns. When Maddie sits next to him, his shout of surprise fills the air, as quickly there as it is gone again.

"You shouldn't be afraid. Maybe there's life inside," she says. "And maybe we're just seeing the echoes."

"There aren't any echoes."

"Not on this side, no, but who knows what's on the other side."

"Maddie, there's nothing. Can't you see that?"

"If you're so afraid of it, why do you come here every night?"

He sits up straight. She smiles.

"I'm keeping tabs on it, that's all," he finally says.

"But why? It will come for us soon enough. Then we'll know."

He grabs her shoulders and gives her a shake. "What's happened to you? How can you be so damn calm?"

She takes his hands away and presses a kiss to each palm in turn, her mouth warm against his skin. "I can't," she says, her words small and quiet.

He bites back a sound halfway between a groan and a laugh. "What do you mean, you can't?"

"I know you don't understand, but I can't be angry. I

can't be afraid anymore." Her voice breaks; she takes a deep breath. "I know it won't do any good, and if I start crying, I don't think I'll be able to stop. I pray every night that this is all a mistake, that everything will be fine in the morning." She rests a fist between her breasts. "It hurts too much to be afraid. It's better this way. Trust me."

"Oh, God, Maddie." He pulls her close.

She trembles in his arms then pushes him gently away. "Let's go home."

"I'm scared, I'm so scared—"

She puts a finger to his lips. "Shhhh."

They make love long into the night and fall asleep with their legs entwined.

He wakes alone. He knows before he lifts his head from the pillow; the weight of the apartment has changed, lifted, the trapped exhalation belonging only to one, not two.

No, oh, no. Please let me be wrong. She wouldn't leave me. Not like this. Not now.

She left a note, her handwriting spidery and thin, on a small scrap of paper lying in the center of the kitchen table, one edge held in place with the salt shaker, a silly ceramic pig they'd found at a yard sale.

Joshua,

I'm sorry I couldn't wait any longer, and I knew if I told you, you'd try to stop me. I believe that when it's all over, we will be together again. Instead of saying goodbye, I will say until then. I love you.
Always and ever,
Maddie

He crumbles the note into a ball and throws it against the wall. Bites back a shriek. No, maybe he isn't too late. He flees from the apartment, not bothering to lock the door, and runs along the edge of the world where flat meets real, calling out her name, knowing she can't hear, but calling anyway. Tears pour down his cheeks, and the hurt turns every heartbeat to pain. He can't believe she's gone. He refuses to believe she's left him like this.

Then he skids to a halt. There. His Maddie. Standing with a small smile on her face and the paper rose held in one hand. Her other is extended, palm up, beckoning him closer. Fingers stiff, he traces around the shape she's made, standing so close that every exhalation warms his cheeks.

"Why did you leave me? Oh Maddie, why didn't you wait?"

He thinks about the paper flower, the way she'd tipped her head back and laughed when he'd presented it, feeling foolish, but right. The way her fingers twined round his own.

And the tears won't stop; he can't make them stop. He sobs until his throat aches, until his eyes are swollen and the world is a blur.

I would've gone with you, if you'd asked me to. If only you'd asked. It isn't better this way. Not for me.

When he wakes the next morning, the buildings across the street are captured in russet and amber. The sidewalk in front of his building and most of the street is still safe, still the color of real. Not the color of past.

He can no longer see Maddie, but he knows she is there.

Somewhere.

He hopes she isn't afraid. He hopes she isn't in pain.

A loud rumble of thunder wakes him from a deep sleep. Fat drops of grey are falling from the sliver of sky, dark clouds roiling in the small space.

He sits at the kitchen table with his head in his hands, listening to the storm cry its rage. After a time, he takes a napkin, folding it by memory, his movements sure and careful. When he finishes the first rose, he makes another and then another, until a dozen lay on the table.

I'll see you tomorrow, Maddie. Tomorrow. Even if you don't know I'm there.

In the morning, rain still falls, but of a gentler sort, and mud spatters the street. The last of the tea tastes like tears on his tongue. He ties the roses together with a purple ribbon, Maddie's favorite color. Bouquet against his chest, he traces his fingers over their wedding photograph and says goodbye to all the things they bought together. The soft smell of her lingers in the apartment, and he breathes it in, willing it to memory.

Then he hears a shout, not of dismay, but wonder and, with heavy feet, he walks to the window. The rain has washed everything clean, and the mud isn't mud at all, but a mix of umber and sienna. All the colors have been stripped away, leaving behind a stark landscape of black, white, and grey.

He stumbles as a woman approaches one of the black and white buildings and disappears around the side and sinks to his knees when she returns. "You have to see this," she cries. "Everyone, please, please, come and see!"

Several people emerge from buildings on the real side

of the world, people he vaguely remembers from the time before, people he passed on the sidewalk or almost bumped into at the corner coffee shop. They follow the woman through the door, their voices trailing behind in syllabic streamers of anticipation.

Joshua races from the apartment. All around him stands a forest of paper dolls and thin scraps of buildings, the fronts and backs pressed against each other, the interiors locked away, tucked inside like flowers pressed between pages of a book.

He runs again until he finds her, motionless and still.

Ignoring those running in circles around him, shouting out 'whys' and 'hows' and 'what nows' (he doesn't care about any of their questions. He doesn't need reasons), he touches Maddie's face. Her skin, the texture of good paper, warms beneath his palm. He clenches a fist to his chest. His heart hurts in a place he didn't know existed.

"I wish," he says, a catch in his words. "I wish you'd held on just a little longer."

He swallows his sorrow. He won't leave her in the street. He can't. She belongs at home, with him, not here. He lifts her with gentle arms, and though the weight is wrong, it will be better soon. He knows it will.

Careful not to bump her on the door or the walls, he carries her into their apartment, puts her in bed, and tucks the covers around her shoulders, ignoring the way the sheet clings to flat lines and angles instead of curves. He sets the paper roses on the nightstand so she'll see them

if

when she wakes and sits on the floor beside the bed.

"Everything will be okay," he says. "I know it will."

As the sun arcs across the room, his back aches and his stomach growls, but he's afraid she'll fade away into nothing if he moves. If he were a painter, maybe he'd know how to bring her colors back, but all he can do is keep still and hope.

When the room turns to shadow, he joins her in their

bed, imagining he can hear a tiny breath forming deep in her lungs, waiting to emerge, waiting to push her back to real.

"Please come back, Maddie. Please come back to me. You're all I have."

He falls asleep with one hand curled under his cheek and the other holding hers, dreaming of paper cuts and maybes and time.

DAMIEN ANGELICA WALTERS

Damien Angelica Walters is the author of *Paper Tigers* (Dark House Press, 2016) and *Sing Me Your Scars* (Apex Publications, 2015). Her short fiction has been nominated twice for a Bram Stoker Award, reprinted in *The Year's Best Dark Fantasy & Horror* and *The Year's Best Weird Fiction,* and published in various anthologies and magazines, including the 2016 World Fantasy Award Finalist *Cassilda's Song, Nightscript, Cemetery Dance Online, Nightmare Magazine,* and *Black Static.* Find her on Twitter @DamienAWalters or on the web at http://damienangelicawalters.com.

ALL PROCEEDS GO TO

association

https://www.stroke.org.uk/

The UK's leading stroke charity, changing the lives of all those affected by stroke and funding cutting-edge treatments.

There are over 1.2 million stroke survivors in the UK with 100,000 strokes happening in the UK each year. That's one stroke every five minutes.

Even though you are now twice as likely to survive a stroke compared to 20 years ago, stroke is still the fourth single largest cause of death in the UK.

We know we need to change how people think about stroke and challenge the myths surrounding it. We push for greater awareness of stroke and its warning signs and campaign for better stroke care.

We believe:

- strokes can and should be prevented
- everyone has the right to make the best recovery they can after stroke
- research has the power to save lives and ensure people make the best recovery they can.

These beliefs drive us forward to change the world for people affected by stroke.

ACKNOWLEDGMENTS

I just want to thank each and every author contained within this book, who either wrote something specifically, or offered a reprint of their work. Your time, work and words is hugely appreciated, and made this project a reality. Thank you.

I have to say a big thank you to Adam Millard, for proofing this and sorting out all that fun stuff.

A nod and a drink to Nev Murray over at Confessions of a Reviewer, for organising the launch party, and allowing me to spend some time waffling on about the stories in this book, appreciated.

Thank you to Siobhan Casson over at the Stroke Association. Without your help, this book would probably not exist.

Finally, to each and every one of you who buys this book, your support is hugely appreciated.
You rock.

OTHER EYECUE TITLES

EC1 – CLASS THREE
(Zombie comedy)
EC2 – CLASS FOUR: THOSE WHO SURVIVE
(Zombie survival horror)
EC3 – BOOK OF ISHTAR
(Both of the above books combined into a limited edition)
EC4 – CELBRITY CULTURE
(Bizarro novella, liable to turn your brain into a slinky)
EC5 – PRIME DIRECTIVE
(Sci-fi/horror novella)
EC6 – HEXAGRAM
(Time spanning, historical EPIC horror novel)
EC7 – CHUMP
(Zombie short story collection)
EC8 – TRAPPED WITHIN
(Charity horror anthology)

All books except for TRAPPED WITHIN, are written by Duncan P. Bradshaw.

www.duncanpbradshaw.co.uk

www.ingramcontent.com/pod-product-compliance
Lightning Source LLC
Chambersburg PA
CBHW020507260626
47156CB00006B/1897